A NOVEL

IN JUSTICE

ALAN SEARS

WinePress **WP** Publishing™

WinePress Publishing (PO Box 428, Enumclaw, WA 98022) functions only as book publisher. As such, the ultimate design, content, editorial accuracy, and views expressed or implied in this work are those of the author.

ISBN 13: 978-1-60615-013-9
ISBN 10: 1-60615-013-8
Library of Congress Catalog Card Number: 2009927857

DEDICATED

To the ministry of the Alliance Defense Fund, the ADF team, and our allies who are committed to keeping the content of this book fiction, and to all of the dedicated law enforcement officers who stand on the front lines every day to keep us safe, who cannot imagine doing the things described in this book that someone someday may attempt to require of them . . .

"Every heresy is a truth taught out of proportion."

—G. K. Chesterton
Daily News, June 26, 1909

"The pointy-headed busybodies have yet to enfold these youngsters in the iron-clad conformity of cultural diversity's embrace."

—P. J. O'Rourke
Wall Street Journal, May 20, 2009

| PROLOGUE |

April 2015

The room was silent except for the scratching of a fountain pen's nib as it trailed black ink on a yellow legal pad. The pen was old, even older than the seventy-six-year-old man who held it. It had belonged to his father and come to him four decades before at his father's passing.

Reverend Theodore Benson—Pastor Teddy—set the pen down and looked at the numbers he had written. He saw nothing but bad news. Once again, the offering was off, and he would have to choose between his paycheck and paying the utilities. How many times had he made that decision in the last six months? Far too many. Still, he never complained.

He moved his eyes from the desktop and traced the familiar images of his office. He had been a young man of twenty-five when he came to Chapel Street Church in Nashville. "Fifty-one years." He shook his head, struggling to believe the number. Could it really be that long?

The lone light in the room came from a banker's lamp sitting on his marred oak desk. It cast shadows on the old, dark-stained paneling that covered the walls of his office. On one wall—near the door with its frosted, pane-glass window that bore "Pastor Theodore Benson" in gold letters—hung his college degree, his seminary diploma, and his ordination certificate. All had yellowed over the decades. They weren't the only things to have grown old with the years.

Chapel Street Church sat nestled in a changing community. Those who attended were retirees too close to death to want to move. They had supported him through the years. They had built the church, paid for its building, taught its children, and now did what little they could.

"How much longer do you figure we got, Pastor?" Mick Tolbert had asked just before services last Sunday. "The way I see it, we ain't got but a few months left before we close and padlock the doors."

"Nonsense, Brother Mick. This church will outlive us and our grand-kids. We're just going through an adjustment period."

"You know I'm no troublemaker, Preacher, but I know how to count. We got more going out the door to the cemetery than we got coming in to worship."

Mick was five years younger than Pastor Teddy, but it seemed like there were decades between them. Mick was the last deacon left. Remembering the conversation pained Pastor Teddy.

"Oh, Lord . . .," Teddy said to the empty room. It was as much of a prayer as he could muster.

Most men his age would have retired a decade before, but Teddy couldn't bring himself to do it. Even ten years ago, the church had lacked a sufficient congregation to support a full-time pastor. Besides, he thought, retirement was the first long stride on the road to the cemetery. That reason alone would have kept him from leaving, but another reason rooted him in place—he was incapable of surrendering hope. If he left, the church would die within months, the doors locked and the windows shuttered. Every week he stayed gave the church one more opportunity to make a difference for the kingdom of God.

His unflagging hope kept Teddy going. He had mobilized a small group of volunteers to reach out to the poor, elderly, and disabled in the neighborhood; and even purchased gospel tracts and Bibles at his own expense to distribute wherever he could. He knew that the social ills that had befallen his community had their roots in the abandonment of God. Faithfully and tirelessly, he shared his message of salvation through Christ alone. He shared it from the pulpit, shared in direct mail to his community, shared it wherever he could. He was old now and he could feel his vitality slipping away. The day would come when he could no longer stand in the pulpit or go door-to-door to reach those without Christ. The day would come when he would have to step down—but that day wasn't today. Still, the knowledge gave him new urgency.

Teddy acted on his God-centered social responsibilities to the neighborhood without abandoning the deepest convictions of his faith. Sin was sin. Immoral behavior needed to be pointed out. He did this pointing out with increasing frequency and fervency. Though his congregation was small, his words loomed large, garnering criticism and threats from local groups who didn't appreciate his outspoken stance. He railed against the popular notion, even among fellow believers, that "tolerance" was a biblical principle. For Pastor Teddy, character mattered. Right and wrong mattered. And those principles never abandoned him. Even the recent threatening letters from a man two blocks down had not slowed Teddy. Despite neighborhood turmoil and dangers from theft and vandalism, he stayed and served.

Teddy looked at the clock and saw it was time. He punched a button on the radio alarm clock on his desk that served as his office stereo. He could listen to the program over the Internet if his service was working, but Teddy wanted nothing to do with the computer tonight. No tuning was necessary. Teddy only listened to one station, and he only listened to one show.

Teddy was a small church minister by choice. He held little regard for mega churches and scoffed at their dapper-dressed preachers, with their expensive haircuts and watered down gospel, but he made an exception for one man: Pastor Pat Preston of Rogers Memorial Church. The church was less than ten miles from his own but light-years away in success. Teddy didn't mind Preston. Preston was a "straight shooter," a man who spoke with the courage of his convictions, just like Teddy—except Preston delivered the word to thousands at a time, and Teddy spoke to forty seniors—mostly widows—on a good Sunday.

Teddy leaned back in his office chair. It protested with a loud squeak. Music, an upbeat version of "Amazing Grace," poured from the speakers. That would irritate Wilma. She believed the old hymns were sacrosanct, never to be touched or altered in any way. *Old woman. Never could keep up with the times like me.* He chuckled. He was as mired in the past as she, but he liked to tease her about it nonetheless. It was the music that kept her from listening to the broadcast, and that was one of the reasons he worked late every Sunday night.

Teddy listened with his eyes closed, waving his right hand as if directing a nonexistent choir in his office. He stopped abruptly. Had he heard something? He sat unmoving, straining ears that were becoming more useless every year. He reached for the radio and turned down the volume.

Nothing.

He turned it up again. *Just my imagination.* The neighborhood had several rough elements. Twice in two months, burglars had forced their way into the building. For several years the church had paid for a monitored security system, but as attendance had dropped and tithes had dried up, the service had become one of the first victims of an empty checking account. Good ol' Mick had brought a gun into the office when the alarm company cut off the service. He'd left it in the pastor's desk drawer.

"Our tellers count money in this office, Preacher. You know that. I need to be able to protect them." He knew what Mick was doing. Teddy had shared with him the threatening letters he'd received. Mick was, after all, the last deacon. The thought of Mick wielding a weapon was terrifying. At first, Teddy resisted, but arguing with Mick was like debating a stone—no amount of talking could change him.

Again he leaned back in the chair. Pastor Preston's welcome prayer oozed from the speakers. There was a time when Teddy would have paid good money for a voice like his. Teddy knew Preston was a good-looking man too: tall, straight, thin, with intelligent eyes.

Preston's voice filled the room. "The gospel of John is unique in many ways. Eighty percent of its material can be found in no other gospel. That includes our passage for today."

Teddy smiled. Very few pastors took the time to educate their people. Consequently, the modern church was filled with folks who learned their doctrine through "seven-eleven" praise music—seven words repeated eleven times. He paused his thinking, then chastised himself. The thought was only partially true. There were still many faithful ministers who aimed for the parishioner's mind as well as his heart.

Another sound pressed through the walls.

Teddy lowered the volume on the radio. There was another thud, followed by footsteps. Fast-moving footsteps. Someone was in the church building . . .

. . . in the hallway . . .

. . . near his door.

The frosted glass in the door kept Pastor Teddy from seeing clearly, but he saw several shadowy figures and heard the shuffling of their feet.

He reached for the phone to call the police. No dial tone. They hadn't paid the phone bill in two months. Had the phone company cut off the service, or had the men in the hall . . . ?

The silhouette of a man played on the glass. He held something—something long and straight. A gun. A shotgun.

Teddy pulled his desk drawer open and grabbed the .38 service revolver Mick had insisted on leaving. Teddy had never fired a weapon, and the weight of the gun surprised him. He raised it with both hands and pointed at the door. Maybe the sight of the weapon would send the intruders fleeing. Maybe it would frighten them back into the shadows. His hands shook. He wondered if he pulled the trigger, would he kill the robber or hit the doorjamb?

"*Stay away*! I'm . . . I'm armed!" As he shouted his warning, he thought he heard one of the men yelling at him. He couldn't make out the words. "I said, 'Stay away.'" He could see at least three figures through the glass.

In a single second the doorknob turned, and a man wearing dark clothing and holding a shotgun pointed directly at Teddy plunged into the room. "Federal—"

Teddy's gun went off, although he didn't remember pulling the trigger. The gunman's head snapped back. Blood splattered the office. Teddy saw a bullet hole between the man's eyes. The man dropped to his knees then fell face-first on the rug. Teddy's eyes followed the man to the ground. Large, white letters blazed across attacker's back: POLICE U.S. MARSHAL.

Teddy glanced up and saw the other uniformed men, saw muzzle flashes, and saw the ceiling as he fell to the floor.

Words poured from the radio. Pastor Pat Preston was reading from the gospel of John. "I tell you the truth, unless a kernel of wheat falls to the ground and dies, it remains only a single seed. But if it dies, it produces many seeds . . ."

So cold. So dark.

The first sentence from Deputy U.S. Marshal Rick Dickenson's mouth was a string of six obscenities. Seated in the communication van parked in the Chapel Street Church lot, he had just witnessed the death of two men and seen it on three video monitors.

He keyed his mike. "Officer down. Shots fired. We need medical, our location, immediately. Repeat: Officer down. Shots fired. We need medical."

Deputy Dickenson watched the video feeds from the on-helmet cameras his fellow deputies wore. The whole event had been recorded from beginning to end. Video had become standard operating procedure for such incursions. Modern juries loved—even expected—video.

Dickenson's eyes skipped from monitor to monitor. He had seen his fellow deputy, Ronnie Lee Jefferson, turn the doorknob and swing the door open. The camera caught the dim image of an old man holding a handgun. Less than a second later, Jefferson's camera flashed on the ceiling then settled on the carpet. In a moment of hopeful self-deception, Dickenson thought Jefferson's helmet had slipped off. That was before the video feed revealed a widening pool of dark fluid.

Two other agents had cameras mounted to their headgear. Both showed the flash from the handgun and the subsequent flashes from the automatic weapons they carried. The old man crumpled behind his desk. The agents approached, kicked away the handgun, and confirmed the killer was dead.

They turned to their fallen comrade. Their monitors showed the dead agent in full detail. The radio link filled with words worse than what Dickenson had uttered moments before.

John Knox Smith had received a text message to watch CNN. It was six thirty, and he had just finished his last bite of bagel. That bite, like all the ones that came before, had been gently dipped in a cup of black coffee. John had a complicated mind but simple tastes.

Like most mornings, the large-screen television in the living room filled the space with news accounts. John switched from MSNBC to CNN. The morning anchor, looking far too chipper for the hour, was talking about a police action in which a federal marshal and pastor had been killed. John turned up the volume. "We warn our viewers that the video you are about to see is graphic and may be disturbing to some, especially children. Please use discretion."

The video filled the screen. A dark hallway. A door with frosted glass. A doorknob being turned. The flash of a gunshot. The camera landed on the floor. John assumed that it was still attached to the agent's helmet and that the helmet was still attached to his head.

The video cut to another camera and John watched an old man die. It occurred to him that the sight would stun the country. Sadness would be expressed, as would outrage that a minister had killed a deputy marshal who was doing his job. John would express the same shock and disgust, but for the moment, he smiled and remembered something one of his heroes, a founder of the ACLU, had said. "Use every crisis to advance the agenda."

He called the office of his assistant at the Department of Justice and waited for voice mail to pick up. "Andrea, I want all the info you can get on the marshal who was murdered last night, Ronnie Lee Jefferson. Also, find some time for a team meeting this morning. I think we just got our Alamo."

Pastor Pat Preston sat on his sofa, thumbing through a two-week-old issue of *Time* magazine he had been meaning to read since it had arrived in his mailbox. Pat freely acknowledged his addiction to news and information. He subscribed to a dozen print and online magazines—most he never had time to read—and two newspapers. He could change channels from CNN to MSNBC to FOX without looking at the remote in his hand.

Monday was his day off, but he still rose early. He always rose early. A day off gave him time to recharge his batteries and feed his hungry mind. His wife didn't share his love for early mornings. He took a sip of coffee laden with flavored creamer and glanced at the television screen when he heard "minister killed."

He set the magazine down.

Eight days later

"There's someone here to see you, Pastor." Ava Raitt, Pat Preston's personal secretary, slipped into the office and closed the door behind her. "I don't have her on the schedule for today. Shall I tell her to set an appointment and come back?"

"No, you shouldn't. She's not on the schedule because I forgot to put her on my calendar. You know I can't remember to do those important things."

"You scheduled her?"

"I did. This morning. I was in early when she called. I told her to come by."

"But . . ." Ava paused.

"But what, Ava?"

"It's her . . . the wife of that preacher."

Pat smiled. "I know. I recognized her name. Even if I didn't, she told me who she was."

"But . . ."

"Show her in, Ava. It's rude to keep her waiting."

Ava frowned and exited the office. A moment later, a woman with hair that had long ago moved from gray to white entered. She walked without a cane and seemed steady on her feet.

"Sister Wilma, come in." Pat rose from his chair, rounded the cherry wood desk, offered his arm, and escorted her to one of the visitor chairs situated near a plush sofa. "Please, have a seat. May I get you anything? Coffee? Water?"

"No, I'm fine, thank you."

She wasn't fine. Pat could see it in her eyes. Her shallow breathing and hunched shoulders told him she was a woman on the edge of physical and emotional collapse.

"Shall I stay, Pastor?" Ava asked.

"No, thank you, Ava. I'll call if I need you."

"But . . ."

Pat's gaze carried a message. Ava slipped from the room and closed the door behind her. Pat sat on the sofa nearest the chair where the elderly woman sat. He was close enough to hold her hand, which he did.

"Thank you for seeing me. I'm . . ." Tears rose in her eyes.

"It's my pleasure. I just wish it were under more pleasant circumstances."

"I feel bad, like I should apologize."

"To me? Why on earth do you feel you should apologize to me?"

"My husband loves . . . loved your sermons. He listened to them often—on the radio in his office."

"That's quite a compliment, Wilma, not a criticism."

"I . . . I've always been critical of pastors with large churches."

Pat laughed. "Me too. Some of those guys are crooks."

Wilma gazed at him for a moment, then chuckled. "I think you should know that before I ask what I've come to ask."

"I appreciate your honesty. Maybe I can win you over with my charm." Pat leaned toward her. "How are you holding up?"

"I'm still in disbelief. The empty house tells me the horrible news is true, but part of me refuses to believe it."

"You've been a pastor's wife for many years. You know that's normal."

Wilma nodded. "Knowing and feeling are different things." She pulled a facial tissue from her purse, dabbed her eyes, then scrunched it in her free hand. "I have a favor to ask, but I think I know the answer. Still, I have to do something." She gazed into his eyes, and for a moment Pat thought she could read his soul. "Our church isn't part of a denomination, so I don't have an organization to turn to. I've asked other pastors in the area, and they've turned me down. Most had ready excuses, but I think they're trying to put distance between themselves and my husband. They think he's a hate monger, a murderer. The video . . . the reporters . . . the government. It's been more than I can bear. Still, I have to make arrangements, and I don't . . ."

"Yes. I'll be happy to do it."

Wilma blinked. "I haven't asked my favor yet."

"You want someone to perform the funeral service for your husband, right?"

"Yes, but you didn't know my husband. By doing the funeral, people might think—"

"I don't care what people think. I care about what God thinks. Let me ask this: Would your husband have turned someone in your place down?"

"No. He was always doing things for strangers."

"Then I won't turn him down."

"He's not what the press says he is. He's never been in trouble. The gun wasn't his. The federal marshals said they tried to phone, but no one answered. The phone had been cut off earlier. We've been having trouble paying the church bills, and . . . and . . ." Wilma's hand began to shake.

"Are you sure I can't get you some water?"

Wilma shook her head. "I'm afraid the press will make a mess of the service."

"There will be no press, Sister Wilma. I'll see to it. I can't keep them from doing what they do on public property, but I can keep them out of the chapel and the graveyard."

"How can you do that?"

"One of my trustees owns a local mortuary. He's a good man. He'll do what's right."

Wilma lowered her head. "I can't pay you much for your time."

"You can't pay me anything because I won't let you. I make a good salary. I don't need an honorarium. Are you—I'm sorry to be blunt—able to afford the funeral costs?"

"The people in the church are trying to raise the money. We didn't have life insurance. Never could afford it."

Pat rose, moved to his desk, and pulled a card from one of the drawers. "This is the mortuary I was telling you about. I'll call my trustee and let him know you'll be contacting him. You make whatever arrangements you want. Our church will cover any shortfall."

"I can't—"

"Yes, you can. Please don't deprive us of the blessing of giving."

Wilma began to sob.

Pat gave her a few moments, then said, "Now, tell me about your husband."

| CHAPTER ONE |

A slate-gray Mercedes E320 with Maryland plates pulled up and stopped beside the Department of Justice building at the corner of 10th and Constitution in the heart of the nation's capital. Although the luxury sedan had begun to show its age, it appeared well kept and newly polished. The driver, a young woman in her early thirties, turned slightly and spoke to her passenger. John Knox Smith turned to his wife and offered a polite smile, then returned his attention to the vanity mirror in the passenger-side visor. He saw a handsome young man in a dark blue suit. Dark, intelligent eyes stared back. John straightened his red tie, opened his door, and slipped from the vehicle.

Once outside, he adjusted his collar and cuffs and smiled at his reflection in the side window. After buttoning his custom-made, double-breasted suit coat, John nodded an almost imperceptible good-bye to his wife before turning to go into the building.

A noise across the street drew his attention. A small group of men and women stood along the curb on the opposite side of the street. Nine or ten shabby-looking people held signs and placards with illegible writing. They shouted and waved their fists at him.

They were far enough away, across the busy Constitution Avenue brimming with traffic, on the sidewalk in front of the Natural History

Museum, so he felt no danger. But he found them offensive and couldn't restrain the sneer that grew on his lips.

They're just another ridiculous group of fundamentalist whackos, standing there as if their presence could make a difference. He looked at them with scorn and shook his head. He would have preferred to shake his fist, but the street was a public place and every cell phone had a camera.

As the Mercedes pulled away, he turned sharply and walked to the security checkpoint just inside what was once called the "attorney general's entrance."

He went through the motions, passing his BlackBerry and his Burberry calfskin briefcase through the screening equipment. John found the procedure all too familiar. He had been going through the process since he first came to work in the AG's office six years before. But security remained an issue in every government building, including the Department of Justice. John knew the guards by their first names, and they knew him on sight.

"Have a good day, sir." An older guard handed the BlackBerry and briefcase to John.

Once he cleared the security area, John allowed himself to relax. The past six years had passed in a blur and felt much shorter. He loved this town, this building, this place. This was his turf—the place where he knew he belonged.

With his new position as assistant attorney general and director of the Diversity and Tolerance Enforcement Division, he would be coming through these VIP doors a lot more often. *And who knows? One of these days the big office on the fifth floor may be mine as well.* The thought pleased him. But he was content for the time being. This was his big day and nobody was going to mess it up.

Upstairs in the attorney general's office, he was scheduled to meet briefly with the vice president, the recently appointed chief justice of the Supreme Court, and the attorney general of the United States to coordinate the order of the march and make sure everyone was on the same page. But before going up on the elevator, he couldn't resist the urge to take a look inside the Great Hall, where the morning's announcement would take place.

John loved being where so much history had been made. Official programs, placed on stands around the atrium, offered a reminder of the building's history. John picked one up and read:

> Dedicated in 1935, the Justice Building is a 1.2 million-square-foot structure and renamed the Robert F. Kennedy Justice Building in 2001, in honor of the former attorney general and presidential candidate who was assassinated in 1968. Fronting on Pennsylvania Avenue, mid-way between the White House and Capitol Hill in the Federal Triangle area, this magnificent building has often been referred to as "the heartbeat of American justice."
>
> The DOJ includes the Federal Bureau of Investigation, the Bureau of Prisons, the Board of Parole, the Immigration and Naturalization Service, and the Drug Enforcement Administration. Altogether, there are eight major divisions, a half dozen federal agencies, and at least three dozen separate offices and bureaus administered by the DOJ, along with the newest federal agency, the Diversity and Tolerance Enforcement Division (DTED).
>
> As head of the Department of Justice (DOJ), the attorney general is a member of the president's cabinet and is responsible for enforcement of all federal laws. The attorney general represents the president in all questions of law and advises federal agencies and departments on legal matters. As the popular humorist Will Rogers once observed, "This is where the long arm of the law begins."

Looking across the magnificent atrium of the Great Hall, John realized that at long last he had earned his seat at the center table. His career had been on the fast track ever since law school, but now he was in the center of it all—exactly where he was meant to be.

He glanced briefly at the two enormous statues on each side of the Great Hall—the male figure known as "the majesty of law" and the female figure representing "the spirit of justice"—both nude and both without the traditional blindfold. Elegant tile work and magnificent paintings surrounded the entire room. The atrium reflected the opulence and sophistication of the Roosevelt era with all the excesses of the 1930s. *The scale of this place is imposing*, John thought, *but certainly appropriate for an arm of justice with the authority to reach into every aspect of American life.*

Beyond the Great Hall, John passed the large paintings of famous lawgivers from former times, including Socrates, Solon, Sir Edward Coke, Justice Oliver Wendell Holmes, St. Thomas Aquinas, Moses with the Ten Commandments, and even Jesus. They were portraits of men who had left their mark on history—whether they were real or merely legends.

By any measure, the Great Hall was a grand and elegant place, and shortly a contingent of the most powerful people in the country would gather here to participate in his crowning achievement. It would be the beginning of a new era in American jurisprudence.

The thought made John smile. He turned and made his way back to the elevators and up to the fifth floor. As he walked the hallway to the AG's office, he paused to look at the portraits of the former attorneys general who had presided here. He was especially fond of the picture of Robert Kennedy, captured with such a solemn and pensive expression on his face, as if he had some premonition of what was to come.

It pleased John Knox Smith to realize he was part of this history now. One day his own image might hang in that corridor, right after the portrait of his boss. When he passed through the door into the attorney general's suite, his assistant, Andrea Covington, was already there and eager to see him.

"Good morning, John." She seemed buoyant. "How was the drive down?"

"Good morning, Andrea. Everything was fine, except for the whackos across the street."

"You mean the protesters? Yes, I saw them. But don't worry. They'll be gone shortly."

"Good. I hope you're right."

"They were on the sidewalk in front of the building when I came in," she said. "So we asked the police to move them over to the other side of Constitution."

John nodded his approval and turned his focus to more urgent matters. He was there to meet with the dignitaries, Vice President Angela Baxter-Brown, along with Chief Justice Isaiah Williams and his boss and mentor, Attorney General Alton Stamper. They would take a few minutes to meet and greet before going downstairs together. But it was apparent that pomp and circumstance would be the order of the day, and nothing could have pleased John more.

Andrea was elegantly dressed, as always. Her brown and white St. John knit suit accentuated her shapely figure, shoulder-length blonde hair, gold appointments, and red-soled Christian Louboutin shoes. He could sense her pride at standing with the newly appointed head of the Diversity and Tolerance Enforcement Division.

Despite his efforts to appear modest about the new appointment, John had made no secret of his delight or his ambitions. He believed this was his destiny, and he knew the promotion to assistant AG was just the first giant step on his way up. There would be many more.

The challenge that would become his today was enormous, but he was completely committed to the mission. He reminded himself he was no hypocrite. He was a true believer in the mission and had been pushing for a new era of transformative justice for a decade or more—at least since his first year at Princeton. He had already shown that he could be relentless when he knew what he wanted. He had come a long way from the southern Colorado town where he grew up.

The thought of his boyhood home confused him. Some men remembered their hometowns with fondness, others with loathing. The best emotion John Knox Smith could muster was ambivalence. Washington, D.C., fit him in a way Colorado Springs couldn't. The memories of those days seldom made it out of the mental iron safe John kept them in. Colorado wasn't a different state to him; it was a different planet.

An only child of Margaret and Chester Smith, John had grown up in a warm and caring home. He thought of his father, a fine, upstanding man. Not a high achiever or ambitious man, Chester still set an example of self-discipline. He took his family to Cottonwood Church each week, but faith had never become the center of the family. They went to church because most the people in their neighborhood did. It was what respectable Colorado people did.

Those Sundays had an impact on John, but not in the way his parents expected. The hours spent in Sunday school and worship services inoculated him against the misguided pabulum served up in classes and from the pulpit. He thought of those days as a good shot of penicillin that kept him from contracting any faith-related diseases. By college, John loved his mind more than any soul he might possess. Intellect was the spirit that moved him to his true calling.

His intellect, coupled with discipline and ambition, had brought him to this special day, and he was only thirty-three. There were those who thought John too young for such an important promotion and responsibility. He didn't care what they thought.

His promotion had not happened by accident. Everything had fallen into place because he had a plan—a plan he worked every day. Now, his superiors were handing him a chance to change history.

He thought of the protestors across the street. The powerless, pathetic protesters standing outside could only offer a dramatic contrast with the reception he was about to receive. Let them protest. He was about to stand on the same platform as the vice president, chief justice of the United States, and attorney general. All eyes would be directed at him, not at the handful of malcontents with handmade placards.

By the time John and the other officials made their way downstairs, the Great Hall was alive with excitement and anticipation. The atmosphere was electric, and Justice Department employees and Washington dignitaries of all stripes packed the hall. It was standing room only. Secret Service and FBI agents were scattered throughout the crowd, whispering into their sleeves and listening to voices in their earpieces.

John Knox Smith, the assistant attorney general designate, entered the room and mounted the stage with three of the most powerful people in the world. The fanfare was sensational; it was everything he had hoped it would be. John smiled humbly and stood to the side, giving the others preeminence in position on the stage.

Some who had come to observe the ceremony were guests of the administration—men and women who had contributed in one way or another to this landmark occasion. Seated in the front row were Senators Heywood and Borden, who had carried forward the legislation for the creation of the DTED. There were four or five congressmen sitting together a few rows farther back; these were the brave ones who had pushed the measure through the House of Representatives. They sat beside a group of White House staffers and several members of the Senate Judiciary Committee.

Others seated in places of honor were the real troops, the ones who fought trench warfare in communities across America—warriors like Ben Braden of the ACLU and Nabil Medina of Americans for the Separation of Politics and Religion, along with a group of federal judges and a scattering of academics and liberal clerics. Each had played a part in his ascendancy, and John was pleased to see their faces in the crowd.

Representatives of the Human Rights Campaign were there as well, along with members of the executive committees of three of the largest mainline denominations, and a well-known Catholic college president from the West Coast who had fought what he called "the forces of darkness" in his own church to see these events come to fruition.

John continued to scan the crowd. There were others there, others he would rather not see. He had no idea why they would attend a ceremony that glorified their staunchest opponent. The presence of pastors from two of the largest Protestant churches stunned John. To make matters worse, Dr. Jim Stockman, head of Christian Family Forum, sat in an aisle seat, leaning to the side to improve his view. Next to him sat Larry Jordan, the bulldog head of the Alliance's Washington office— the Christian legal alliance that seemed to oppose all John cared for. Both men had fought unceasingly against the federal initiatives John championed and had done so for two years. The sight of the men made every muscle in John's body tense and his stomach turn. He motioned for Andrea to approach, then whispered, "How did *they* get in here?"

Andrea glanced over her shoulder. "Stockman and Jordan? We couldn't keep them out. They made a formal request and Stamper signed off on it. I think he wants you to get a taste of what is waiting for you."

"It'll take more than those two jokers to rattle me."

Andrea smiled. "I know that."

John returned his attention to the audience, nodding at friends and occasionally waving. He tried to focus on his supporters, but his eyes kept drifting to Larry Jordan. The man sat as comfortably as if he were in an easy chair in his home. He gave no indication of hatred or animosity, but even over the distance that separated them John could sense the man's determination. That determination was a sharp stone in John's shoe.

The Alliance, through its regional office in Washington, had sent witnesses to Capitol Hill to testify in opposition to the legislation founding the DTED. As a legal group, they were seldom involved in public policy debates, but somehow they always managed to get involved in what they called "religious liberty" and "free speech" cases. Now that President William Blaine had signed the new law making the DTED a fact instead of a concept, the Alliance could do nothing more than arrange for one of their people to be in attendance at John's swearing in.

Jordan will go back to his office and write an angry, right-wing hit piece on the event then circulate it in one of his famous fund-raiser letters sent to all their supporters in "flyover country." No doubt he will distort what happened here today. A lot of good that will do you, you sanctimonious, religious snob.

Month after month, for more than two years, the Alliance had sent lawyers, detailed briefs, and written testimony to the House and Senate committees, opposing everything John and his supporters were trying to accomplish. They held private meetings with congressmen on the Hill, explaining why the bill was bad for advocates of religious liberty. Because of their constant agitation, a small cadre of legislators fought the Respect for Diversity and Tolerance Act of 2014, and they had forced proponents to scrap important parts of the bill.

"Ladies and gentlemen, Vice President Angela Baxter-Brown." A male voice thundered over the loudspeaker, pulling John's attention back to the moment. He stole a glance at Larry Jordan and Jim Stockman. Would they rise, or would their arrogance glue them to their seats? They stood, mildly disappointing John.

The vice president stepped to the podium and pulled the microphone toward her. The audience broke into applause for the former California governor and Internet entrepreneur. She motioned for everyone to be seated.

"Just over 240 years ago," she began, "our ancestors declared that the pursuit of happiness was the right of all Americans. One hundred and fifty-four years ago, President Lincoln spoke of freedom for all

Americans. Fifty-four years ago, the Reverend Martin Luther King, Jr., spoke of a dream of equality for all Americans. And three years ago, when he was elected president of the United States, William E. Blaine, the senator from Maine, spoke of a dream of acceptance, equality, and inclusion for all Americans."

She paused to give the crowd a moment to respond with applause. John admired the way the vice president could seize an audience's attention. She was a consummate speaker.

"Today," the vice president continued, "we move a step closer to that vision of a unified and compassionate society. Not merely the opportunism and individualism of the founders, but a vision of a government absolutely neutral and removed from all the intolerance of sectarian dogma, and a nation as free as possible from the prejudices associated with bias, intolerance, and religious bigotry.

"We come here today to celebrate the right to hold beliefs of our own choosing and to repudiate the platitudes of intolerance and hypocrisy that, for an unconscionable length of time, had been driving our world to the brink of self-induced madness. This, my friends, is a new day, and we have come here to applaud the building of a fresh, new, and impenetrable wall of separation between church and state, and to renew the values the First Amendment was meant to ensure.

"I want to say thank you, first of all, to the stalwart members of Congress who fought for and gained approval for the anti-bigotry statutes signed into law by President Blaine yesterday in the Rose Garden. As you know, these new laws, so long in the making, call for the immediate creation of a powerful new division in the United States Department of Justice, to be staffed by up to one hundred federal prosecutors and assisted by all the investigative and regulatory agencies of the federal government."

My division, John thought with pride.

"From this day forward, Americans can be assured that this administration will do all it can to eradicate hate and end the destructiveness that religious-based hate and intolerance have brought upon the people of this nation. I bring you that message with the blessing of the president."

Cameras flashed from the press corner. Baxter-Brown paused to allow the media enough time to capture her image.

"I'm honored to be here on this occasion, but I know you didn't come to hear me. It's my duty and my distinct pleasure to introduce the chief justice of the United States Supreme Court, who will administer the oath of office to John Knox Smith, the first and only choice of the president for this key position." She turned and motioned to Isaiah Williams. "Mr. Chief Justice."

The recently confirmed chief justice stood six feet six inches tall and looked the perfect person for his job. He was a man of dignity and obvious authority. His prematurely gray hair and billowing black robe highlighted the eminence of his position and the task at hand. As he approached the microphone, another round of applause echoed through the Great Hall.

The chief justice had assumed his office only a few months earlier, but millions knew the inspiring story of his rise from poverty, to starring as a power forward in college, on to the NBA, to Stanford Law, to a short tenure on the federal bench, and now to the highest judicial office in the land.

"Ladies and gentlemen," Williams said, "before beginning the swearing-in ceremony, I'd like to pause for just a moment to say thank you to all the guests in this Great Hall for coming here today. You've all worked long and hard for this day, and I'm pleased that so many have come out to be part of this celebration.

"But now, without further ado, let's proceed to the business at hand." Williams turned and motioned for John to join him. John's heart doubled its pace.

John Knox Smith, impeccably attired in his handsomely tailored navy blue suit and accompanying red tie, stepped to Justice Williams and repeated the oath of office. "I do solemnly swear to uphold the Constitution of the United States of America and to faithfully perform the duties of the office of assistant attorney general of the United States to the best of my ability."

Before he finished speaking the words, the audience stood and applauded, and the massive hall reverberated with the sound.

Williams used no Bible during the swearing in. John shared Williams's view that the old book was a mockery to what they had achieved.

Finished with his assignment, Chief Justice Williams shook John's hand and then moved from the microphone, taking a seat beside the vice president. As the applause died down, John nodded to the members of his staff seated in the front two rows of the audience, then stepped up to the microphone without notes.

"Thank you, Mr. Chief Justice, and thank you all. I'm honored by your show of support and the encouragement you've given me. I'm especially grateful to Vice President Baxter-Brown for being here; she has been a tireless fighter for the values we all cherish. I also want to say a special word of thanks to my dear friend and colleague, Attorney General Alton Stamper.

"To paraphrase a former president of the United States who was called upon to serve in a time of healing: Ladies and gentlemen, our long national nightmare is almost over. Thanks to the wisdom of the Blaine administration, the United States Congress, the American people, and many of you here today, we have finally been given the legal tools to bring organized bigotry and hatred to an end in our lifetime."

When the crowd applauded, John looked at Larry Jordan and Jim Stockman. Neither man joined in the applause. Both sat like statues, revealing nothing of their thoughts or emotions. No matter how placid they pretended to be, John guessed they were seething inside—and he took great satisfaction in that.

"Just a few days ago a hero gave his life for justice and equality. Deputy United States Marshal Ronnie Lee Jefferson was killed by a gunshot to the head while attempting to make entrance into a pastor's study to deliver a search warrant and remove illicit materials and weapons. He and his fellow marshals had been warned by an informant that the suspect pastor was armed and dangerous."

John left out much of the material Andrea had discovered about the event. He saw no need to mention that the informant proved to be an unbalanced man, angry at the church for some minor offense, or that no hate materials were found anywhere in the church. Ronnie Lee Jefferson had died for a psychotic's lie.

"Ronnie Lee Jefferson left behind a beautiful wife and two small children. You've seen the news reports and saw their grief on television. Jefferson was a decorated veteran and was rightly buried at Arlington National Cemetery with full military honors. This genuine hero came from poor southern roots, but through hard work he made something of himself—something about which his father could feel proud. Ronnie served two tours with the marines in the Middle East and earned the rank of staff sergeant. After serving his country in the military, he continued to serve our great land by joining the Marshal Service. Just days ago, his life ended at the hands of a lunatic clergyman.

"Why have I chosen work in the Department of Justice? Because of men and women like Ronnie Lee Jefferson, who risk their lives to make us safe and fight evil. I can think of no better career than serving the public by seeking justice for everyone. Justice and equality are our rights in this country—no one has a right to take them away—no individual, no ministry, no church, no organization.

"It is nearly impossible to imagine the harm that has been done to this country and in the world under the banner of faith-based bigotry and intolerance. It is impossible to imagine because it is so vast with an ancient history of oppression and injustice. As we have seen, almost all wars—and certainly most of the terrorism we've endured in this country and around the world—spring from hate motivated by religious and ideological intolerance.

"Since it is impossible to acknowledge all the religions and belief systems of the American people, it is our view that any acknowledgment, favor, or accommodation of a particular faith tradition must be seen as an illegal establishment of religion and in direct conflict with the First Amendment. Furthermore, they are a violation of the statutory laws of the nation. Those who wish to practice their religion openly must understand that respect for diversity, tolerance, and equality is no longer optional. It is mandatory.

"The Bible, which is still considered a holy writ in some religious traditions, is, in my view, the most misused, misquoted, and misunderstood book in history. It is the very symbol of judgmentalism, intolerance, and hate, and a book through which great evil has been done. Yet even that book, with such a history of intemperance, affirms the statement

'Blessed are the peacemakers.' And that is my commitment to all of you today as we begin this new enterprise: to lift high the banner over a new era of peace, tolerance, and equality for all people.

"Those of you privileged to serve in the United States government will have much to be proud of as these new plans take shape. In coming months and years, and with due diligence on our part, you're going to see the dream of America as 'One Nation After All' become a reality and not merely an empty chant. Those of us involved in law enforcement will be the peacemakers. The criminal and civil penalties that Congress has provided will be applied swiftly and surely against the purveyors of hate and intolerance who violate our laws. It is what Ronnie Lee Jefferson lived for. It is what he died for. It is what I pledge to work for.

"So, once again, let me say thank you, Madam Vice President; thank you, Mr. Chief Justice; and thank you, Mr. Attorney General, for the confidence and trust you've placed in me today. I pledge by every living thing and all that is dear to my heart that I will fulfill this office with enthusiasm, and I will not relent until we see true justice enforced across this land. In time, this will yet become a nation of equality, acceptance, and tolerance. Justice will have new meaning, and there will be renewed hope for all who've felt left behind.

"Thank you."

As John Knox Smith stepped away from the microphone, his staff leaped to their feet and surrounded him, bathing him with praise and congratulations. The crowd began to disperse. As they did, John saw Jordan talking to Stockman. Even across the hall he could see the disappointment on their faces. For a moment, John's eyes locked with Jordan's. He expected to see hatred. Instead, he thought he saw pity.

It infuriated John.

| CHAPTER TWO |

Andrea Covington followed her boss, doing her best to match his stride, an effort made more difficult by the two-inch heels she was wearing. What was it someone had said about Fred Astaire and Ginger Rogers? "All Ginger had to do was copy Fred—backwards and in heels." Andrea held no doubt that John Knox Smith was the Fred Astaire of the Justice Department, and she was doing her best to be his Ginger Rogers. Some days were more challenging than others. She had thought today would be a breeze until she saw him staring at Larry Jordan and his Bible-thumping buddies.

Today should have been JKS's moment of joy. At just thirty-three, he had been appointed to one of the highest positions in the DOJ. Andrea had watched that joy drain from her boss's face when he caught sight of Larry Jordan. He had been able to hide his disgust from everyone but her. She knew him too well, maybe better than his wife, maybe better than he knew himself. That knowledge led her to her next action: she followed him to his old office and closed the door. The office was close to bare except for the furniture. Workers would have his new office on the fifth floor ready within the next two hours.

"I can't believe Jordan would have the unmitigated gall to come to my swearing in." John stepped behind his desk and shoved his executive chair to the side. It slid on plastic wheels until it impacted the side wall. "Why? There's no logic to it. He and the others came just to see if they could throw me off my game. They can't. No one can."

"Of course. It was stupid of them." A pair of leather guest chairs sat in front of the desk, but Andrea remained on her feet. She wouldn't sit unless John did.

"Jordan and his cronies have done nothing but hinder the progress we've been making. Every time someone tries to lay down a straight and smooth road to help our country climb out of the dark ages, people like Jordan and his Alliance pop up, making our work ten times more difficult than it should be. You'd think the pounding they took on FACE II would have shown them how futile their efforts are."

"FACE?" Andrea already knew the answer, but she also understood how much her boss needed to vent. He was expected at a reception in ten minutes and needed to get this out of his system.

"FACE, the Free Access to Clinic Entrances bill. It was first fought in the courts years ago. I was in junior high school at the time, but I followed it closely. Then it was amended and *whoa*!"

"That one went to the Supreme Court, right?" She spoke softly, hoping John would do the same.

"Yeah. The Alliance argued against the bill on the ground of freedom of speech. Freedom of speech . . ." He lowered his voice. "What the Alliance really wanted was to make it difficult for women to exercise their legal right to reproductive care. A woman facing an abortion has plenty to think about; they don't need to push their way through a line of fundamentalists waving signs and shouting, 'Shame.'" He shook his head. "Fortunately, the Supreme Court eventually saw through the sham. It had nothing to do with free speech but free access. The Court saw that even though they still struck down part of the law."

He pulled his chair over and sat. "That decision made it possible to prosecute protestors trying to intimidate women who were just exercising their rights. It also laid the ground work for the new Respect for Diversity and Tolerance Act. Without that series of precedents, we had no hope of stopping religious extremism. It broke the back of much of the so-called right-to-life movement, and now we build on it to break the religious kooks."

Andrea sat, then cleared her throat. "When the religious dissenters realize that, not only are they going to be arrested for acts of hate and intolerance, but they're going to wind up doing serious jail time. Then they'll stay away from such disruptions in the public square in droves."

John smiled. "You memorized my whole CNN interview from two days ago?"

"Not all of it. Just the really impressive stuff."

"You know how to flatter a man like me."

Andrea's darkly tanned face warmed. She hoped it didn't show. "Just trying to be the best assistant in the DOJ."

"As far as I'm concerned, you are. I'm surprised the AG himself hasn't stolen you."

"I'm happy where I am."

"Good, because I'm keeping you."

"Maybe Larry Jordan was here because he's too stupid to stay away."

John raised a finger. "Careful. Never underestimate the enemy. Larry Jordan is anything but stupid. The Alliance's lawyers have led federal courts astray for years. The man has argued before the Supreme Court several times and won some key cases. No, he's not stupid. Misguided maybe, but not stupid. The Alliance is well known in D.C. So is Jordan. Jordan has been fighting what he calls 'religious freedom' issues for decades. He has friends. Some of them were in the room this morning."

"You mean Dr. Jim Stockman?"

"Him and others. Secretary of the Interior Dan Spencer was there."

"But he's a progressive, isn't he?" Andrea shifted in the chair but never took her eyes off John.

"I thought so. Well, he is on many issues. He's been a strong defender of the environment, but I learned a little while ago that he and his friends are evangelical Christians. You could have knocked me over with a feather."

"You're kidding. How did he get confirmed?"

"I don't kid about these things."

Andrea was glad to see John lean back in the chair. He was relaxing.

John looked at the ceiling. "I even saw a couple of congressmen who fought against the RDTA, especially the enforcement aspects."

Andrea scooted forward until she was perched on the edge of the chair. "I think you should forget about them. The VP was there; the AG; the chief justice, as well as several members from the president's cabinet. Every major news outlet covered you. Of course you have opponents. All great men do. But you also have many friends and allies."

"True, but there are many challenges ahead. There are those who think I'm too young for this post."

Andrea shifted back in the chair, as if trying to put distance between her and the concept. "Nonsense. Nonsense from beginning to end. Why should you wait until you're older? Your talent is clear and has been clear from the beginning." She took on the tone of a proud wife. "You made a name for yourself in college. What was the name of your valedictorian speech at Princeton?" She already knew.

"The Age of Intolerance."

"That's right. And didn't the *New York Times Magazine* publish it? And didn't it cause a stir in the judicial community?"

"Well, yes—"

"You were much younger then, but you still left your mark. I imagine people were talking about you back then. Then after Harvard Law, you clerked on the D.C. Circuit Court. Just eighteen months later, you clerked for Justice Stephen Brewster at the Supreme Court. Then in 2009, at just twenty-seven, you came to the DOJ through the new Honors Litigation Program . . . then became lead prosecutor for the DOJ's Hate Speech Task Force—"

"Andrea—"

"Just a few years out of law school, President Blaine appointed you, and the Senate unanimously confirmed you as assistant attorney general—"

"Ms. Covington—"

"Those in the know don't question the appointment. Not only that, you earned this spot. It didn't come by political favor. The Hate Speech Task Force, which you led, won thirty felony convictions. You argued and won the *Liberty Free Church v. United States of America* in 2012 before the Supreme Court. How old were you then?"

"I was thirty, but—"

"You see, that's my point. How many thirty-year-olds have done that? Not many, I can tell you that. It made you a household name for a while. And what about the new law provisions drafted by your team? More than 80 percent were successful—"

"Andrea, stop talking."

"And . . . I'm sorry. What?"

"Stop talking. I know these things. I was there. Besides, if some public relations exec hears you, she'll hire you away from me and pay you lots more than you get from the government."

Andrea smiled. "Thanks, but I'm not going anywhere." She looked at her gold Rolex watch. "But you are. I've got to get you to the reception."

Larry Jordan didn't go back to the offices of the Alliance. Instead, he drove Dr. Jim Stockman to the Ronald Reagan Washington National Airport and returned to his home in Virginia. He parked the car and entered his two-story home. Before he entered, he straightened his back, took several deep breaths, and stuffed his depression deep into his gut. No need to upset Marla.

He walked in, set his keys on the foyer table, removed his coat, and strolled into the kitchen.

"Is that you, Larry?" The voice came from upstairs.

"No, it's your favorite door-to-door salesman." He heard her laugh.

"Aren't you supposed to knock first?"

"Haven't you heard? There's a new sheriff in town, and requiring me to knock is intolerant of you."

Marla appeared in the kitchen. She was tall, had Catalonian features with long mahogany hair and brown eyes, and looked younger than her forty-eight years. "Maybe it's just me, but that sounded a tad bitter."

Larry sighed. "Sorry. Watching Smith's swearing in and hearing his little speech have made me . . ."

"Cranky?"

"That'll do. Maybe more furious than cranky."

Marla smiled, and the sun seemed to shine brighter. Setting the basket down, she stepped to him and put her arms around his neck. He pulled her close and inhaled her scent. "He got to you, didn't he?"

"No, not really. It's just that his appointment, the passing of the RDTA . . . this whole thing has pushed the cause of liberty back. We win some, we lose more." He pulled away, moved to the refrigerator, and removed a bottle of flavored water.

"Can I fix you anything?"

Larry shook his head. "No thanks. I'm going to go into my study and think awhile."

"Maybe you should pray for a while as well."

He chuckled. "I've been praying all day."

"Okay, but you're taking me to dinner tonight."

Larry blinked several times. "I am?"

"Yup. You're depressed and need to spend time in my scintillating company."

"I didn't say I was depressed." He took a swallow of water.

His office was out-of-date by the day's standard, but he didn't care. He liked dark paneling, the old fireplace, and the rows of books that lined one wall. He sat in a leather desk chair that had once belonged to a judge he clerked for soon after leaving law school. The man had been his mentor. After he died, the widow gave the chair to Larry. He'd had it repaired several times over the decades, but he would not let it go.

Once seated, he set his water on the table and admitted to himself that he *was* depressed. He seldom allowed such emotions into his life, but as he grew older, his emotions grew stronger. On his desk rested a leather-bound Bible and a thick printout of today's court of appeals decisions. Light tried to press through the shut mini-blinds over the window.

He took another sip and attempted to put his thoughts in order, but his mind raced as if his brain were floating in high-octane caffeine.

John Knox Smith might have more power now than ever before, but God wasn't dead, and no amount of wishing on Smith's part would change that.

"Marla," Larry said to the empty room. "You need a steak."

| CHAPTER THREE |

After the festivities and the public reception were over, John Knox Smith made his way upstairs to the conference room of his office suite, located just around the corner from the attorney general's office on the prestigious fifth floor of the Justice Building. His first staff appointees were assembled and waiting for him. A worker was tacking the last corner of thick, new, dark red carpeting in place. Someone had taped a laser-printed sign to the office door, which read "Diversity and Tolerance Enforcement Division." Below that someone had scrawled in red ink, "We Stop the Hate!"

Around a massive antique conference table sat the handpicked DTED team: Donna Lewis, chief of staff; Joel Thevis, lead attorney; and Special Agent Paul Atoms, head of the new DTED Enforcement Unit and liaison to the Federal Bureau of Investigation. Next to Paul sat Postal Inspector Sandra Evans from the Prohibited Mailings Section; Special Agent Bob Maas, Internal Revenue Service Criminal Investigation Division and Public Policy Enforcement Exempt Organizations; and the Blaine administration's outside liaisons; the Reverend Lynn Barrett of the Metropolitan Urban Church, representing religious minorities; and Reneé X, of OneAmerika, representing racial and sexual minorities, and former counsel for the ACLU.

John had handpicked the members, and Attorney General Stamper had personally approved each one. The law enforcement group had a proven track record of pursuing "targets" and a hunger for personal advancement. To John, they were tireless defenders of justice and equality. The outside liaisons were a first for the Justice Department, which had never before paid for full-time advisors—another distinction for the DTED.

Some on the team had served with John on the national Hate Speech Task Force. Their effort had led directly to the landmark 5–4 Supreme Court ruling of *Liberty Free Church v. United States of America* three years before. That ruling had helped make the new initiatives possible. The case, involving a reexamination of all previous broadcast laws and regulations, had made it clear that "the free speech guarantees of the First Amendment were never intended to shield bigoted or hateful expression that harms another person's or group's sense of equality and acceptance."

That victory was not only the highlight of John's career as a young litigating attorney but a triumph in every way. At age thirty he had accomplished something lawyers twice his age could only dream of—arguing and winning a decision before the Supreme Court. The decision upheld the Federal Communications Commission's cease-and-desist order against reading certain Bible passages and sermon comments over publicly owned airwaves, and eventually forced the Virginia-based national television ministry of Rev. Jeremiah Helton to shut down.

Normally, the solicitor general, supported by a team of FCC and DOJ lawyers, would have argued the case, but since John had done such an impressive and thorough job of pulling everything together, Attorney General Stamper had made a special appeal for John to make the argument. The overlap of the Liberty case with so many of the ongoing hate-crimes investigations within the DOJ at that time was too great to ignore. It was John who had formulated the charges, tracked down the critical evidence, and made the case against Helton in the first place. It was only fair that he should be the one to head the litigation effort.

John had moved the case through the district court and the court of appeals, predicting all along that it would eventually land in the high court. When it did, Alton Stamper convinced his colleagues to put everything in John's capable hands. John led the joint prosecution, and his victory helped propel him to a lead role in passing the new RDTA legislation. Those successes had led straight to his groundbreaking promotion and leadership role at the DTED.

When Assistant Attorney General John Knox Smith entered the room, the team rose and applauded. The outpouring of affection and support from his team threatened to overwhelm his emotions. Tears welled in his eyes. John circled the conference table, shaking hands with the staff, addressing each one by name, and thanking them for their support.

At six-two with his blond hair and piercing blue eyes, John was a strikingly handsome man. His good looks and quick mind made him a standout in any crowd. It hadn't always been that way. Growing up, he had been the smallest, skinniest kid in his class, something he had lived with until his sophomore year in high school.

John had adapted quickly and his personality had blossomed, but he never forgot that he had been a neglected and undervalued child. Everything he achieved was a form of compensation.

When the room was silent once again, John took his seat at the front of the group. "Friends, as I said at the ceremony this morning, our long national nightmare is about to be over, once and for all, but we've got a lot of work to do to get there. As you may know, I studied ethical theology and sociology at Princeton before I went to law school. One thing I learned was that the history of this world is one long epic of hatred, intolerance, and violence motivated by religious bigotry. World leaders of the last century killed millions in the name of their fatuous religious beliefs and narrow view of truth.

"Untold millions died because of distorted biblical justifications. The former autocrats of the Catholic Church, John Paul II and Benedict XVI, endangered the health of millions around the world by convincing their followers that there was something wrong with a woman exercising her reproductive right to choose. I've spent years studying religious activity in our society. It's clear to me that a new era of intolerance and terrorism is right around the corner if we don't do our jobs well."

John nodded toward Reneé X and Paul Atoms, who had backed him up and provided devastating evidence in a dozen or more cases over the past two years.

"I've known some of you for a long time," John said, "and I know your dedication to our mission. But I also know that none of you would ever let your personal opinions or beliefs cloud your judgment about the importance of what we do here. For the next few minutes I'm going to give each of you some marching orders and answer your questions. Then I'll try to make it home in time to see my son's soccer game this evening. Is that all right?"

The personal touch brought laughter. John continued. "You may have noticed that I didn't ask my spouse or child to come to today's ceremony. My purpose was to avoid any suggestion of bias for anyone who may hold other views on marriage and child rearing. I also want you to know that I've been active until recently in a church where I've served on the board of equals. To avoid the appearance of impropriety, I will be formally resigning that membership this week, and I will stop attending services.

"I'm asking each of you to think about your own organizations and affiliations, and how they might reflect on your work here. I hope you'll resolve any potential conflicts in your private life and think about how your appearance, your speech, and even the clothing and jewelry you wear could reflect on the team. We're all judged by the company we keep. We don't want to give anyone reason to question our ethics or our motives as we move forward."

John turned his attention to his chief of staff. "Donna, your staffing report shows that we've got three or four applicants for every prosecuting attorney slot on the team. That's great, but I want to start slowly with a crack team. I'd like you to pick the top twenty Ivy League candidates, preferably those currently with Justice, and get them transferred to us before the week is out. Be careful to exclude anyone who has any known religious preferences or biases."

"Sir," Donna said, "will there be any particular criteria for orientation, gender, or racial mix that you'd like me to use in addition to the department's standard minimums?"

"No, not for now. As we ramp up, we'll probably want to increase the mix in some areas for special expertise. We want to make sure all the oppressed minorities are represented on the team, especially gender-differentiated persons, who really understand the effects of religious intolerance and hate speech in this society. But for now, see what you come up with in the current pool of applicants."

"Got it," Donna said.

John nodded at Andrea. She passed around a small stack of documents that included John's first same-page memo, designed to keep all the team leaders on the same page, along with a copy of the agency's "Organizational Objectives." Then, turning to the keyboard of his laptop computer, he flipped the switch on a large, flat-screen projector and said, "Okay. As I outlined in my testimony before Congress last week, here are the key goals of this organization."

John read each item aloud:

Organizational Objectives:

All: Identify organizations and individuals in open and flagrant violation of the United States Respect for Diversity and Tolerance Act (RDTA) of 2014.

All: Create a national interdepartmental and agency database on organizations and individuals engaged or suspected of engaging in violations of RDTA. This list should include religious organizations where sexual and other bias is advocated. The list will be maintained by the Department of Justice with Department of Treasury, Postal Service, and Internal Revenue Service cross-reference.

Agencies: Investigate and prepare criminal case prosecution reports against organizations and individuals engaged in serious violation of RDTA for DOJ prosecutors.

Justice: Prosecute violations of RDTA, seeking penalties for organizations and individuals up to the maximum levels allowed by law.

Justice: Prepare civil lawsuits to obtain prohibitory orders to stop all use of the United States Postal Service by organization or individuals engaged in violation of RDTA. Most hate-based sectarian organizations cannot function without direct mail solicitation.

The United States Postal Service must put an end to all mail that promotes or enables hate.

Agencies and Justice: Supply non-grand jury investigative data to the Federal Communications Commission for actions, including suspension or revocation of broadcast licenses for stations carrying content in violation of RDTA.

IRS: Prepare administrative cases, to be backed by civil litigation, to eliminate tax exemptions for—and the deductibility of charitable contributions—to all organizations engaged in violation of RDTA, especially Christian and Jewish schools that openly oppose Darwinian and other scientific truth.

Justice: Prepare civil Racketeering and Influenced Corrupt Organization Act (RICO) lawsuits to seize all of the property—especially homes, churches buildings, and commercial property—hate literature such as tracts, films, videos, electronic storage media, and other publications owned or controlled by organizations or individuals involved in violation of RDTA. As soon as we develop an RDTA case, we should move with RICO.

Justice: Work with the public news media to provide maximum publicity within the bounds of legal ethics to ensure awareness of and compliance with the law.

Justice, in liaison with congressional leaders: Review all sections of the United States Code and identify inappropriate language for updating. Seek and remove all authorizations for bias from law, specifically including the misnamed "Equal Access Act," the illusory claim "In God we trust" from currency, any funding for education or backing of student loans where the institution allows unlawful, public religious acknowledgment.

Justice and State Department liaison: Coordinate with international law enforcement community, the United Nations, and the International Court of Justice to ensure that the United States is in full compliance with worldwide efforts regarding tolerance and equality. Determine which international conferences and events may merit the DTED's active participation.

When John finished, Special Agent Paul Atoms was the first to react. "John, I want to thank you for what you're doing here. I consider myself very fortunate to be part of the team. It's a dream come true for me. I can name a dozen progressive FBI agents who are fed up with prosecuting white-collar economic crimes. They'll want to leave the old-fashioned ways of the Bureau and join the team. What you've just laid out is a chance to change history; I, for one, can't wait to get started."

"Thanks, Paul. I'm glad you feel that way."

"Your decision to push Congress to set up your own investigative unit was brilliant. You just couldn't depend on a lot of those at the FBI. They have an archaic view of what 'fidelity, bravery, and integrity' means; they're about two generations behind in their understanding of where law enforcement needs to be."

Atoms had more to say. "Does anybody remember the famous raid in Miami back in 2000, when the DOJ snatched that Cuban kid who was being held illegally by his right-wing relatives? That story made front page news for weeks. We all know how dangerous some of those Christian leaders can be, and we know a lot of them have weapons. That's why the raid went down with such a show of force."

Atoms turned to John. "If you agree, sir, I'd like to begin my project by cross-checking gun registrations, hunting licenses, National Rifle Association memberships, and all the data I can get my hands on to determine who we need to keep an eye on. As long as we know which ones are armed and dangerous, we'll be able to make arrests with a full detail of protective forces when the time comes—if it comes to that."

"Good point, Paul. I agree. Safety is a huge concern. I don't want you taking any risks when you investigate these cases. Be sure that any time you go into one of these dangerous places, you take plenty of firepower. I don't want federal employees getting hurt. We can't have any more murders like Ronnie Lee Jefferson's. I would rather conduct a handful of raids with twenty or thirty agents than a lot more with inadequate safety precautions. Be sure you let the major news networks know when we're going in. We want to give these arrests all the coverage we can. Media coverage helps with deterrence."

Paul nodded. "Yes, sir, I can do that."

"I appreciate this kind of proactive thinking, Paul. When we were building this team, I asked each agency for their best people, and you've just shown me that we've got 'em. As we recruit for our DTED Enforcement Unit, be sure to weed out those FBI folks stuck in that old mode; we can't afford to let anything slow us down."

IRS agent Jason Harrier entered the conversation. "I agree with what Paul said earlier. This is the opportunity we've been waiting for. These so-called hate-preaching 'ministries' are going to think twice when their funds start drying up. We'll see how faithful their wealthy donors are when they can no longer get a tax write-off for contributions. When they see that the American taxpayers are not going to subsidize their bigotry and intolerance with tax breaks, the show will be over. These nutcases keep saying that Jesus is the only way. Let's see how long they stay on radio and TV when we get through with them."

Several members of the group laughed. John joined in. "Jason is right. Exclusivity claims by Christians won't last long when the loudest and most intolerant ones learn they're going to be facing prison time and the loss of their property and their fat payrolls. But we need to lay a lot of groundwork before we can take them on directly. A lot of careers are going to be made by those, like you, who help us rid the nation of that kind of bigotry. Don't forget, but it will take a while. As you work with the support staff in your agencies, I hope you'll spread the word. We want the best and brightest to work these cases. We want every indictment to lead to a conviction and maximum punishment. Can we do that?"

Everyone in the room spoke at once. All assured John Knox Smith and their colleagues that they were on board with the plan and eager to get started. John had the affirmation he needed.

He called for silence. "Do we have any specific violations to discuss?"

Reneé X raised her hand. "Mr. Smith—"

"Call me, John. I'm uncomfortable with formalities except when absolutely necessary."

"Yes, sir . . . John." She smiled and cleared her throat. "Over the last few weeks I've been compiling audio and video clips to give everyone a good look at some of the most dangerous hate mongers on the airwaves today." She glanced at her notes. "Their profiles are similar. Most are old white guys. They preach what they call 'biblical inerrancy,' which basically means they believe the Bible's contents are literally true—if you can imagine that—and most are graduates of fundamentalist evangelical or old-style Catholic seminaries.

"One of these guys runs a radio and TV program called the *Children's Bible Story Hour*. Every weekend he fills these little ones' heads with hate. His whole thing is this exclusivity garbage, that no one can know God except by this guy's favorite formula."

John could read the frustration on her face.

Reneé continued. "He's a bad one. But the guy who really gets my goat is the leader of the so-called Christian Family Forum. He hosts a radio show that goes all over the country. Most of his listeners are in the South and West, but people all over the country listen to this stuff, day in and day out. It's just one diatribe after another, attacking freedom of choice and everything else we care about."

John said, "You're talking about Dr. Jim Stockman, aren't you, Reneé?"

"Yes, that's right."

"He was at the swearing in. I saw him sitting next to Larry Jordan."

Reneé grimaced. "I missed that. Lucky me. I call him Doctor Holier-than-Thou. He incessantly preaches against the gay community, saying homosexuals suffer from a—get this—'disordered' personality. Almost as bad is the Catholic bishop in the Midwest with his *Radio Altar* program, on which he rambles about the 'holocaust of abortion,' attacking freedom of choice and health-care providers who offer a full range of services. He says priests in his diocese have to teach what the fifteenth-century throwbacks in Rome put in their catechism. It suppresses the freedom of the other priests who would prefer to be teaching how to love instead of how to hate."

John motioned to Lynn Barrett at the end of the conference table. "Lynn, isn't this what you call 'religious genocide'?"

"Yes, it is precisely that," Barrett agreed.

"For those of you who may not know," John said, "Rev. Barrett is our liaison from the Metropolitan Urban Church and a special appointment of the president. Lynn, tell everyone what you mean by 'religious genocide.'"

Rev. Barrett leaned forward. "Glad to. When these Bible-pushers Reneé is describing can't engage in actual physical genocide, they try to eliminate ethnic, religious, and cultural minorities by religious seduction—what they call 'conversion.' Their goal is to eliminate all other beliefs but their own. They say they're trying to save the lost, but they're really trying to make clones of themselves."

"So everyone who isn't just like them," Reneé X interjected, "has to be converted."

"Exactly. Their predecessors did it with crusades, with gas chambers, or with bullets. Now they do it with emotional intimidation and with unceasing talk about sin and eternal judgment. These are some of the most troublesome hate mongers we will ever deal with, John. They ought to be the first ones you go after."

"I've already started my list," Reneé said, "but I need to point out that some of these organizations have multimillion-dollar campuses and thousands of donors and supporters backing them. Do you have any idea how much real estate they own?"

"Yes, I do. But go ahead and roll the tape, Reneé," John said. "Let's see what you've got."

Andrea punched a remote control and handed the remote to Reneé. The lights dimmed, and a video played on a flat-screen television mounted to the front wall. Several in the group shifted their seats to gain a better view. The video began, showing a heavyset man standing behind a large Plexiglas pulpit. The subtitle identified him as the senior pastor of Cornerstone Fellowship in Atlanta. He held an open Bible in his right hand as he spoke. Andrea increased the volume slightly. The preacher's voice echoed in the room:

"Hear me, dear ones! The Word of God is clear on this. Any man or woman who will not repent of the wickedness of homosexual sin—the very sin of Sodom and Gomorrah, with all the evils of homosexual and lesbian behaviors—and give his or her life to Jesus Christ will be condemned to an eternity in hell. That's what it says right here!" He lifted the Bible above his head. "This is the truth. There's no way around it."

After a short pause while the congregation responded with applause and muffled shouts, the preacher backed away from the pulpit and said, "What does this mean for you and me? It means we must stand firm in our opposition to every effort of the homosexual community to redefine who can marry and who can rear children. They want to recruit your children into that lifestyle, God forbid! But that's their goal.

"These people are well funded and well organized. We need prayer. I want you to pray with me now. Pray in Jesus' name; pray for all those who are confused and trapped in that deadly lifestyle. The forces of darkness are on the march. Pray that, by His grace, this nation will turn back the shadows of darkness from our land before it's too late."

When Reneé paused the video, there were muffled expletives and groans all around the room.

John rubbed his eyes as if he were trying to squeeze the images from his eyes. "Unbelievable," he muttered and looked up. "That's precisely what I've been talking about. That kind of talk is unacceptable in this day and age." He leaned back in his chair. "Do you know what really scares me? We may not be able to get a conviction on a madman like that. The jury might vote to acquit this guy on the grounds of insanity!"

There was a moment of silence as John and the others reflected on what they had seen. "No normal person would believe that anyone in America could still speak that way," John continued. "He's not preaching a sermon, he's launching a crusade. To make matters worse, this character is a preacher, a person who claims to teach love. Rev. Barrett has it exactly right. Instead of love, he's preaching hatred and bigotry. It is spiritual genocide. We've got to shut these people down. If any of us—"

"Here's the thing, John," Reneé interrupted, "this guy is only one example. I can give you a dozen worse than this one."

"I know. Believe me, I know," John said. "At some point I want everyone to see them all, but this example really makes the point. I appreciate the good work you're doing. Keep it up. From here on out, our top priority must be to deal with guys like this. He and his kind need to be stopped."

"It's going to be a war," Reneé said.

"I'm ready for that. We all are. Let's hope it's like the FBI's war on the Mafia back in the eighties. Once the Mafia dons and fat cats were in jail and their assets seized, it was easy to nail their subordinates. It's amazing how little courage these folks have when they lose their money and their limousines, do a 'perp walk' in front of the TV cameras, and are looking at twenty years in federal prison."

The discussion continued until John was satisfied that the salient points had been discussed and the first steps of the action plan were in place. "You have your assignments. Let's get this place fully staffed and let the cases roll. For any organizations with television, radio, or Internet programming that reaches Washington, we'll want to try those cases here in D.C. If any of those groups use the Internet or if their broadcasts reach the District of Columbia in any form, we automatically have venue. I know a Washington grand jury will be responsive and act swiftly to see that justice is done."

John stood. His team followed suit. "Any problems? Any questions? No? Then, thank you all."

John was pleased with the way everything had gone. Despite his earlier claim, attending his son's soccer game never crossed his mind. Instead, he spent the next hour and a half reviewing media coverage of the day's events and writing personal notes of appreciation to the influential friends who had attended his swearing-in ceremony.

By the time he returned home, delivered by a hired limo service, Cathy and Jack were in bed, fast asleep in their Silver Spring home.

| CHAPTER FOUR |

The Outback Steakhouse on North First Street in Arlington, Virginia, buzzed with people. Larry and Marla Jordan waited in the cramped lobby.

"Must have been a pessimist," Marla said.

"What? Who's a pessimist?" Larry asked.

"The architect who designed this place. The lobby is too small. I guess he didn't think they'd do enough business to have customers waiting."

Larry raised an eyebrow. "He? How do you know the architect was a man? Women can be architects too, you know."

"Of course I know that. A woman would have been optimistic and designed a larger space for waiting."

"That a fact?" Larry decided not to push the issue. It was one of those discussions no husband could win. He resorted to "Yes, dear."

Ten minutes after arriving, they were seated near the bar area. Flat screen televisions hung from the ceiling. Two showed NBA games, and one was tuned to the news. None had volume, but each had captioning turned on. Larry wasn't interested in any of it.

The waiter appeared at the side of their table and offered them drinks from the bar. He seemed disappointed about their order of water with lemon. Marla ordered king crab legs and sirloin; Larry chose a center-cut filet.

"I'm not that hungry," Larry said when the waiter stepped away.

"Is that why you ordered the nine-ounce filet instead of the seven-ounce?"

"Force of habit. Besides, a man can't be seen ordering a small steak when a bigger one is listed on the menu."

"Mr. Cro-Magnon."

"That's Mr. Cro-Magnon, attorney-at-law to *you*, if you please."

Marla grinned. Her smile warmed Larry. As lousy as the day was, he could find reasons to thank God—Marla led the list.

"Thanks for suggesting we go out," Marla said.

"I thought it was your idea."

"It was, but I don't mind if you take the credit."

"You know, I've argued before the Supreme Court several times, endured their questions, and sidestepped every effort to unravel my argument. Somehow, however, I can never seem to keep up with you."

"Just the way it should be. I like being the brains behind the brains."

The waiter brought dark bread and whipped butter, then disappeared.

"He's hopping tonight," Larry said. "It must be tough."

"A night for good tips."

"I suppose so . . ." Larry tuned his head and caught sight of the television with the news show playing silently. The image of John Knox Smith dominated the screen, his hand raised as he took the oath. "Now my appetite is *really* gone."

Marla followed his gaze. She reached across the table and touched his hand. "He won a battle, not the war."

"He won a big battle." Larry looked away, unable to face the screen. "Unbelievable power has been placed in that man's hand."

"Did God lose all His power in the process?"

"Of course not, Marla. It's just that . . . that . . ."

"That what? That unbelievers have acted in such an unbelieving way? You know that Scripture teaches the unsaved can't think like the saved. He's acting according to his nature. He actually believes all that equality stuff. He has no way to understand that 'tolerance' is not a Christian virtue."

"That excuses him?" The words came out more sharply than he intended. "I'm sorry. I don't mean to be terse."

Marla went on. "I've never verified it, but I've often heard that G. K. Chesterton once said, 'Someone who believes in nothing can tolerate anything.' That's where this is leading us. We've been married a long time, sweetheart. I know the kind of passion my husband has. I don't expect anything less. It's just . . . never mind."

"Oh no, you don't. You can't 'never mind' me. Say it."

"It just seems that you're taking defeat harder these days. You've had plenty of successes, but you seem to forget those."

He squeezed her hand. "I haven't forgotten them. It's like climbing stairs. A person doesn't pay much attention to the steps behind him, just the ones in front—and we have so many steps ahead. The Alliance has been fighting this battle and defending churches and ministers for a long time. We've stood in case after case against the government and the ACLU's push for 'equality,' which in reality means surrendering to their totalitarian agenda. We fight, we win, but in the end, it seems like we make little progress. I know why so many give up."

Marla pursed her lips. "Are you thinking of giving up?"

Larry studied the glossy finish on the wood tabletop. He didn't answer.

"I shouldn't be surprised," Marla said softly. "I've seen you give up many times before. I've seen you walk away from everything for as long as fifteen minutes. Then you clench your spiritual and legal fists and head back into the ring to fight another round."

"Wait a minute. Did my delicate wife just use a boxing metaphor?"

"Maybe. I'd use them more often if I could figure out why they call a square boxing area a ring." She paused then said, "Have I not commanded you? Be strong and courageous. Do not be terrified; do not be discouraged, for the Lord your God will be with you wherever you go."

"Joshua 1:9. How many times have I quoted that in speeches?"

"Hundreds of times. Every once in a while, you need to hear it." She leaned back. "I think you *should* quit. Contemplate going back into a private practice. Give yourself the whole night off. Plan a new future. But when the sun comes up tomorrow, pick up your shield and walk to the front line again."

"You think you're smart, don't you?"

"I did take one class on basic psychology in college. Think I can hang out a shingle?"

Larry chortled. "I think you could do anything you want, but the Alliance needs your marketing skills."

"I'm here for the Alliance, but most of all, I will always be here for you."

Larry looked back at the monitor. The image had switched to a high-speed chase, but Larry spoke as if John Knox Smith were still on the screen. "We still have business. Serious business. Enjoy your day because the battle has just begun."

"I'm sorry?"

Larry turned. The waiter looked stunned as he held two salads. It took a second for Larry to make the connection. "I didn't mean you. I was just talking out loud."

"Whew. I thought I'd done something wrong." He set the salads down and slipped away.

Marla stared at Larry. "Great, now you'll have to double the tip."

The picture on the television set faded away, and the image of John Knox Smith disappeared. Chester Smith sat back in his armchair and stared at the dark screen. Placing the remote on the table beside him, the older man raised his hands to his face, rubbed his eyes, and sighed. "You've come a long way from Sunday school lessons and church picnics, Son."

There was no one in the room to hear him. Since his wife had died, Chester lived alone in the house where the family had resided ever since moving to Colorado thirty years before. Those had been different days then. He was a different man now, and John . . . ? Well, John had changed in ways Chester couldn't understand.

Chester had named his son after John Knox because his family had descended from the fiery Scottish reformer. Even though his own faith was not particularly deep or personal, he had tried to raise his son to be, at the very least, a moral man. In one sense he had been successful. John had an honorable job, had made a name for himself, worked for justice—at least justice as he saw it—and lived the life of a law-abiding citizen. So why did disappointment gnaw at his stomach and soul like a rat chewing through a cardboard box?

For most of his adult life, Chester had managed a successful construction business, employing nearly two hundred people. Along the way, he had built a lot of churches, schools, and government and professional buildings. He had made money in his time, and he had been able to live comfortably in his early retirement years. But caring for his ailing first—and then second—wife had been costly. He was no longer a wealthy man. Providing his son with a Mercedes E320 as a graduation gift from Harvard was the limit of Chester's discretionary spending, but he knew it would mean so much to John to arrive at his first big job with the appropriate image.

At one time, John's mother, Margaret, had been a social worker, but emphysema had put an end to that. Her long convalescence and early death had left Chester to raise the boy alone. "I made a hash of that," he said to himself. "The boy needed a mother."

When Margaret died, he'd tried to get closer to his son, but it was too late. John had found a new life of his own—a life filled with school work, student council activities, and the varsity debate team. Chester had tried to ease his pain through work. He couldn't blame John for burying himself in things outside the home. At the time Chester had felt relief that John had chosen a positive path of self-healing instead of turning to drugs or worse.

Chester slid forward to the edge of his easy chair and rested his elbows on his knees. His gaze fixed on a small stain a few feet away, but he never saw it. Other images filled his mind.

"Fourteen," he whispered. "Just fourteen. Far too young to lose a mother."

Men and sons; sons and men. The thought emptied him. Some fathers and sons bond early and forever. Others, especially fathers so busy with fighting for and supporting a family they fail to mold it, drift apart. By the time Chester realized that he and John had slipped miles apart, it was too late. John had lost a mother, and he didn't need a father, especially one who was absent much of the time.

Chester held out some hope that having a new wife would help bring everyone together. It hadn't. John had written off the family. Home was a place to sleep and eat. Everything else for John had revolved around his education. He'd became consumed with being the best at everything he tried. It had been John's response to loneliness. Chester could figure that much out.

Chester had always been generous with his son and never mean. However, like John, he hid beneath a blanket of activity: building things or working with the various charitable ministries at their former Presbyterian church. Chester's special interest was a series of building programs for senior citizen retirement housing.

Rose, Chester's second wife, had done her best to be a mother to the teenager, but John had never given any indication of accepting her into the family. Chester looked up to the fireplace mantle and saw Rose's image in a silver picture frame. She had died just two years ago after a long illness, leaving Chester to rattle around in a house too big for him.

Chester wondered if John ever thought about him.

Pat Preston closed his Bible and stepped from the lectern at the front of the mortuary chapel. The setting sun shone through the stained-glass windows and painted vivid splotches of gold, blue, red, and white on the floor and padded oak pews. Everything about the place was designed to help the bereaved feel comfort. The background music played old hymns in mournful tones; the carpet was plush and dark blue; the walls wore a coat of pale beige. Every day people came to this chapel to say good-bye to a family member or friend.

For the past forty minutes, Pat had done his best to bring words of comfort and insight from the Bible to the twenty people who had sat on the pews. All had been elderly; only a few had been men.

A dark wood coffin rested on a metal stand with wheels. Inside the box lay the body of the Reverend Theodore Benson—Pastor Teddy— faithful husband, diligent pastor of Chapel Street Church for fifty-one years, and to some, a murderer.

When Pat had arrived at the mortuary, he had driven past a gaggle of reporters, several of which had recorded his arrival with cameras. He had ignored them and thanked God that the mortuary owner had been able to convince the local police to keep the reporters off the property during the funeral.

Pat had dismissed the congregation so they could make their way to the grave site for the last part of the memorial. He had moved to Wilma Benson and sat by her side. She had no family to sit with her through the ordeal. Seeing her seated alone had twisted Pat's heart so much that for a moment he thought it would stop beating.

"Thank you, Pastor. I don't—"

He put an arm around her. "It's almost over. Soon the healing can begin. But . . ."

"But graveside is the most difficult. I know."

Pat nodded. As a young student preacher, he had asked the senior pastor of his church what he should say at graveside services. The pastor, half in jest, replied, "It doesn't matter. No one will hear you anyway."

The comment had caught him by surprise. A few funerals later, Pat had understood. The sight of the coffin hovering over an open pit could seize a person's attention and never let go. Good funeral homes covered the opening with a tarp of artificial grass, but it fooled no one, especially the family. As the wife of a minister for over fifty years, Wilma certainly knew that.

The small crowd came by, shook Wilma's hand, and expressed their sorrow. Normally, Pat would have stood to the side, but he couldn't allow Wilma, a woman he had known for only a few days, to sit alone any longer.

After the last well-wisher passed, Wilma gazed at the coffin and said, "I wish it could have been open casket. The funeral people said it was 'ill-advised.'"

Pat knew why. The bullets from the marshal's automatic weapons had done too much damage. "That would have been nice," he said.

Wilma took a deep breath and rose. Pat joined her. "I'm ready," she said. He offered his arm. They would ride in the hearse to the graveside. "You know, Teddy used to say that no one hears what the preacher says at funerals."

Pat smiled. "I've said the same thing myself."

"He was wrong. I heard every word you said, Pastor. I will never forget it."

He patted her arm. "I'm glad."

| CHAPTER FIVE |

T he day had flown by like the once-mighty Concord with a tail wind. John Knox Smith made it home by 10:30. As he expected, his wife and nine-year-old son, Jack, were in bed. He could have been home sooner, but he and several of his team had decided to dine together, then go out for drinks. A small measure of guilt nagged him about his home responsibilities, but he had learned to ignore it over the years.

Sleep was still a good two hours off; his mind bubbled with excitement from the day. He slipped into his office and checked his e-mail. He found a message from Special Agent Paul Atoms, head of the DTED Enforcement Unit and his liaison with the FBI. It contained a link to a video site that compiled news coverage from around the country. A few moments later he was watching a reporter standing in front of a stone pilaster and iron gate. A bronze plaque read "Gentle Rest Mortuary—Nashville."

John turned up the volume on his computer.

". . . that's right Michele. I'm here in front of the Gentle Rest Mortuary, where services for Rev. Theodore Benson, the clergyman who killed Ronnie Lee Jefferson as the deputy U.S. marshal was attempting to execute a warrant on Rev. Benson. As our viewers are sure to recall, video of the event was recorded as the tragedy unfolded. To protect themselves, other deputies fired and killed Benson as he stood with gun still in hand.

"Jefferson was buried at Arlington several days ago, but funeral services for Benson were held up as investigators continued to gather evidence. The Reverend Pat Preston, popular minister of the mega church, Rogers Memorial Church, performed the memorial and graveside services. Reporters were forbidden to attend. Many in Nashville know of Pastor Preston, as do many across the country. His sermons are carried on radio, television, and over Internet media.

"All requests to interview Pastor Preston have been declined. As yet, we do not know what connection exists between the two ministers.

"This is Jerry Howard—"

John hit the pause icon, silencing the report.

Pat Preston? John couldn't believe his ears. How long had it been? He didn't bother with the math. It was enough to know that he hadn't seen Pat since they graduated from Princeton.

A bank of books stood along one wall of his home study—several hundred volumes from college, law school, and general reading he had done over the years. He kept every book he read. Each stood as a testimony of his keen mind. On the bottom shelf were several yearbooks from his time at college. He pulled the most recent from the shelf, settled into an overstuffed chair, and turned on a reading light.

Flipping through the pages, John found the 2002 photo of Pat Preston. The image opened floodgates of memory. John had many acquaintances in college but only a few friends—two to be precise. Only two would tolerate his polemic ways. Pat was one of the triad of friends.

MARCH 2002

Thirteen years earlier

"Anyone who actually believes the Pollyanna version my opponent is defending," John said, "has been hoodwinked by a right-wing conspiracy to hide the actual motives of so-called 'patriots.'"

John's eyes traced the crowd in the Richardson Auditorium of Alexander Hall, reading their body language like a man reads a book. Their faces were turned toward him, eyebrows neutral, mouths relaxed. A few leaned forward and several nodded. He was pulling them in.

"If there's a conspiracy," Pat Preston, John's opponent in the debate, responded, "then it is perpetrated by educators who want to make you think history is irrelevant and therefore not worthy of the time to study it. How can you expect anyone to have an interest in learning history if all students do is memorize a bunch of mind-numbing treaties and dates and events with no context? No wonder the average student's knowledge of history is paper thin."

Pat's words garnered an immediate response. Some students cheered; others booed. The moderator banged the gavel repeatedly, calling for order, but it was obvious this debate had hit a sore spot. When decorum returned, Pat continued:

"Most kids just blow it off. Even here on this historic campus, most students slide by without learning anything about the sacrifice made by patriots. They paid a high price for our freedom. For most, the goal isn't to learn about history; it's to memorize just enough to pass the tests. Anything learned is promptly forgotten. Most of our university graduates don't know enough history to vote responsibly or to even know what candidates should stand for or against."

Such arguments infuriated John and his liberal friends. His impulse was to interrupt, to stop the flow of Pat's presentation, but the rules of debate had been clearly drawn. He would have to wait his turn. All he could do was smile as if his adversarial friend were telling jokes rather than arguing forensic points.

Pat's limited time ticked by. It was time to start bringing the argument home. "We meet inside a place of history. Over in Nassau Hall at the heart of Princeton University we are surrounded by history that changed all our lives, including that of my opponent. That great hall, Nassau Hall, once served as a barracks and a hospital by American and British soldiers at various times during the Revolutionary War. When British soldiers tried to take refuge there in 1777, a cannon ball fired by Alexander Hamilton's men decapitated a portrait of King George. The patriots who preceded us used the frame for a portrait of George Washington. Be honest with yourself: How many of you knew that?"

Murmurs and moans floated in the air, but there were no loud protests. "If it weren't for one of our professors who still believes that history matters—and by history I mean *accurate* history, not recast, reformatted, remade history—I wouldn't have known that fact either. As Professor Roberts of the Witherspoon Philosophical Society noted, 'Postmodern scholars have been rewriting history to fit their pet theories that facts have been buried in a blizzard of reinterpretation, "facts" that cannot and do not resemble the truth.'"

Pat reached beneath his podium, pulled a freshman history textbook from a shelf, and held it up. "Look familiar? This text is required reading for American History. This book contains multiple-page essays on current figures in American history, all of whom turned out to be people the political left calls heroes: people like John Dewey, Alfred Kinsey, Margaret Sanger, Saul Alinsky, and Noam Chomsky.

"In this text, there is a story about the Old South Church in Boston, the famous meeting hall during the American Revolution. It has since become a museum and the repository to a collection of plaster statues of all the liberal heroes who have spoken there. One is Margaret Sanger, the founder of Planned Parenthood. It shows her wearing a gag. She often wore a gag when speaking in public to show how society was 'oppressing' her for her views. This book has a picture of her statue, but not a word about Sanger's support for eugenics, her bigotry in which she called certain parts of the human race 'human weeds'—faces I see in this room tonight. It makes no mention of the abortion industry she helped create.

"That alone should be enough to cause concern, but there is more." He flipped through the pages. "Here it is, a short article about George Washington with a tiny, black-and-white picture showing Jean Houdon's famous bust of Washington. It refers to him as 'the man some have called the father of his country.' The essay says George Washington was a wealthy slaveholder who participated in a war to preserve his right to own slaves and increase his fortune. That is the entire coverage of America's first constitutional president."

For effect, Pat snapped the book shut. The sound rolled through the auditorium. "The hero of the era, according to this author, was Thomas Jefferson, who made sure the government protected the principle of 'separation of church and state.'" Pat sighed. "As every history professor knows—or should know—Thomas Jefferson was four thousand miles away at the time and had no input into the Constitution or the Bill of Rights. When the founding fathers penned those documents, Jefferson was serving as the ambassador to France. I hope I don't need to tell anyone here there was no instant messaging or Internet in those days."

The comment brought laughter.

"Let's take another step to historical accuracy." Pat set the book down. "The phrase 'separation of church and state' is used a great deal today. But where did it come from, and how was it originally used? It is true that Jefferson wrote those words, but he did so in a letter to the Baptist church in Danbury, Connecticut. When the entire letter is read, it is clear that Jefferson meant the government had no inherent right to interfere in religious matters. Were you taught that in history class?

"The document Jefferson did write," Pat continued, "is the Declaration of Independence. That document proclaims that our freedoms come not from kings or governments but from the Creator. President Kennedy said essentially the same thing two hundred years later. Anyone who tells you the founders meant to keep religious life completely separate from public life—as my worthy opponent is doing—has swallowed the bait and hook of revisionists who wish to alter history—history you have a right to know. It's the duty of every patriot."

It was John's turn to rebut and he didn't waste a second.

"Patriots?" Although John's podium held a microphone, he projected his voice to the back row. "Patriots? We have used that term so frequently and so haphazardly that it has lost all meaning. One man's patriot is another man's terrorist. True patriots hunger for truth and balance, for equality, not a one-sided, self-limited view touted by cheerleaders waving pom-poms of aggrandizing historians who wish to make gods of the flesh-and-blood men who wrote our early legal documents. We are educated men and women who need not fear an accurate history even if the history reveals the founding fathers to be a bunch of slaveholding rich people who didn't like paying taxes to King George.

"The English parliament only asked our forefathers to pay a reasonable tax, just as our government demands today. The colonies were expensive to support and manage, not to mention a long way across the ocean. Furthermore, two-thirds of the colonists were against independence and never dreamed of going to war. Rich landowners pushed the British into war because they refused to pay their fair share, just like so many wealthy of today."

John took hold of the podium and leaned forward. "We all admire the framers of the Constitution, but if we are to be intellectually honest—led by our minds and not our hearts—then we have to admit the document was written by rustics who were limited to the knowledge of their age. If they lived today, they would argue to amend the Constitution to reflect the values of our own time."

The booing began before John had finished the sentence, but a second later applause erupted, drowning out the expressions of disfavor. Sensing the majority of the crowd shifting his way, John added, "When Jefferson wrote that 'all men are endowed by their Creator with certain unalienable rights,' he knew what he was doing: he was writing for the unwashed masses who still hung to religion, whose votes would eventually be needed. Besides, Jefferson was one of them himself. He owned slaves, didn't he? He was sleeping with the help and didn't know the first thing about true equality. You may as well admit it. The past was corrupt. The founders were corrupt. There's nothing we need to learn from the founders except not to be like them. What matters is our ability to overcome the handicaps they created for us, from slavery to prejudice to intolerance to religious dependency.

"In 1898, H. G. Wells wrote *The War of the Worlds*. Make no mistake, what we have in the intellectual community and the country at large is a 'war of the worlds' or better yet, a 'war of the worldviews.' I think it is best, I think it is noble, I think we can honor our founding fathers by being honest in our view of them and the country they started."

John closed the yearbook and let it rest on his lap. He leaned his head back against the chair and closed his eyes. Those had been good days. The debates between him and Pat had been fought in places other than the university auditorium. They had argued in classes, in the cafeteria, and over restaurant tables. The debates had revolved around politics, history, and most of all, religion. Of course, Pat had never called it "religion." He had called it "faith." Whatever. A rose by any other name.

Even though their interests differed, John and Pat had been well acquainted at Princeton. Their mutual interest in student government had often meant competing for the same leadership positions as class officers and ultimately in the race for class valedictorian. They had often shown up at the same place at the same time. Several times they had taken the same classes.

John wondered how a man of such keen intelligence and superior academics could go so far wrong and chase after myths and legends in the church. Truth was, as great a student as John was, Pat was better. The difference lay in individual ambition. John had it; Pat didn't.

He could still replay the give-and-take they'd had over religion. Pat would listen to John's well-reasoned arguments but never seemed influenced by them. Instead, he had quoted from the works of C. S. Lewis, Francis Schaeffer, and Russell Kirk, but had never descended into personal argument. It was one thing to debate on stage but another to be offensive face-to-face. John still suspected that Pat feared driving him away from God, as if he hadn't already traveled far away enough. He never pushed his advantage. In fact, he often deferred to John whenever they came to an impasse—except on spiritual matters.

Both had run for class president their senior year. It had looked as if it were going to be a hard-fought race. But rather than go against John publicly, Pat had decided to run for vice president, leaving the top job for his opponent and friend. Mid way through their last semester, they had learned that both were finalists for class valedictorian. They'd had precisely the same grade point average.

To settle the tie, the university president had asked faculty members to vote for the student they believed to be most deserving of the title. Knowing this, John had gone to Professor Saul Peterson, and the two of them had begun lobbying the faculty. Eventually, enough of the faculty had agreed to vote for John to assure his victory. If Pat had felt slighted or resentful, he had never let on to John.

Pat's humility kept John unsettled. He knew how to deal with ambitious people but not humble ones.

Within hours of graduation, Pat had returned to his family home in Owensboro, Kentucky, and had spent the summer working with his dad at the mill. John had spent a few days with his father in Colorado before heading to Cambridge.

John lowered his feet from the desk, set the yearbook aside, and played the news report again. "What are you doing, Pat? What are you getting yourself into? How can you perform a religious service for a man who killed a federal law enforcement officer? A man with a family?"

John dictated a note to himself into his new BlackBerry:

"Have team look into Pat Preston."

| CHAPTER SIX |

Keith Gentry was waiting for Pat Preston when he stepped into the church study that morning. Pat's stomach dropped like an elevator slipping several floors. Forcing a smile, Pat entered his office and slipped off his suit coat, hanging it on a walnut coatrack made by one of his parishioners, and took a seat behind his desk. Pat liked to have a large object between him and his chairman of the deacons.

"I'm sorry, Keith, I must have forgotten our meeting."

Gentry forced a smile that seemed to cause him pain. "I'm not on the schedule. I thought I'd just stop by and say hi."

You never stop by just to say hi. "That's nice of you. Would you like some coffee? Oh, I see Ava has brought you some." As if she had read his mind, Ava appeared with a coffee mug filled with Pat's favorite brew and set it on Pat's desk. She set it down and left without speaking. She held less love for Gentry than Pat did. Pat took a sip of his coffee.

"She makes a strong cup, Preacher." Gentry was a thick man with a thick neck and very thick skin. He needed a hat and thick heels to reach five foot eight. If humans were machines, then Gentry was a bulldozer. For forty-two years, he had worked for the highway department of Tennessee and had taken an early retirement earlier that year. He spoke plainly and often without regard to how his words landed in the ears of others. Still, somewhere in his barrel chest beat a pretty good heart.

"That's my fault. I like African coffee, and some of that can be a tad strong."

"I prefer a good American cup o' joe myself. Don't have much use for the fancy foreign beans. Maxwell House has always worked for me."

"Technically, Deacon, all coffee is foreign."

"Why did you do it?"

Pat tilted his head. "Why did I switch to African coffee?"

"Don't be cute, Pastor. You know what I mean. The funeral. Why did you do it?"

"Ah. You mean Pastor Benson's funeral."

"Right, although I don't think he deserves the title 'Pastor' after what he did."

"I performed the service because his wife needed and deserved to have someone officiate at her husband's burial."

Gentry sipped his coffee without taking his eyes off Pat. "I'm a little surprised that you didn't run it past me and the other deacons."

"Why would I do that? We do a lot of funerals. Do you really want me to call every time someone asks me to do a funeral?"

"This wasn't just any funeral."

Pat sighed and pulled his coffee cup closer. "What's on your mind, Keith?"

"God has given us a great church here. We need to be good stewards and protect it."

Pat felt his ire reaching a boil. "I think the church can survive a funeral."

"There were reporters there. It was all over the news. Your name and the good name of the church were plastered all over the radio and television news."

"I saw the reports. It will all blow over in a week."

"Maybe, maybe not. Burying a cop killer is bad for our reputation."

Pat closed his eyes for a moment and then opened them. "Our reputation?"

"Of course. We have a good reputation in this community and in all of Nashville. Because of our television ministry, we are known throughout the world. We can't afford this kind of scandal."

Pat wanted to bite his lip but feared biting through it. "How about our reputation with God? I don't think I heard you mention that."

"You know what I mean."

"Yeah, I do, Keith, and that's the problem. My concern is that this church does as Jesus wants it to do. Benson's wife came to me for help and I gave it. If I had to do it all over again, I wouldn't change a thing."

"That right there keeps me up at night. You're a good preacher, but you sometimes come up short on the wisdom side of things."

"Gee, thanks."

"You know me, I don't try to offend anyone, but I do tell it like it is."

Pat rubbed his eyes and wondered if he'd heard correctly. "You would have sent Mrs. Benson, a sister in Christ, away? You would have said, 'Sorry, Mrs. Benson, we're not going to help you'?"

"I wouldn't have been that crass, but yeah, that's what I would have done."

Pat pushed back from the desk and stood. "Keith, the day this church becomes more concerned about its image than about its mission is the day it stops being a church." He paused. "Was there anything else you wanted to talk about?"

Gentry set his cup on Pat's desk and stood. "I see you're not much in the mood for talking. Still, I had to come by and tell you to be careful. You need advice about these things. You should have come to the deacons first."

"Thank you for coming by, Keith."

Pat walked to the door and waited for his chairman of the deacons to leave. As soon as the man crossed into the outer office, Pat closed the door. Ten minutes later he was finally able to sit down.

From the first day he arrived at Rogers Memorial Church, Pastor Pat Preston made a huge impression on the Christian community, not only in Nashville but also far afield. Within three months of his inaugural sermon, his voice was being broadcast on radio and television stations across the country. The network of stations had been established by Pat's predecessor, Pastor Bill Richards. The responses from the shows, however, soon outstripped Pastor Richards. Before long, Pat was receiving requests for speaking engagements from every corner of the country. Within two years he was considered one of the leading voices of the church in America.

By the middle of his third year at the church, Pat and Becky had a two-year-old son, Luke, and an eleven-month-old daughter, Phoebe. It was apparent to the congregation that Pastor Pat was taking Rogers Memorial Church to a new level. In less than four years the church grew from just over 4,500 to more than 10,000 members, with an average weekly attendance of 6,000. That pattern continued even during Pat's leave of absence to work on a doctorate at Oxford.

The opportunity to study at Oxford came unexpectedly. During his third year at Rogers Memorial, one of the best-known Christian philanthropists in the country invited Pat to fly to Grand Rapids, Michigan, for a meeting. The elderly gentleman, who insisted on remaining anonymous, said he had been aware of Pat's love for Christ ever since he heard him speak at a Young Life conference many years earlier. He had gone to that event as a sponsor but had been watching Pat ever since. He read a paper Pat had written while at Southern Seminary and then got a copy of his senior thesis from Princeton. When he read the document, he decided to help Pat take the next step of his education.

The old gentleman told Pat he had a long-time connection with Oxford University in England, dating back to his own undergraduate study there a half-century earlier. Over the years, he had sponsored the studies of several promising young scholars, both in America and Britain, and helped at least one young man complete a doctorate at Keble College, Oxford. He wanted to do the same for Pat.

"I never considered going to Oxford. What would I study? Would I get to decide that or would someone else?"

"Basically, you decide. You will have to find a tutor who shares your area of academic interest, which I presume to be theology, but with your academic credentials and my financial support, I imagine you can do whatever you like."

It didn't take Pat long to make up his mind. "I would want to work on the writings of C. S. Lewis."

"Excellent. I was hoping you would say that."

"Then I'd be more than honored," Pat said, "to accept your generous offer."

"Splendid. Then it's settled. I propose we make a call early tomorrow morning to my good friend on the faculty of theology, and we'll see where that takes us."

Pat had already done so much reading and study on the life and work of Lewis that he was able to complete his readings and examinations in less time than expected. He wrote a dissertation and successfully defended it. In less than two years, with a substantial portion of the work done from his home in Tennessee, Pat earned his PhD or, as they called it at Oxford, a DPhil. He spent one full term and part of another in Oxford and returned with his family for the robing and graduation ceremonies.

He had his picture taken in full regalia with his tutor on the lawn of Liddon Quad, standing next to the elegant Gothic Revival chapel. He never had the photo framed and hung on his office wall. He kept it instead in a nightstand by his bed. On rare occasions, he took it out as a reminder of God's provision when he least expected it.

The new credential would have added to Pat's prestige, had he used it, but he decided not to put DPhil on his business cards or stationery, nor did he use it as part of his official title. Instead, he asked everyone to refer to him as they always had, as "Pastor Pat." Nevertheless, the study and travel in the United Kingdom had left a mark on him, adding a new level of security in the faith and a greater passion for sharing the gospel.

Except for those wonderful—but all too rare—hours of discussion and debate in his tutor's rooms at Keble College, Pat had to battle his way through the Oxford experience. He discovered that in Britain the Christian faith is all but dead. Less than three percent of the people there attend a Christian church.

The Muslim population, at nearly 10 percent of the nation, was very active in the local mosques. A sizable percentage of Britons might claim to be Christians, but there was little evidence of faith in their lives. Furthermore, Pat's professors and fellow theology students generally agreed that religion was little more than a convenient myth—a moral fable or emotional crutch. At best, it offered a set of organizing principles for a comfortable life—sort of like an old pair of shoes.

On top of everything, his work on Lewis eventually had to be watered down in order to survive the review process. He never compromised on the essentials, but he did cut portions of his paper where he had explained Lewis's view of "salvation through Christ alone" as the only logical way of responding to the gospel. He had originally quoted Lewis's statement, in which he said, "A man who was merely a man and said the sort of things Jesus said would not be a great moral teacher. He would either be a lunatic—on a level with the man who says he is a poached egg—or else he would be the Devil of Hell." But he had to cut that.

On returning home to America with Becky and the children, after all the celebrations were over, Pat made up his mind to "fight the good fight" as the apostle Paul had called Timothy to do. He was determined to do what he could to keep his country from the depths of apostasy and hopelessness that the formerly Christian nations of Europe were enduring. Over time his sermons, speeches, articles, and radio and TV broadcasts became more impassioned, focusing on the claim that "either Christ is Lord of all or He is not Lord at all" and the fundamental truth that "Jesus is the only way to God." He believed that Christ's teachings ought to influence every aspect of the culture.

Over time he developed a personal motto: Preach Jesus in word; preach Jesus in action.

| CHAPTER SEVEN |

OCTOBER 2015

Six Months Later

Matt Branson removed his overcoat and hung it on a hook near the door to his office. He shivered. October had arrived in D.C. and begun its annual work of freezing bone marrow wherever it could. Matt hated the cold yet always seemed to land in parts of the country where snow and cold dominated the winter months. Princeton wasn't Alaska, but it was plenty cold in February. After college, Matt had moved to law school—in Michigan. His next stop was Washington, D.C. It seemed he was doomed to spend part of his year longing to be in some sunny part of the country. Why couldn't the Department of Justice be in Florida?

Retrieving a University of Michigan coffee mug from the top of his desk, Matt stepped into the corridor and marched to the coffee pot. Moments later, the fluid began to warm him. He settled in behind his desk. He had arrived twenty minutes early, thanks to unexpectedly thin traffic.

Since college his life had been a struggle to put in twenty hours of work in every twenty-four-hour day. It had been that way at Princeton, in law school, the two years he had clerked in the U.S. District Court for the Eastern District of Michigan, and the year he had clerked for an appellate court judge. Matt considered hard work not only the key to success but also a sacred duty. That attitude had so impressed the judges for whom he clerked that both had made personal appeals to the attorney general. Alton Stamper had been quick to accept him into a nonpolitical deputy assistant's slot for the Office of Professional Responsibility.

On his desk Matt kept a small plastic cube with the text of the Apostle's Creed, the Lord's Prayer, and the Ten Commandments on three sides. On the fourth side he had placed his favorite photo of his wife, Michelle.

Matt tasted the coffee again.

"You need a warm up?"

Matt looked up to see Lisa Denton, his personal aide. She was short with dark eyes and long, black hair that curled around her shoulders.

"You're in a little early."

"Yeah," she said. "Traffic was light this morning. Go figure."

"Take your blessings where you can find them, Lisa. Tonight traffic might not be moving at all."

"No doubt. Anything you want me to start on?"

"Let's pick up where we left off."

"The assistant attorney general for the DTED called. He wants to have lunch again."

Matt grinned. "Did John say he was going to pay?"

"No, and I didn't ask."

"I'm just kidding, Lisa. We always split the ticket. After all, we're both poor civil servants."

"He wants to have lunch with you today. It's been a while."

"I imagine he has his hands full. I know I do."

"Do you keep up with all your college buddies?"

Matt shook his head. "Not really. We've all gone our own ways. Most of us lost contact when we went to grad school. John went to

Harvard; I went to Michigan. I didn't see him again until I started here. We've always worked in different areas of the law."

"So he's the only one?"

"I keep in touch with a couple others, but most live in other states. John and I happened to go to work here at Justice. When did he call?"

"Right before I left," Lisa said. "He seemed surprised you were already gone for the day."

"I hope you told him I was in a hearing."

Lisa grinned. "Of course I did. You work as hard as he does."

"Great. Go ahead and confirm the lunch. Did he say where he wanted to meet? Wait, let me guess: Terri's Italian."

"But do you know what time?" Lisa smiled and cocked her head.

"Um, noon."

"Lucky guess."

Matt walked the two blocks to Terri's Italian, a small bistro-style restaurant with a too-small common dining area and two large rooms in the back that could be reserved for meetings or parties. The rooms were often the choice of high-ranking government employees who needed a place to meet outside the office.

Matt arrived first, and the hostess showed him to one of the rear rooms. He took a seat at a round table with the requisite red-and-white-checkered tablecloth. Overhead hung empty Italian wine bottles. It looked like every other mass-produced Italian restaurant Matt had ever been in.

Five minutes later, John Knox Smith walked in wearing a charcoal-gray suit, emerald-green tie, and a stark white shirt. "Sorry to be late, Matt." He slapped Matt on the shoulder then removed his coat and draped it over an empty chair. "Glad you could make it."

"Thanks for inviting me, John. I'm surprised you offered to buy."

John laughed, "I didn't make that offer, but I get the hint. Wish we could do the National Gallery and lunch there more often. With the cheaper prices, you could afford to pay for mine without complaining."

Matt laughed in reply, "We've both got pretty demanding jobs, and we're not exactly after the same things."

"We work for the same guy, after all."

"True, but there's a world of difference between the DTED and the Office of Professional Responsibility.

"OPR is an important post. Keeping us government attorneys in check is tough work."

"We do what we can," Matt said.

"I'm just having a salad. How about you?"

Matt thought for a moment. He seldom ate lunch away from his desk. "Antipasto sounds good to me."

A waitress took the order and delivered the salads and diet drinks a few minutes later.

"I'm sorry I didn't arrange an invitation to the swearing in," John said.

"You've already apologized for that. You only had so many seats available to you. I saw it on the news."

"I still feel bad about it. I didn't have many friends in college. You were one of the few who could tolerate me."

"Who said I tolerated you?"

"Cute. Do you still have the tired old BMW you left Princeton with?"

Matt shook his head. "I kept it for a long time, but a few years of Michigan cold and snow did a job on it."

"Not to mention the road salt. I still have the Mercedes my dad gave me, although I have to put more and more money into it each year. So, how's the family?"

"Fine." Matt doubted John had come to ask about his family.

"Do you ever think about our college days?" John asked.

"Sometimes. I remember trying to keep up with you and Pat Preston. I always felt a few steps behind."

"Nonsense. You were a brain—*are* a brain."

"I lacked the academic skills you and Pat had. I always had to work twice as hard just to stay even."

"Nothing wrong with inspiration. You still a Christian?"

The question came so suddenly, Matt had trouble formulating a response. "Yes, of course. Why?"

John shrugged. "I remember you and Pat shared that conviction. I saw one of your old mentors at the swearing in."

"A mentor of mine? Who?"

"Larry Jordan. You know him, don't you?"

Matt set his fork down. "I've met him, yes. He's head of the Alliance here in D.C. He was at your swearing in?"

"He was, as well as a couple of his . . . friends." John took another bite of his salad, then asked, "Didn't I hear that you went to one of their programs or something? It was while you were in law school."

"I think you mean the Madison Scholars Academy. It was after my second semester."

"Sounds fascinating. Tell me about it."

Matt picked up his fork but did nothing with it. "Not much to tell. It's a summer study and internship program. It's nine weeks long."

"Where does it meet?"

"You can get that info from the Internet."

John looked wounded. "Ease up, Matt. I'm just trying to catch up with an old friend. This isn't an inquisition. I saw Larry Jordan at the swearing in, and it made me think of you."

"That was six months ago, John."

"True, but seeing you again brought it to mind. Look, if you're ashamed or—"

"Ashamed? It was the best summer of my life. It helped put faith and reason together."

"Now, you see, that's what interests me."

Matt inhaled deeply. Maybe he was overreacting.

"As you know, the Alliance is dedicated to protecting our first freedom: religious liberty. The right of free speech, right of peaceful assembly—"

"'Congress shall make no law respecting an establishment of religion, or prohibiting the free exercise thereof; or abridging the freedom of speech, or of the press; or the right of the people peaceably to assemble, and to petition the government for a redress of grievances.'" John raised an eyebrow. "They made us study constitutional law at Harvard too."

"Okay, the Alliance seeks to protect that. I applied to attend the Madison Scholars Academy to get a perspective on a few things I was wrestling with. We met at a campus not far from Chicago, and then I interned with a D.C. law firm."

"Did you learn anything?"

"I learned a lot, John. Do you remember the debate where you squared off with Pat on revisionist history? Well, I learned Pat was right. There is a social, cultural, and religious history that has been expunged from our high school and college history books."

"Pat would agree with you about that."

"I had been struggling with what I thought were conflicts between faith and science, faith and reason, faith and law. The parish I grew up in had a tired pastor and an aging population. I'd never heard what my church really believed, and I learned that no conflict exists between theology and those things."

Matt paused, then said, "I used to listen to you and Pat debate those issues and always left more confused than informed. Pat knew what he believed; you knew what you believed. I wasn't so sure. The Madison Scholars gave me the information I needed to make up my mind. Turns out, I wasn't alone. There were many people like me at Madison. For a while, I thought I was the only law student in the world still trying to be a Christian. Turns out there are a lot of Christians in law who love America and want her to be great again."

"I know a lot of law students driven to prayer by law school." John chuckled at his joke.

"They challenged us intellectually. David Barclay did a full day of lectures on the religious roots of America. Dr. Jerome Berlitsky, who teaches natural law at the University of New Mexico, challenged the way we think. He quoted others who said, 'There are some things we can't not know.'"

"'Can't not know.' That's awkward wording." John pushed his bowl of salad away.

"Awkward but powerful. He quoted the apostle Paul, who said some things are written on the heart."

"Sounds like you had a good time."

"Well, it's not Disneyland. David Barclay's lecture lasted five hours. It seemed like one hour. I can't believe how little I knew about our founding fathers."

"Sounds like you managed to keep you faith through law school, clerking, and your time in the DOJ."

"Why the sudden interest in my faith, John?"

"Do I need a reason?"

Matt stared at him for a moment. "One time back in college, I told you I had a personal relationship with Jesus Christ. I told you because I hoped it might lead to further discussion, but you just shrugged it off and changed the subject. Are you giving Christianity another look?"

"Not like you mean it, Matt. I still have my syncretic belief system. I draw from all faiths. Jesus is in the mix. The goal is equality."

"Jesus is in the mix?" Matt couldn't help himself. He laughed. "How's that working for you?"

"You need to remember, Matt, 'Every shaking advance of mankind towards equality and justice has come from the radical.'"

"John, don't quote Saul Alinksy to me. As a Christian, I agree with Jefferson's declaration that all men are created equal, that we all have value in the eyes of God, and we're free to become whoever He wants us to be. As to equality, one-time British Prime Minister Margaret Thatcher said, 'The single biggest intellectual error . . . has been to confuse freedom with equality. Equality is usually the enemy of freedom.'"

John smiled. "Matt, let's not go back to those debates at Princeton. The Department of Justice's official role now is to ensure equality, so you'd better not be quoting ancient Brits. And speaking of those old debates, do you ever talk to Pat Preston?"

Another question from left field. "No. We exchange Christmas cards every year. That's about it."

"Did he talk to you about the funeral?"

"He hasn't talked to me about any funerals."

"Not even the one he did for the preacher who shot the U.S. marshal in the head?"

Matt's mind began to whir. As one of the lead lawyers for the Office of Professional Responsibility at the DOJ, he had developed a sixth sense when wayward prosecutors were lying to him. "No, we haven't spoken or exchanged mail in years. Why do you ask?"

"He's doing well, you know. Went to Rogers Memorial Church a few years back. It was a big church then, about forty-five hundred in attendance; it's over ten thousand now."

"How do you know this? Are you investigating him?"

"What's to investigate? He does, however, have an annoying habit of descending into hate speech topics in his sermons—sermons that are broadcast over radio and television and streamed over the Internet. It's disconcerting."

Matt pushed away his half-full salad bowl and drink, then leaned over the table. "You *are* investigating him. You're trying to get me to deliver a message."

John looked at his watch. "Wow, look at the time. I've got to go."

"It's been less than half an hour, John."

"We should take a long lunch soon and head over to the National Gallery of Art. You know, break up our usual routine. It's just two blocks from the office. They have a great new traveling exhibit of some modern art and architecture, including I. M. Pei, who designed the East Building. And let's go see my favorite: Alexander Calder's seventy-six-foot-long mobile. It's hung high in the atrium—"

"John, what do you want?"

John pulled cash from his wallet and tossed it on the table. "Maybe you should send your Christmas card early." He didn't wait for a response but turned and marched out of the restaurant.

| CHAPTER EIGHT |

From his position in the Justice Department, John Knox Smith was able to incorporate many of the ideas he had learned from his professors at Princeton and Harvard Law into the departmental procedures employed by his staff. He was glad to know that fewer and fewer people still believed the old myths about the country's founding era. As John read it, people were concerned about the future and had developed a desire for fairness and equality—at least most people. Hate mongers still existed.

Thanks to the progressive administration of President Blaine and his supporters, there was now a generation of bright, young, equally progressive judges being appointed to the federal courts who understood and who were dedicated to changing the world. Thank goodness the curmudgeons are mostly gone, along with their antiquated ideas about the Constitution and the law—originalism and precedents and textualism and the intent of the founders. What were they thinking? The republic couldn't have lasted another fifty years if that outdated view had endured much longer.

Some of John's older classmates from Harvard had already been appointed to the federal bench. The president understood that letting attorneys get too much "experience" before being placed on the bench could be deadly to the progressive agenda. These were bright young people who understood that the Constitution was only the starting point and not holy writ. What wisdom the founders had was that they understood that all those things would have to change, so they provided a judicial system and a mechanism for revising, updating, and amending the Constitution to keep that living, breathing document relevant to the needs and wishes of generations yet to come.

The law that established the Diversity and Tolerance Enforcement Division was, by any measure, an amazing piece of work that cut through decades of red tape and interdepartmental feuding. The country had long been divided into ninety-three federal districts, including territories such as the Marshall Islands, the Virgin Islands, Puerto Rico, and so on. At the same time, there were twelve federal circuits and federal courts of appeal, including the District of Columbia. This meant that like all other federal laws the district courts, circuit courts, and ultimately the Supreme Court of the United States were empowered to hear and decide the cases that John and his staff were prosecuting. Unlike other laws, any challenge to the constitutionality of RDTA moved immediately to the top of the docket for review.

In each federal district, there was also a U. S. attorney appointed by the president and confirmed by the Senate. These people served at the pleasure of the president, and the president did not have to show cause to fire any or all of them. Normally they were the chief federal law enforcement officer in their territory and called the shots.

But one of the most remarkable features of the RDTA provided that prosecutors in D.C. would no longer need the cooperation of the U.S. attorneys in the ninety-three federal districts. It was all John's idea. The RDTA made it possible for the DTED, working with the DTED Enforcement Hate Crimes agents, to empanel a grand jury in any federal district and pursue hate crime cases under their own authority after simply notifying the locals. Equally amazing was establishing the special enforcement unit directly within the DTED, allowing agents like Paul Atoms direct investigative, arrest, and related powers.

All this meant they didn't have to follow normal Justice Department protocols. And none of this could have happened without Will Blaine's consent.

It also meant that John Knox Smith could have, in effect, thousands of Justice Department lawyers, all ninety-three U.S. attorneys' offices, the FBI field offices in every state, the FBI headquarters in Washington, plus all the agents and liaisons in the D.C. headquarters working for the DTED as need be. At the same time, he had direct authority over the Postal Inspection Service and other federal enforcement agencies.

The RDTA legislation framed it so that the director of the division had up to one hundred full-time, top-notch prosecutors to carry out departmental mandates. Congress had never before enacted new criminal laws on such a scale. It was one of the largest justice initiatives in history, and John felt he was sitting in the catbird seat. There was no question that President Blaine had helped put him there.

Within their first month at the DTED, John's people had conducted raids and confiscations in many parts of the country, just so the people would begin to realize there was a new lawman in town. Every citizen needed to know that there was an overwhelming urgency to obey the law and to cooperate with this powerful enforcement agency. John's team had wasted no time in getting the word out.

They had made sure the judicial and law enforcement networks knew what was happening because John wanted to send a message. "It's not that we're vindictive," he had explained in a letter to the special agents in charge of federal law enforcement offices. "We just want people to know this is serious business. There is no such thing as a slap on the wrist anymore. These cases are felonies. The only way to wake people up is to put habitual offenders away."

Adding to the impact of the new litigation was the fact that the American Civil Liberties Union—in cooperation with other civil liberties groups and nongovernmental organizations, most of which became eligible to receive federal funds—was waging its own campaign of intimidation, closely coordinated with the DTED and the hate crimes units. In some cases, ACLU lawyers augmented ongoing prosecutions with investigative input or legal assistance; in others, they brought civil suits or conducted full-scale media campaigns on their own. No one was more appreciative of the ACLU's equality enforcement efforts than John Knox Smith, who had been a card-carrying member of the ACLU ever since his time at Harvard Law School. He had attended their events and contributed to the organization while studying under Dr. Saul Peterson at Princeton, but to avoid any appearance of a conflict of interest, he had dropped his formal association with the group when he was named head of the DTED. However, like many others in the justice system, including members of the Supreme Court, he had kept an informal and business relationship with the group, a relationship he was proud of.

Although part of the ACLU was recognized as a private, nonprofit, public-interest law firm, attorneys in the group's D.C. headquarters were intimately involved in case selection for the DOJ. They were a tremendous source of intelligence and frequently sent damaging information on religious figures and organizations to John, Joel Thevis, and other prosecutors on the staff with the names of targets they deemed "ripe for an indictment." With their help, John believed the DTED would be able to make a substantial contribution to the dream of the group's founder and guiding spirit, Roger Baldwin, and some of its recent leaders, to "separate these people from society." Baldwin had little patience for any person or group who disagreed with his worldview and who would try to impose their morals on others.

John couldn't agree more.

| CHAPTER NINE |

Eighteen months later

John was on the fast track now. He had already argued and won another case before the Supreme Court, upholding sections of the RDTA legislation he had helped draft, sections that made it possible for him to hold his new position. In direct contrast to that sad-looking bunch of losers standing on the street corner the morning of his swearing-in ceremony two years earlier, he had risen to prominence. President Blaine hailed him as a superstar. The vice president called him a "miracle worker." To Attorney General Alton Stamper, John could do no wrong.

Key members of Congress took turns praising him, as well as leading academics, broadcasters, journalists, and law enforcement officials from around the world. As good as the praise was, John felt best about the unfailing loyalty of his handpicked staff of lawyers and investigators who were eager to take the ball and run.

The DTED staff was young, but every one had a stellar background. They knew what they were doing, and they believed John was the kind of leader they had always wanted to work for. John said he didn't like being the center of attention, but he did like being at the center of the action.

Loyalty naturally accrues to those in positions of power, but John's staff also knew that whoever made the boss look good ended up looking good as well. Each member of the DTED team worked overtime to burnish John's reputation.

The staff's temperament varied greatly. Some had chips on their shoulders from previous work they had done and previous insults they had suffered. Reneé X fit that mold. Still, they were special and industrious, or else they wouldn't be there. Most had come up through the system or had been recruited from other departments and divisions of the federal bureaucracy. John had handpicked a few because he had seen something in their background or accomplishments he believed made them ideal for the new department.

The number one requirement was youth and energy. John had come to the DOJ at twenty-seven years of age, and he had been a ball of fire ever since. Now, four years later, he knew that youth was on his side. That's why he insisted on assembling a staff of young, energetic, and motivated men and women from the best universities. While a fifty-year-old prosecutor might be more nuanced, balanced, and deliberative in making his case and going after the target, these young people were fast on their feet, impulsive, and ready to do battle at the drop of John's hat. That's exactly what John was looking for.

Every agency of government used a system of annual employee appraisals, measuring five levels of performance. Federal employees received ratings of "outstanding," "exceeds fully successful," "fully successful," "minimally successful," or "unacceptable." Anyone performing in the top two levels received a pay raise and, in some cases, an annual bonus as well. Some employees worked hard for those high ratings. On the other hand, individuals rated in the bottom two categories were subject to immediate reassignment or dismissal.

For the wired-in agents and lawyers on John's staff, it was all about getting high marks and extra kudos in those reviews. Because competitiveness, hard work, and the ability to get things done in a timely manner were attributes of those in the highest categories, John only brought people on board who had shown themselves to be high achievers, consistently appearing in the top category in their annual performance ratings.

There were still a few agents in Washington who loved to investigate the old-fashioned kinds of crimes and catch bad guys. Those were the traditional gumshoe detectives from the pages of crime fiction—basically a dying breed. There was another kind of agent, one whose primary motivation was to work his or her way up the ladder to a high spot on the food chain. They didn't reflect much on what was happening with the people around them or on whether the right guys were in charge. They were only interested in getting convictions, whatever it took. If they could get the right technical charges, they could make a case; if they could slam a perp with a conviction that made all the papers, so much the better.

The more convictions they got by plea or by trial, the faster they could rise, the better they looked, the more places they could go. It was a volatile combination that, in the wrong hands, could spell disaster for the target of an investigation, especially when someone was being targeted not because of what they did but because of who they were and what they believed.

Even before the Diversity and Tolerance Enforcement Division was formally commissioned, a lot of legal research had been done to lay the groundwork for John's legal "bulldozers." Case workers established networks of informants and made preliminary contact with like-minded agencies and even international nongovernmental organizations, called NGOs, letting them know that the doors of the agency would soon be open for business.

By the time Chief Justice Isaiah Williams finished giving John the first handshake and slap on the back, there were writs and cease-and-desist orders sitting on John's desk, ready to be sent to individuals and organizations judged to be in violation of the new laws. Within weeks there were lawsuits, search warrants, and legal actions in process.

Over the previous two years, John had tried to make clear to everyone that the people who worked for him were not bad people. They didn't do this work out of hatred or bitterness. They did their jobs, working for a larger house, a better car, and a bigger paycheck. Some had been attracted to government jobs because they liked the feeling of power. For a few, perhaps, it was the "little man, big gun" syndrome— ordinary people with a little too much power. John wasn't looking for perfection, just a good, healthy balance and a penchant for getting convictions.

As far as he was concerned, the more aggressive his team members became and the more convictions they racked up, the better the media coverage would be. John had become very media savvy. He was poised, handsome, quick on his feet; and he loved making media appearances.

He had been at the DTED less than two months when Harvard Law invited him to give the graduation address. It was a coup for someone so young to speak at commencement. While there, he met with deans and professors, urging them to send the best and brightest graduates his way.

More invitations rolled in. He spoke on NPR, CBS, MSNBC, and other networks. He even made the cover of *Esquire* magazine as one of Washington's most fashionable young executives. John served as a guest lecturer at Georgetown University Law Center and took part in several widely publicized media events.

In record time he made the list of social invitations and became a regular at some of the most illustrious progressive think tanks in Washington and a regular guest at the Human Rights Campaign. His public affairs people, who were allowed to promote John's public appearances beyond the scope of ordinary DOJ guidelines, were kept busy making arrangements with the media. John, however, was selective in what engagements he accepted. He took only shows and interviews that would reach the intellectual segment of the population. He would never go on Fox News, for example, or give interviews to right-wing periodicals. His time was much too valuable, and he spoke only to those news outlets that could help him move the ball forward. The one exception was an interview by *USA Today*, which he agreed to only because he knew it would give him and the agency exposure to thousands of business travelers.

Success, however, didn't come cheap. Long hours, less sleep, and growing stress at home exacted an emotional price.

John took his seat at the head of the conference table. Camped around the table's perimeter sat his team. He had called his key players together to identify some of the issues and individuals they needed to deal with. Truth was, things had begun to slow down, and John wasn't happy about it.

He listened to reports and drummed his fingers through each account. He let the room fall silent, then said, "Listen, people, we have a terrific program here and a federal mandate that allows us to get whatever we need when we need it, whether it involves federal or civil cases, mail fraud, or Internet and broadcast violations. We're empowered to charge in and get the goods, but we haven't been doing much charging lately. Will somebody please tell me what's going on?"

Silence dominated the room until one of the newer attorneys said, "It's all about time, John. We're busting our fannies trying to get everything done. There's just so much paper you can push through the legal pipe at one time."

"I don't buy it. Of any department in the DOJ, we have the greatest freedom, the largest latitude. I know you're working hard, but you're not working harder or longer than I am. Lately, we've fallen off our game. Where are the big cases? To achieve our goals, we not only have to prosecute cases, but we must prosecute cases that get media coverage. It's the only way to get word out that we mean business."

DTED Special Agent Paul Atoms, who had been quiet during the meeting, spoke up. "I'll tell you what's eating me, John. It's these people in the western states that won't do anything to stop the hate speech going on in their jurisdiction? It's everywhere you look out there. If you go into any of those churches on a Sunday morning, they'll be preaching that stuff. You can hear it on the radio in your car. If you get their junk mail—which I do now and then—it's always the same thing: they just keep preaching their hatred. What's wrong with these people? What's it going to take to get their attention?"

The words struck deep in John's pride. Atoms was right, but hearing the words spoken aloud touched off John's already short fuse. "I'll be run out before I let that go on any longer. So help me, we're going to show these people they cannot resist the United States government!"

There was a stir as the members of the team reacted to John's intensity, but John continued. "Congress has given us a free hand to do whatever we have to do to get the job done. They wrote us a good law, but it's useless if we don't use it. Like all laws, the courts will have to interpret what it means, and that's why the litigation you all do is so important. But can't somebody make something big happen?" John shot to his feet and began to pace.

Lead attorney Joel Thevis cleared his throat. John fixed his eyes on him. Lately, John had come to believe that Thevis was slowing things down with his insistence that every detail of every case be vetted.

"We can't assume the other side won't fight back, John," Thevis said. "I don't think you can always count on open-and-shut cases. It may be well and good to rally the troops, but caution is still the better part of valor."

"Is that a fact? Better part of valor? Give it a rest, Joel!" John's word carried an edge. "The other side will have their lawyers defending their arguments. So what? I don't doubt they'll trot out their old First Amendment dodge, but that's not going to work anymore. The First Amendment was never meant to protect hate speech. That's the law."

"Even if we win at the district court level, John, you know they'll come back at us over and over again."

"Meaning what?"

"Meaning that some cases are not slam dunks, even when it looks like we're winning. I've studied some of the cases where that group, the Alliance, has been involved. They don't give up just because some government agency is involved. They routinely beat the ACLU. They've got a lot of experienced people, and they won't take a solid beating lying down. But win or lose—and you have to admit, they win a lot—they're never going to lie down just because the DTED is coming to town."

John's first impulse was to lash out. Mention of the Alliance brought his blood to a boil. Instead of unloading on Joel, John took a deep breath and shoved his anger down. "Understood, Joel. That's why it's so important to have someone like Chief Justice Isaiah Williams on our side. He understands the importance of the RDTA legislation and why it was written the way it was. It's a short ride down Independence Avenue to the Supreme Court from here, and anything we take to that level, we win."

"John, there is more than one man on the Supreme—"

John slammed his hand on the table. The sound echoed in the large room. "I know how many members sit on the Supreme Court, Joel. Don't lecture me about constitutional law or the Supreme Court. I've argued before them. If anyone in this room understands the court, it's me."

"I wasn't trying to lecture you, John. I'm saying it would be unwise to assume a victory there, even with Chief Justice Williams on our side."

John waved Thevis off. "Look, we've got people all over the country who understand what we're doing here and why it's important to establish some benchmarks. By that I mean I want some strong cases that will send a message to every man, woman, and child in America that hate speech is going to stop. Do you hear what I'm saying?" He turned to Paul Atoms and Bob Maas of the IRS. "I want you to call in your assets. You've got informants. Use them. Stop fooling around. Get us some earth-shaking cases we can go after."

Atoms nodded. "I'm with you, Boss. Here's something we can use. I know these two guys over in Arlington across the river who set up a Web site and an overnight 800 number to report hate speech violations. Anybody who witnesses an open display of bigotry, hate, or intolerance of any kind can go to that Web site and report it. The information comes right back to us. Unless I miss my guess, within a few weeks these guys will be flooded with phone calls and e-mails, and we'll have more cases than we can handle."

"Okay, see how it goes, Paul," John said. "It's a good start. But you may need to come up with some sort of reward system for people who bring us tips that lead to convictions. We don't need any more small potatoes—just the big stuff. If they give us a tip that results in a successful prosecution and conviction, they ought to get a tax-free reward or something like that. See what you can come up with. We can work it out, I'm sure. Spread the word that there's a paycheck for cooperating with this agency. Who knows what you might turn up?"

The frequency of raids increased. DTED officers and agents with the nationwide Hate Crimes Task Force went into churches, ministry offices, and charitable organizations, arresting staffers and volunteers, and marched them out in front of the media. There were dramatic photos of men and women in handcuffs doing what the headlines referred to as the "perp walk" or the "frog march." It was an unforgettable show of force that had enormous PR value for the DTED.

Most of those arrested were never convicted. Some were charged, all were humiliated, and many lost their jobs. Their families were publicly embarrassed, yet most of them never went to trial, and some of those who did were eventually exonerated.

The presumption of innocence until proven guilty, the heart of the Bill of Rights, kept many of the arrestees out of jail. The DTED worked differently. In the new cases brought by John's team, there was a presumption of guilt, whether they could substantiate it in court. The public scandal devastated the individuals and the religious organizations involved and made ministry fund-raising next to impossible.

John had made it clear, in light of years of "church shootings" and religious violence, that he didn't want his agents to get hurt. He frequently reminded them of Ronnie Lee Jefferson's murder. Whenever the action teams went on raids, they were ordered to show plenty of force and, when necessary, use it. For John, the object of the raids was the shock value, sending a loud warning to anyone who might be tempted to resist that there would be a price to pay for their foolishness.

In some cases, they sent a dozen agents in full assault gear to arrest a couple of unarmed, middle-aged women. The agents on DTED operations looked more like commandos than law enforcement officers. There were special agents in POLICE windbreakers with helicopters buzzing overhead. They called in local law enforcement and used bullhorns to command everyone in the building to exit. People came out with their hands up, some in tears.

There were scenes on the six o'clock news of police investigators working in areas cordoned off with yellow tape and crime-scene technicians hauling out computers and files in cardboard boxes.

One case drew national attention. Two men from Gideons International were handing out Bibles on a public sidewalk in front of an Albany, Georgia, high school. The principal of the school called the police. When the Gideons, both in their late sixties, tried to explain to the officers that the First Amendment protected such an activity, one of the officers grabbed a Bible from the man's hand and slapped him across the face with it. The second Gideon, without thinking, knocked the officer's hand away.

A student with a cell phone caught everything on video, and the footage was broadcast on the evening news for weeks. The local reporter said on the air, "People once thought of Gideons as law-abiding citizens, but these pictures tell a different story." A police department report indicated that the officer suffered severe bruises and emotional stress as a result of the incident. A spokesperson for the city said it was apparently no accident the Gideons had taken the name of an ancient warrior and bigot. But despite excellent media management, some reporters and news outlets, especially in smaller communities, questioned the need for such massive shows of force for otherwise seemingly peaceful "ministry operations." This began to build steam, and some national programs raised questions. John had to become more proactive with the media.

When these first signs of blowback appeared, John went on television to refute allegations that his people were overreaching, overreacting, and using excessive force. He told a CNN reporter, "I shouldn't have to point out that the police officers and federal agents responding to these cases are upstanding, hard-working men and women, doing the jobs they've been trained to do. These are red-white-and-blue Americans. They're proud to be serving their country in this way." It was a message he repeated in every interview.

John kept to himself that none of the agents and officers carrying out the DTED's directives had enough information to make important decisions on their own. John had been furious when he learned a policewoman had told a reporter, "We just follow orders and leave the rest to the people who get paid to give orders."

When John's department issued writs and apprehension orders, as many as a half dozen departments and agencies would be mobilized and mixed. The officers conducting the raids were from different units and seldom knew each other. Under orders, they simply went in, using force when necessary, and apprehended a group of suspects they had been told might be armed and dangerous. None of them thought of asking the task force commander why they were going in. If they had an arrest warrant signed by a federal magistrate or judge, then they had all the explanation they needed.

John Knox Smith explained some of these procedures on another nationally televised interview program hosted by Jonathan Kooper and specifically mentioned the Gideons case. Unlike previous television interviews, Kooper had arranged to have a defense attorney from the Alliance present. The split-screen interview soon turned hot. John struggled to keep his temper. To make matters worse, the Alliance representative was Larry Jordan. Though two years had passed, John had been unable to erase the image of Jordan staring at him as he took his oath of office.

"Mr. Smith," Larry said, "you know very well that the Georgia Gideons are honest citizens. These are Christian men who volunteer their time to give Bibles to whoever wants them. They're men of peace. Your agency is trying to paint them as hoodlums."

John's composure slipped. "Don't make me laugh. These are men who lashed out at a police officer, causing bodily harm. That's assault and battery, counselor. That's basic law. You should know that. How dare you call them men of peace!"

Kooper stepped in. "You must admit, Mr. Smith, that most people would agree the Gideons in this case are ordinary, honest citizens."

"Do they? Do you have an opinion poll for that, Kooper?" John shifted in his seat. "If true, then it shows how wrong people have been about this bloody religion that wants converts at all costs."

Larry pounced on the comment. "Mr. Smith, that's a slander. That's basic law. You should know that. You're attacking the religious beliefs of—"

"I'm not attacking anything." John raised his voice. "Read your own history. Your religion started two thousand years ago with a blood sacrifice—a human sacrifice at that. The people in your churches are absolutely fixated on blood. You sing songs about it and perform rituals in which you drink the blood of Jesus. Can you deny that? If you scratch the surface, even the most peaceful Christians will eventually show their true colors."

Before Larry could reply, the grainy cell phone video began playing in a loop, repeating only the portion of the dispute where the Gideon grabbed the officer and shoved him away.

Larry objected. "Show the whole thing, Jonathan. Show the cop hitting the Gideon. You've cut out the part where the police officer strikes our client across the face."

Kooper said, "We'll be back." The network cut to a commercial break. When the show returned four minutes later, Kooper moved on to another topic but did so over Larry's protest. Larry did manage to slip in, "The full video can be seen at our Web site or at any number of video sites on the Internet."

John felt he had won that debate, but he was outraged nonetheless. His dream job would turn into a nightmare if the media gave the religious whackos support. He was under pressure on the job, fighting a war at home with his never-happy wife, and for the first time the agency was getting resistance from members of the media. He had heard that some of his colleagues at DOJ thought the DTED was moving too fast. John remained confident that the agency could deal with resistance from right-wingers around the country. There were still some pockets of unredeemed red-state adherents out there, but it was much harder to deal with resistance from inside the camp.

The team leaders who had watched that interview on the television in John's private office were thrilled with his performance—none more so than Andrea Covington, who called his BlackBerry immediately after the broadcast. "John," she said, "you were fantastic! It took my breath away, seeing you like that, speaking so forcefully and looking so . . . so authoritative. I am proud of you. We all are."

Hearing those words from Andrea's lips was the best gift anyone could have given him. It was the kind of feedback he needed.

Larry Jordan slipped into the hot water of his spa, found his favorite seat, and let the jets of air and hot water massage the back of his neck.

"Jim Stockman called right after the interview," Marla said. She moved to a spa seat next to him and took his hand. She wore a jade-green swimsuit. "He said you were at your best."

Larry chuckled. "I hope that's not my best. Smith got too many licks in and dominated the conversation—something Kooper said he wouldn't allow. Then . . . the way the network handled the Gideon tape! I should have done more to make them show the whole thing." He leaned his head back and looked at the stars overhead. The scent of freshly mowed grass in their backyard filled the air. In the distance, a neighborhood dog barked at something only he could hear.

"What could you do? They don't let you run the video equipment."

Larry's muscles, caressed by the spa's hot water, began to relax. "I toyed with refusing to change subjects. You know, sit there like bump on a log until they did as I asked."

"Why didn't you?" Marla asked. She laid her head back and stared at the same stars.

"You know how these interviews work, Marla. The network thinks their viewers are too stupid to follow a topic more than a few minutes. It's ping-pong journalism. Talk about this for eight minutes, run a commercial set, talk about that for six, run a set of commercials. It's formulaic. If I tried to stay on topic, Kooper would have defaulted to Smith, and he would have run the whole segment." Larry closed his eyes, took a deep breath, and exhaled slowly.

Marla said nothing.

"Whose idea was it to get a spa?" Larry asked.

"Mine. The idea came to me when I could count the number of knots in your neck and shoulder muscles."

"You're a genius."

"Of course I am."

Larry opened his eyes. "I have moments when I think we're losing, Marla. Smith and his DTED people are getting away with so much.

The rate at which they're conducting their raids is increasing. Many of those arrested turn to us. It's an honor to represent them, but we're getting overwhelmed." He sat up and gazed into the dark water. "I can't believe our country has backpedaled so much over the last two years. This is what our founding fathers feared, and now it's happening. Faith is being criminalized. Freedom of speech is being trampled. Historically freedoms have been trampled under military boots. Now our freedom is being trodden by people in the latest-style loafers and expensive suits."

"All in the name of tolerance."

Larry cupped his hands and splashed water on his face. He could smell the chemicals in it. "When I was a kid, my father told me that if you can name something, you can control it. Smith, Congress, and the president have assigned the labels used by media and lawmakers. Preaching the gospel is now hate speech. Speak out against any social ill except poverty or the environment, and it's suddenly hate speech. The government is for equality and tolerance; churches are for hatred. The sad thing is, people are starting to believe it."

"If you tell a lie long enough, it becomes the truth."

"That's right. That's what we're fighting."

"And," Marla added, "you're having some great successes."

"Many of which we've won by the skin of our teeth. Smith is smart. In some ways, he's a genius. He knows the law, he knows people, he knows the media, and he's convinced himself he is doing something worthwhile—something noble."

Marla ran her hand up and down Larry's back. "That's the difference between you and John Knox Smith. He thinks he's doing something noble. You know you're *called* to do something noble."

They fell silent for several minutes. Larry watched the bubbles on the water as if one of them might burst, releasing the one answer he needed to make the growing nightmare end. Thousands of bubbles burst, but none offered more than the air they held.

"Ready for bed, hon?" Marla asked.

"Can't I sleep here?"

"Only if you want to look like a prune when you go into the office. Prunes aren't known for their leadership abilities."

Larry laughed. "Okay, you win. Tomorrow, the battle continues." He rose, and the cool night air chilled him. So did the thought of the fight he felt obligated to wage.

| CHAPTER TEN |

For John, one of the most dangerous things about the evangelical church's intolerance remained the seemingly ever-present preachers on the airwaves and Internet. Some, like Reneé's favorite targets, Jim Stockman of the Christian Family Forum and Ron Wilder of the North American Christian Network, had daily radio and Internet broadcasts that reached coast-to-coast and even around the world. It was hate speech on a macro level, using the Bible to bash homosexuals, social progressives, oppose equality, and people of other religions. It was bringing in outrageous sums of money in the form of donations from supporters all over the world.

As the confrontations continued to escalate, John began to think the warnings from Joel Thevis were coming true. The Alliance and its allies were fighting back and winning far too many cases. To get his agents back on track, John decided on a more direct approach. He called the whole team into his private office and told them he wanted everything they could get on the Alliance itself. "I want to know who these guys are. Get me every name. I want to know everywhere they've been, everything they've done, and every penny they've spent for the last five years."

"We know Larry Jordan leads the group—" Reneé X began.

"Larry Jordan is one person in the Alliance. He's the head, but there are other people doing his dirty work. I want to know about them." He pointed to Special Agent Bob Maas. "Maas, I'd like you to be in charge of this. I want you to find out who's paying the bills and what their endgame is. How big is the outfit? One way or another, we're going to stop these guys. Get with Sandra and find out about their direct mail and e-mail operations. Who puts all that together? How many pieces do they send out? I want us to know every name on their lists. I particularly want to know how they put together their cases and how they always manage to come up so strong against our guys at the worst possible time. Can you do that, Bob?"

Maas nodded. "Check. We'll get started right away."

"Good. I want you to do whatever it takes. We've been looking the other way too long, and these guys have been eating our lunch. Get me the goods on the Alliance, and do it fast."

When a staffer on the Hill learned complaints were coming from his district, he usually asked, "How many people are we talking about? Ten or ten thousand?" If it were ten, he'd say he didn't have time to deal with it. If it were one thousand, he'd do what he could. But if it were ten thousand, he'd take the matter seriously and make whatever promises were necessary. Before long, the issue would figure prominently in the next campaign.

It may have been cynical, but old-timers believed there was more truth than fiction in that view. Such was the mindset of John and the DTED agents working to learn everything about the Alliance and those who spearheaded its work. They knew enough about Larry Jordan and the Washington staff to know they were determined and aggressive. But none of that had mattered until the Alliance had become a major threat. Now John wondered what lay in the deeper levels of the group.

How were they able to show up so consistently when the DTED brought an action? If the Alliance were just some right-wing outfit working out of a storefront, John and his team could ignore them, but they were much more than that. They were a large organization with a huge support base. They couldn't be ignored any longer.

John knew he couldn't go up against the more than four hundred thousand churches, synagogues, and mosques in America, but he believed most of them would be cooperative if they had a better grasp of how federal policy worked and how the system he administered functioned. The DTED existed for the well-being of the community. What's not to like?

To help bridge the growing chasm between the churches and the government, John approached the White House about establishing funding for what he called Faith-Based Action Centers, to be established in every church and religious organization in the country. Building on the remnants of the old Faith-Based and Community Initiatives program, John's idea was to set up a national Web site to coordinate the activities of these action centers. They would host a series of issue-oriented forums around the country to support the new citizen-led committees and help them organize training programs.

The Faith-Based Action Centers or FACs would help people understand and incorporate federal policies established by the new laws. Above all, they would encourage respect for diversity, tolerance, and equality in the homes, schools, neighborhoods, and churches of America.

President Blaine enthusiastically supported John's plan and brought in Senator Elizabeth Borden and leaders of the House Committee on Financial Services and the Committee on Oversight and Government Reform to secure the necessary support and funding from Congress. The White House Office of Legislative Affairs vetted the final version of the bill, and when all the behind-the-scenes work was completed and it had quietly passed both houses, President Blaine signed the bill and announced the new initiative to the public at a televised ceremony in the Rose Garden.

"For too long, people have believed that the important doctrine of separation of church and state means that government should have no interest in the faith community, but that's not the case. Our public servants in Washington, in the federal and state legislatures, and in city and county governments all over this country care very deeply about what happens in the religious community.

"More than fifty percent of Americans say they have some sort of religious affiliation. This is not something government can ignore. The initiative we're announcing today—to set up Faith-Based Action Centers in churches, mosques, and synagogues all over America—will help bring us all together to ensure a closer, friendlier, and more cooperative relationship between the government and the American people, with grants and operating funds for church leaders who promote the healthy separation envisioned by America's founders.

"Along with this new program of Citizen-Led Action and Mobilization Programs—CLAMPs—the centers will help members become more involved in the important issues of the day. This is where faith and political action legitimately work together. It means that faith-based funding will be available to churches, synagogues, and mosques that teach and embody the principles of diversity, tolerance, and equality, helping to make us a more caring and sensitive nation."

Matt Branson grew uncomfortable with John's recent actions. He had first felt the disquiet eighteen months before when John pumped him for information about Pat Preston. Nothing had come of that, but John's recent tactics left Matt puzzled and concerned.

Matt couldn't believe his old friend had gone so far. John wasn't the same person he had known in college. The fact that three of the highest ranking officials in Washington had praised John so lavishly, giving him their seal of approval, was impressive; but the things Matt was hearing about John and the cases he pursued were troubling.

The distance between them expanded. Their once-weekly lunches and twice-monthly trips to the art museum became less frequent. Weekly lunches became biweekly; biweekly became monthly. It had been six months since Matt and John had walked the shiny floors of the National Gallery of Art.

It wasn't until he began hearing rumors inside the DOJ and seeing the news coverage about DTED operations in the South that he started to wonder what John was really up to. Those concerns magnified when he overheard part of a conversation between a pair of college students at a restaurant in Old Town Alexandria.

One young man sitting at the bar, a few steps from where Matt was having dinner, told his friend, "I'm totally up against the wall, man, because of something I said on my blog. I mean, I was jokin' around, you know?"

"Geez, what'd ya post, dude?" his friend asked.

"All I said was I was afraid the homos were taking over. I mean, it was a joke! But a couple of days later this guy from the DTED Hate Crimes calls me at home and goes like totally berserk. A couple of days later, I get this long, threatening letter from some guy—Smith or something like that—and before I know it, all these detectives are snooping around. I mean, they've got everything but tracker dogs on my tail."

Smith? John Knox Smith? It fit with the DTED Hate Crime visit. Matt gazed at the meatloaf and potatoes on his plate. He had planned to go back to the office, but home was looking better.

Overhearing that bit of conversation got Matt's attention. It also started him thinking a lot more about the policies John and his team were carrying out. He grew concerned about how the tactics the agency was using affected real people. In the beginning, Matt had been curious but not skeptical about John's work. He didn't believe in conspiracies, and he didn't listen to gossip. He had debated enough philosophy and religion with John to know he wasn't a bad guy. John had different views, but he was open-minded. He enjoyed a good debate, and they'd had many of them. John had even taken the time to meet with Matt to drop an unmistakable hint for Matt to ask Pat to be careful. That was months ago, but John seemed to be changing with every turn of the calendar page.

What Matt heard that evening frightened him. He had read a few things about the DTED in the *Washington Post* and had seen comments posted on the Internet. It made him wonder. Still, he had ignored most of that. Now his interest was piqued. Matt began listening more closely to the office gossip. The more he learned about the DTED, the more he suspected something improper was going on. Things were changing. It wasn't looking good for people who didn't take a seat on the diversity and tolerance bandwagon.

For the first time, Matt began to consider that his old friend, John Knox Smith, might be a very dangerous man.

The dichotomy between Matt's beliefs and those of John made him think of his experiences at the Madison Scholars Academy during his student days. The Alliance believed what Jesus said in John 14:6: "I am the way and the truth and the life. No one comes to the Father except through me." They believed Jesus is the only way to God and defended that view openly. Their theme verse was John 15:5, where Jesus says, "I am the vine; you are the branches . . . apart from me you can do nothing." The old John would have debated the issue or maybe mocked it; today's John would blow a fuse.

There were probably a few ministries in the country that could withstand a full-scale assault from a big agency like the DTED, but they'd better have some pretty good ammunition. Matt knew the Alliance had plenty. On his first day that summer in Chicago, he had heard Alex Stanton—the Alliance head at the time—describe how they work. What got his attention was hearing that the Alliance believed that God favored their efforts. For someone like John, having a Bible verse as an organization's motto would be a big enough threat. But saying that God is blessing their efforts?

One of the instructors in Matt's seminar at Madison had characterized John's way of thinking well when he said, "Most of these people know what Christianity teaches. What they oppose isn't religion. They certainly don't oppose what we would call loosey-goosey liberal Christianity. What they oppose is Jesus on the cross with His arms extended to embrace the world. What they're against is the claim that Christianity has something to offer and requires us to respond."

When someone had asked if there was some sort of conspiracy to wipe out Christianity, the lecturer said he didn't believe that. "Our opponents don't have a problem with religion," he had explained. "But Christians claim to have the truth—truth with a capital T. That's what they hate. They much prefer the view that Christianity is just one of many paths. If it's no big deal and one 'truth claim' is as good as another, then there's nothing to argue about. But if we actually believe and publicly proclaim that Jesus is the only way to heaven, then we've got a problem."

Matt learned there were dozens of legal battles about those issues taking place all over the country. Alliance lawyers were engaged in as many as four hundred lawsuits and legal challenges every day of the year. Meanwhile, the Alliance had become the largest religiously oriented legal alliance in the world. They weren't fooling around.

For nearly three decades they had been doing strategy, training, funding, and litigation for cases involving religious liberty, traditional marriage, family issues, and life issues such as abortion and euthanasia. One area where they were particularly successful was equal access cases in which they defended the right of Christian groups on university and public school campuses to have access to the same facilities and opportunities as any other group.

In their first ten years, the Alliance had taken on and funded more than three hundred equal access cases, including six that had gone to the Supreme Court. The Court recognized their standing and their right to bring actions challenging a lower court's ruling. All but one of the equal access cases in which petitions of certiorari were granted by the Supreme Court—meaning they'd hear the appeal—were litigated by the Alliance attorneys. The justices took the cases in order to settle the matter of equal access. They decided the Alliance cases were the best to use to decide the issues.

By the time Matt attended the Academy, they had already taught more than two thousand lawyers how to mount a defense and bring legal actions in their legal areas. In addition, more than twelve hundred law students from the best schools in the country had gone through the Madison Scholars Academy. Matt felt lucky to have been one of them. Yet outside Christian circles, hardly anybody had ever heard of them, which is why Matt began to think John and the DTED agents had been ignoring them for so long. No one in Matt's law class at

Michigan could understand why he wanted to go to Chicago for a summer program like that in the first place.

A thought surfaced in his mind so suddenly it took him by surprise. *I once said I want my life to matter. I want my faith and my legal training to count for something. Now I'm finding out that one of my friends is in charge of the biggest threat to Christian beliefs since the age of martyrs. Can I stand by and watch that happen?*

The next evening Matt went back to the restaurant in Old Town in hopes of finding the young man he had overheard. Thanks to a helpful waiter, he eventually came up with a name. Back at the office he was able to locate the young man's address and phone number on the Internet. He placed a call and explained his reason for making the call. They agreed to meet confidentially the following day.

Matt had to think twice before taking the step. The Justice Department had a strict rule prohibiting government lawyers from pursuing a case that might be detrimental to the department. Matt was not one to even stretch—much less break—an ethics rule. Since there was no case at the moment, Matt decided to move ahead. If things turned out as badly as Matt feared, then he might have to make some life-changing decisions. In the meantime, he could at least find out what the young man had done and why he felt threatened. Matt knew it was risky, but he knew he couldn't look the other way—not any longer.

Matt drove to Alexandria at the appointed time. The coffee shop bustled with activity. Having eaten here before, Matt knew the place was busy and noisy—just what he wanted.

"You couldn't have chosen a quieter place?" Zach Willard asked.

Matt studied Zach for a moment. He was thin, fighting a skin condition, and had nervous eyes. After what he had been through, Matt didn't blame him for being nervous. "Sometimes noise is good."

Zach blinked several times. "I get it. You don't want to be overheard. Why not?"

"How old are you, Mr. Willard?"

"Twenty-two. I'm a junior in college." He paused. "I started late."

"Nothing wrong with that. Did you bring the letter Mr. Smith sent you?"

"Yeah." Zach pulled it from the back pocket of his jeans and shoved it across the table. Matt pulled the rumpled page closer. It bore the DOJ letterhead. "You guys scared me to death. It was a joke."

"Exactly *what* was a joke, Mr. Willard?"

"Look, can you call me Zach? I feel like I'm on trial here."

Matt smiled. "Sure, Zach, and you're not on trial. I'm not here to harass you."

"Then why are you here? I mean, I want to cooperate as much as I can, but I'm a little confused. You guys came on pretty strong."

"I can't go into detail, Zach. I'm following up on the activities of some DOJ staff. There's nothing to worry about."

"If you say so."

"I do say so. I went to your blog site and didn't see the piece that started all the trouble."

"Are you kidding, man? After the phone call from your Justice Department goons . . . I mean *people*, I yanked it down as fast as I could. I want nothing more to do with that stupid blog post."

"But you brought me a copy, right?"

"Maybe. I'm not sure I should give it to you. You might try to use it against me."

"It's smart to be cautious, but the DTED already has it. I'm hoping you can save me the trouble of asking for it."

This time Zach studied Matt. "That would take like . . . what? Ten seconds? You don't want them to know you're asking around, do you? Sorta a right hand keeping the left hand out of the loop kinda thing."

"I can't comment on that, Zach. I can tell you that I'm not here to trick you. I would just like to read it."

Matt gave him several moments to think it over. Finally, Zach reached into his back pocket and removed a printed page. It looked as if he had printed it from a Web site. "I ain't proud of that. I was just goofing around, you know, making a joke."

Matt read the piece. It was less than 250 words. Only about 20 percent dealt with the homosexual agenda. True, Zach had used several offensive terms in making his case that the homosexuals "were taking over." To Matt, it looked like the kind of thing a person straddling the threshold between adolescence and adulthood might pen after a long night of video games and too many energy drinks. Matt pushed the blog post back to Zach. He studied John's letter one more time.

"Okay, here's the deal. This is a form letter meant to scare you into compliance. It has no real teeth. My guess is the whole thing will be forgotten in a couple of days. The form that came with the letter is a simple way for you get rid of the whole thing. Basically, you're saying that what you did was a mistake. Now listen closely, Zach. I am not your attorney. You need to seek legal advice before signing any legal form. However, I can tell you that this is pretty routine."

Matt could see Zach relax. "You mean, it's all over?"

"Probably." Matt removed a business card from its case. "If you have questions, feel free to contact me. I need you to listen closely again. Are you listening?"

"Um, yeah—I mean yes."

"I am not involved in this case. I'm from a different department, so I can't give you answers about an ongoing investigation. However, if you think you're being singled out, get an attorney and have him contact me. Got it?"

"You'll make it go away?"

"I didn't say that. The man who sent you the letter is several pay grades above me. I'm just doing a little investigation for my department. Understood?"

"Understood."

Matt gave the DOJ letter back to Zach.

When they parted company, the kid seemed satisfied. For Matt, it was a different story. His friend John Knox Smith ran an agency that was trying to change the country. Matt's job, his life, and his beliefs were at risk. He knew John was a smart, determined, resourceful guy who had been handpicked by the president to implement and enforce new directives. Nothing would stand in John's way. Anyone with genuine faith would be at risk.

Including Matt.

| CHAPTER ELEVEN |

When John Knox Smith told the team he wanted to stir up as much publicity as possible, he wasn't doing it to make the public aware of the need for more government regulations. It wasn't even about cracking down on hate crimes. His plan was to use the media's coverage to make any person or organization the DTED went after look evil and to make anyone speaking against him or his tactics look stupid.

This was one reason so few organizations ventured to challenge the DTED. It was nearly impossible to confront the agency without looking stupid, intolerant, insensitive, or filled with prejudice. No one wanted to end up on the wrong side of the Department of Justice. So far, John's plan had worked beautifully. Even if the Alliance lawyers challenged him in several important cases, his team of agents and advocates were making life miserable for hate speech offenders in district courts all over the country.

In one case, a federal district judge in Texas told a group of high school students who were planning to pray at graduation exercises, "If any of you mention the name of Jesus, God, or any other deity, you will regret the day you were born. You will spend up to six months in jail." DTED lawyers were in the crowd on graduation day to make sure the young people complied.

In another case, the director of a Christian school in the Midwest, based on DTED threats for refusing to allow investigators into the building, barricaded himself in his home, terrified by what the government might do to him. A judge in Kansas City ruled that sending kids to a private Christian school was a truancy violation. At first the principal had been defiant, demanding a fair hearing. But as the pressures increased, he simply gave up.

Another U.S. attorney general ordered the FBI and the Bureau of Alcohol, Tobacco, and Firearms to shut down a religious school in a family compound in Arkansas. After a long, costly confrontation and a series of tragic, complicated errors, a fire broke out. Eighteen innocent men, women, and children died in the flames.

John, who always remembered that incident without regret, wanted to terrify those who refused to comply. He was seeing the fruit of that desire every week.

When IRS Special Agent Bob Maas and Postal Inspector Sandra Evans returned from Chicago with their report on the Alliance, they had more information than anyone at the DTED could have anticipated. They brought the team leaders into the conference room, where Bob had set up his laptop and a monitor. As soon as the lights dimmed, he said, "John, here's the stuff you asked for. Let me say first of all that I believe we can beat these guys, but it's not going to be a cakewalk.

"We discovered the organization is bigger than we realized. They have a full-time staff with district offices in several major cities. With allied attorneys and their staffs in just about every major city in the country, we estimate they may have as many as twenty-five hundred lawyers on call 24/7."

"Are those all full-time people?" John asked. He was having trouble processing the number.

"Not all of them," Maas said. "But that doesn't matter. Even the volunteers and pro bono lawyers are available 24/7. For these zealots it's not about the money."

"I understand. What else?"

"Well, the Alliance was founded in 1994 by a group of national ministry leaders, broadcasters, a financial planner, and a pastor from Florida who propagated the worst myths of America's Christian origins. Its first head was Alex Stanton, who served as general counsel and CEO. He did a lot of public speaking on the Alliance's behalf. For years he was all over radio and TV, speaking across the country, promoting their right-wing causes."

"Of course," John said sarcastically. "I imagine he was doing a lot of fundraising while he was at it."

"Don't they always?" Sandra said with a laugh. "They've had a lot of big donors paying the freight. But most of their support comes from small- and medium-sized contributions. They have supporters all over the country. True believers."

John shook his head and laughed. He understood that legal work was incredibly expensive. Without fund-raising there would be no charities or nonprofits, but he would never say that out loud—publicly or privately.

"Stanton was a federal prosecutor at one time," Maas continued. "In fact, he was the director of the Commission on Pornography that Ronald Reagan set up back in the eighties. Some of you may remember that. They did a lot of mischief back then. It took years to finally get things back to normal for First Amendment protection. When Sandra and I were going through newspaper clippings from that era, we were shocked to see how much trouble it caused. Fortunately, the commission doesn't exist any more."

"Who's running the Alliance now?" John asked.

"When Stanton retired, he was succeeded by Scott Freeman, who is another former DOJ lawyer and a member of the D.C. Bar."

"Where did he go to school?" John asked.

Sandra answered the question. "University of Virginia. Both undergrad and law school."

"As the group grew," Maas continued, "they became a sort of legal clearing house and law school at the same time. They take on cases in three areas: first is what they call religious freedom and equal access; second, what they call 'sanctity of life' or what we would call 'anti-choice,' creating havoc with women's health; and third, 'protecting marriage and family,' which is really just another way of saying anti-equality and anti-LGBT."

"When we started looking at what they actually do," Sandra added, "it didn't take long to see what they're up to. They promote bigotry in the name of religious freedom. They want the courts to say fundamentalist preachers, priests, Bible-thumpers, and even Orthodox Jewish rabbis can say whatever they want from the pulpit without restraint."

As Sandra spoke, she handed John a copy of a report showing the types and total numbers of mailings sent out by the Alliance. On a separate sheet she had listed several kinds of legal alerts sent daily over the Internet from the firm's national headquarters, along with a list of some of the other Christian ministries that were set up as Internal Revenue code 501(c)(3) law firms to handle public interest legal defense cases—firms that worked with the Alliance or received grants and funding from them at one time or another.

Scanning the page, John saw the names of dozens of tax-exempt organizations. They were sending millions of pages of questionable information every day of the year. Almost all were Christian ministries. The list sent a chill down his spine. John pushed the report to one side. "Bob, can any of these outfits besides the Alliance mount a serious defense if we go after them?"

"Not if we could just take them on one at a time. But the Alliance always works together. Even when they squabble internally, they keep working together. A few of these groups have their own lawyers on staff. Several have law firms on retainer. They all have access to the Alliance or one of a half dozen religiously oriented public interest law firms that take on religious liberty cases."

"Don't . . ." John paused and lowered his voice. "Don't use that term. That's their term. You mean religious bigotry cases."

"Understood. The problem is that Alliance lawyers are everywhere. They have as many as four hundred cases in litigation around the country at any given time, most handled by their allied attorneys. We came across one document that said they have commitments for as many as two hundred million dollars worth of volunteer pro bono legal services."

"If that isn't bad enough, John," Sandra put in, "they've put more than three thousand pro bono lawyers and law students through their various training programs. They call the law school component the 'Madison Scholars Academy' and its graduates 'Madisonians.' Each year, their Alliance lawyer training sessions bring in lawyers from every state in the union as well as territories like Puerto Rico, Guam, and Samoa."

"They even get a few from the European Union and Latin America," Maas added.

John decided not to tell the group he knew someone who had gone through a summer of the Chicago law student brainwashing.

"The graduates of these programs are in the courts, law firms, and government offices in every state. They've been in the White House and are now in the legal counsel's office, as well as the Senate Judiciary Committee staff. Two won seats in Congress. Some are at the DOJ."

"There aren't any Alliance people on staff with the members of Congress we've been working with," Sandra said, "at least, not as far as I'm aware. But we know some of their people have been pushing for a congressional inquiry to look into our operations. They've been supplying information to our opponents on the Hill."

"I find that hard to believe," Joel said. "Are you sure about that?"

The newest member of the team, Mike Alden, raised his hand. "Sir, I can tell you there are Madisonians in some of the biggest law firms in this city. They have people in the Defense Department and the Judge Advocate General Corps, in all branches of service. They're the ones propping up that Catholic general who's running the Marine Corps. In fact, there are at least six Madisonians here in this building."

"Bob," Joel interrupted, "are you suggesting some of these people are involved in cases we're handling now?"

John stiffened. It was one thing to know that Matt had gone through the program but quite another matter to learn that he wasn't the lone

Madison Scholars Academy graduate in the DOJ. It unsettled him. "They have informants in this building? Are you kidding me?"

"I wouldn't kid you, sir," Alden said. "I know some of them from college and law school. They were top students and seem to get top jobs everywhere. I see them around the building all the time."

Bob Maas continued quickly, "I agree, John. It is unbelievable. We'll look into it. Maybe Alden can help with that. Wait until you hear this: Sandra learned that a couple of their people are working for the major news networks in New York; one is a producer at Fox News. At least four of them have been appointed as federal judges and have issued rulings in direct opposition to the antidiscrimination laws you put through."

Pointing to information on the video monitor showing the number of Alliance-connected judges, lead attorney Joel Thevis said, "I can confirm that, John. We know one judge in Oklahoma who has been causing a stir down there. He wrote an angry letter to the American Bar Association saying he's upset that the ABA has been promoting—as he put it—the 'homosexual agenda.'"

"Homosexual agenda?" John said. "Is he talking about equality and fair treatment for the most oppressed minority in this country? I can't believe it. Who is this guy?"

"Judge Dossett in Oklahoma City. I was told he's a Madisonian."

"What did the ABA have to say?"

"They objected, of course," Joel answered. "They put the word out on their Web site that any attorney litigating cases on behalf of individuals in the LGBT community needs to stay away from this guy because he can't hear their cases impartially. Believe me, the ABA chapter in that state—and all the attorneys we know in that part of the country—are watching him."

Looking from Joel to Agent Maas, John said, "There was a rule passed by the bar association in San Francisco a few years ago that said judges may not hold memberships in any organization that promotes discrimination. It said that no responsible officer of the court should be a member of the Boy Scouts or serve as a Scout leader or anything of that sort. It's been a problem for a long time. California's Bar Association made it clear that any judge who's involved with organizations known to be anti-equality, antichoice, or anti-LGBT either needs to cut those ties or get off the bench. Why can't they have something like that in Oklahoma?"

"Good idea," Joel responded. "They're working on it, but it's not as easy as it sounds."

"Any lawyer who belongs to a group that calls homosexual behavior a sin," Mike Alden chimed in, "should have his license revoked. Those people don't need to be in our profession."

"The problem," Joel continued, "is that we don't have a lot of friends in some parts of the South. It will take a while to get the bar associations in those states to go along with us. Just because it worked in San Francisco, John, doesn't mean it's going to fly in Oklahoma."

John glanced at Joel. Once again, his lead attorney seemed to be making excuses for their delays in progress.

Bob Maas closed his laptop and turned up the lights in the room. Before anyone could speak, he said, "Sir, there's one more thing. As a byproduct of our research, we discovered that among the approximately one thousand federal judges in the country, as many as two hundred of them have indicated on anonymous questionnaires that they accept the traditional beliefs of their religion as being true."

"They *what*?"

"Basically, sir," Maas said, "as many as a fifth of the judges appointed by President Blaine and his predecessors are unreformed Bible-thumpers still hanging onto their backward religious beliefs. I'm sure some of them are from the more enlightened varieties who believe in diversity and tolerance, and affirm our values. But unfortunately there are still some Protestant evangelicals and conservative Roman Catholics who remain unreformed, still clinging to their guns, religion, and a theology from the Middle Ages. There are even a few Jews who adhere to the teachings of Moses and the prophets."

Reneé X leaned forward. "John, there are some old-line Roman Catholics in that group as well, along with the Baptists, Presbyterians, and Pentecostals. Some of them openly say that they believe in the old ways. Privately, some of the judges Joel mentioned would say they believe that some people are sinners. You know that belief in moral absolutes has got to affect their objectivity. That's why we have to get these people off the bench."

"Reneé is right, John," Maas said. "Congress has the authority to remove these guys by impeachment, and I think it would be the right thing to do. It wouldn't reflect on us, and it sure would be helpful if someone like Mike Alden or one of the young lawyers could get us the names of those judges. If there are Alliance people on the bench in this country, we need to know who they are and where they are."

Joel looked at the newest member of the legal team. "Can you do that, Mike?"

"Yes, sir. I believe I can. Give me a few days, I'll get as many names as I can."

John smiled. "That's great, Alden. Do it. But don't count on those cowards on Capitol Hill to take on sitting judges. We'll have to look at other ideas."

Mike Alden wasn't through. Raising his hand like a schoolboy, he said, "Sir, with your permission, I would like to suggest that we also begin an investigation to find out where the other Madisonians are working. We need to know who they are, where they're employed, and where they stand on our issues. Once we know who stands with us, working for diversity and tolerance, we can do whatever it takes to weed the rest of them out."

John thought of Matt but kept the thought to himself. "Absolutely. Do it. I want the names of every one of those graduates working in this building. I want to know who they are, who they work for, and what they're doing here. I want to know where they live, where they shop, who they hang out with. I'll give you two weeks. Can you do it?"

Alden hesitated. "There's just one thing. If I do the kind of research I need to do, there's a good chance word will get out what we're up to. They'll know what I'm doing."

"Good. They need to know we're on to them, and they're not getting away with anything. We're for truth and justice. This isn't something you have to do secretly. We have nothing to hide. On the other hand, we don't want to be so open that they'll be able to hide evidence if they're imposing their faith views in their job. If shaking the trees gets us what we want, shake it. But get me whatever you can find, Mike." John looked at his lead attorney. "Am I right, Joel?"

Joel nodded. "As always, John, as always."

John sat back in his chair and folded his arms across his chest. "When Mike's finished his investigation, every one of those suckers on the public payroll will be ousted and identified so the whole world can see what we're up against. If they're doing what we think they're doing, they'll learn what happens to people who promote hate and bigotry in this country while living on the taxpayer's dollar."

Since arriving at the DTED two months earlier, Mike Alden hadn't done much. John had only picked him for the team because Senator Heywood had been a friend of Alden's father at Yale and recommended him. When Donna Lewis had checked into his background and found out the kid had graduated from a Catholic law school in Indiana, John wasn't so sure Alden was the right person for the job.

But so far the kid was looking pretty good. John thought this new assignment would be a good way of checking him out. Either the kid would prove he was up to the challenge, or he would prove he wasn't, in which case John's friend Heywood would have some explaining to do.

John told Andrea to make sure the kid knew how to get messages directly to him, bypassing Joel Thevis. He didn't want to take any chances that Alden's report might be shared with outsiders.

To John, caution was better than trust.

| CHAPTER TWELVE |

By the end of their first two years in operation, John and the DTED team had prosecuted and won dozens of cases. But to their annoyance, too many other cases had been challenged, dropped, and some lost, thanks to the Alliance. At least the media wasn't reporting on those cases. Along the way there had been muted protests and small pockets of resistance here and there, mostly in small towns and rural areas, in what John and the team referred to dismissively as "flyover country." But it wasn't until the DTED began aggressively targeting a large group of evangelical pastors and ministry leaders, shortly after the government seized control of a half dozen faith-based hospitals, that John started to worry about how large the backlash might become.

The hospitals had recognized so-called "conscience claims" by their personnel who refused to administer morning-after pills, to perform abortions, or to help with assisted suicides. For some reason, the media decided to give full coverage to the hospital employees' arguments.

A growing number of people were frightened by these DTED actions and angry about what they saw happening. Some cried for help. So far, the courts had been an effective steamroller for the agency, mowing down the opposition with full search-and-seizure arrests. They periodically put convicted felons behind bars and—in the case of the hospitals—simply enforced the contracts the hospitals had signed to receive Medicare and Medicaid funding. But it was becoming apparent that John would need new strategies to deal with the dissenters and growing media coverage of them and to counter the legal defense mounted by the Alliance.

One of John's primary objectives, to improve the odds of winning difficult cases, was to target opposition leaders. Churches, ministries, NGOs, and private hospitals operated under federal statutes, and they had to abide by federal regulations. Those who refused to follow those guidelines were in violation. John's team could bring the power of the IRS, the FBI, and a dozen agencies, including the Postal Service, the FCC, and the Departments of Commerce and Transportation, down on their heads with great economic impact if they so chose.

When Dr. Jim Stockman went on the air in an attempt to mobilize his base of two million listeners to resist the growing enforcement efforts and new government restrictions, John decided they would have to go after Stockman and his organization by any means necessary. "This garbage shouldn't be allowed on the airwaves in the first place," he said. "Bigots shouldn't have radio programs. They can't be allowed to send out seditious and inflammatory materials through the U.S. mail—it's a violation of federal law."

That's why John had requested that a tough investigator like Sandra Evans be assigned to his team. She was the first person he went to when he decided to turn up the heat on Stockman. "Let's get busy on this, Sandra. I'd like you and Bob Maas to come up with a plan. We'll come down hard on these guys when they least expect it."

Sandra nodded. "The DTED characterizes hate speech as sedition, and the Christian Family Forum is in the center of the bull's-eye. The Interstate Transportation of Obscene Materials law, which has been virtually useless since the Reagan and first Bush administrations' wars on pornography, will actually come in handy when we go after these ministries. We have the amendment to the bill passed by Congress, which makes it illegal to mail any literature that displays antichoice propaganda, attacks gender or sexual orientation, or shows propaganda photos of 'missionaries' conducting cultural genocide. We can bring felony counts against offenders.

"That goes for material sent by any instrumentality of commerce, including FedEx, UPS, and any other parcel service."

John was pleased she had taken his instruction so seriously. "Law enforcement agencies can identify the illegal transport of forbidden literature across state lines by any ministry and present the individuals responsible for prosecution."

"There will be resistance in flyover country from people who want to hang on to their old habits," Sandra said. "They will never stop trying to block the progressive agenda. That's why we have to keep pursuing them."

"I'm glad to hear you say that, Sandra," John said. "I think we're on the same page."

"Thank you, but . . ."

"But what, Sandra?"

"I'm not telling you anything new, but the truth is there is a growing anxiety across the country, a sense that our agency is . . . well, the phrase I'm hearing is 'out of control.' So far, no one has found a way to slow us down. Most of their elected officials, the media, and even local law enforcement are on board with the new policies. Those who dare to stand up and make a racket are being peeled off one by one."

"We knew this would be one of the obstacles we'd face, Sandra. All progress faces opposition. Remember Roger Baldwin and Saul Alinsky's most basic teachings. We will continue to fight hard and fast. It's the only way to bring about the needed changes. In time, even those people will see how right we are. You believe we are right, don't you Sandra?"

"Of course I do! I believe we have truth and justice on our side."

John wondered if she meant what she said.

The most serious cases of rebellion involved hate speech posted on the Internet or mail sent directly to local officials. There were also several cases of apparent resistance involving vandalism, arson, random shootings, and bombings of government facilities. Some of those cases included serious injuries. In three of them—in Texas, Oklahoma, and Arizona—there was loss of life. The media, always looking to push the borders of the story, investigated the lives of the perpetrators, several of whom had tenuous and distant links to some religious group. Any violent act that could be linked to a church or parachurch organization, no matter how tenuously, the media felt compelled to report.

John had made up his mind early on that he wasn't going to allow protests to slow him down. He told the staff to keep an eye on those incidents; to monitor when, where, and how they happened; and to find out what was being done in response. He wanted to be able to jump in as soon as possible with legal action or, if need be, one of the SWAT units.

Arrests continued to be made, and as far as John was concerned, the bigger the controversy the better. One way or another, he had to make clear the point that no one could successfully resist the DTED or the laws his unit had been commissioned to enforce. Nevertheless, as they entered their third year in operation, dramatic confrontations were taking place much more often. People realized that there was a new lawman in town, but no one was beating their swords into ploughshares.

In the wake of every random attack, no matter how flimsy the link to religion, there was always a tough crackdown by the police. In some cases, law enforcement collared fundamentalist pastors and charged them with hate speech violations. In other cases they handcuffed individuals in airports, restaurants, shopping malls, and theater lobbies and brought them in for questioning. Overheard remarks people made that might have seemed insensitive or crude a year or two earlier were now an enforceable federal offense. A few cases received scathing reports by the remaining conservative media or on Internet blogs that helped fuel the public's growing negative reaction.

A few weeks later, one of the most sensational and widely publicized busts took place in Colorado Springs, when Special Agent Paul Atoms and Postal's Sandra Evans led a multiagency task force, along with local law enforcement, on a raid of the international headquarters of Stockman's ministry. Pushed by John, they had moved up this assault months earlier than Sandra Evans had thought possible. Officers pushed their way through the front door of the Christian Family Forum and marched six ministry executives and twenty-nine staff workers and volunteers out of the building in leg bracelets and handcuffs, surrounded by officers in riot gear, doing the "perp walk" for the television crews.

The postal inspector had a breakthrough when she found massive use of the mail for the Forum's counseling practice. Stockman had stirred up a major controversy by promoting what his organization referred to as "reparative therapy" for men and women who, as he put it, wanted to "break free from same-sex addictions and other sexual sins."

Counselors at the CFF Treatment Centers held advanced degrees and were fully licensed, but the RDTA lawyers determined the language referring to "reparative therapy" was a hate crime. So the agents assigned to the DTED went to a local magistrate, who issued the search warrants and signed arrest warrants for Stockman and anyone else in a leadership position with the organization.

Sandra Evans, Paul Atoms, and the other agents and police officers on the bust held a brief press update, carefully following ethics guidelines on their comments. While doing so, they lined up the subjects arrested on the sidewalk so the media could get good, clear shots. Some of those photos and video would appear in the national media as a further deterrent to others.

Stockman was traveling when the raid occurred, but that evening he told his national radio audience that he had been shocked by the raid and the arrests. "We have done nothing in secret. All aspects of our ministry are open, detailed on our Web site, and approved by state licensing boards. We will not roll over and give up. With the help of the Alliance and dedicated Christian lawyers, we will fight this case all the way to the Supreme Court. What we're saying to the government and to anyone else listening to this program," Stockman broadcast, "is that almost every one of the men and women who has contacted us seeking help has made a life-changing decision to follow Jesus Christ. They have laid aside years of pain and stopped their self-destructive behavior. Our counselors will never waver in our promise of support for them. We will never water down the message of hope that God has called us to share." From the moment he spoke those words, Stockman was himself in violation of federal law. It was what John Knox Smith had hoped for.

In the midst of the growing enforcement efforts, the media began reporting on the most baffling acts of resistance, which took place over a period of several months, beginning with a series of explosions along the East Coast and mid-Atlantic region. They happened so suddenly and randomly that the attacks left the police and FBI baffled. Investigators noted that they always occurred on the site of DTED enforcement action a few hours or days earlier.

Whoever was behind the attacks used crude, homemade explosive devices, which made John believe that it would be a only matter of time before those responsible were caught. Evidence piled up; signature patterns that crime scene ATF investigators could trace appeared. As the toll of injury and damage continued to grow with the intense media coverage, the public grew agitated by the lack of resolution. The explosions usually happened near government buildings, but some occurred at shopping centers. They almost always resulted in serious casualties. One of the worst happened in Richmond, Virginia, where a blast during Monday morning rush hour took the front off a neighborhood police station, killing four officers and injuring two others, along with an elderly couple who were inside the building waiting to see their son, who was in custody.

Even though the explosives and accelerants used by the assailants were remarkably simple, solid evidence was slow in coming. The cases perplexed law enforcement and enraged John Knox Smith. They appeared to be a direct challenge to the DTED.

The biggest news to hit the networks that summer concerned a "kook" in a beat-up camper with expired West Virginia license plates and a crucifix dangling from his rearview mirror. Charles Wesley Spurlock had a long history of abuse and resistance to authority in the community of Rocky Summit, West Virginia. He had done time in a dozen different jails for everything from public drunkenness and reckless endangerment to armed robbery. His rap sheet included at least one felony and a half dozen misdemeanors. He had been on a rampage ever since the ATF, backed by a local FBI agent, raided his cabin and seized his guns a year earlier.

Spurlock wasn't a quick thinker, but he was persistent, and he could hold a grudge as well as anyone. Despite his namesake, he had never been to church in his adult life. However, during one week the previous winter at a homeless shelter in Charleston, West Virginia, he'd spotted a large, metal crucifix on another man's bunk and stolen it.

After the raid on his cabin, Spurlock plotted his revenge for months, using whatever "science" he had learned from the survival magazines he collected. He had been the East Coast bomber, setting off explosions everywhere he read or heard about an FBI raid or arrest. He had not connected his actions to the DTED—he just went wherever he heard the FBI had interviewed or arrested someone within a few hours' drive of his cabin. Now, after loading his fifteen-year-old camper with sawdust, a dozen plastic jugs filled with gasoline and other accelerants, and twenty-seven bags of an ammonium-based fertilizer he had purchased at Wal-Mart, one forty-pound bag at a time over a period of months, he made the 250-mile drive to Washington, D.C., and set off an explosion outside FBI headquarters.

Spurlock, it turned out, hoped the blast would be a lesson the world and the FBI would never forget. If everything went as planned, he would not only get his revenge, but he believed there was a good chance he might even become a celebrity in the process.

If the ignition device Spurlock rigged had worked, the damage would have been much worse—perhaps not on the scale of the Oklahoma City bombing of 1995, although that was clearly his intent. But even this ineffectual arsenal would have been enough to terrorize the District of Columbia and kill or injure dozens of federal employees. However, Spurlock only succeeded in blowing himself up and setting his camper on fire.

Flying glass and debris from the blast injured a group of tourists on a tour bus, and two small children were hospitalized with second-degree burns. Doctors indicated the children would be fine with time and proper care, but a short time later one of the girls died from an unexpected infection. The funeral, held at a large, multiracial church in Baltimore, was covered by the national media. Emotions ran sky high.

It wasn't long before investigators linked the FBI bombing and Spurlock to at least six other attacks, including the police station bombing in Richmond, as well as an explosion on an elementary school playground, where a principal who read the Bible aloud at staff meetings was arrested. The school blast had taken the lives of three third-graders and a twenty-two-year-old student teacher. The explosion and fire in D.C. happened directly across the street from the Pennsylvania Avenue entrance to the Department of Justice. John Knox Smith and his staff were working at the time, and John had just returned from an appearance on CNN. Their first realization that something had happened outside their own building came when Andrea heard sirens, turned on the television in John's office, and saw the on-site report broadcast on Channel 7. Several of the team members rushed into the office to watch the coverage with John and Andrea, while a handful of the others went outside to see the carnage for themselves.

Half an hour later they came back shaking their heads. This was what John had feared. It was as if someone were sending them a message. In a sense, it's what they were here for. Their job was to stop the hate and intolerance that could lead to this sort of terrorist attack, no matter how long it took or who became tangled in their net. It was troubling, to say the least, when the hate showed up on their doorstep.

As the investigators went through the burned-out hulk of Spurlock's camper, they found little that would help them identify the perpetrator—some old books, magazines, and fragments of assorted religious tracts mixed in with Spurlock's charred remains and bits of clothing that could provide DNA evidence. There was no personal identification, nothing but a partially melted crucifix still attached to the camper's rearview mirror. Every news service used the image in their coverage. Within hours Spurlock became known as the "Crucifix Bomber."

The crucifix, the bomber bearing the name of an infamous British religious dissenter, and shreds of tracts proved to John that the explosion had been an act of terrorism carried out by a right-wing fanatic with a grudge against the DTED—and thus against him—the work of a crazed, fundamentalist Christian.

John was elated with the way the media displayed the religious image. He saw this as a potential "tipping point," a moment when things could really start to pop. Finally, the dissent in the media began to fade. Who could defend the Crucifix Bomber, a man who had killed little boys and girls? Though truly sad for the victims and their families, John thought this series of events was so sweet.

Within twenty-four hours of receiving the forensics reports, John dispersed DTED agents over the entire region. They knocked down doors in Virginia, Maryland, and Delaware; teams of agents traveled to Tennessee and West Virginia to follow up on leads where individuals had reported seeing an old, tan pickup with a camper matching the description on the evening news.

John felt certain the secretarial staff and office workers were confused to see him looking so cheerful over a tragedy that had taken place right outside their building. He had been angry and morose for weeks, but the repeated media image of the charred crucifix had made his job easier. That put a smile on his face.

For weeks, pictures of Spurlock's smoking wreck lying in the middle of Pennsylvania Avenue flashed across TV screens in every city in America. The wreckage of the camper and the dangling crucifix became iconic—an emblem of the hatred and intolerance boiling over in Middle America. The cable talk shows brought in experts, lawyers, police detectives, and forensics specialists to debate what had happened. They talked about public access to public buildings and whether authorities should allow certain types of vehicles in the cities. Citing an increase of "far-right, Christian" violence, Attorney General Stamper ordered the U.S. marshals to increase security at other potential targets, especially women's healthcare providers who offered third trimester treatment. This had the double effect of protecting such providers as well as keeping many in the antiabortion crowd from terrorizing patients. When publically identified, "Crucifix Bomber" Charles Wesley Spurlock got his desired fifteen minutes of fame. John got much more.

After the long dry spell in which it often seemed to John's team as if the DTED couldn't buy a positive story in the major media without "balance" or voices of dissent, John was suddenly back on page one, and the DTED was being praised by all the right people for their quick response. The one sour note was that many times after his agents made an arrest, Alliance attorneys showed up, looking into the charges, butting into John's plans, and gumming up the works. Even when they chose not to get involved, they were still spoilers with their questions. When the Alliance *did* get involved, they made the DTED's work a lot harder.

John was troubled that there were still some federal district judges in the hinterlands who refused to follow the DTED's interpretation of the law. Consequently, John's team was constantly preparing appeals at the circuit court level, while keeping their eyes on everything that was happening out there. Consequently, his lead prosecutors and investigators were running in too many directions.

While some of this proved exciting and rewarding for John personally, it was a drain on the members of his team. Meanwhile, the chaos in John's home life grew. The long hours and nerve-racking demands on his time were making the impossible situation at home immeasurably worse. It had been a mistake to marry so young while still in school. Without Andrea's emotional support and superb work ethic to lean on, his load would have been unbearable.

The entire staff stayed on the fast track, and their cases were moving swiftly. Under ordinary circumstances, most of the cases would have taken years to settle. But because of the priority Congress had given them and the incredible range of resources at John's disposal, the really important cases were getting through the legal system, from indictment to final appeal, in a matter of months. This meant that the pace was often frantic, and time was a problem.

For John, there weren't enough hours in the day. The forty-minute drive to the suburbs was a daily battle, and when he was home his wife was constantly on his case. Even when Cathy was in a good mood, which wasn't often, she could be demanding and insensitive to his needs. She refused to understand that he could not waste time at home entertaining her impossible demands when he was bringing a new era of justice and equality to the world. John was sorry he had married the Connecticut doctor's daughter, who thought getting to a soccer game or attending a school meeting trumped an arrest or staff meeting. She pestered him about her ridiculous van troubles, the work that wasn't getting done around the house, and the problems of raising a son as "a single parent." Just because she had grown up with a nanny and a housekeeper didn't mean it was an essential need now. John was fed up with her complaints about his lack of income as a government lawyer. Didn't she know that changing history was far more important than money? Then there were her suspicions about what John was doing when he was gone for days at a time. Every week was a struggle not to walk out on her and her self-centered behavior.

| CHAPTER THIRTEEN |

The original DTED legislation had made it through Congress by the slimmest of margins. But now, with the Crucifix Bomber and the earlier murder of Ronnie Lee Jefferson shifting public opinion, many of the politicians who had resisted the original bill read the polls. They quietly amended the obscenity laws and other laws, and almost overnight there was a seismic shift in public opinion. Even the most relentless obstructionists were getting on board.

Seeing the momentum building, John went back to Senators Heywood and Borden, who had carried the bill the first time. He convinced them to go back for all the measures that had been cut from the initial legislation, including measures that even John's lawyers doubted could survive an appeal to the Supreme Court. President Blaine instructed his legislative council at the White House, "You can send through the full package now with my blessing."

The president had stayed on the sidelines during the early wrangling over the original legislation involving the DTED to make sure his fingerprints wouldn't appear on it in case things went badly. But after Charles Wesley Spurlock's bungled bomb attack, he was more than willing to give the team at the DTED and their allies in Congress his full support. Within weeks the bill was back on the Hill, now known as the American Citizens Equality, Safety, and Freedom Act. Insiders called it "DTED Squared."

The *Washington Post* quoted the president's press secretary: "This is a very difficult topic. Admittedly, we've seen some extreme things happening, but in the current climate, I think we all agree something has to be done. The public now understands the risks involved, and it's vital that we step up to stop the hate and bitterness that is lurking in some parts of this nation. Equality for all Americans is not a meaningless phrase; it's a pledge we make to every citizen."

Larry Jordan stood at the window of the Alliance conference room and gazed at the people who wandered the street. Lunchtime had arrived, and the amount of foot traffic on the Chicago sidewalk just off Michigan Avenue and the "Miracle Mile" shopping district swelled. He wondered about the men and women who went about the day's business—accountants, lawyers, bank employees, tech company workers, and more. They moved from place to place as they had the workday before and as they would tomorrow. The country was changing around them, but he was sure that most gave little thought to the changes.

Larry turned and faced the other Alliance leaders who sat around the long conference table. Michael Larson from Atlanta sat to Larry's right. Next to him, Caroline Silvers of New York pushed a potato chip around on the paper plate in front of her. The sandwich on her plate remained untouched. Natalie Grossman had arrived from Miami that morning. Los Angeles-based Alexander Barons was the only one to eat his whole sandwich. His size indicated that he usually finished every meal.

Each person present represented the Alliance in the city and region they lived. There were many others who could be here, but Larry felt a smaller group of the best and brightest would be more productive.

Larry, who preferred to think on his feet, forced himself to sit at the head of the table. "Scott Freeman is still overseas, but he didn't want to lose any time. He asked me to gather a brainstorm team. You're that team."

"They've been turning up the heat," Barons said, pushing his plate back. "They've got wind in their sails now, and they're feeling confident." He didn't need to define who he meant by "they."

"I can't believe Congress went for this," Natalie said. "The language in the expanded DTED empowerment bill is much harsher than before. They have dramatically increased the penalties for conviction. Five-year prison terms and $250,000 penalties were bad enough, but $1 million fine is beyond reasonable explanation. They have lost their corporate minds."

"Not to mention the forfeiture component. It's way beyond RICO," Caroline added. She was an ebony-skinned woman who looked a decade younger than her forty-two years. Many new legal opponents assumed her good looks came at the expense of intelligence. They made that mistake only once. "They're treating our clients as if they were spies for a foreign country or drug dealers."

She tapped a fingernail on the table. Her jaw tightened. "They're not criminals. Not in any sense. These are good people, honest people. We've seen it time and time again: someone feels a call to do something worthwhile, to spread the gospel, to bring spiritual light to a dark world, to protect the unborn, the innocent. Then guys like Smith charge in and ruin them. I don't know how anyone with intelligence can look at these organizations and not see the integrity of the men and women who lead them. They follow stringent guidelines for nonprofits, allow their organizations to be audited, file endless reports to the government, have strong, independent boards of directors; and they leave themselves open to all possible scrutiny. They work hard and are paid a fraction of what they'd make in the private sector. What do they get for it? Persecution and loss of property."

Michael Larson spoke up. "The forfeiture presumption in the new law says that wherever a 'crime' occurred—in a home, a business, an automobile, or anywhere else—that property automatically transfers to the government. This has been the case in admiralty law for many years, where the government has the right of seizure of vessels on the high seas. Later, it was expanded so that if an individual carried illegal drugs in a boat, airplane, or other motorized vehicle, from the moment they placed the contraband in it, that vehicle belonged to the government.

"With these amendments," Larson continued, "when an individual or organization violates the hate speech law, the person's property that is used to further the offense—whether a home, a vehicle, a church, a synagogue, or a radio station—becomes the property of the government retroactively from the moment of the offense. It then becomes the burden of the former property owner to prove whether or not there was any lawful defense for their actions."

Larson, who looked like a nineteenth-century Samuel Clemens and a silver-tongued trial lawyer, tapped the tabletop with his little finger. "We must make the case that this is an egregious overreaching by the government. Taking property without due process of law is a violation of the First, Fifth, and Fourteenth Amendments. I've done everything but pay the media to make this known, but they haven't been so inclined."

"For more than a century," Larry said, "the FCC has argued that the government owns the airwaves and possesses the authority to regulate not only who uses those airways but how they use them. These new laws have reached the point where government can exercise similar authority over all property—both public and private—to ensure that no property of any kind can be used for purposes it had banned. Government directives argued that 'whatever emanates from a property is of public interest,' and the law will no longer allow private property to be used for what it declares deleterious purposes."

"I heard John Knox Smith interviewed a few weeks ago," Barons said. "He argued that the new law is simply a logical extension of the Supreme Court's ruling in *Kelo v. City of New London*, et al., which allowed cities to seize private property for commercial or other uses in the public interest, like taking houses to put up warehouses or grocery stores. He said . . . hang on a sec." Barons closed his eyes and leaned his head back. "Got it. He said, 'It's logical. When anyone uses a church or any other public venue for hate speech and that fact is brought to the attention of law enforcement, the government has an obligation to seize the property and transfer it to someone who will use it for a better public purpose.'" Barons opened his eyes. "I almost had to call the paramedics to restart my heart."

"They're going after church property and church schools," Larry said. "They're using their favorite skeleton key, hate speech, to do it."

"The local governments are turning a blind eye," Larson said. "And why wouldn't they? Churches and church schools are tax-exempt entities. If their property is turned over to a tax-paying enterprise, then the city, county, and state governments get a boost of cash."

Larry couldn't sit still any longer. He stood and stepped behind the high-back chair. "Pray the Supreme Court will put that mischief away. The Alliance's caseload is growing geometrically. The more the government continues to prosecute, the more we have to step up our efforts. Since the new law has gone into effect, our caseload has tripled, but our income has not. And every case comes with backlash. For every pastor, rabbi, priest, or parachurch leader who is arrested, there are scores of others who water down their teaching or get out of the ministry. Attrition rate is staggering. Parachurch organizations are having trouble hiring employees, contributions are off as well, and not just with them, but with churches, too."

"And the Alliance?" Natalie prompted.

"We have the best supporters an organization like ours can have, but we have seen a dip in contributions. Our first president said, 'It's a matter of supplies.'"

Silence filled the room for a moment as they waited for Larry to take the lead.

"Here's what we need to buckle down," Larry said. "We have won many of our cases. Like you, I'm thankful to God for everyone, but the playing field has changed and changed to our disadvantage. I know you are all working more hours than anyone has a right to ask, but we need to do more. If we don't, we may win battles but lose the war. I want to hear ideas. I don't care how crazy they are, I want to hear them. Then we'll take some serious time out to pray over them, asking for discernment and wisdom."

Barons smiled.

"Something funny, Alexander?" Larry asked.

"Years ago, I read a biography of Bobby Kennedy. When he was attorney general, he went toe-to-toe with teamster leader Jimmy Hoffa. Late one night, Kennedy leaves his office. As they drive down the street, he sees the window to the office used by Hoffa. Bear in mind, this is well after normal work hours. Kennedy sees the light and assumes Hoffa is still working. He makes his driver turn around and goes back to the DOJ. He used words I won't repeat here, but in essence he said, 'If Hoffa is going to work late, then I'm going to work later.' Somehow Hoffa hears of this and decides to leave his light on all night every night."

"That's not a bad idea, Alexander."

"What? Leaving the lights on?"

"No—making certain that John Knox Smith and his pals know we are in this for the long haul. We challenge them at every turn. We work every case as if we're arguing before the Supreme Court. We take every case that should go to the high court. They need to know that we aren't going away. Not now. Not ever."

The more arrests they made, the more cases initiated—whether taken to trial or not—the better John felt. In some districts the dockets were so full and the demands on judges, prosecutors, and other government officials so great that the whole system was slowly grinding to a halt. When one of the deputies to Attorney General Stamper called to speak to John about the predicament, John had a ready response.

"You need to get rid of the dead wood," he said.

"Dead wood? What does that mean?"

"It's simple. We need more firepower, but what we don't need is the obstructionist rat pack gumming up the works. We need to weed out the traditionalist judges and get new ones. And while we're at it, we need to double the number of judges in the appellate system."

"Fire everybody? Is that what you're saying?"

"No, of course not. That would create a stink. There's a better way, and the time is right."

At that point John offered to meet with the attorney general to lay out a plan that would solve their problems, guarantee fast and efficient implementation of President Blaine's policies, and make life in all the department's agencies and bureaus more tolerable. To help lay out the details, he asked Senator Heywood to join them, since his plan would involve important new legislation.

The end result of that meeting, which both Alton Stamper and Will Blaine were glad to endorse, was a new law hailed by the media and progressive think tanks as the most far-sighted and far-reaching law in the history of modern American jurisprudence. Since the caseload for federal judges had been so extraordinary the past two decades and since so many federal district and appellate judges were being forced to work intolerably long hours for months on end, the administration and the Congress, led by Josh Heywood, were able to settle on a remarkable solution, proposed by the head of the Justice Department's Diversity and Tolerance Enforcement Division.

The National Judicial Expansion and Retirement Act was a sweeping new law that offered all federal judges of any age and who had served at least ten years on the bench a one-time option of early retirement at 100 percent of their current salary, with inflation and cost-of-living adjustments for life. Furthermore, there were no limitations on nongovernmental employment. The only requirement for judges to take advantage of this opportunity was that they had to exercise their option and step down within six months of the enactment of the new law.

In addition, the bill created two judicial positions for every existing position, doubling the number of federal judges, dramatically decreasing the workload of the officers of the court and leading to a greater "administration of justice." Members of Congress who supported the fast-track initiative were motivated by the fact that the new law would help to clear the courts of any remaining "original intent" types and would allow the current administration to gain incomparably greater influence in the federal courts without the need of a constitutional amendment, which would have been too slow and messy.

Rather than creating a firestorm of dissent from conservatives, who were simply labeled as the "Party of No" by the media, these fast and decisive moves by the administration and Congress, in changing the structure of the courts and expanding its role, were well received by the public—a public who had little understanding of the workings of the court system but knew it was terribly backed up.

The added pressure this new law applied to churches and other religious groups failed to result in, as Joel Thevis had once predicted, a backlash. Instead, many of those groups grew more cooperative.

"Avoiding the press?"

Pastor Pat Preston looked up from his nearly empty paper coffee cup and saw the familiar face of Skip Warner. He stood two inches shorter and at least twenty inches rounder than Pat. The overhead lights of the Atlanta conference hall anteroom reflected off his brushed-back, white hair. The suit he wore looked tailored for his large frame.

"The press hasn't shown any interest in me, and I thank God for that." Pat motioned for Warner to join him. "You want a coffee or a soda?"

Warner sat at the round table and brushed away a few crumbs left over by the people who had been there before them. "My stomach can't take any more acid or carbonation."

"How about some water?" Pat noticed that neither of them made eye contact. Warner kept his eyes fixed on the table. Pat watched the ebb and flow of denominational leaders and mega church pastors flow in and out of the rented conference hall.

Warner waved off the offer. "I imagine you're disappointed in me."

Pat sipped his coffee to buy a few seconds of time. "Yeah, Skip, I am."

Warner nodded. "I figured as much. Truth is, I'm pretty disappointed in myself."

"Then why do it?"

Warner picked at something stuck to the table's surface. Pat didn't know what it was and didn't care.

"Our country has changed, Pat. This isn't the same government we grew up in. Things were very different when we started ministry."

"I can't argue with that," Pat said. "Still . . ."

Warner chuckled, but Pat heard no humor in it. "Seems like several lifetimes ago since I stepped behind the pulpit at The Harbor Church in southern California. There were forty pairs of eyes looking back at me. Every week, we had to make decisions about which bills to pay and which to let visit with us longer. Did you know that several times I went without pay?"

"I didn't know that. The same happened to me in my first church during my Southern Seminary days."

"We were younger then, more flexible in every area of life."

"Skip, we're not that old. You talk like we're sitting in rocking chairs on the porch of the old folks' home."

"I'm ten years older than you, Pat, and ministry has a way of aging a man."

"That's certainly true. The work isn't for the faint of heart."

Warner looked up. "Do you think I'm faint of heart?"

Pat hesitated. "I've always admired you, Skip. I've followed your career, and I listen to your sermon every week over the Internet. You have been an inspiration."

"Until now."

"I'm not your judge, Skip. God is."

"You don't think I should have spoken up in favor of accepting the government's new policies on hate speech and taken the funding?"

Pat set his cup aside and leaned over the table. "What we do is not hate speech. It is not intolerance."

"The government thinks it is."

"The present government does. They won't be in office forever."

"This won't go away, Pat. This kind of thinking is here to stay. That's why there are so many key leaders from the Christian community here. This is probably the largest gathering of mega church pastors in history. They all came for the same reason, to discuss the errors of our ways."

Pat clenched his jaw and prayed for a civil spirit. "I've heard your sermons. You've made no errors and neither have I. All we've done is preach from the Bible. We proclaim the truth of Scripture. We don't do it with hate. You know that. Everyone is welcome in our church. If a homosexual comes to our service, I don't point them out and call for a stoning. I preach whatever God has put on my heart for that morning, just like you do. I don't point out adulterers or fornicators or liars or thieves. I preach Christ and His love. Some respond; some don't, but what I do—what *we* do—is not a crime."

"It is now. Thanks to Congress, the president, and the attorney general."

"And John Knox Smith."

"What's that I hear in your voice? Disappointment?"

Pat nodded. "I went to school with Smith. We used to debate every-thing. It was an odd friendship. I knew he was a man of ambition and passion, but I never saw this coming."

"I want to tell you something, Pat. I want you to hear it from me and not through the media."

"I'm listening."

"I'm going to hold a press conference and apologize to all who may have been offended by my sermons and writings."

"By which you mean . . . ?"

"Primarily members of the lesbian, gay, bisexual, and transgendered community."

"But your church—"

"My board is behind me on this."

Pat rubbed his eyes. "You have a ten-thousand member church. You built that church up from forty people, Skip. God built that church through your biblical preaching. To back away from your previous teaching is bound to create problems."

Warner lowered his voice. "Doing nothing will cause greater prob-lems, at least for me."

"What does that mean?"

Leaning closer to Pat, Warner spoke just above a whisper. "I got a call shortly before coming here. We have a member who has a com-munications firm that handles Internet security for several California law enforcement agencies. He also handles their intranet systems—the network that only law enforcement can access. He, unintentionally mind you, came across a plan to raid my church. The member called me immediately. DTED Hate Crimes units are just days away from kicking down our doors. You've seen the news, Pat. You know how they do this. They arrest the heads of the ministry and parade them around for the media to see. Tell me that won't knock the legs from under my ministry."

"It grieves me to hear that. I know what it feels like."

"Really? Forgive me, Pat, but how can you?"

"Not long after John Knox Smith started shaking things up, I heard from a mutual friend Mr. Smith and I share from our college days. He said John hinted that I should be careful about what I do and say. It came after I did the funeral for a pastor who was gunned down in his office."

"As I recall, he gunned down a U.S. marshal."

"I don't think we'll ever really know what happened," Pat said. "All I know is that the government never found what they went in looking for. Word got to my old friend, and he seems to think I made a mistake by doing the funeral service."

"So what did you do after the warning?"

"The same thing I've been doing since entering the ministry—proclaiming the Word of God and the love of Jesus."

"You didn't back away?"

Pat shook his head. "I couldn't come up with a good excuse to tell God why I feared men more than I feared Him."

"That's great preacher talk, Pat. I've said the same thing myself, but things have changed."

"So you say. The question is . . . has God's will changed?"

Warner sighed. "Do you know who Father Francis Perone is?"

"He's a parish priest in New York, right?"

"Long Island," Warner said. "He spent much of his time preaching about what he called 'the abortion crisis.' His sermons went out over television, radio, and Internet—just like us. The local bishop refused to quiet him despite requests from the DTED. The guy kept at it, taking the state's most prominent health providers to task. He went so far as to name them in his homilies.

"Some of his own parishioners felt he had crossed the line, but Perone would not shut up. Reports of his hate speech violations mounted; still he kept at it. During a nine o'clock Mass, agents entered the church and arrested him. He was right in the middle of his message. These guys not only arrest you; they do so in a most embarrassing way. They could have taken him before or after the sermon or even during the week, but they chose the middle of the service. Do you know what happened?"

"No," Pat said.

"I had one of my staff do a little research. A few parishioners made phone calls, and a few conservative bishops complained to the press. That was it. No one raced to his defense. After a few days, people stopped complaining. The whole thing just disappeared, and Father Perone was left to defend himself."

Warner sat back. "That could have been you, Pat. If I don't step back a little, it will be me." He stood. "I know you don't agree. You probably consider me a coward. But I hope I can still call you a friend."

Pat stood and held out his hand. "I wish you'd reconsider, Skip, I really do. Nonetheless, you can count on my friendship and my prayers."

Warner's eyes glistened. He tried to speak, but the words never came. He turned and melded into the milling crowd.

That night, Pat watched Skip Warner on the evening news. He stood behind a lectern outside the main entrance of the Atlanta conference center. Behind him stood several nationally known pastors and parachurch leaders.

Warner's voice broke and his lip quivered. "I and many of my brethren wish to offer a heartfelt apology to those who may have felt slighted by our preaching and teaching. Scores of ministers have gathered at this meeting to evaluate our past behavior and treatment of people from certain important and valuable segments of the community. We have weighed ourselves in the balance of fairness and justice and have found ourselves wanting."

Warner paused and inhaled deeply. A tear trickled down his right cheek. He let the tear fall before speaking. "After acknowledging our guilt, many of us have agreed to be more cautious in our speech and more open in understanding. To set the tone for these changes, I wish to apologize and seek forgiveness from the homosexual and transgendered community. I further promise to lead in efforts to make equality and acceptance of such groups a reality. No longer will we discriminate in areas of marriage and sexual conduct. God's love is broad enough to encompass everyone, and we wish to be His agents in expressing that love. To paraphrase Jesus, 'Come to me, all you who are weary and burdened, and I will give you rest.'"

Pat turned off the television and began packing his bags.

| CHAPTER FOURTEEN |

One of the unexpected public reactions to the new laws and frequent prosecutions was the unity it brought to people who were serious about God and His Word—a unity that spread across faith lines. Nobody pretended there weren't differences in the various faith traditions, but in areas where they could agree, they began working together to defend their common interests.

The closing of ranks came into play in Baltimore, when a small Orthodox Hebrew school that had been teaching Hebrew Scriptures came under fire from antireligious groups and ultimately from IRS Agent Bob Maas and the investigative team at the DTED. The main provocation was the headmaster, a well-known rabbinical scholar and author. He had taught a lesson in which he said Moses had literally come down from Mount Sinai with two tablets written by the finger of God.

"Furthermore," he said, "those ten laws are still relevant every day of our lives. We all know people who violate those laws and commit sins, even though they know that God hates sin." Then he said, "Sin in any form is an offense to God, and many of the things being pushed on young people by the popular culture—especially outfits like Pop-Teen Television Network, which promotes homosexuality and other types of sexual experimentation—is sinful and ought to be avoided at all costs."

When word of that lesson made its way to one parent estranged from the faith, a parent who happened to be a major stockholder in PTTN, the roof crashed down on the rabbi and the school. Threats and accusations were leveled at the headmaster and the school board. Soon the ACLU and IRS were brought into it. As the feud escalated, one parent, afraid for the future of the school, called the Alliance. Scott Freeman, the Alliance head, agreed to take a look at the situation. Within a few days, he sent Larry Jordan to investigate.

Larry visited the school and spoke to the headmaster. The Alliance agreed to take the case. This wasn't the first time the Alliance had aided the school. Some of the city's movers and shakers had been working for years to put the school out of business for other reasons. They tried issuing zoning violations, parking inadequacies, nuisance restriction, and every other trick they could think of. In those early years, the Alliance stood by the Hebrew school, successfully defending every case brought against them and doing battle with the city. Larry led the charge and won each challenge—but not easily. It seemed to Larry that every case was a steeper hill to climb. In the end the Hebrew school continued to exist and teach.

The story made news on several fronts. John Knox Smith watched every act of the legal play. The loss annoyed him. The fact that the Alliance represented the school pro bono irritated him even more. More cases were won simply by the crushing cost of mounting a defense. The Alliance was getting on John's last nerve.

In some parts of Washington, D.C., gangs of rebellious teens of all ethnic origins and backgrounds banded together to prey on anyone who had the audacity to drive through their neighborhoods. The situation had provoked a number of dangerous confrontations, one that metastasized overnight into a national scandal.

With cap-and-trade taxes on carbon consumption in effect and gasoline prices hovering near five dollars a gallon, the only people still driving for fun were the wealthy and those who lived in family groups or shared a car. Teenagers in the inner cities felt frustrated. Cruising was part of their culture, and now even that had been taken away from them.

One summer evening a group of teens from southeast D.C. had been prowling around the DuPont Circle area looking for trouble. They spotted a group of well-dressed young men in a BMW convertible going around and around the circle, laughing, joking, and gesturing to people on the sidewalks and in the shops.

The gang thought the guys in the Beemer were perfect targets. The teens wanted their ride, and they managed to surround the luxury car at a traffic light. They fought. In the end, one of the men was seriously injured and later died of his wounds.

The three who survived the attack claimed they had been targeted because they were gay. Furthermore, three of the teens had been wearing their gang symbol: a large, gold cross on chains around their necks. They had crosses tattooed on their arms or shoulders. When police arrested the teens, they were booked and identified. Police did background checks and discovered that one of them was the grandson of a well-known African-American pastor in the D.C. suburbs.

In most cases, police remove all jewelry before taking mug shots, but since the crosses were associated with their gang symbols, they made an exception. Associated Press photos appeared in the local newspapers and on the Internet. Soon the media identified the gang members as a Christian hate group. One headline read, "Christians Target Gays in DuPont Circle: One Dead, Three Injured."

In their official statement, the teens said they were offended that anyone would be driving like that in a luxury car. It was an insult to everybody who had to walk. They had no idea how the BMW's occupants engaged in sex. Their statements never appeared in print.

An editorial in the *Post* read, "Who in this country still criticizes gay men for their genetic identity? Who would think of stomping a gay man to death because of his choice of lifestyle? Is there any doubt where this sort of intolerance originates? This religion-driven ideology continues to breed hate and violence in our cities. How long can we afford to look the other way? When will it end?"

Readers had no doubt it was "true believers" behind the DuPont Circle killing. Only those who read to the end of the story on page 6B would have learned that the young thugs were not active in any church. The crosses were nothing more than gang signs. As the story spread, with more emphasis on the photos and less on facts, public outcry grew. In response, pastors all over America rushed to denounce the act of faith-driven violence.

Conservative pastors and church leaders, who had once resisted allowing Faith-Based Action Centers to be organized in their churches, began coming around. A group of them met at the National Press Club in Washington to encourage all Christians to join them in sending a "message" to America that loudly proclaimed, "Stop the Hate!"

Many Christian radio stations changed too. A federal judge in upstate New York issued an opinion broadening the Supreme Court ruling that declared that the free speech clause of the Constitution does not apply to hate speech. The Court held that any sermons and programs used to raise funds for any ministry that advocated inequality and intolerance could not claim First Amendment protection. No one had forgotten what happened to Rev. Jeremiah Helton, whose TV and radio broadcasts had once reached as many as twenty million households each week. In order to broadcast and publish Helton's sermons, books, and commentaries, the ministry had grown steadily over three decades, from a small, family-run operation to more than four hundred employees and an annual budget topping sixty million dollars. At that time, Liberty Free Church was one of the best-known churches and one of the most respected ministries in America.

When the ministry first came under assault from the DOJ's Hate Speech Task Force, Helton immediately employed the services of outside legal counsel from one of the most prestigious law firms in Washington. The firm was known for their work in the regulatory arena with the Federal Communications Commission and had represented broadcasters and some of the largest broadcast networks in New York, Washington, and L.A.

They were great lawyers who did an excellent job for their clients. The level of trust was high. Their loyalty to the case was beyond question. Furthermore, Helton understood that, off the record, some of the attorneys agreed with the ministry's message. They were not, however, constitutional religious liberty lawyers. So when the going got rough and charges came down from the hate crimes unit and the FCC, Helton's lead counsel had only one overriding goal: to reduce the amount of exposure and the personal risk to his client.

In the initial stages of representation, they refused all offers of help from the Alliance. They were concerned that any connection with a "conservative religious liberty" ministry would jeopardize the client's chance of a positive outcome. The senior partner said the Alliance was "too radical." He admired their winning track record but said, "They have a great group of lawyers and the most impressive list of pro bono attorneys I've ever seen. But the Alliance is in danger of being stripped of their own IRS exemption. Believe me: the same people going after Jeremiah Helton have the Alliance in their sights, and that's one headache we don't need."

As Helton's case proceeded through the courts, the Alliance offered to submit an amicus brief on Helton's behalf. Then-Alliance CEO Alex Stanton personally called Helton, offering staff support for his legal team. Initially, Helton said he was grateful for the offer. Two days later the offer was rebuffed, and the filings the Alliance had submitted to bolster Helton's case were opposed by his own lawyers.

Just days before the writ of certiorari was issued, allowing Helton's attorneys to present their case before the United States Supreme Court, Helton called Alex Stanton and begged him to stay away and not let it be known that the Alliance had ever expressed an interest in the case. Despite that request, Alliance lawyers tried to file an amicus brief on their behalf. But since both parties in the case had opposed it, the Court dismissed the brief, meaning at least three fundamental, constitutional arguments, which could possibly have made all the difference in the outcome of the case, were never heard by the court.

When the Court's ruling came down the following June, authored by none other than the chief justice himself, Helton's team lost on all counts. His ministry of more than thirty years was immediately shut down.

In the few years since the *Liberty Free Church* ruling came down, most Christian ministries had avoided confrontations and ignored the long-range implications of that decision. The DuPont Circle killing, the D.C. bombing, and the Nashville pastor's slaying of the young U.S. marshal, however, brought it all back to the surface. The media wasted no time in making the connections. It was becoming increasingly apparent that John Knox Smith and the prosecutors at the DTED would soon be going after bigger game.

Faced by the prospect of losing their licenses and livelihoods, scores of Christian station owners, managers, and hosts from around the country met to participate in a debate at the quarterly owners' conference hosted by their broadcast association in Nashville. Many resolved that it was no longer wise or profitable for any ministry to resist government directives concerning what the DTED had identified as "aggressive programming."

In a prepared statement read to the media by the group's senior vice president and director of industry standards, they said, "Religious broadcasters don't want to appear to be obstructionist on this issue. We have never condoned hate speech on our affiliated stations. Furthermore, for most of our stations, preaching programs are no longer the principal source of revenue. It's certainly not smart to allow a few troublemakers to turn this debate into a battle for the rest of us."

Over the next several months many Christian radio stations changed their formats. Most went to a mix of music, news, and entertainment programming, along with slick, highly packaged infomercials that allowed the station owners not only to avoid the hassles of a Washington crackdown but also to increase profits beyond anything they had previously known.

In a live broadcast on his own weekly program, the association's new president said, "We will fight censorship up to a certain level, but we're never going to give hate mongers access to the airwaves. The minute anyone who has been identified as a hate monger tries to buck the system, we will take them off the air. That's our pledge." This was, he said, the view of the association's entire board of directors.

A notable exception, along with the former broadcasters' president, was Rev. Ron Wilder of the North American Christian Network, who had a group of small stations across the Midwest. He insisted that "the gospel is still the gospel" and said he would never compromise.

As soon as he spoke those words, a member of the task force took the digital recording to the DTED, and Donna Lewis, John's chief of staff, had it transcribed. From that moment, Wilder became a top target of the DTED Hate Crimes Task Force. He was "aiding and abetting hate speech." Within days, the DTED, using the new forfeiture procedures, seized those stations, and the ministry was shut down.

John was shrewd. He didn't get where he was by accident—not at his age. He understood that keeping the media on his side was essential. Even before the raids and confiscations started, he had been busy letting people at the FCC know which way the wind was blowing. He had already taken steps to get them on board with the DTED's agenda.

When President Blaine first took office, the FCC had several vacancies because the new Congress refused to confirm the former president's appointees. When the shake-ups began, they were able to fill many of those slots with people who understood they had to take definitive action to stop the hate.

The "Kindness Doctrine," which had been signed into law by the former president, guaranteed that hate speech would not be allowed in broadcast media. The airwaves were public property, owned by the government, and the government wanted what was best for the people. Why would they allow public property to be used to send out information that made people feel unwanted and discriminated against? It was their duty to protect all Americans from expressions of hate. One way they achieved this was by scrutinizing America's airwaves.

As John had promised, the Faith-Based Action Centers being set up and funded in churches and religious institutions of all faiths had been the biggest boost to the DTED initiatives. FAC committees in the churches—organized and implemented by lay leaders in each congregation with taxpayer funds—were changing the cultural dynamics in the faith community. They introduced a whole new constituency to the objectives of diversity, tolerance, and equality.

Under the new initiatives, program directors in Washington were able to provide nationwide, interactive video conferencing, beamed into every participating church in the country by satellite, with the latest and best information on the battle for fairness and equality.

The most distinguished clergy in America often led these sessions with pastors, priests, rabbis, ecumenical teachers, and scholars from many faith traditions. In addition, matching funds were made available for up-to-date computers, video equipment, and satellite links to make it all possible.

It soon became apparent that more churches were eager to get involved. The FACs brought new equipment, programming, a greater sense of community involvement, and much-needed funds for additional staff to manage it. In some cases there were large financial stipends for senior ministers to cover the time and effort they put into reviewing and supporting these new programs.

The literature made it clear, however, that government funds could not be used to promote any particular religion. On the contrary, the government would have to be completely unbiased in its support for religious freedom and the right of all Americans to be affiliated with any (or with no) religion. "In every case," the literature said, "government's concern is limited to diversity, tolerance, and equality."

The program was fully supported by the ACLU and other religious watchdog groups because it was helping all Americans understand what the separation of church and state was all about. Rev. Lynn Barrett, one of a handful of leaders who participated in every panel, discussed how the Bible and other major religious texts clearly taught the principles of diversity and tolerance.

Bestselling authors, media personalities, musicians, and popular sports figures participated on the programs, as well as young people, parents, and senior citizens who had been through the training and were eager to share how the new ideas had changed their lives. For the first time, they had found meaning and purpose in their lives.

Father Jerome Filcher, who headed the reform group Catholics for Reality explained how the Catholic Church was being threatened with extinction under the leadership of a series of reactionary pontiffs, but that program never aired. The ecumenical review committee felt the message was inappropriate since the former priest had injected religion into his discussion of the failings of the church.

Overall, the FACs proved to be a tremendous success. John's initial spearheading of the initiative brought him even wider exposure, both in this country and abroad. For the first time since launching the agency, conference bulletins, announcements, and calls for academic papers on judicial reform were coming to him from around the world. On more than one occasion, John had been approached about attending these events, but Washington was too demanding. He couldn't find the time.

As a rule, the DOJ didn't provide assistant attorneys general a staff car and driver, except for official business during the day. However, because of heightened security concerns and the mission-critical status of the DTED, Attorney General Stamper arranged for John to have a car and driver assigned to him. After agonizing over what to do with his old Mercedes, which was rarely driven and becoming an eyesore and an embarrassment, he decided to sell it before he had to pour more money into repairs. The act was another way of severing ties to his past.

Since he wouldn't be driving, it was unrealistic for him to be going back and forth to Silver Spring every day. With the pressures of the job and the complaining from Cathy whenever he was home, he decided to bring in an old leather couch and some bedding and began sleeping at the office. He kept a change of clothes in the closet in his office, and there was an executive shower available. The department would have paid for a hotel room, but John decided it was too much trouble. He needed to be available at all hours. For him the temporary quarters were his best option.

The longer this went on, the greater Cathy's suspicions became. "You're having an affair, John. You might as well admit it. I know she stays late at the office with you. I see you texting back and forth on your BlackBerry."

"Oh, for the love of . . . ! She is my assistant, Cathy. Of course we text and talk on the phone and work late."

"You're having an affair. I can feel it."

"Don't be ridiculous. I haven't touched another woman. There's nothing between Andrea and me."

"That's what I'm worried about."

"Don't be crude, Cathy. It's beneath you."

"And who is beneath—?"

"Don't say it. You want to know why I prefer to sleep at the office? This is why. I work long hours, grueling hours. You have no idea the stress I'm under. When I come home, what do I get? Paranoid delusions, naggings, accusations, and complaints about the car, the house, everything."

"You love your job too much." Tears rose in her eyes.

"I do love my job, which is why you can know that I'm not having an affair with Andrea or anyone else. A thing like that would kill my career. I'm too smart for that."

"Apparently you're not smart enough to realize you're sacrificing your family. You're losing your son."

"You're overreacting as usual. Jack's just going through a phase. It'll pass."

"You hope."

"It . . . will . . . pass."

That ended the conversation.

John's workload was outrageous with cases in litigation all over the country and with the Alliance meeting him on the doorsteps of every courthouse. He had once heard that if a bullfrog is dropped into boiling water it will hop out, but if it's lowered into a pot of cool water which is slowly brought to a boil, it will remain in place until dead. He wondered if he was becoming the latter bullfrog.

John cut away layers of life until all that remained was the office and his consuming cause. He didn't have time to squabble with Cathy, and for the first time since the new legislation was enacted, the DTED was getting effective resistance from some of the right-wing groups besides the Alliance. He had expected this all along, but expecting a confrontation and facing it were very different things. Once again, he had to deal with questions from the media he never had to worry about before. He was constantly putting out fires. Andrea became his only trustworthy confidante; but there were many things he wasn't free to discuss with her.

An unpleasant surprise landed on his desk. A group of dissident congressmen had somehow managed to schedule hearings to look into DTED activities. Members of the minority party normally had a hard time holding hearings on their own, but somehow a group of representatives from southern and western states with long tenure in Congress had pulled together a hearing dealing with what they described as the "excessive use of force" and "organizational overreach" of John Knox Smith and the DTED.

To make matters worse, the media would cover the hearings. They repeated the Alliance drivel put out in the group's unending press releases. They claimed DTED agents were out of control and going beyond their authority, brutalizing and humiliating people all over the country.

When questioned about the tactics of his officers and agents by a wire service reporter, John said, "I think you know why we go into places like that with a show of force. The reason we started doing this in the first place was because we knew there was a risk that someone could get hurt. I hope I don't have to remind you what happened to Deputy Ronnie Lee Jefferson, who was gunned down in Nashville in one of those places, leaving a wife and two wonderful sons behind. How many more officers do we have to lose before people realize it simply has to be this way?"

Playing the devil's advocate, the reporter pressed John further. "I suspect you'll have a hard time convincing people that your average preacher is a menace to society."

The reporter's statement infuriated John, but he maintained his poise, thankful the reporters couldn't hear his heart pounding his ribs. "We've found that virtually every one of these outlier churches has members who belong to the NRA. What does that tell you? These people are gun owners; by definition they're armed and dangerous. Why would an honest citizen need to have a gun?"

"Isn't that a Second Amendment right, Mr. Smith?" the reporter asked, continuing his aggressive tone. "That's what we hear whenever we bring up the issue of gun control."

"Nothing in the Bill of Rights condones butchery," John said. "The Second Amendment is about protecting the nation in time of war, not violence against legal authority. These are people who spend way too much time thinking about blood and death and sacrifices. They worship a book that celebrates the wrath of an angry god; their greatest heroes are people who had violent deaths. Why would anyone be surprised when they resort to violence to get what they want?"

"Do you really believe it's that serious?"

John started thinking about how he was going to punish the press representative on his staff who had allowed this fiasco. "Look. I shouldn't have to remind you of the Crusades, the Inquisition, the Reign of Terror, the wild men shooting up women's health clinics in this country, the Crucifix Bomber, or the DuPont Circle death. Any time these people wrangle their way into positions of power, everyone pays a price. It always leads to violence, and it comes from their belief that they have the only truth and everybody else is doomed to hell."

"Mr. Smith," the reporter said, almost apologetically, "I don't mean to push you so hard, but again, most people believe they have a right to their beliefs, and they also have a right to persuade other people that their way of thinking is correct and desirable. Except for the incident last month at DuPont Circle, we haven't seen many gangs of gun-wielding Christians running amok; and frankly there are questions about that one."

John reached his limit. A bit of his anger slipped into his words. "First of all, there is no question that the incident at DuPont Circle was an attack planned and executed by a gang of fundamentalist zealots against a respected minority. Don't take my word for it; why don't you try reading the newspaper sometime?

"Secondly," he continued, "these people are determined to crush all other beliefs. They're carrying out a vendetta against members of the LGBT community. Their practice of conversion is nothing short of genocide. If they had their way, there would be no Muslims, no Hindus, no Buddhists, no Jews. They would wipe out all those great religions by forcing them to convert to their own bloody beliefs.

"Worse, there's a large segment of the Christian church who believe in 'transubstantiation' and such as a sacred part of their doctrine. Ever heard of that term?"

"No, can't say I have," the reporter responded.

"Look up 'transubstantiation.' The doctrine teaches that by the conversion of bread and wine into Christ's body and blood, Christ becomes truly present in the sacrament. Thus Christ Himself is really present and eaten. There's a word for that: cannibalism. Who in their right minds would countenance a belief like that?"

"Point taken," the reporter said. "Any final comments for the record?"

John paused briefly, then said, "The highest honor for such a Christian is no different than for any other terrorist group. Blood, death, self-sacrifice, wiping out entire populations by conversion. They do it by emotional coercion and the elimination of anyone who doesn't agree with them. Remember that their god was a martyr, hung on a cross. This is the model they expect the rest of the world to follow? What am I missing here?"

The following Sunday the entire interview headlined the feature sections of both the *Washington Post* and the *New York Times*.

| CHAPTER FIFTEEN |

Of all the DTED team members, Andrea Covington was closest to her boss in temperament and ambition. She made John's professional reputation and public persona a priority. She maintained daily contact with the two-person PR team that arranged his appearances. Whenever his ego needed a boost, she pressed the two young women to find media events, speaking opportunities, and other forums at major universities, think tanks, and nongovernmental organizations where John could be seen, heard, and received with favor. Those trips always pumped new life into her boss.

After the recent television debacle, knowing that John was eager to take his DTED experiences to the next level, Andrea had also made connections at the United Nations, the Council on Foreign Relations, and the Global Policy Institute in New York. She forwarded copies of John's curriculum vitae and selected news clips to several important global policy organizations overseas, including the headquarters of the European Union in Brussels and the Club of Rome with its headquarters in Switzerland.

In the list of organizational objectives that John had presented to the staff on their first day of business, he had specifically included a requirement to keep an eye out for international programs dealing with transformative justice. Andrea had been scouting for international events that might appeal to John. She knew the agency could offer new insights on compliance with international law. She also saw it as an opportunity to provide exposure for her boss on a much grander scale, speaking to an international audience about the DTED's perspectives on diversity and tolerance enforcement.

Her interest wasn't entirely altruistic, however. With any luck, she thought, she might be able to accompany John to such an event and share in the experience. She had never traveled abroad and looked forward to the prospect of working in some capacity with the International Court of Justice, the International Criminal Court, or perhaps even the UN-related International Criminal Tribunals and Special Courts that were, by any measure, the most advanced proponents of judicial reform on the planet.

Meanwhile, the Diversity and Tolerance Enforcement Division was clearly the fulcrum of social change in America. Everyone on the staff was competing to see who could make the biggest score and advance the cause fastest. Because of his success, groups like the American Civil Liberties Union, Americans United for the Separation of Politics and Religion, and the Southern Equality Law Center were actively competing to see who could exceed in supporting John's entire agenda.

These organizations weren't just sending new complaints to be investigated by the DTED and the hate crimes units; they were filing bold new lawsuits on their own. They saw money to be made and injunctions to be had, forcing compliance with their agendas. In many places, their attorneys were spearheading private enforcement actions and providing evidence for government bloodhounds, all at the same time.

Ben Braden, executive director of the ACLU, said on a Sunday morning TV interview program that regular church attendees were the most dangerous people in America. "Those who attend church more than three times a month vote consistently against progress and equality. They not only condone the injustice, mockery, and sedition coming out of right-wing pulpits," he said, "but they fund it. These people need to be separated from society. There's no significant difference between the leaders of these groups and the terrorists that flew the planes into the twin towers on nine-eleven."

John couldn't have said it better, Andrea thought. After hearing those remarks, her boss ordered his team to redouble their efforts for the fourth or fifth time. He also made sure his chief litigators and agents understood that he wanted as many indictments as possible to take place in D.C. in the next few weeks, where they would get, as he said, "the most bang for the buck." Andrea drew from his energy. When the fires of zeal burned within him, she felt honored to be his assistant. When he, as he sometimes did, briefly fell into despair, she felt honored to be the one he confided in.

Under federal statutes, venue for adjudication is wherever the crime occurs. If the average person can access an offensive Internet site or hear hate speech on radio or TV in the District of Columbia, the offender is, ipso facto, within the jurisdiction of the D.C. courts, regardless of where the speaker actually spoke.

John didn't like requiring his staff and agents to travel for long periods of time. He told Andrea that he hated them to be away from their families or domestic partners. If they had a venue in D.C., they wouldn't need to travel. It was much better if they could stay in town and sleep in their own beds at night when those long, tedious trials were underway. She thought this was endearing. He spent most of his nights sleeping in the office, but he wanted his team to be able to return home as many nights as possible. She wondered how many others saw John's sensitive side.

Trying as many cases as possible in Washington meant the government wouldn't have to pay for a fleet of lawyers to set up camp in Iowa or somewhere else out of town. As a fair-minded economic conservative, John was protecting the taxpayers, one more thing for Andrea to admire. Never mind that John thought D.C. juries were quick to convict.

To deal with all the cases coming in from all over the country, John decided to bring several new agents on board, in D.C. as well as in other metropolitan centers. In the process, he increased the scope of DTED operations to include a broader range of federal and local agencies. His goal was to cement the government's case against the purveyors of hate speech and religious bigotry, wherever those offenses occurred.

One of his first initiatives under the new expanded program was to ask the federal district court to impanel a series of special grand juries to hear evidence and bring indictments against the offenders. The grand jury was an ideal way to get to all the facts because each member of the jury was allowed to ask questions, and they generally asked a lot of them. But after a grand jury had been sitting for a while—those individuals could be impaneled for several weeks or several months if prosecutors insisted—they tended to become cynical and quick to change.

Over extended sessions, they get to know the agents and officials of the court very well, and they come to trust the prosecutors. When government lawyers brought an indictment proposal, the grand jury would vote in secret to indict or not to indict. More often than not, they went along with the prosecutor and rendered an indictment. Unless the Alliance or other experts in constitutional law interfered, most of the indicted would plead guilty or otherwise settle their case.

John was upset to learn that his old nemesis from Princeton, Pat Preston, had been identified as one of the biggest offenders and was being watched closely by his agents in Nashville. John had been shocked that Pat had performed the funeral for the killer pastor but had not dreamed of Pat's other activities. Pat and John had always been on different wavelengths, but John had never expected Pat to go very far with his brand of primitive thinking.

When he learned the size and scope of Pat's ministry and Reneé X showed Pat's photo on the cover of his favorite news magazine, John could barely restrain his rage. There was Pat Preston wearing an Oxford doctoral gown with an enormous headline across the top that read: "Is This the Conscience of the Nation?"

"I know this guy," John admitted. "We went to school together. He was always a pain in the neck at Princeton, and he apparently hasn't changed." What he didn't say was that he had once considered Pat a friend. *But that was a long time ago.* John tossed the magazine on the desk. Why couldn't Pat have found a small church somewhere, fed the poor, visited the elderly, performed funerals, and done whatever else small church pastors did?

"What's so dangerous about guys like this," added Reneé, "is the number of people—tens of thousands—who tune in on Sundays to hear him preach; not to mention his sermons are all over the Internet. He's in the South and parts of the Midwest on live TV and Internet stream every Sunday morning. He's even on D.C. cable. He preaches against abortion rights and gays, and attacks politicians we know and love—by name. To top it off, he finishes every sermon with what they call an 'altar call' and a time of confession and rededication."

"Another way to capture more suckers," John muttered. This wasn't news to him. Many churches did the same. Pat had tried to explain it to John at Princeton.

"It's a time to make a public statement about their belief. Everyone Jesus called, he called publicly. The altar call is a way of doing the same thing. It's also a time to ask for prayer." John had stopped listening at that point.

What made this so galling for John was that churches like Pat's preached, "Jesus is the only way, the only truth, and the only life." There was no other way to God.

John had taken his first New Testament class in college because his father had recommended it. It wasn't his favorite course, by any stretch, but he had learned enough from his professor to know that the context of Pat's sermons defied common sense. His old friend based a lot of his material on the gospel of Matthew, a New Testament book that talked about the demands of the Christian life. He mentioned this to Reneé.

"Anyone with the least knowledge of the Sermon on the Mount," she said, "should know that the whole point of that text is love and acceptance. How can you love your neighbor as yourself when you're damning his soul to hell? I find it hard to believe that anyone could fall for that line."

John had come to believe Pat only used Scripture to exclude people and attack groups he personally disliked. According to the article Reneé had shown him, Pat said, "A good tree cannot bear bad fruit, and a bad tree cannot bear good fruit. Every tree that does not bear good fruit is cut down and thrown into the fire." The caption under Pat's picture quoted him using that most hated phrase "by their fruit you will recognize them."

After seeing that, John was in a slow boil for the rest of the day. Didn't Pat realize those words would be an insult and a slur against the entire LGBT community? The article also quoted Pat saying, "Not everyone who says to me, 'Lord, Lord,' will enter the kingdom of heaven, but only he who does the will of my Father who is in heaven." John knew the reference: Matthew 7:21.

John tossed up his hands. "How can anyone repeat stuff like this with a straight face? That's the most insensitive thing I've seen in months. I'm shocked that the editors would allow a story like that to be printed."

"Are we going to do anything about it?" Reneé asked.

For a moment, John hesitated. He gave no thought to crushing people he didn't know, but this was Pat Preston. The moment passed. "Of course we're going to do something."

Shortly after returning from his studies at Oxford, Pat began attending the meetings of the ecumenical council each week in Nashville. The group included a dozen clergy members from several Protestant denominations as well as one Greek Orthodox priest, the pastors of two Roman Catholic parishes, and an Orthodox Jewish rabbi.

One of the men Pat met there was an older Catholic priest, Father John Corollo, who had been a highly respected member of the community earlier in his career. But because of his conservatism and strong pro-life positions, he was no longer welcomed by certain groups in the city or, for that matter, in his own church. He was eventually moved aside and replaced with a younger priest who was more receptive of new ideas.

Despite their differences, Father Corollo felt drawn to Pat and encouraged him in his ministry. In some ways he became Pat's confessor, which Pat, a proud, hard-core Baptist, said was impossible. They talked at length about the situation at Rogers Memorial. He offered encouragement and good counsel, but Pat didn't fully understand the advice he was given about watching out for disappointments with congregations and leaders.

"No one should go into the ministry if they're looking for a peaceful, comfortable life," Father Corollo told him. "I know you're perplexed by the resistance you're seeing. What you're discovering, Pat, are the kinds, of pressures that always come to those who focus their love on Christ rather than on the charms of this world. I'm afraid you'll have to go through some hard times along the way, which means you need to bathe these concerns with prayer. Make sure you're always clothed in the full armor of God."

Pat gained a lot from those conversations. He knew there would be challenges if he continued to speak out honestly and openly about his biblical convictions, but that was a challenge he had accepted when he was ordained. He didn't plan on changing his focus now. He had no choice in the matter. He was accountable to God and his congregation. If there were repercussions, he would just have to deal with them.

Although they were years apart in age and disagreed on many things—like the role of the pope and Mary—they enjoyed their times together. They prayed for and encouraged each other.

Pat taught an informal service on Wednesday nights and preached two of the three Sunday services. Almost a year after returning from England, he began a five-part series on Wednesdays called "Why Other Religions Don't Work." Several months later and because of the strong reaction the series stirred up among the members, his associate, Frank Billington, persuaded Pat to repeat the series and expand on his thoughts for the Sunday morning services.

Pat agreed. He renamed the series "The Insufficiency of Hope" and expanded it from five to six weeks in order to wrap up with a suitable summary at the end. During the first five weeks, he explained that the so-called "great religions" were based on wishful thinking and clung to "a hope that could never be fulfilled."

"The Bible teaches the importance of hope," Pat said, "but other religions offer only false hopes, either in some powerless deity, in a mistaken belief in the goodness and perfectibility of man, or, as with the Eastern religions, in the hope of escaping the tragedy of life through death and annihilation, and merging their souls with the cosmos." In his sermons, Pat called this man-made concoction a "death trap."

The first week Pat preached on Islam. In successive weeks he dealt with Buddhism, Hinduism, and the New Age movement. The fifth week he preached on false messiahs of many kinds. He had been planning a wrap-up to the series with a summary of all his major points, along with an appeal on behalf of what he called "Our Only Hope of Heaven," when the hammer came down.

The DTED agents had already classified Rev. Pat Preston as a bigot. He had been on their radar screen for some time. To John, his former friend and school competitor had evolved into a homophobe and a radical pro-life activist who wanted to deny women the full range of health-care options they were due. He insisted there could be only one type of marriage and one type of family, which was not only irrational but illegal.

Most offensive of all, after all that had happened across America, was that "Pastor Pat" had the audacity to attack every other religion in the world and to libel anyone who had a different interpretation of the Bible. He called them "pagans who follow a false messiah."

John and his team had declared war on hate and intolerance of that kind, and it was clear that the pulpits of the remaining fundamentalist churches were going to be the next major battlefield. The DTED lawyers selected a grand jury that had been meeting for several months. The seasoned grand jurors took testimony from dozens of witnesses in all the cases John's prosecutors brought to them. They were tired, but they were battle tested and, from John's point of view, very reliable.

Then a series of new events shocked the nation, including another bombing at a middle school cafeteria in Kingsport, Tennessee. Nine students and several cafeteria workers were killed or injured. Three of the victims were seriously hurt, crippled for life. One fourteen-year-old boy died in the hospital, and two young women had been decapitated by flying debris. Shortly before the bombs exploded, a caller had said, "Remember the Crucifix Bomber." The words and photos shook even the toughest men and women on the jury.

The grand jury had seen numerous examples of how certain people and groups used hate speech to create an atmosphere of intolerance—an intolerance that propelled some people to acts of extreme violence. They were eager to stop it, especially when a pastor from another part of Tennessee was contributing heavily to the atmosphere of intolerance and hate.

Not only did the series on "The Insufficiency of Hope" create a lot of commentary on the Internet, but the national media began reporting on it the first week after Pat preached on the weaknesses of Islam. One of John's strongest supporters from Americans for the Separation of Politics and Religion, Nabil Medina, accosted him at the group's monthly meeting and made it clear how deeply offended and hurt he was by what "that Tennessee outlaw" had said about his religion. John was caught off guard. It was one of the few times he had been directly confronted by his alleged shortcomings in his job. It infuriated him.

A short time later, John was a guest on a TV interview program during prime time. He sat across the table from a pair of Washington notables. The host said he wanted to show John a video clip and get his response. What he showed was a segment from Pastor Pat Preston. Every muscle in John's body tensed.

After showing the clip, the host turned to John. "Our reporter, Devon Hayward, has been following this case for weeks now, Mr. Smith. He tells us that you've been close friends with Rev. Preston for many years, going back to your days at Princeton. Yet you've never mentioned this, and apparently no one at the Justice Department is looking into this case. Is that right?"

It was an obvious "gotcha" situation—an unfair, misleading cheap shot. John felt his face turn red. "That's false—absolutely false," he snapped.

"I resent your implication. I knew Pat Preston at Princeton, that's true, but calling us friends goes too far. My staff is very much involved in this case. We have agents looking into the situation in Nashville at this moment."

Unimpressed, the host continued. "All right, Mr. Smith. We'll come back to that another time. But let me ask you something else. I'd like to get your reaction to another statement from your Princeton buddy, Rev. Preston. This comes from a broadcast earlier this morning on one of the local stations in Nashville. I suspect our viewers would like to know how you would respond to what the minister has to say here. Take a look."

The video showed Pat Preston seated at a table, saying, "There are people in this country and in our own government who want to tell us what we can and cannot say from the pulpit. They talk about tolerance, but they're not tolerant in the least. They talk about diversity, but the only diversity they condone is the practice of evil. What they define as hate speech is the gospel of Jesus Christ. If they could, they would strip this nation of the very freedoms our ancestors died for. Their kind of equality can only occur if the government limits the freedom of everybody to become who God wants them to be. Honestly, I'm afraid that's where it's headed."

Realizing he had reacted a little too strongly in his previous comments, John consciously calmed his emotions and said, "I agree. That's not acceptable. It's unfortunate that Reverend Preston would speak those words on a nationally televised broadcast. But I'm not surprised. We've heard a lot of this kind of talk lately. Take my word for it. We *are* doing something about it."

John stormed out of the studio. He grabbed his BlackBerry and scrolled down to a number Pat had given him years earlier. John knew the number might not work, but it was the only one he had. *I'm going to kill him myself,* he smoldered as the phone rang. *Pat was always strange, but I never thought it would go this far.*

To John's surprise, Pat answered the call on the third ring.

"Pat, is that you?"

"Yes, this is Pat Preston. Who's speaking?"

"Pat, it's John Knox Smith."

There was a long pause on Pat's end, but John didn't waste any time. He said, "Pat, you've humiliated me."

"I what?"

"Humiliated me—with what you said this morning about the government practicing evil. You said it on national television."

"B-but, John," Pat said, stumbling over his words, "I never said anything about you. Our service was on the air this morning, that's true, but it had nothing to do with you. Besides, I don't know how you saw it. Aren't you in Washington?"

"I've just been humiliated in front of twenty million people on national TV, Pat. They played part of your broadcast and put me on the spot." John resisted the growing urge to yell profanities into the phone. "Once upon a time I thought we were friends. Now look what you've done!"

"I would never knowingly humiliate you, John. I'm sorry if I said something that hurt you. Please forgive me."

John wasn't about to listen to an apology. "You know perfectly well what I mean, Preston! Did you say that the only diversity we condone in this country is the practice of evil? Did you say that or not?"

"That's what you're calling about?"

"You weren't like this in college, Preston. You were . . . I don't know . . . I thought we understood each other. Now you're spouting all this sin and hell business, and accusing me—*me*—of being intolerant!"

Pat said nothing.

"Were you always so full of hate, Pat? Were you ever really my friend?"

"I thought so, John. At least I tried to be. I remember you told me once that you thought Jesus was a good role model. You said he set a high standard. Back then, you also said you weren't against God. You were receptive to some of the ideas we talked about. In fact, you said your father—"

"That's enough! Don't you dare tell me about my father. And don't tell me what you think I may have meant years ago. What I want to know is this: if you have something against me and what I'm doing at the Justice Department, then why haven't you come to me directly instead of saying all those things behind my back?"

"John, I tried. I called—"

"That's a lie. You never called me."

"Do you have any idea how many times I've tried to reach you over the last year—calling, e-mailing, writing to you? I sent you at least six letters. Every one of them came back unopened. I called your office at least that many times. I was told by a young woman on your staff, Andrea something, that you would be in touch, but you never called back. After months of that, I finally gave up. I decided you didn't want to hear from me. Besides, John, it's not like you sought my opinion."

The statement stunned John. Was Andrea filtering his mail, calls, and e-mails?

"John, are you still there?"

John and Pat had never been on the same page. Whenever he was around Pat, he felt manipulated. The one thing he knew about evangelicals was their unflagging desire to convert people to their religion. It's exactly what Lynn Barrett had said to him the night before: "People like that only want to strip away whatever is natural and spontaneous and good about life and replace it with their own prepackaged and hopelessly outmoded vision of right and wrong."

"John?"

Bringing up John's father was the last straw. The poor man would have been just like the rest of those Christians if he had known how. He never went for the full dose of God talk, but he spent his spare time building apartments, feeding the poor, and passing out blankets to homeless men on winter nights—all the while ignoring the real-world concerns of his family. John was glad that at least his father's religion was limited mainly to harmless charity work.

"Listen, John, it's obvious you're upset and you blame me. Let's talk about this. We can meet if you want to and—"

John ended the call and stormed down three flights of stairs instead of waiting for the elevator. When he reached his car, he waved off the driver who came around to open the door.

"Take me to the office, now."

John slid into the back seat and slammed the car door. A moment later he was on the cell phone to Andrea. The conversation was short—he made it clear to Andrea that the days of her filtering his mail and phone calls were over.

| CHAPTER SIXTEEN |

When John exited the elevator on the fifth floor of the DOJ building, he grabbed the first DTED attorney he saw in the hallway and said, "Come with me." As soon as they walked through the door of his private office, John spun around, his face bristling with anger. "Get me everything on how the case is developing against Rev. Pat Preston in Nashville, Tennessee. I mean *everything*. Where is he now? What's he doing? What he's saying about me and this agency? Where's the grand jury on his case? Is an indictment drawn up? Get it all, every word of it, and don't leave anything out. Is that clear? I'm going to nail that self-righteous bigot one way or the other."

"Yes, sir. Perfectly clear, sir. I'll get right on it." Then, hesitatingly, he asked, "Just one question, sir. Does this take priority?"

"What do you mean, priority? What did I just say? Of course it's priority. Why are you asking me that?"

"The judges, sir . . . and the Madisonians."

For a moment John felt lost. Then he looked at the young attorney more closely. "You're Alden, right?"

"Yes, sir. Mike Alden. You wanted to know the names of the federal judges that aren't following our directives. You also wanted me to do backgrounds on all the Madisonians at Justice."

"Of course. How's that going?"

"Fine, sir. It's been slow going, but I'm making headway. I gave a preliminary list of all the judges to your chief of staff last week, and I'm still working on a few others. I had some trouble getting the list of all the Madisonians, so I had to get some help from OPR. But I should have the information you wanted in a few days."

"You went to the Office of Professional Responsibility?"

"Yes, sir. They have access to the files on Justice Department employees. That's the only place to get some of this stuff."

"Okay, Alden," John said. "Look, I'm sorry. I forgot about that. It hasn't been my best day. Here's the deal: Preston comes first. Put the other stuff on hold for now and get me everything you can find on him. Then you can go back and wrap up the other assignment, but stay away from OPR. Got that?"

Before leaving, the young man reached over to shake his boss's hand. "Sir, I want to thank you for trusting me with these important projects."

John wasn't sure what to make of it, but he shook hands and said, "Sure, Alden. You're welcome. You'll do fine."

"I know how important this is to you, Mr. Smith," Alden pressed, "and I want you to know that I'm with you on everything. You can trust me, sir. I won't let you down."

That evening John had dinner and drinks with his colleague, Rev. Lynn Barrett of the Metropolitan Urban Church. The Capitol Hill restaurant buzzed with activity, but John ignored it. Instead he focused on telling Barrett how upset and embarrassed he felt after being caught off guard on a national television broadcast.

"The fact is," John said, "it's people like Pat Preston who have made my life unbearable."

"I know." Barrett's tone was sympathetic. "Somehow we have to stop these people. But you've got to stop pulling your punches, John. You have ways to shut these guys down once and for all. This may be just the provocation you've needed to ramp it up a bit."

"Are you saying that breaking down doors and hauling people off to jail isn't ramping it up?"

"You know what I mean, John. There's so much hate, and you could be doing more. What you find when you check these people out is that their whole way of life is devoted to one thing: converting people to their way of thinking. You know what I always say: it's nothing but spiritual genocide."

"I hear what you're saying, Lynn. I want to ramp it up, believe me. But some people are already having trouble with what we're doing. If we're too aggressive with guys like Preston, they'll come back at us because of all the AIDS relief, charities, missions, and things like that. Right-wing Christian groups run so much of that stuff. I mean, my own father did it for years. That's about all he did."

"Well, excuse my French, but that's a load of crap, John. The more dedicated they are—pretending to be kind and compassionate and all that rot—the more deceptive they are. People have to realize that those charities aim at just one thing: conversion. Even their hospitals are motivated by conversion. When your friend Preston was preaching those repugnant sermons about the world's great religions, do you think he was thinking about philosophy or customs?"

"Of course not. I'd prefer that you not refer to Preston as my friend."

"I understand. That was a long time ago. But here's my point. Everything they do is about converting the lost and heaven or hell. It is part of every fiber of their existence. Preston is like all the rest, practicing cultural genocide from the pulpit. If you go soft on him, everything they said about you this morning is going to stick to you like glue."

Responding to the passion in his voice, John said, "I hear what you're saying, Lynn. We've talked about this many times. I agree with everything you've said. I'm not saying we go soft on anybody; you've seen how aggressive we've been, especially over the last few months. I'm just saying we have to think about the public reaction and prepare for possible repercussions."

"Maybe you're right, but the only way to stanch a bleeding wound is to cauterize it. If you care about diversity and tolerance, then you're going to have to turn up the heat. It's time to stop this 'Jesus is the only way' business."

John pushed back from the table and smiled. "The Diversity and Tolerance Enforcement Division. I still like the sound of that, Lynn. I like what I do, and I like doing it here. It's the one true reality of our time. Whether it's religious or cultural, or the expression of our sexual identity, people have to start showing more respect for other people's choices. I like to go to the National Gallery because it's full of strange and wonderful things. If you go to any museum in this city and look at the incredible range of art, culture, and philosophy, you'll see the importance of diversity, and diversity is crucial to the continued success of our nation. If you were to take all the art created by other cultures and religions away, almost everything worth preserving would be gone."

"Imagine a world without lesbians and gays," Lynn said, "with all the beauty and art and imagination that comes from our community."

John nodded. "Take that away, and nothing worth keeping would be left; just the residue of that bloody cross-worshipping cult." John leaned back in his chair and placed his napkin beside his plate. "True believers are the biggest threat we face, Lynn. But somehow we'll stop them. Believe me, we've simply got to."

John was determined to turn up the heat, but that meant he would need the cooperation of the courts at all levels. He knew he could count on Chief Justice Williams and at least four of the associate justices at the Supreme Court to rule in favor of the strong, new amendment to the law and the new RDTA regulations when their cases reached that level. But most cases would be settled at the district and appeals court level. John wanted to be sure his attorneys could count on the judges there to cooperate.

He asked Andrea to connect him with the head of the Administrative Office of the Courts. As soon as he got the director on the line, he said, "We need to talk." Two days later John and Joel Thevis met with the director and explained their concerns.

"We did a lot of hard work to get the new, expanded DTED bill and the National Judicial Expansion and Retirement Act passed through Congress," John said. "They've been signed into law by the president, but we're still not getting what we need from the district courts. The retirements and new appointments are moving too slowly."

The director looked at John skeptically. "What does that mean, Mr. Smith?"

"We thought the offer of early retirement at full pay for judges on the bench over ten years and the doubling of judicial positions would bring in a wave of new talent—people who think like we do. We have a lot of federal judges who are still hanging onto beliefs and ideologies that are in opposition to our core values and policies. We cannot have men and women sitting on the bench who support bigotry and intolerance."

John became animated. "Those people are throwbacks to another century. We can't have people like that in positions of trust. Any judge who is so out of touch that he or she can't read the handwriting on the wall needs to be permanently recused. That puts the ball squarely in your court. We want to know what you're going to do about it."

"If you're saying what I think you're saying, Mr. Smith, you're asking for trouble. We've been through this before. Meddling with the federal courts in any way, short of a full-fledged ethics investigation or a change of administrations, can be a disaster. In any event, what you're asking for would raise red flags in some places, and that could lead to a very nasty constitutional confrontation."

John shook his head. "One more legal battle won't faze me. I wouldn't look forward to a situation like that, but we both know it's time to settle some of the basic questions: What is 'free speech'? What is 'free exercise'? What is our constitutional position on those issues going to be? What has the Supreme Court decided is the meaning of the First Amendment? When are we going to bring our law into alignment with Europe? My agency is prepared to take on a major case that will help settle the matter, but we're going to need a little help."

"It comes down to this," Joel Thevis said, pressing harder. "What does the First Amendment actually mean? This whole concept of unenumerated rights needs to be put to bed. If the courts have said it isn't there, it isn't there. The mistaken idea that some people can trample basic human rights in the name of free speech or their so-called 'religious freedom' is an outrage to human dignity. We can bring the cases, but ultimately the courts will have to settle these questions. That means we need properly informed judges in the district courts."

The director sat forward with his elbows on the desk and his hands folded in front of his face as he listened to Joel's explanation. After another long pause, he said, "Gentlemen, the common interpretation of the First Amendment is that every American is guaranteed freedom of religion, speech, press, assembly, and redress of grievances. That's it." Then, sitting back in his overstuffed chair, he added, "Those are the 'five freedoms' the way the founders laid them out. There's not much wiggle room as far as I can see."

John recoiled at the mention of the founders. "We'd better stop and remember who the founders were. I hope you're not trying to glorify those people. They were some of the biggest hypocrites in history. They put all that flowery language in the Declaration of Independence and the Bill of Rights when their real goal was to avoid paying taxes and to keep their slaves. The reactionaries who try to disguise that fact with talk of 'originalism' aren't fooling anybody. That's garbage."

Leaning forward once again, the director said, "I think I know where you're going with this. You need to be very careful when you start messing around with the federal courts, not to mention the First Amendment. This is still a hot-button issue. As you know, there are at least two justices on the Supreme Court today who believe strongly that the free speech clauses in the Constitution protect just about anything anybody wants to say. Even if I happen to agree that their position is based on a false premise, you're not going to get either Collins or Grouling to go along with you."

Joel glanced at John and said, "We only need a simple majority to win our cases. I'm sure Justices Collins and Grouling are reasonable men. Like anybody else, they can be persuaded, and if—"

"No. Don't go there, Mr. Thevis." The director scowled. "If you try to tamper with the Court—"

"Who's tampering?" Joel protested. "I'm just saying—"

John jumped in to short-circuit the debate. "Joel, let it go. We know what you mean. We're not going to try to influence any of the courts that way." He addressed the director. "Here's the point we're trying to make. There has to be a limit to what people can say without penalty. You know we didn't decide this on our own: it's the law. Unlimited free speech would be a disaster. But we have to find the right case—a case that will help us make the point once and for all—and we want to be sure this office is informed and prepared to help when the time comes."

"I'm still not following you, Mr. Smith. What does that mean, 'prepared to help'?" It was obvious the man was irritated and unhappy with the direction of the conversation.

"I can't say at this moment," John answered. "I'm not sure what will happen when the time comes. I'm just saying it's important that judges at all levels need to be educated and to rule responsibly so we can establish the precedents that will help us do our jobs better. Surely you see what I mean. You know what the law says. If there are no responsible limits on what religious zealots can say in a public forum, then no one is safe. It's as simple as that. One way or the other, we're going to make sure that fact is established by law and that the federal courts allow us to make it a dynamic and lasting precedent."

As John and Joel were leaving his office, the director penciled a note to himself: "Call Alton Stamper. What's going on at the DTED and our courts? This JKS is dangerous."

| CHAPTER SEVENTEEN |

After struggling for so long in a nonexistent relationship with her husband of nearly thirteen years, Cathy Smith realized she'd taken all she could. Countless times, she had tried to get John's attention. She tried to make his home life pleasant and inviting. She tried to keep young Jack busy and out of John's hair as much as possible. She tried to be more loving and ever more expressive, but he treated her like a cardboard cutout. Nothing helped. John remained distant, and they argued constantly. And now he had moved to his office.

"John," she said one evening when everything came to a head, "I'm here day and night, taking care of you and your son and looking after a house you hardly use anymore. The least you could do is pay a little attention to your son. I don't expect you to care about me anymore. I know you have other interests, and I—"

John, she knew, seldom tolerated confrontation, especially from his family. Drawing to his full height, he snapped, "Cathy, what's wrong with you? I think you're losing it."

"Losing it? You think *I'm* losing it? Okay, if that's how you see it. Why do you think I'm losing it? Could it be because you're not part of this family anymore? Could it be because you're enjoying a full, rich life with your pals downtown while Jack and I sit here day after day, waiting for you to give us the time of day?"

"Cathy, will you please get a grip? Can't you be serious?"

With that smug rebuke the level of tension in the room escalated. Cathy began to shake. "Serious, John? Is that what you want? Okay, try this. I'm not sure who you are anymore or what sort of world you belong to. You always seem to have plenty of time for your dance lessons and your speech lessons and sending some poor sap to prison and who knows what else. You spend every spare nickel on your precious wardrobe and grooming. You talk incessantly about your little girlfriend, Andrea, and her awesome wardrobe. What am I supposed to think about that, John? How serious do you want me to be?"

John switched into prosecutor mode. She had seen it many times before. His eyes narrowed and his nostrils flared. "I don't believe what I'm hearing! You are the most self-righteous, hyper critical, overly possessive woman I've ever known. You've never been a wife to me, and you're not even half a mother to that boy. You spend all your time schlepping from one coffee klatch to the next—"

"I do those things because I hunger for adult involvement, something I never get from you."

"I'm not going to listen to this."

"You never do. You never listen to anyone except yourself."

Cathy watched her husband's face turn crimson. For a moment she expected him to throw the mug of coffee he'd been holding into her face.

"You wonder why I'm not here more often? Ask yourself, who would want to come to this place and listen to you? I'm leaving."

He set down the mug and reached for his BlackBerry on the coffee table. Before he could pick it up, Cathy snatched the phone and hurled it across the room with all her might. It broke into pieces against the stone fireplace.

"Cathy! Have you lost your mind? Look what you've done!"

"Good. I'm glad I did it. Now maybe you'll try talking without that prosthesis attached to your ear."

"That phone is the property of the United States Department of Justice. Do you know what you've done? You've committed a federal crime—a felony. I could have you locked up."

"Locked up? Go ahead. It will be a great addition to your resume." Cathy was hurt, furious, frightened, and overwhelmed.

"You're being ridiculous." John picked up the pieces of the phone and studied them.

A bitter realization settled in her mind. Her marriage was over. This was it. She couldn't keep up the pretense any longer. Their marriage was a fraud and had been since the day she'd dropped out of Boston College to marry the young law student, thinking he loved her like she loved him. Tears streamed. She pressed both hands over her mouth, sobbing, gasping for air. Somehow, she managed to utter the words, "Good-bye, John. It's over. I'm going home this time."

"No you're not. In a few hours, you'll settle down and realize how good you have it." He walked to the door. "I think it's best if I sleep at a motel tonight. We can talk when you've regained your reason." John walked out.

Twelve hours later, Cathy loaded the van with clothes, valuables, and other personal items. Then she called the school and arranged to pick up Jack during his lunch hour.

Because her son had always been so hard for her to handle, Cathy sent him to stay with his grandfather in Colorado. "It's temporary," she promised him, "just until I get things figured out." She expected the boy would argue and complain. Leaving school without an opportunity to say good-bye to his teammates and friends and leaving behind everything he valued gave him the right to complain, but he didn't. Somehow that made her decision more difficult. She reminded herself that Jack never liked going to Connecticut with her and her parents, who had shown no interest in Jack or his life.

John had even suggested on one occasion that Jack would be a lot better off with his Grandpa Chester. "Those two think alike," he had said. Cathy called her father-in-law to see if he was receptive to the idea and learned he was delighted at the prospect of having his grandson for a visit. Ever since Rose had died, Chester had been feeling a growing sense of uselessness and isolation. Having his grandson around the house would be a breath of fresh air for him—a new beginning. In a sense she was doing Jack and her father-in-law a favor. She told herself that repeatedly, but it never felt right.

After throwing some of Jack's clothes, sports equipment, and other essentials into a duffle bag, she drove him to Baltimore's Thurgood Marshall Airport, bought him a one-way ticket to Colorado Springs, and put her only child on the plane to Grandpa's.

For several weeks Matt Branson immersed himself in his study of the Diversity and Tolerance Enforcement Division. Thanks to some careful but always ethical interdepartmental data snooping, he was able to download public case files and records of arrests and confiscations. He examined how the charges against people like Jim Stockman and others had been filed. In every case DTED lawyers had shopped the cases to sympathetic judges. They were trying all their cases in D.C. courts, the first to have a full array of new judges under the Retirement and Expansion Act. They used grand juries that were stacked to make sure every juror would be sympathetic to the prosecutor's case.

It was while Matt was immersing himself in these discoveries that Pat Preston called his office phone. He hadn't seen Pat since graduation. When Matt had left Princeton and headed to Ann Arbor, Pat had been on his way to Louisville to become a Baptist preacher. Matt knew from Christmas cards and a wedding announcement that Pat had finished Southern Baptist Seminary, been ordained, and moved to Nashville to serve as the senior minister of a large Baptist church. Recently, Pat had been interviewed on radio and TV stations. Matt had tuned in a few times. It hadn't surprised him to hear Pat was taking heat for some of his uncompromising positions. But when he heard that John Knox Smith and the DTED were on his case, his heart had sunk.

"Tell me what's going on, Pat," he said. Pat explained about John's phone call and the growing sense that someone was investigating him.

As he listened to Pat's story, Matt could see it playing before his eyes. The pieces were coming together, not just with Pat and John, or where all this might be headed, but he suddenly saw what was happening in his own life. He understood for the first time what his calling was all about: fulfilling his passion for defending the defenseless.

Only the week before he had been thinking, *This is what God has been doing with me all along. I couldn't figure it out, but now I think I understand. This is why I've been so troubled in my spirit ever since I got here, and why I felt I ought to be doing more with my life. This is it!*

He now understood that all the research he had been doing on the DTED had a bigger purpose than he imagined. His conversation with the kid in Alexandria and now Pat's situation—they were part of the same thing.

"There are things I can't go into, Pat, but I can say that you are the kind of target John and the DTED love to prosecute. Still, I can't believe he'd go after an old friend."

"I don't think he considers us friends, Matt. He was really angry on the phone and blamed me for his embarrassment. It's hard to believe how different we turned out."

"You need to get a lawyer, Pat. That's all I can say at this time. I don't know if John has you in his crosshairs or not, but he's not likely to tell me."

"You think I need an attorney?"

"If he comes after you, you're going to need one—a good one." Matt wondered how much further he should go. "Pat, if I say anything beyond telling you to get legal counsel, then the DOJ can fire me. I could have my license revoked."

"I understand."

"Listen, Pat. I can't advise you, but that doesn't mean I don't care. I'm going to give you my private mobile number. Will you stay in touch?"

"Yes. I can't . . . Matt, I can't back away from the truth, even if John decides to make an example of me. Do you understand?"

"I understand." Matt hung up and rubbed the back of his neck. He had done nothing wrong, nothing in violation of DOJ operating principles, but he felt the attorney general himself was going to kick down the office door.

His instincts said to back away, to protect himself. His soul said something else. *Can I afford not to get involved? Morally? Can I just ignore an injustice of this magnitude?*

Pastor Pat was an all-American guy, a graduate of top schools, a gifted minister, and a capable young man. He had built a large following in Nashville because he was genuinely warm and caring. But as the pressures continued to mount, he realized that some people in his church were beginning to pull away. Publicly they were all smiles, but privately, according to what his staff had said, they were saying, "We've known this man for years. We always thought he was more or less normal, but we're not sure any longer. We're seeing a whole new side of Pastor Pat."

A few bolder members told him that ever since he had returned from his time in England, he seemed different. Many in the congregation had noticed the changes, and they talked about it with their friends. It was true that his sermons were stronger now, and he was more passionate about preaching the gospel, but some members felt he was less tolerant of behaviors and lifestyles he disapproved of and much too judgmental.

The media played a role, often naming Pastor Pat and Rogers Memorial as an example of religious intolerance. A local television station broadcast a series of investigative reports in which one of Pat's most trusted supporters was quoted saying, "The government has been showing us the face of bigotry, up close and personal, and some of us feel we've been betrayed by our church's leaders."

This was the same man who had told Pat after his installation service, "We're here for you, Pastor Pat, no matter what happens. We know God has sent you to us." The man was one of the most trusted and influential leaders in the church. However, when he saw which way the social wind was blowing, he changed his tune. Other friends who had often invited Pat and Becky into their homes seemed to be running the other way as well. Not because they were thoughtless or insensitive, but, as Pat concluded, because the outside pressures were too intense.

Several of the old guard in the church, including some of the charter members who had been faithful church supporters for more than thirty years, came to the office and told Pat, "If you get yourself into hot water with this stuff, Pastor, it's going to change everything around here. We have to think about the future. We can't keep living in the past."

One woman shook hands with Pat after the Sunday service. Instead of thanking him for the sermon, she said, "If you keep saying the kinds of things you've been saying lately, Pastor, it's going to change your life. This church will survive, but you'll be ruined, and your family will pay the price. You should think about these things."

The warnings were upsetting, but each time he heard these comments, he swallowed hard and promised to pray about it. And he did. One afternoon as Pat was putting his papers away and preparing to go home, Frank Billington, his most trusted associate, stopped by the office, purportedly to see how Pat was holding up.

"I'm going to be fine, Frank. Thanks for asking. But I have to admit, I'm definitely feeling the pressure."

"I can imagine," Frank said.

"I don't know where it will end, but I feel God has given me a message, calling sinners to repentance. I can't walk away from that, no matter what happens."

Frank grimaced and looked at the floor, as if embarrassed by what he had heard. "You know, Pat, a lot of people think it would be better for all of us if you would bend with this thing rather than let yourself be broken by it."

Pat wasn't sure if he'd heard him correctly. "Frank, what are you saying? You've always been a strong advocate and friend. You've been a mentor and confidant to me ever since I got here. Are you saying I should back away and preach some other gospel?"

Frank had taken Pat under his wing when he first arrived in Nashville and had helped bring him along with wise counsel and encouragement. Pat thought of him as his Rock of Gibraltar. "We have to be strong, Frank, even if they send in the marines. The truth is still the truth, and you know that's not up for grabs. Even if they bring the entire weight of the government down on our heads, we can't compromise God's truth. Did the apostles run when persecutions came? Did Peter run from Nero's wrath? Did Paul jump ship?"

Frank sighed and rose to leave. Before walking out, he looked back and whispered, "Pat, I don't know you anymore."

The words broke Pat's heart. Tears were forming in his eyes. "You too, Frank? Apparently, I never knew *you*."

On the drive home, Pat's thoughts churned. What would he do now? If Frank Billington could turn on him, what would the deacons do? What about the members? What would he say to Becky, who was already a long way beyond nervous about what was happening to them?

When John Knox Smith had hung up on him after that bizarre phone call a few days earlier, Pat had felt he was in trouble. He had prayed, "God, help me. I'm really going to need it." He had uttered the same prayer countless times since.

When he arrived home that evening, he stood in the kitchen while Becky was busy cooking dinner. He shared with her all Frank had said. She said very little. He saw her trying to be brave in the face of terrifying possibilities. He took her hand and they prayed. Her hand shook.

| CHAPTER EIGHTEEN |

Pat had never dreamed he would need a lawyer, but he needed one now. His first inclination was to call Matt Branson, but he hesitated. Matt had made it clear that his job with the Department of Justice kept him from directly helping Pat, but . . . Matt had said he wanted Pat to keep him informed.

At three on a muggy Thursday afternoon, as Pat sat in his church office reviewing reference materials for his Sunday sermon, his assistant Ava Raitt, trembling from head to toe, opened his office door. Three deputy U.S. marshals walked in and presented him with a subpoena.

The subpoena demanded the original written text and original digital recordings of every sermon he had preached since arriving at Rogers Memorial Church.

"You're kidding. Every sermon?"

"We don't kid, Reverend. Whatever you have—printed material, digital material, video of your sermons—we want them. And we want the originals, not edited or monkeyed-with copies."

Pat didn't speak.

One of the marshals turned up the heat. "Reverend Preston, you have a choice to make. You can give us those sermons now, or we'll be back with search warrants. And believe me, if we come back we will take everything we need—with or without your help. Whichever way you'd like it, Reverend. You decide."

Pat cleared his throat and tried to force his heart back to a normal pace. "I'm not trying to be obstinate, but there's no way I can pull all that together on short notice. Some of my sermon notes are easy enough, but I'm not a technician. I wouldn't know where to begin to make copies of digital material. I don't know how to operate the equipment; the CDs and DVDs may not be complete. We have the more recent material, but if you want originals of everything back to my first sermon, well, I don't think that's possible."

"So you are choosing not to comply."

That irritated Pat. "Listen. There are many things I struggle with, but communication isn't one of them. I did not say I wouldn't comply. I'm telling you that some of the material may not be readily available."

"You want us to come back with a warrant?"

"I will give you everything I can, but it will take time to get you everything."

"We'll be back, Reverend Preston—with a warrant." They walked from the room.

"Pastor? What is this all about?" Ava asked, eyes wide.

"Someone doesn't like my sermons." He looked at the subpoena and thought about his former classmate John Knox Smith.

"It was like they didn't want you to be able to comply. They're asking the impossible."

"I think you're right. With a search warrant they can do the searching themselves. Maybe they hope to find something incriminating."

"What should I do?"

"I want you to gather all the notes from my previous sermons and box them for delivery. Call in some help, someone you trust. No gossips, Ava. Pull together copies of whatever we have on CD, DVD, and the like. Make a list of what's missing, and we'll see what we can do to get those items."

"You're giving them what they want?" Ava still trembled, and she looked on the verge of tears.

"Of course. I have nothing to hide, and I've said nothing I'm ashamed of. Understand?"

"Yes, Pastor."

He smiled. "It's going to be all right, Ava. Take a few moments to gather yourself, then get busy."

"What are you going to do?"

"I need a minute to gather myself," he said with a chuckle, "then I should make some calls."

Ava slipped from the office, closing the door behind her.

Pat closed his eyes and prayed. His heart tripped, his palms were wet, and his stomach twisted into a knot. It was happening.

A few minutes later, he picked up the phone and called Matt Branson on the cell number he had given Pat. Matt answered on the third ring.

"Matt, the situation down here isn't looking good. I think I'm going to need some help."

"I know, Pat. I've been doing a little looking around. I learned you're on John's public hit list. You need to be careful. Don't give the agents any problems. Have they contacted you yet?"

"Agents? No, just the marshals."

"What did they say?"

"They demanded the originals of all my sermons, but I told them it wasn't possible. We don't keep them. We make hundreds of copies, but I rarely see the originals once they're gone. I can give them my notes, but they're not originals either. They won't be identical to the recorded material."

"That's probably why they want everything," Matt said. "They may not believe you at first. They're not good at compromising, and John is trying to make a statement. I think you'd better do whatever you can to pull that stuff together."

"I have my assistant working on it. Can you help me, Matt, or can you give me the name of a lawyer here in Nashville who can help me?"

"I want to help you, Pat, but if I do . . ." Matt hesitated.

"I know. I shouldn't ask. It could cost you your job."

"Yes, it could." The line went silent for a moment. "Pat, let me think. There are some things I have to take care of first. In the meantime, I want you to get in touch with the Alliance office here in Washington and let them know what's happening. Ask for Larry Jordan. I can't call him myself because that could be construed as hampering an ongoing investigation. It must be you who makes the call."

"I understand."

"I want to check out some things at the office."

"I understand," Pat said, greatly relieved that Matt was being so helpful. "Matt, there's one more thing. The marshals said they were coming back with a warrant, and I'm afraid they're going to tear the place apart."

"That's why you need to do whatever you can to cooperate. Call me if they do come. Don't give them any provocation. Do whatever you can to cooperate with them. That's very important." He gave Pat the phone number for Larry Jordan in D.C. and told him to call the Alliance.

Pat rose and paced the room.

Pat felt like he had just finished his second marathon for the day. He slept poorly. Adding to his burden was Becky's fear. Normally, the first to fall asleep, Becky lay awake for two hours before surrendering to sleep. Pat lay awake and listened to her breathing. He could always tell when she was awake and when she was asleep. What little sleep Pat got was fitful and choked with unpleasant dreams. He rose early, drank too much coffee, and tried to settle his mind by watching an old movie.

After breakfast he went to the office and helped finish organizing as much of the material as the subpoena demanded. As he expected, there were lots of holes, and there were no original recordings at the church at all.

The door to his office snapped open. Pat jumped up from his chair. Ava stood in the doorway. "I just saw them through the window."

"Who?" Pat asked.

"Men. Armed men. They're coming to the office."

"Men? You mean federal agents?"

"Yes."

Pat quickly dialed Matt Branson. "Matt, they're here."

The door to the outer office flew open. Pat watched beyond Ava's figure as the three marshals he had met before stormed in, joined by half a dozen other men and women dressed in windbreakers that read "DTED," "Police," and "U.S. Marshal" in big letters.

Ava turned and stepped in front of the first man in the doorway. "Excuse me, you can't just barge in here—"

One of the marshals shoved her aside. She fell forward, landing hard on the floor. She screamed in pain.

Pat set the handset down and rounded his desk. "Take it easy."

He started for her, but a man in a windbreaker boasting POLICE in yellow letters grabbed his arm. Pat felt the meaty grip but could only see Ava writhing on the floor. Without thinking, he jerked his arm free and knocked the agent's hand away. He crouched next to his administrative assistant. "Ava, are you hurt?"

Before he could touch Ava, he felt himself pushed to the floor. "On the ground. On the ground!" Pat didn't know who uttered the words, nor did he know whose knee was pressed in his back. The agent or marshal jerked Pat's arm behind his back and twisted his wrist. Pain shot up his arm like lightening. "Ow, you're hurting me."

"Stop resisting."

"I'm not resisting."

"Stop resisting!"

The agent pulled Pat's left arm behind him, and Pat felt the cold, hard metal of handcuffs.

Ava continued to writhe in pain. "My knee. My knee." She began to cry.

"Matt!" Pat shouted into the phone. "Matt!"

When things calmed, the warrant team placed Pat in the backseat of one of the marshal's cars. For over an hour he sat in the rising heat. The sun was intense. The pain in his back where the agent had ground his knee made breathing difficult. He watched while two DTED agents and three U.S. marshals removed the boxed material Pat had provided. From his position in the backseat, he could see the agents opening doors to the church building.

A woman police officer took pity on Ava and called for an ambulance. Fifteen minutes later she was on her way to the hospital. Pat wished he could apologize to her for what had happened.

Several times the searchers came outside, yanked the car door open, and demanded to know where his personal records and the original recordings were hidden. Pat was indignant, but, remembering Matt's caution about being cooperative, he tried to be respectful and never shouted back at the officers. He became more and more disoriented, sweating profusely, and on the verge of passing out. He wanted to pray but found he could only weep.

| CHAPTER NINETEEN |

When they arrived at the police station, the officers put Pat through the booking procedure. They took his wallet, his shoelaces, his belt, and everything in his pockets. They filled out all the forms and made him sign a release. Every act made him feel humiliated. Then they placed him in a holding cell. For an hour he sat in the small room, wondering who had been confined here before. Normally a disciplined thinker, his mind stumbled over every thought. What would he tell his wife? What would he tell the church? How badly hurt was Ava?

He lay down on a hard bench and tired to focus. It didn't help.

An hour later, the door to the holding cell opened, and a man with a large envelope motioned at him. "Let's go."

Pat rose. "What's happening?"

"You're free to go."

"What do you mean?"

"We're releasing you. Go home."

"You're not filing charges?"

"Look, buddy, if you don't get out of here, I'll find some charges to file. You're done for now, so go on home."

"May I use your phone?" Under the circumstances, Pat hadn't been able to grab his cell phone before agents hauled him out of his office.

The officer rolled his eyes. "Follow me." When they got to the booking desk, the policeman picked up the phone and dropped it on the counter. "You get one call."

Pat called home and asked Becky to come down and pick him up at the county jail. "I'll explain later," he said three times. She arrived a half hour later. Neither spoke a word on the long drive across town. Pat pleaded that he needed to clear his head.

Until that moment, Pat had managed to ignore the pain in his chest, but on the way home his ribs were aching so badly he could barely breathe. His kidneys felt on fire. During the arrest, he had been as passive as possible, but he had taken a knee to the back, his arms and ribs had been twisted, and he could remember something hitting him in the ribs several times.

He suffered emotional pain as well. How would the media handle this? What would the members of his congregation say, and what would his family back in Owensboro think if they found out he'd been thrown in jail, even if was for less than a full afternoon? Would he be humiliated in print? What would he say the following Sunday? What about the ministry's radio and TV broadcasts? How would he go on with his life if this became a bigger deal?

Before the raid on his office, the marshals had alerted the media. There had been a photographer outside the church when the agents pulled Pat from his office and shoved him into the back of the local police patrol car. By the time he and Becky got home, one local television station had aired the story.

"When are you going to tell me what happened?" Becky's voice carried concern, fear, and anger. "I think I have a right to know."

"Of course you have a right to know. It's just that . . . I'm stunned."

"I can believe that. So am I."

"Remember I told you last night about the marshals and the subpoena?"

"You said you had already pulled much of the material together."

"I had, and we gathered even more this morning. It's not everything. I don't know that we can find the notes and original recordings of every sermon and Bible study."

"And they arrested you for that?" Becky went to the kitchen and removed two bottles of water from the refrigerator. She gave one to Pat.

"Yes . . . well . . . no. They came back today with the Department of Tolerance and a couple of local police. They barged into the outer office. Ava was standing in the doorway between our two offices. They pushed past her—or maybe they shoved her. It's not clear in my mind. All I know is, she fell to the floor and screamed. I rushed to her aid, but one of the men grabbed my arm. I pulled away."

"You pulled away?"

"I wasn't thinking about being arrested. I was thinking about poor Ava. She sounded hurt. Next thing I know, I'm on the floor in pain."

"They beat you?"

"They treated me pretty rough." Pat stood and removed his shirt. Purple bruises ran down his side. He also had bruises on his arms and wrists from where he'd been grabbed and cuffed.

"Oh, Pat!" Becky stood and approached him. "Turn around."

He did. She gasped.

"What?"

"You've got a big bruise there, too." She gently touched his skin. Her touch hurt. "We should take you to urgent care."

"I'm all right."

"No you're not. It sounds like you're having trouble breathing. Are you?"

"A little."

"Put your shirt back on." It was an order.

"Yes, ma'am." He smiled. "I'm sorry, Becky. I never imagined this."

"You've done nothing wrong."

"You seem angry."

"You don't know the half of it, but I'm not mad at you." She retrieved her purse. "Come on."

"Can I use your cell phone?"

"You really want to be making calls?" Becky opened the front door and waited for Pat to tuck in his shirt. He grimaced with each movement. "Wait." She closed the door. "Take off your shirt again."

"You're kidding. Why?"

"Just do it. I'll be right back." By the time he removed his shirt, she returned with a digital camera. "Hold out your arms."

"What are you doing?"

"Taking photos of your injuries."

"Why?"

"I don't know. They do it on all the lawyer shows."

Pat called Matt first. As Becky drove, he sat in the passenger seat, which had he reclined to help his breathing, and held Becky's cell phone to his ear.

"I've been trying to get you for hours," Matt said.

"I was a little tied up."

"Tied up? Is that a joke?"

"I default to humor when I'm scared out of my wits."

"The whole thing scared me pretty good, too, and I just heard it over the phone," Matt said. "This is getting out of hand. Are you in a car? It sounds like you're in a car."

"My wife is taking me to urgent care."

"You're hurt? How badly did they hurt you?"

"I'm okay, just bruised here and there."

Becky frowned at him.

"This tears it for me, Pat. I'm flying down there."

"You can't. You work for the DOJ."

"I'll quit tomorrow. As soon as my resignation is official, I'll become your attorney of record."

"You're not going to quit your job on my account, Matt. We're not at that point yet. For now, let me do this my way. I'm not ready to make a federal case of it yet."

"Is that another joke? It's *already* a federal case or at least very close to being one."

"Let's not react, Matt. Let's be proactive. We don't know if this is going to go any further. Give it a little more time. Besides, I have to think about the church."

"Take my advice, Pat. Think about yourself for a change."

Matt set the down the phone and stared at it. He had been wondering if he should leave the DOJ, if he should undertake a different course in his legal and spiritual life, but he had never uttered the words out loud. Hearing the words "I'll quit" come out of his mouth filled him with concerns. Somehow he would have to find a way to break the news to Michelle that he was planning to leave his position at the DOJ. After that, he wasn't sure where things might go. There would have to be an exit interview at the office, which could become confrontational if they discovered that he was going to take Pat's case. For the moment, however, his only plan was to pray for wisdom and guidance.

Pat spent his time in the urgent care center thinking about what faced him at the church. Becky sat with him, holding his hand and rubbing her thumb on the back of his hand until he was certain she'd soon reach bone. It was what she did when she was nervous.

Becky was not only smart but also intuitive. She knew when something chewed at Pat's mind and heart. He had no idea how she knew so much without his telling her. More than once he had accused her of being a mind reader.

Something was chewing at Pat. Not just the brutal arrest, not just the fact that the DTED led by his old friend was poking around in his life, but that he would have to face the church. To be a pastor was to live in an aquarium. A large church like his meant there were more people peering in.

His first concern centered on the congregation, but his mind soon shifted to the chairman of the deacons, Keith Gentry. He would have questions. Lots of questions. Lots of accusations. Keith and his wife, Kaylene, had been less than enthusiastic about Pat's coming to Rogers Memorial from the beginning. They had been afraid he was too young and too conservative. No doubt this news would push them even further away. In fact, he suspected it could lead to a big division in the church. The tense conversation they had had after Pat performed the funeral for the slain pastor wouldn't help.

"What about Sunday?" Becky asked.

"I don't know yet."

"This is Friday; Sunday's coming."

"That's the thing about being a pastor: Sunday is always coming." He paused. "Maybe I should do all three services. Tell the people what happened."

"The longer you wait, the more tongues will wag, and . . ." Becky nodded to a television mounted near the waiting room ceiling. Video of Pat in handcuffs being led to the patrol car played on the scene. Once in the car, the cameraman stepped closer to the window. Pat's face filled the screen.

Pat felt as if a spotlight were shining on him. He scanned the room. No one looked at him. They were lost in their own sets of problems. He looked at Becky. Tears ran along her cheeks.

"It . . . it must have been horrible for you."

"It was worse than attending a senior ladies' luncheon."

"I'm going to tell them you said that. You think you have bruises *now*?" She tried to smile, but more tears came.

Pat put his arm around her, which sent pain shooting along his back and down his side. He did his best to conceal the pain.

When Pat arrived at the church on Sunday morning, he was still confused and stiff from pain. The Vicodin made him drowsy. The doctors found no broken ribs but promised he'd be sore for a few weeks.

Church members and visitors filled the first service, and he had no doubt the other two morning services would be filled to capacity as well.

At the 9:30 service, at the beginning of his sermon, he laid his notes aside for a moment and changed directions. He wasn't up to finishing his six-part series today. He was going to give the congregation a little background on what had happened to him on Friday. Most of the members had seen the news reports and were expecting an explanation. But Pat's comments were so vague and disjointed that he created only more confusion. When he said he was planning on wrapping up the series on "The Insufficiency of Hope" the following week, someone in the service groaned, "Oh, please, no."

Pat hesitated, confused and unbalanced by the comment. When he tried to return to his sermon topic, he felt dizzy and disoriented. He misquoted the Scripture verse and stumbled over his words. When he tried to ad lib and get away from his notes, he lost his train of thought completely. Embarrassed, he said, "I'm sorry. I guess I'm still a little out of it."

The church emptied quickly at the end of the service. No one came forward, but several deacons rushed to the front to speak to him. They asked if he was feeling all right. They said they could see that something was wrong, and they wanted to know if he was ill. Was he on medication?

"Just a prescription of Vicodin before daylight." He took a shallow breath. "We should talk. Let's go to my study."

The deacons brought in extra chairs and closed the door.

"I need to bring you up to speed," Pat said. He remained standing, partly to exert a sense of authority, but mostly he had less pain when on his feet. "I'm sorry I didn't let everyone know sooner, but it was only Friday, and I've been . . . distracted. Here's what happened."

It took ten minutes for Pat to give the basics about the subpoena, the return of agents, Ava, the arrest, and his trip to the hospital after being released from the holding cell.

Keith Gentry was the first to speak. "Still, you should have called me. It's my job to know what's going on at the church."

"I was in no condition to call on Friday—not physically, not emotionally."

"But," Gentry said, "they delivered the subpoena on Thursday. Why didn't you call then?"

"I don't know. I guess I was focused on getting the material together."

"It only takes a minute to make a phone call. Maybe I could have prevented this from happening."

"How?" Pat asked.

"I don't know. Now, we'll never know."

Howard French asked, "Pastor, why were they here in the first place? I don't get it."

Pat shook his head. "I don't know exactly, Howard. They wanted originals of all my sermons and all the original recordings. I told them that wasn't possible. I didn't have them."

"Come on, Pastor," Gentry said. "You know why they were here. You've been pretty rough on other religions in this last sermon series. You know the government has been cracking down on such things. You brought this on yourself. And Ava got hurt in the process."

Those words pierced Pat like a hot knife. "What happened to Ava shouldn't have happened. The agents didn't need to get into my office that quickly. I was just sitting behind my desk."

"So was the preacher that shot the deputy marshal," Gentry said. "You know, the one you did the funeral for. He'd been preaching some pretty rough stuff in that little church of his."

Pat tried to ignore him. "For those of you who are interested, Ava is fine but will be taking some time off. She twisted her leg when she fell and suffered a spinal fracture. She'll be in a cast for a while. I'm sure she'd enjoy a visit."

Gentry wasn't ready to switch gears. "Pastor, you know very well that U.S. marshals don't just barge into a church like this unless they've got a doggone good reason. I believe what you're saying, but I have to believe there's something missing in your story. We need to get to the bottom of this."

"I think we should meet," Howard said.

"We *are* meeting," Pat said.

"I mean the deacons."

Pat stared at him. "You mean *only* the deacons."

No one spoke.

Pat shrugged. "Okay. Go ahead. I'm sure the adult classrooms are still unlocked. I've got to get ready for the eleven o'clock service." Pat moved to the door and opened it. The deacons filed out. Pat tried to read their faces. Some seemed burdened, others angry.

Alone in his office, Pat sat in his high-backed leather chair. A moment later he leaned forward and rested his head on his hands and wished to be someplace else—anyplace else—and he told that to God.

After the third and final service of the morning, Gentry and Howard met Pat at the front of the church.

Howard did the speaking, but Pat held no doubts that Gentry was doing the pushing. "Pastor, the interests of the church come first, and we need to make some decisions. We think it would be a good idea if you could meet with us again on Wednesday evening, here at the church. Say, six o'clock. Will that be all right?"

Pat said it would. "Maybe we should pray together about this—"

"We would love to, Pastor, but we've already kept our wives waiting longer than usual. You know how that is."

Howard and Gentry turned.

Pat stood alone in the large auditorium.

After the service, the assistant youth minister, Bobby Douglas, hung around, chatting with a group of teenagers likes he did every Sunday morning. He shooed the young people home and headed to the parking lot. As he unlocked the car door, four large men in DTED

Windbreakers with big, shiny badges and firearms on their hips surrounded him.

"Are you Robert Douglas?" The man who asked was tall with brown hair cut close to his scalp. His mouth looked incapable of smiling.

"Um, yeah. But I go by Bobby—"

Before Bobby could finish the sentence, he found himself being bent over the hood of his car and handcuffed.

"What are you doing? I didn't do anything wrong." The metal cuffs closed on his wrist.

"Come with us, please."

"Where? What?"

They led Bobby to the backseat of a dark sedan and forced him in. Thirty minutes later, Bobby sat in an interview room at the local FBI office, a room the DTED had commandeered.

What the agents had discovered was that Bobby wasn't the morally upright young man he seemed to be.

"My name is Special Agent Curtis Young," the dour-faced man said. You like the Internet, Bobby."

"I guess so. Why am I here?" Bobby rubbed his wrists where the cuffs had been.

"You guess so? How about chat rooms, Bobby? You like those?"

Bobby felt his blood ice over. "They're . . . um . . . they're okay."

"Here's the thing, Bobby. I'm a busy man. I have lots on my plate, so I'm going to get to the bottom line." He opened a file. "It says here you have some tax violations; misrepresented your income. That true?"

"I think I need an attorney."

"It also says here that you once tried to use a false name to open a credit card account."

"That was a mistake."

"Mistake? You forgot your name, Bobby?"

"No. It was a college gag. A bunch of us filed for credit cards using the names of guys on the third floor of our dorm. They had been bugging us about making too much noise on the fourth floor. You know. A little rivalry. What's the worse that could happen? They get a credit card."

"I see. You were trying to teach them a lesson. Is that it?"

"Sure."

The agent's frown deepened, something Bobby didn't think was possible. "The problem is, Bobby, you used someone else's name and Social Security number, then put your own address down. That looks bad, son. Real bad."

"That was a mistake. We were doing this late at night, and I was sleepy. I put my own address down by mistake."

"What about the chat rooms, Bobby?" Young studied the material in the folder. "I have transcripts of chats you've had with teen girls. They're pretty graphic, son. Do you think you should be making such offers over the Internet?"

Bobby couldn't speak.

"Let me tell you why this looks bad. Some of those girls are pretty young. Minors. And you're *not* a minor, so that makes you a sexual predator."

Bobby's face grew hot. "I should talk to an attorney."

"Sure, sure, that's your right. You'll get your call, I want to make sure you have enough information to talk intelligently to your lawyer—or will you be going for a public defender?"

"I . . . I . . ."

"It doesn't matter. It's none of my business. Bobby, we got three sets of very serious charges. If you're tried for any of these offenses, it's going to be a felony conviction. More than likely, you'll be going to prison for a very long time. Do you understand that?"

Agent Young laid out records of phone calls, credit card receipts, and even some magazines with swimsuit photos of young women taken from his office at the church. Just as Bobby was wondering what he was going to tell his parents, and worse, how he would explain all this to Pastor Pat, Agent Young got his attention. "You're in big trouble, Bobby, but there's a chance we may be able to reduce the charges. We might get these charges thrown out completely if you help us out with another matter."

"What other matter?" He sounded more eager than he intended.

"Your boss, Pat Preston. We want to know everything about this guy, Bobby. What does he do in his spare time? Why does he keep saying those things, preaching that other religions are wrong and sinful?

Why does he do that? Doesn't he know that kind of talk doesn't fly anymore?"

"You just want answers? That's all?"

"Pretty much. In a sense, you'll be a police informant." Young leaned over the scarred metal table that separated them as if he were about to whisper a secret. "Bobby, you have the right to lawyer up and cut off all communication between us if that's what you want to do. I would never interfere with that. Guilty people have a right to a lawyer. You can let your lawyer tell you how much time you're facing. By the way, he'll tell you that you're facing fifteen years in a federal pen, but you don't have to take my word for it. What I want to do here is offer you an opportunity to make things right. Do you understand?"

"I understand."

"The prosecutor makes the final decision, but we might not have to take the next step if we can get certain information. If you can tell us the inside scoop on Pat Preston and what the guy is really up to and what's behind all the hate, I think we may be able to do something for you. Would you like that?"

The idea of spending his best years behind bars with a bunch of hardened criminals horrified Bobby.

Young leaned back. "Let me tell you what we need, Bobby. I'm not looking for lies. That won't help. These are the kinds of things I want you to tell me." He listed the evidence he needed to nail Pastor Pat on what he called "intent."

Bobby listened for all he was worth.

| CHAPTER TWENTY |

Most of Pastor Pat's radio and television audience had no idea what had been happening at Rogers Memorial Church. Pat still had an important broadcast ministry as well as speaking and teaching commitments. He knew there were some things he couldn't discuss for the time being, but he wanted people to know what his ministry stood for, why his church preached the gospel, and why he and the staff did what they did.

After the last meeting with the deacons, Pat decided this was no time to run away and hide. Instead, he needed to make as many personal appearances as he could over the next few days to let the community hear his side of the story.

When Pat stepped into the pulpit on Sunday mornings, he always looked perfect. He was upbeat and optimistic, and he knew how to deliver a sermon. He generally worked on his message all week, and when he stood to preach, he knew there was nothing else he wanted to do. He did a great job in the studio as well, recording the opening and closing segments of the *Just One Life* daily broadcasts. The crew selected short portions of his sermons to use for the teaching segments, and it all came together so well because Pat's tone and delivery were always consistent and appealing.

But Pat wasn't quite as savvy in other ways. He didn't understand when others had questionable motives. When interviewers on local radio and TV programs started asking the "gotcha" questions, he was not as cautious as he should have been. On one local station, an interviewer asked, "Reverend Preston, are you trying to say that—out of all the preachers in this state—federal agents or whoever they were just happened to pick you at random? Are you saying that United States marshals put you in the back of a patrol car for no reason?"

According to the official documents filed with the search warrant and return—which practically everyone in the media had seen by that time—Pat had created a climate of fear and intolerance in the community. When federal agents and local police officers had come to his office to speak to him about it, he had physically attacked them and had to be restrained with handcuffs.

An interviewer from Nashville's Channel 5 buttonholed Pat. "If you expect us to believe your story, Reverend Preston, then you're telling us these law enforcement officers are lying. Is that right?"

When Pat stumbled over the question without giving a satisfactory response, the interviewer went on to say that the officers who had filed the incident reports were church-going men themselves. "All four of the marshals who took you to jail that night, Pastor, are members of local congregations in and around this city."

When he was unable to respond to that bit of news, the station ran the video clip of Pat being hauled out of the church and shoved into the back of a patrol car. Seeing the report on the six o'clock news changed a lot of people's minds about Pat. Pat noticed that even Becky was beginning to question some of the things he had told her about the arrest. She acted like she wanted to believe him, but he sensed her growing doubt.

"Pat, the problem is you're far too trusting. Someone needs to follow you around to make sure you take care of the little things that get you into trouble."

They prayed together often. At first, Becky's prayers were simple requests for wisdom. As pressure from the media and the church increased, her prayer changed. "Lord, please help Pat and please help me help him. Help him not to forget what has happened. Help him understand how serious this is. Lord, please help me."

The words stung Pat's soul.

Despite the negative feedback and frequent misinterpretations of what he was trying to say, Pat continued to speak to anyone who would listen, explaining his situation. He wasn't totally inept, but he had trouble realizing how poorly he appeared in his own defense. A couple of people, including the staff at the church, advised him to back off for a while, but he refused. He told them he wanted to be "proactive." *Proactive* had become his favorite new term.

One of the associate ministers took him aside. "Pat, there's a time to talk and a time to let others do the talking. For you, this is that time."

Pat disagreed. "You know I'm not being prideful. I want people to hear the truth. God is still God, and I'm confident He'll make a way. In the meantime, I'll just let the chips fall where they may."

The associate pastor shook his head. "At times, Pastor, you're impossible to deal with."

Pat met with the deacons on Wednesday night. It was clear from the first that Howard French was upset. As he unfolded his prepared remarks, he told Pat he had something important to say and wasn't going to allow interruptions.

"Pastor," he began, "you know we love you. You've made a lot of progress since you came to this church, and you have taught us a lot. I suspect you've learned many things as well. As a board of deacons, we have tried to be your friends and support you. We have paid you well, and we even helped you and your family when you were away in England, working on your doctorate. But I must also point out that our job, first and foremost, is to protect the interests of this church."

Pat opened his mouth to respond, but Howard cut him off. "Not now, Pastor. Please, just listen. Rogers Memorial Church is a large congregation with a huge financial commitment. We have a multi-million-dollar campus and lots of important and expensive programs. All of this demands order and consistency in church operations. In addition, the well-being of the 160 good folks employed by this church depends on what happens in that pulpit every Sunday."

Once again, Pat tried to speak. But Howard held up his hand. "As much as we love you, Pastor, we can't let anything damage the work of the church and school next door. Rogers Memorial can't go forward if our pastor becomes a detriment rather than an asset to the work we're trying to do here."

This time Pat made no effort to speak.

After a long pause, Keith picked up the thread and said, "Pastor, it's obvious what you've done for the church. No one's disputing that. You've taken us from twenty-five hundred people on Sunday mornings to more than six thousand in the combined services, and we can see the Lord's hand in that. We have nearly ten thousand members on the rolls now, but there are still a lot of questions to be answered. The first thing we're asking you to do is to discontinue the series you started on the other religions."

Pat gave no response.

French continued. "You told us there would be six sermons in the series. I believe the next one was going to be where you wrap it up and go over everything one more time. We believe you're too caught up in recent events, and honestly we can't let you preach that sermon. We know it's an emotional situation for you, but we need to turn the corner."

"And there's something else we've done, Pastor," Gentry said, breaking his out-of-character silence. "We've gone ahead and hired a lawyer to represent the church, just in case."

"In case what?" Pat said. "What do you mean? You've hired a lawyer to represent me?"

"No," Howard said quickly, "to represent the church. Our number one goal as fiduciaries has to be to take care of the church."

"So I'm not part of the church anymore? I believe I'm still a member."

"Well, sure you are, Pastor," Keith said. "You know what we mean. Don't make this more difficult than it has to be. If you think you need a lawyer, you should look into it right away. But we have to look after the church. That's our first responsibility."

One of the other deacons spoke up. "Pastor, we're not telling you not to preach. We want you to preach, and the folks expect it. What we are saying is, don't preach that sermon. Save it for another time. Go back to what you were doing before all this commotion got started."

"Talk about the importance of walking the walk and talking the talk," Gentry added. "Talk about the miracles that happen around us or something like that."

Pat's expression didn't change, but the words felt like the first stab of Caesar's men. Hurt and anger swirled inside him although he tried not to let it show. He felt chastised, but more than that, he felt deserted by the men who had once promised to be his defenders and friends forever.

Being told by these men not to preach a sermon he believed God had laid on his heart injured him most. He had been building a train of connections for five weeks, all in order to get to sermon number six. That was the message that brought it all together. He believed God had given him sermon six as a special revelation. The first five sermons, which had come from his Wednesday night teaching series more than a year earlier, were the stepping stones to what he really wanted to say—what God wanted him to say.

Pat had pledged to follow the counsel of the deacons—he had signed an agreement to that effect when he accepted the call. But he was deeply conflicted now and worried about how he would respond to their demands. From the deacons' tone of voice, they were only a step away from cutting him loose. The thought of being fired was troubling enough, but the worst part was what it would do to Becky if he lost this position. She wouldn't be able to handle that.

"I'm sure you agree with our assessment, Pastor," Keith said.

"Really? What gave you that impression?"

"Surely you're not going to go against our advice. We are unanimous in this."

"I didn't say that either. I'm going to pray about it and seek God's leadership on the matter—just like you did. You did pray together about this, didn't you?"

No one spoke.

Gentry twitched in his chair. His face grew red. "Pastor, the Bible says a wise man listens to counsel. It's in Proverbs somewhere."

"I'm glad you hold the Bible so highly, Deacon. Here's another verse for you. It starts at Acts 4:19. 'But Peter and John replied, "Judge for yourselves whether it is right in God's sight to obey you rather than God. For we cannot help speaking about what we have seen and heard."'"

The next few days were some of the worst Pat ever endured. He hadn't agreed to step aside, and he hadn't told the deacons exactly what he was going to do on the following Sunday. But he did agree to postpone sermon number six for a time.

Normally he would have spent most of the week working on his sermon, a sermon he would have delivered with passion. Reading the Scripture had become a chore. He found it impossible to concentrate, let alone pray, except for the most casual prayers over meals with his family. He had a hard time talking to Becky or playing with the kids. God seemed far away, and the sermon he eventually prepared late on Friday afternoon was little more than a warmed-over devotional. It was exactly what Keith, Gentry, and the other men had asked for, with just one brief reference to a comment by C. S. Lewis from the book *Surprised by Joy*. But even with that familiar subject, Pastor Pat was anything but joyful.

| CHAPTER TWENTY-ONE |

When Pat and Becky arrived at church on Sunday morning, the signs of what lay ahead were obvious. The parking lot was less than two-thirds full, and the sanctuary was half empty. There was none of the customary chatter. The place was almost silent, and there was a mood of doubt and anxiety. For the first time in his life, Pat felt like he was floating outside his body, looking objectively at the chaos around him. It wasn't a pretty sight.

No one said anything to him about his situation. There were no embarrassing questions, no acrimony, just polite smiles and gracious words from a few old friends. But he felt the uncertainty, suspicion, and aloofness of the members, and it hurt.

When Pat went to his office after the first service, he fell into his chair and sat silently at his desk for several minutes. He couldn't focus on his sermon or anything else for that matter. The music leader stopped by to make sure Pat was still satisfied with the hymns he had selected for the 9:30 and 11:00 services. Pat simply nodded. Black clouds of fear, disappointment, anger, and pain hovered above him. The only sound in the room was the ticking of an antique clock on the wall. With every *tock* that followed every *tick*, Pat's despair grew. Ten minutes before the service was supposed to begin, Pat lumbered down the hall to the office of one of his associates, Chuck Childress, and told him he couldn't preach.

"Chuck, I can't do this. I'm too stressed right now, and the congregation is obviously upset with me. I think I need time to think this over and regroup. I'm sorry to ask you this, but would you . . . *could* you possibly take the services for me?"

"You mean now? You want me to preach? Today? The organ is already playing. The service starts in ten minutes." Chuck's face went white.

"Yes, I know," Pat said, looking down in embarrassment. "Can you do it? I know you have something in reserve—an old sermon you can use. I've seen you do it before. You're awfully good on short notice."

Chuck shook his head as if he were about to say no, but after a brief hesitation he looked at Pat and said he would do his best. Pat knew Chuck could take over for him very well. He was a gifted speaker and a quick study. Pat also believed that the members would be much happier to see Chuck in the pulpit—at least on this occasion.

Sure enough, Chuck's presentation for the 9:30 service was flawless. Anyone would have thought he'd been working on it for weeks. The choir, the soloist, and the hymn selections were perfect as well, and Pat was relieved. By the 11:00 service, however, Pat was on the verge of tears not only because of his concern for what was happening to him but also because of his concern for what was happening to his flock.

They had taken him in, loved him, and taught him what it meant to be the minister of a large and vibrant church. They had rewarded him in ways he had never anticipated and for which he could never repay them. As he looked around the room, names and faces leapt out. Grayson Webb, the first to call him and champion his candidacy, and his wife, Cindy. On every row sat men and women who had become a part of his life. These were people who had invited him into their homes and shown such affection for Becky and the children. It felt as if he had spent a lifetime in this place, and he loved it so much. But now he felt like a convict on the gallows, waiting for the trap door to fall open and the rope to snap around his neck. Just imagining that grisly scene made him gasp for air.

As he sat on the platform, Pat was too full of his own sorrow to pay much attention to what was happening. Without realizing it, the words of the offertory hymn drew him in. The choir was singing a wonderful old classic he had sung so often as a child growing up in Owensboro, "O Sacred Head, Now Wounded." The lyrics were familiar and the music consoling, but as he focused on the words of that ancient sermon composed centuries ago by St. Bernard of Clairvaux, it was as if he was hearing it for the first time.

His emotions, which he had tried so hard to smother, ignited and were soon fully involved. By the time the choir began singing the middle verses of the hymn, tears were welling in his eyes. He made no attempt to brush them away. He sang along, quietly:

> O sacred Head, now wounded,
> with grief and shame weighed down,
> Now scornfully surrounded with thorns,
> Thine only crown;
> O sacred Head, what glory,
> what bliss till now was Thine!
> Yet, though despised and gory,
> I joy to call Thee mine.

His voice could now be heard in the first several rows, faintly, but filled with emotion:

> What Thou, my Lord, hast suffered,
> Was all for sinners' gain;
> Mine, mine was the transgression,
> but Thine the deadly pain.
> Lo, here I fall, my Savior!
> 'Tis I deserve Thy place;
> Look on me with Thy favor,
> vouchsafe to me Thy grace.

In his mind, Pat saw the image of the crucified Christ on the cross, lifted high above the heads of the congregation. As he gazed at the miraculous tableau of the Son of God in His agony, in the anguish and rejection He endured, Pat's heart raced and his temples throbbed. Jesus had lived with humiliation throughout His earthly life. Even though it was God's plan from the very beginning, sight of the suffering Jesus tore Pat's soul open.

As the choir sang the final stanza, the words of that ancient hymn pierced his heart. He couldn't restrain the words as they came from his lips, more loudly now:

> What language shall I borrow to thank Thee, dearest friend,
> For this Thy dying sorrow, Thy pity without end?
> O make me Thine forever, and should I fainting be,
> Lord, let me never, never outlive my love to Thee.

Christ's agony on a Roman cross made Pat's own struggles seem pathetic and pale. Yet here he was, sitting in front of his congregation and feeling sorry for himself, terrified of what was to come if he couldn't—or wouldn't—preach the message God had laid on his heart.

As the music ended and the ushers were coming forward to present the offerings at the altar, Pat leaned over to Chuck with tears in his eyes and whispered, "Chuck, I have to say something. I can't just sit here. I have to speak to them. Will you forgive me?"

Chuck looked at him knowingly. "I understand, Pastor." When the music ended and the ushers had returned to their seats, Pat stood and walked to the pulpit with nothing in his hands but the Bible.

Looking out across the sanctuary he saw many faces he knew and many dear friends he loved. They had welcomed him with open arms, but in the terror of the moment as their church and their traditions were being threatened, they were wavering. How could he blame them for that? He was every bit as weak. He would have walked away himself, if it weren't for the power of the vision he had just witnessed. And so he spoke to them.

"'What language shall I borrow to thank Thee, dearest friend; for this Thy dying sorrow, Thy pity without end?' How many times have we sung those words, and yet how little do we consider their meaning. When Becky and I pulled into the parking lot this morning, I confess, I wasn't thinking about the reality of that sacrifice. I wasn't thinking about the scandal of the cross or the gift of eternal life that was delivered to me on that day two thousand years ago.

"Frankly, I was thinking about my own sorrow, my own fears, and my own humiliation. The events of the past two weeks had shoved all my noble intentions aside. Until a few days ago, the only time I had ever been inside a jail was to visit a young friend in Kentucky who was involved in a tragic car accident. But now I've been humbled and personally threatened.

"Being knocked to the floor, handcuffed, and hauled off in the back of a police car is a terrifying experience and not something I'd ever want to repeat. But I have nothing to apologize for, and I'm not afraid anymore. I have seen the evidence of God's love demonstrated before my eyes. Just now as the choir was singing that magnificent hymn, I had a vision of God's love for me."

Pat studied the congregation. Some looked confused, and a few looked frightened. He glanced to an area were several deacons sat. They looked worried.

"Our Lord, who lived a perfect, sinless life," Pat continued, "suffered so much more than we could ever imagine. Although He had the power of God Almighty in His right hand, Jesus Christ never lifted a finger to resist the punishment men inflicted on Him. How can I, a man of unclean lips, do less than stand on the promises of God in my own time of testing?"

Pat smiled as he looked across the congregation although his heart was full of tears. "I must tell you," he continued, holding up his empty palms, "I don't have my sermon notes with me today. I left them in the study this morning because I asked Pastor Chuck to speak to you. I was feeling sorry for myself, I suppose. But that's okay. I don't need them now. I'd like to speak to you from my heart."

When Pat glanced briefly at Chuck, their eyes met. Pat saw that Chuck was apprehensive. Still, he continued, "Sitting here just now, I realized I cannot be silent any longer. I can't run from the intimidation and accusations that are being thrust at me. My friends, there's only one absolute and ultimate truth in this world, and His name is Jesus Christ, the Savior of men and the only hope of this broken and lawless world. He alone is the Savior of the world.

"There are people among us today, maybe even some of you in this room, who think they can break the law of God with impunity. They believe that if they can pass a new law or convince enough people to vote a certain way, maybe they can establish a new order of the ages. They've become a law unto themselves. But I must warn you: No one can break God's law without paying a price. You can't break God's law; you can only break yourself. God's law is not up for a vote. The Creator on Mount Sinai handed it down, and not one syllable of that law has changed in four thousand years.

"If every politician and bureaucrat in America were to come together on one day and declare a new moral law, it wouldn't make the slightest difference. God's law is eternal, immutable, omnipotent, and inescapable. Sooner or later every one of us will stand before the Judge and give an account of ourselves. None of us will survive the judgment because of our goodness but because of the mercy of Jesus Christ. This is the promise to everyone who puts their trust in Him."

Pat paused briefly, his eyes scanning the sanctuary. "It breaks my heart to think of all the men and women, all the kings and rulers, and all the great nations throughout history that have hurled themselves against God's law only to be shattered into a thousand pieces. You can see the evidence of those shattered lives today in the cemeteries, asylums, prisons, and gutters of this city. How many more will end up there before all is said and done?"

Some members of the congregation shifted nervously in their seats, whispering to each other. Pat ignored it. He had gone too far to turn back.

"My dear friends, I believe we're living through what the New Testament refers to as the last days. Jesus told us these days would come. Now we know it's true. There has never been such an age of lawlessness with so much hostility and rebellion against God's law. The leaders of this nation have turned their backs on God, and I've come up against the reality of that rebellion over the last several days. Leaders at the highest levels of government have tossed the Ten Commandments overboard and knowingly plunged themselves into a sea of wickedness and perversion. The one thing they cannot abide is the truth that God is the ultimate judge and that He hates sin.

"But, again, Jesus said these days would come. In one of His parables, Jesus speaks of a nobleman who went to a far country, leaving his beloved servant in charge. But the rebellious citizens of that country rejected the one left in charge. They shouted, 'We don't want this man to be our king!' Dear friends, this is not just a colorful parable; it's a true story. It is our story. We're the ones Jesus was talking about. We're the ones in rebellion against the Father. And we're the ones who have to decide whether or not we will obey the Lord's anointed.

"Recently I spoke to a man who said, 'Well, Pastor, I believe you're only accountable for the light you have, whatever that may be.' I said, 'What a nice idea! But that's a fairy tale. My Bible says, "This is the verdict: Light has come into the world, but men loved darkness instead of light because their deeds were evil."' We all want to have it our way, don't we? Wouldn't it be nice if we could just make up our own salvation? But Jesus says that's not good enough.

"Those who are antagonistic toward the gospel like to embarrass Christians. On a television interview not long ago, I was one of three ministers who had been invited to discuss the teachings of our various faiths. At one point the host turned to me and said, 'Reverend Preston, don't you believe that anyone who's not a Christian is going to hell?' I knew what he was doing, but I went ahead and said I believed the words of Jesus in John 14:6, where He says He is the only way. At which point the host sprang the trap and said, 'Aha! So you believe that Rabbi Goldman, sitting beside you there, is going to hell. Is that right?'

"Well, I know Rabbi Goldman. We've been on many programs to-gether over the last few years, and I've had him in my home for dinner. I have no animosity toward this man or his religion. I simply said, 'Sir, I don't know what God will do. He has unlimited power, and His ways are greater than my ways. He may have plans that I know nothing about. But as a Christian minister of the gospel, I'm responsible to follow the Word of God.'

"As a Christian, my job is to share the good news with everyone I can, in the hope that some of them will come to Christ. I know it works because the Bible says it does, and I've seen the evidence. I don't know what else God may have up His sleeve. He may have other ways He hasn't shared with me. Then I told the host there was one more thing I could say about that. I said I looked forward to spending a lot more time with Rabbi Goldman, both on earth and in heaven one day."

Glancing at the clock in the back of the sanctuary, Pat said, "I think I've said enough, so let me wrap up my thoughts this way. Before I ask the deacons to come forward to speak to those of you who would like to learn more about how you can have the certainty of eternal life, let me pose a question. Do we want to conquer sin? Do we want to see converts coming to Christ? No one is going to be won by a cowardly gospel that, as Paul says, has a 'form of godliness' but is lacking in power. When Jesus said, 'Blessed are the meek,' He didn't say, 'Blessed are the wimps.' The meek are blessed because they're humble, not because they're wimps. They're willing to stand up for what they believe.

"As followers of Christ, we're called to be different. Jesus said, 'All men will hate you because of me, but he who stands firm to the end will be saved.' The meek whom Jesus blesses are those strong enough to endure the curses and insults, and despite everything the world throws at them, they fight the good fight. Dear friends, that's the commitment I make to you today.

"There are people who say, 'It's not the job of the church to talk about the issues of the day.' But can that be true? Did Jesus talk about the issues of His day? Did He challenge the tax collectors and scribes and teachers of the law, calling them whitewashed tombs full of dead men's bones?

"And what about the abolition movement that freed the slaves? How did that happen? It was godly men like William Wilberforce in England and Alexander Hamilton, John Jay, and Benjamin Rush in this country who led the struggle. There were righteous men and women in the government in those days. They were defenders of religious liberty, men who dared to take a stand against evil. I pray that you and I may be half as strong."

With those words, Pat stepped aside and asked Chuck to come forward and give the closing prayer. As the organist began playing the hymn of invitation, Chuck asked all those who would like to make a commitment to follow Christ to come forward. At least fifty people walked down the aisle.

No one was more stunned than Pat.

Many of the members felt that the Lord had used Pat's words, and they told him so. But the reaction of the deacons to Pat's extemporaneous sermon was less than positive. His defiance shocked them. He had, against their expressed wishes, given another sermon in which he had attacked the government and the administration. Several of the men brushed past Pat, ignoring his outstretched hand.

At home, Pat and Becky sat at the dining room table eating their afternoon meal. The kids had bolted down their food and were outside playing. The moment they left, Pat felt the tension in the room rise. Becky had been bottling up her emotions, just as he had, and he could see the bottle was full.

"Pat," she said, "why is this happening to us? Why do you have to stir up trouble like this? I can't take much more of it."

"Becky, I know you didn't do anything to deserve this, but you've seen what's happening. It's the government. They've taken a few cases completely out of context in order to use it as a weapon against people of faith, and they're making me out to be the bad guy. If we didn't have a successful broadcast ministry in this church or—I hate to say this—if I'd never met John Knox Smith, probably none of this would be happening."

"But why? What did we ever do to them?"

"Don't look for logical answers, Becky. They have an agenda that's motivated by their belief system, which has nothing to do with the Christian values we once took for granted in this country. They see people like us as dinosaurs from some ancient world who hold back their visions of government-enforced equality. We're defenders of that other vision—the vision of the founders and our Christian forbearers. For them, that makes us the enemy."

"I can't take this."

Pat laid his hand on her shoulder, but she shrugged it off. "Becky, do you remember what we learned at Southern Seminary, when you were working in the president's office? That the 'renewal of the church will come only when from pulpit to pulpit we preach as a dying man to dying men'?"

"Pat Preston, that's all well and good, but you know my daddy, who was a preacher for forty years, would never have put Mama in a position like this. He never would have put her . . ." Her words and her strength faded away.

Pat struggled to hold back his own tears. The pressure was mounting, and he knew Becky wasn't going to be able to take much more. She had done some volunteer counseling with the women in the church the past couple of years. Such things were never her calling, but at least she was willing to lend a sympathetic ear. It wasn't until she started hearing complaints from some of those same women about her husband's hard-line preaching and intolerance—especially referring to homosexual behavior as sinful—and about how that upset their neighbors, that she realized how difficult being a pastor's wife could be.

"Do you know what one of the ladies said to me after services today? She said, 'Where is your husband taking this church? Why is he always talking about things that are so scary and controversial?' What bothered me most was I didn't have an answer."

"People shouldn't say things like that to you. If they have a problem with me, then they should come to me."

"But they *do* speak to me." She drew a hand under her eyes. "Pat, wherever you go, you have been the star. That's okay. I enjoyed that. You have always been my strong, masculine hero; always the provider and defender of our family. But suddenly you seem . . . weak. I don't know how to deal with that."

"I'm the same man I always was. I may have lost my emotional footing for a few days—"

"People are treating me like I'm part of a conspiracy. I'm a good woman. I love God and do my duty. I've been faithful. I've given you two beautiful children and served the people of our church. Why are you doing this to me?"

"Becky, I'm not doing this to you."

"You didn't have to stand up there and blast the government again. Have you forgotten what they did to you?"

"Of course not. I still have the bruises."

"Then why risk more? You can soften your sermons for a while. What do I tell the kids when you end up in jail again or when they see your face on the news? What happens if the DTED agents or U.S. marshals or marines come to the door and drag you off while our children watch?"

"I don't think that's going to happen."

"Did you expect what happened last week?"

"Of course not."

"I think it'd be best if I take the kids to their grandmother's for a while."

"But they're in school."

"I can make arrangements with the district for homework assignments. Things are too . . . too . . . volatile for them."

"You're really going to go back to Louisville?"

"Mom can help me with the kids. It's been a while since we've been there. We've only visited a couple of times after Daddy died. It will be good for the kids."

"You mean it will be good for you, don't you?"

"What if it is? Would you begrudge me that?"

Pat thought for a moment. "No, I wouldn't."

The next morning, immediately after breakfast, Becky and the children backed out of the driveway and drove away.

| CHAPTER TWENTY-TWO |

Mike Alden's report on the identities of Madisonians at the Department of Justice held a reminder—a reminder that ate at John Knox Smith as he opened the sealed packet and scanned the list. There, near the top of the list, the first name under "B," was his college friend Matthew W. Branson, Office of Professional Responsibility. He felt no surprise. He and Matt had talked about the Madison Scholars over a meal at the Italian restaurant, but that was months ago. Back then, John found Matt's blending of Christian faith and law amusing. He also found it uncomfortable. Things had changed. The fight against hate speech had intensified, and the DTED had gained ground and momentum. John couldn't afford to be careless. Matt might be one of "them." If so, then his presence in the DOJ created a dangerous situation. The word *spy* came to mind.

John ignored the tiny buzzing of guilt in his mind, grabbed the telephone, and dialed the direct number for the DOJ's director of human resources. "Hey, Barry, it's John Knox Smith, DTED. I need the complete personnel file on Matthew Branson."

"Is this in regard to his resignation?" Barry asked.

"Resignation? What resignation?"

"He announced his resignation a short time ago. I think he's return-ing to private law."

Thoughts ricocheted in John's mind. Something didn't feel right.

"Did he mention anything about Pat Preston?"

"The preacher? Not to me. I just received his formal resignation."

John picked up a pen and tapped in on a notepad. "Did he make any complaints about the department?"

"The OPR?"

"The Department of Justice, Barry, or any of its internal depart-ments." John struggled to hide the irritation he felt.

"Not that I know of. If he did, he didn't complain to me."

John set the pen down. "Listen, Barry, I need you to keep this little conversation under wraps. Can I rely on your discretion?"

"Are you investigating the man?"

It took a moment for John to respond. "It's too early to speak about the matter. I'm just checking into a couple of things. Let's keep this call between us for now. Okay?"

"Sure. Anything you say. You still want that file?"

"I do. I also want to know what he's been working on."

"Can't help you there, John. I'm just a lowly HR guy."

"Just thinking out loud, Barry. I'll have someone get that info for me."

"If you need anything else, just let me know."

"Thanks, Barry." John hung up. Alone in his office, he said, "What are you up to, Matt?"

Andrea entered the office. "I have a pile of messages. You look distracted."

John looked at Andrea. He always felt better when she was in the room. "Matt Branson has resigned."

"Matt Branson? Your lunch buddy from the Office of Professional Responsibility?"

"That's the guy. We go way back to college. Bright guy but lacks drive."

Andrea looked concerned. "The OPR has access to privileged infor-mation. They get into a lot of dirt."

"We've done nothing wrong. I don't have any worries on that count."

"Can you imagine what sort of classified information Branson may have in his possession?"

"You sound paranoid. Paranoia is *my* job."

"Maybe it's contagious. You don't have any worries about his resignation?"

"You know me too well, Andrea. It's spooky."

"I just care about you and what you do, that's all."

John's thoughts drifted back to Matt. "Matt and I went to the same college and have a common acquaintance: Pat Preston."

Andrea narrowed her eyes. "Matt is friends with someone our department is investigating?"

"Yeah. That's what I've been thinking about."

"That seems more than a little suspicious to me."

"I have HR sending over his file. I also want to go over his casework."

"What happens if he's been helping Preston?"

"If he provided any help before his resignation or used DOJ information to warn him, advise him, or anything else, then I'll make sure he never practices law again. His law degree will be useless except as a drink coaster." John stood. "Let's see if we can't uncover a few things that might be of interest to the exit interview panel."

When Matt showed up for what he expected to be a routine exit interview, he ran into a buzz saw. For some reason—and Matt suspected John Knox Smith was the reason—the investigators seemed determined to find improper behavior during Matt's tenure with the DOJ. As part of OPR, Matt had served on exit interviews, but no one had been scrutinized as thoroughly as this panel had delved into his career. OPR and HR seemed committed to destroying his reputation.

For the next several days, Matt's life was a living hell. Every record and file he had ever touched the panel reopened and reexamined.

During the investigation Matt submitted a letter revealing, as required by law, that he planned to go into private practice. He attested he had not and was not being paid by any client and had not formally accepted an offer to be put on retainer. In the letter he revealed he had taken calls from Rev. Pat Preston in Nashville about handling his case, which did, in fact, involve the DOJ, but they had not met to discuss the details of the case, and no specific information had changed hands between them. For several days Matt waited for the guillotine blade to fall. He knew he had done everything properly and within the guidelines of the DOJ, but he feared the panel would see things otherwise.

The gut-wrenching experience left Matt worn and exhausted, but in the end he survived, and the Department of Justice declined to pursue the issue further. Before Matt could relax, he heard that John had registered a protest with the director of the OPR and Attorney General Stamper. Both men refused to intervene. Matt's record was clean, his ratings were high, and it was clear that he had not broken any laws or violated any departmental regulations.

When word of the final HR review came back, the statement read, "Over the last four years, Matthew Branson has been an exemplary employee of the United States Department of Justice, has met or exceeded all expectations of his supervisors, and has earned the affection of his coworkers at all levels. It is with great sadness that we say good-bye to our friend and colleague, and we wish him much success in all his future endeavors."

For the first time in over a week, Matt slept an entire night.

Within days of his departure from the DOJ, Matt began looking into Pat's case. He quickly discovered it was going to be almost impossible to get any new information out of the DTED or the police; and his prospective client was less than helpful. Matt knew it wasn't uncommon for police agencies to deny defense attorneys access to information until formal charges were filed. After a major tactical raid, it could take weeks or even months for the suspect and his lawyers to find out what was happening and to learn whether the authorities would file charges at all. The investigators and DTED agents on Pat's case seemed to be going out of their way to make life difficult for the accused and to stonewall Matt.

After serving a search warrant, officers file a Return of Service document in which they provide statements about what they did and make an inventory of what items they removed from the scene. Ordinarily a simple, nondescript document, Pat Preston's ROS became a multi-page essay about Pat's belligerent behavior. Prosecutors filed it as an open record with the court. Anyone could read it—including press and the deacons of Rogers Memorial Church.

Matt kept track of every article in print or on the Web and every news broadcast. They were stacking up.

In just days, Pat's arrest and the growing wave of news reports created a major crisis at the church. Every time Pat's name appeared in the press, Rogers Memorial Church appeared with it. *Just One Life* ran on three hundred stations across the country, and donations from the on-air ministry provided much of the church's budget. Stations uncomfortable with the media reports about Pat and fearing the new FCC regulations stopped running the programs. Money from those programs dried up, but the ministry bills did not. Although Just One Life, Inc., was a separate corporation from the church, Rogers Memorial was bleeding cash.

The board of directors for Just One Life, Inc., which included some of the church's deacons, called an emergency session.

"We're here to proclaim the gospel of Jesus Christ," Keith Gentry said. "We're an evangelistic organization, but Pastor Pat has put our whole ministry in peril by going away from what we know and taking an unnecessarily critical position on what other religions may or may not believe.

"We've got to get back on the air soon before this ministry goes bankrupt. We're going to ask our lawyer to go to Washington and find out what it will take for that to happen. We'll do anything that doesn't violate our conscience, but we've got to move fast."

There were a couple of dissenters on the board who wanted to stand with Pat, but Gentry and Howard French dominated the discussion. Pat's few supporters were outnumbered and emotionally outgunned.

"We have three years' worth of recorded sermons Pat preached before he got on this kick. He was much more reasonable back then. We also have a talented team of program editors. We could create new material from old broadcasts."

"What we need to do," Gentry said, "is to go back to the stuff before Pat went to Oxford. Pat hasn't been the same since he got back. If that doesn't work, we have at least ten years of Bill Richards's sermons we can use."

"Great idea," Howard said. "Maybe we should ask the folks at the FCC and DTED to help screen some of those sermons—tell them which ones would be best on the air and which would cause the least public disturbance. It will make the church look innocent of Pat's behavior and willing to make amends for any crimes he committed."

That week Gentry, Howard, and their lawyer held a telephone conference with the FCC. It didn't take long for the FCC to squash the idea. "We'll be delighted to put the program back on the air. You've got a good show. Apparently it's very popular, and you've got a lot of support around the country. We also know you've got millions of dollars at stake here, but you'll need to put somebody else on the air. We can't support you if you continue putting Rev. Preston on the broadcast; there's too much bad blood there."

Gentry wasn't disappointed.

A few hours later, Keith Gentry called Pat at home and arranged a meeting with the deacons for later that evening. Pat arrived, his stomach a twisting wad of emotions. Stress started taking a toll on him. His back hurt, he had trouble sitting, and indigestion followed every meal.

The deacons had set the meeting in the same adult classroom where they had held their private meeting a few weeks before.

When Pat stepped through the door, every deacon was seated around folding tables set end to end. Coffee cups rested on the surface of the table. Most were empty. They had been meeting before his arrival.

"Thanks for coming, Pastor," Gentry said as Pat took a seat at one end of the table. Gentry sat at the other.

"Just say it, Keith," Pat said.

"What do you mean?"

Pat leaned over his end of the table. His brain felt lodged in an ever-tightening vise. "I'm not an idiot, Keith. The deacons don't hold several meetings without the pastor unless they're getting ready to show him the door. I know about your meeting with the One Life board."

"We only want what's best for the church, Preacher."

"I want what's best for Jesus."

"They're the same thing, Pat," Keith said in a menacing tone.

"Not in this church. Not anymore. It seems most of you want compliance with the government rather than with God."

"As I understand the Bible, Pastor, that's one of the duties of the church."

"Really? Well, that explains a few things." Pat straightened as if he were walking into the pulpit. "The earliest Christians had to make a choice. Part of the Roman tax-paying procedure was to hand over the money and state, 'Caesar is Lord.' Early Christians paid their taxes but refused to make the proclamations. The Romans executed a pastor named Polycarp who refused to comply."

"This is the twenty-first century," Gentry stated.

"Jesus hasn't changed. The church's mission remains the same."

"We asked you here—"

"Summoned."

"What?"

"You didn't ask me here, you summoned me."

Gentry glanced around the room. Most of the deacons studied the tabletop. Only Howard French kept his head up.

"Please don't make this more difficult than it already is." Howard spoke softly.

"This is difficult for you? You? I've been hurt and arrested for no reason. The media keeps repeating the nonsense about me attacking an officer when all I was doing was helping an injured woman. I was booked, had a mug shot taken, and was forced to call my wife to pick me up from jail. I'm facing legal problems I can't begin to understand, and you feel *you're* going through difficulty?" Pat rubbed his eyes. "Just do it, Keith. No more pretense about concern for me or the church; no more talk about doing what is right. Just do it."

"We took a vote and agree that you should go." Keith blurted the words. "The vote was unanimous."

"Not a single spine in the group," Pat muttered to himself. He knew this was coming, but hearing the words struck him like a knight's lance to the heart.

"What?" Gentry asked.

"Nothing. Carry on."

"We've prepared what we consider a generous termination agreement with a one-year severance package, a reasonable relocation allowance, and certain other benefits. But there's just one caveat: you have twenty-four hours to read and sign the document. There are additional penalties if you go beyond that time."

Pat sat in silence. Had Rogers Memorial been a typical Baptist church, the deacons wouldn't have had so much power. The congregation would be the only ones who could dismiss the senior pastor. Rogers Memorial wasn't typical. It was a mega church. Before Pat had been called, the congregation had transferred many of its powers to the deacon board, which served as a board of directors.

"It really is generous, Pastor," Howard said.

"Forgive me if I'm not overwhelmed with gratitude." He held out his hand, and Gentry passed a manila folder down the table.

Pat rose and walked from the room.

"Pat, you must not sign this agreement." Matt's emotion came over the phone undiminished by distance. Pat had faxed the document to Matt the moment he had gotten home.

"I'm not sure I *can* refuse."

"Look, Pat. This isn't a bunch of guys who put their heads together and drew up an agreement. This thing is loaded with legalese. It makes some very harmful admissions. If I were a betting man, I'd bet my house they've retained counsel against you."

"What difference does that make, Matt? The result is the same. They're playing hardball. They want me to drag my feet. If I miss the twenty-four hour deadline, they cut my severance package and other benefits in half."

"I understand—"

"I still have a family to support. A year's salary will make that possible for a while." He thought of his family, who were still with Becky's mother. He hadn't talked to Becky yet and doubted he would until this was all over.

"Pat, you have a right to fight this. Give me a chance to contact their attorney. The guy knows he can't get away with this. Once he hears you have strong representation, I'm sure he'll take a few steps back and give you more time."

"I'll think about it, Matt."

"Promise me you won't sign this thing."

"Good night, Matt."

Pat hung up.

| CHAPTER TWENTY-THREE |

A week after his phone call with Pat, Matt Branson couldn't decide whether he felt anger toward the man or pity. Once he was able to get a handle on what was coming against his friend, Matt discovered that not only had Pat not been forthcoming with him; he hadn't been cautious either. He had waited until the hammer was coming down to ask for legal counsel, at which point he was already in serious trouble. He had signed the letter from the church; he had signed what amounted to a full confession—against Matt's counsel—potentially admitting to crimes he had never committed. He hadn't even asked to make a statement in his own defense. Matt had a lot of ground to make up and not much time. He realized his best efforts might not be good enough.

Matt had also spent hours learning as much as he could about John Knox Smith's DTED team and tactics. Before he left the DOJ, Matt had considered investigating Smith's professional behavior but doubted he could have made enough headway to help Pat. He also doubted he could professionally survive the process himself.

Matt had investigated as much as he could before resigning. What he had learned convinced him that Smith's team, probably led by Joel Thevis, would review years of Pat's recorded sermons if they hadn't already. They would analyze every article posted on the church's Web site and examine every speech he had given on abortion, same-sex "marriage," or other controversial topics. Some of those comments had been made long before RDTA even existed, but the lawyers would insist the tapes showed how bigoted and insensitive Pat's preaching had become over the years.

Once they had gathered the evidence, they would take the case to the grand jury, where the jurors would vote on each count presented by the prosecutor. Since there could be more than one hundred counts filed, members of the grand jury would certainly find something to act upon. Pat's sermons had gone out over radio, TV, and the Internet; and printed literature had been mailed to cities and towns across America, meaning that each offense could be charged separately. Altogether, they would add up to a tremendous hate speech case against Pastor Pat.

Matt learned that prosecutors had successfully requested that the term of the special grand jury be extended, lengthening the time of their service. They had already served for nine months and been well conditioned to deplore what the prosecutors described as "the venom of hate and intolerance."

Matt felt the Justice Department was manipulating the system, but the action was legal, and the DTED clearly understood the advantages of keeping a group of jurors who could be expected to respond their way. For weeks John's senior prosecutors had been putting together lists of witnesses and physical evidence to present to the grand jury on the Preston case. They had established venue in D.C. because Pat's *Just One Life* broadcasts were available in the area on radio, cable TV, and the Internet in the District and surrounding states.

There was no doubt in Matt's mind that his opponents had thoroughly reviewed the sermons in the "Insufficiency of Hope" series and had gotten detailed critiques from a team of experts, who would bolster their position that the messages were the product of bigotry and disruptive to the peace of society. They would paint Pat as exclusionist, racist, xenophobic, homophobic, and any other label they could think up.

Something else worried Matt: Pat's salary. His client's after-tax income was much higher than other ministers. Pastors were supposed to be poor. The fact that Pat ministered to a ten-thousand-member church, gave much—some years over half—of his money to charity, and lost much of his income to ravenous tax laws would be overlooked. His client would be presented as a money-hungry man who used hatred to fill the coffers of his church and line his pockets.

Day and night, Matt labored to formulate a plan to rescue his friend. When he spoke to Pat, he did so with encouraging words, but once off the phone, Matt plummeted into despair. He had left his job at the DOJ to take an impossible case.

Matt loved the study and practice of law, but he thought it had a seamy side, an underbelly unpleasant to see or to acknowledge. In cases like Pat's, the defendant has no right to appear before the grand jury and is not privy to anything that happens behind closed doors. When Matt contacted John, the assistant attorney general let him know that Pat's case was being considered by the grand jury, but he refused to reveal anything more. John's refusal to offer anything more than the other basic information wounded Matt, but not nearly as much as John's cold, barely hidden anger. What shreds of friendship might have existed between them was long gone.

Matt hired a paralegal to sit outside the jury room and keep an eye on anyone coming and going and to make notes on anything she could pick up. That was the best he could hope for at that point. After her mission was over, all the woman reported was the constant ebb and flow of federal agents and DOJ attorneys. Some remained in the jury room for three or four hours at a time. When the door opened, she saw several large-screen televisions and an array of speakers. After a few days she ventured to ask one of the attorneys if they were still dealing with her client. "Yes, of course. This is going to take a while." It wasn't what Matt wanted to hear.

Questions chewed on Matt's mind. Would a grand jury actually indict a pastor for saying that Jesus was the only means of salvation? Preachers had been announcing that message for two millennia. Ten years ago, Matt would have laughed at the idea. Now the question kept him awake at night.

In the flesh Pat feared the unknown. He could walk the fields of theology, doctrine, and human nature. He could work in the New Testament's original Greek and work comfortably in Old Testament Hebrew. Yet the world of courts, subpoenas, and federal law baffled him.

When Pat asked Matt what he should do, Matt said, "I'm not going to recommend this, Pat, but as your lawyer, I'm obligated to tell you the options. One option in your situation is to speak to the prosecutor before an indictment comes down."

"And say what?"

Matt hesitated. "Ask for mercy."

"Ask for mercy?"

"If you do, you might be able to influence the outcome."

Although Pat agreed to think about it, he couldn't toss off the feeling that it would be one more disgrace to add to everything else he had experienced. Wasn't asking for mercy the same thing as admitting guilt? Saying he shouldn't preach the gospel as revealed in the New Testament?

Pat's thoughts ran back to Polycarp. He had used the late first-century bishop's name when chastising the deacon board. The elderly man had been arrested by Rome for being a Christian. Rome considered Christianity a dangerous political cult. The proconsul tried to give the old man a way out. "Just put a pinch of incense on the fire and say Caesar is Lord, and you will go free."

Polycarp softly refused. "Eighty-six years I have served Christ, and He never did me any wrong. How can I blaspheme my King who saved me?" While an angry crowd jeered, officials tied Polycarp to a stake and burned him to death.

Could Pat apologize for serving Jesus? The thought sickened him.

That evening Pat called Becky at her mother's house. His first desire was to know how his wife and children were faring. After a few minutes, he told her about Matt's efforts and his comment about asking for mercy.

"Pat, you only have one choice. You've got to go in there and tell them you want to make a deal. You've got to go in there, hat in hand, and apologize for what you said. Tell them you're sorry. Tell them you're going to turn over a new leaf and that it won't happen again."

Her words told him his worse fears had arrived. At first, Becky had been mildly supportive, but fear and worry were pirating her resolve. A sensitive woman, she absorbed tension and held it close to her heart.

"Becky, I don't think I can do that. I'd be selling out everything I stand for—everything Jesus stands for."

"Pat, I can't take this any longer. I can't subject our children to this kind of humiliation."

"I need you to stand with me, Becky. I need to know you're with me in this."

Pat heard her voice crack, then the sound of her hanging up.

For the first time in his life, Pat felt fully alone.

For the first time in months, John Knox Smith felt he had a little room to breathe and could put the preparations for Pat Preston's prosecution into the hands of his team. It was also the first time he felt free enough to follow up on something that had caught his eye several months earlier when Andrea had showed him the announcement for a major international conference in Italy on transformative justice sponsored by the United Nations.

"Wouldn't I love to be part of a program like that!" he said to Andrea.

Andrea stood next to him as he sat behind his desk. More and more, he noticed her desire to stand close. "You'll have to respond immediately if you intend to go. Arrangements have to be made with the UN and the DOJ."

"Tempting as it is, I have the Preston case to deal with."

Andrea laid a hand on his shoulder. It felt good. "Joel Thevis can keep the Preston case on track. You should be able to attend the event and enjoy a full week at an elegant, resort hotel and conference center in Florence. It's only one week."

"It's tempting."

"I have more temptation for you." She paused. John turned in his chair, uncertain what to expect. "They would like you to pull together a presentation on the development of the DTED and the new laws it's enforcing. You would be speaking to one of the most distinguished professional audiences in the world."

"A presentation?"

"A full forty-minute lecture, translated into six languages."

"How did that come about?"

Andrea smiled. "I made a call or two."

John laughed. "I suppose you think you should come along . . . to what? Keep an eye on me?"

"I *am* your administrative assistant, and I do have a passport." She gave his shoulder a squeeze.

"Okay, you win. Fill out the forms and draft a letter of acceptance." John let Andrea take care of all the details, something she excelled at.

| CHAPTER TWENTY-FOUR |

John sat in the grand jury room and watched Joel Thevis earn his salary. John had made it clear to Joel and the rest of the team that the Preston case would be their biggest score. The courts had taken other religious programs off the air and fined and censured several pastors, but Pat's case would make history. Well known to the media, he would garner a great deal of attention, just what John wanted. Pat would be the first minister indicted for exclusionist preaching—all the others had had other issues such as gender hatred involved. His sermons touting Jesus as the only way would doom Pat and make sure the federal courts sent a message to America no one would ever forget.

Joel and the two attorneys who had managed the grand jury process appeared before a magistrate judge. As instructed, the grand jury foreman said, "Your honor, we have a sealed indictment. The name of the accused will not be revealed." Then, as each of the various counts was presented, the judge polled the jury members, asking, "Is this your vote?" and each member answered in the affirmative.

Warrants were signed and delivered to a representative of the U.S. Marshals Service. Copies of the documents were sent electronically to the marshals' office in Nashville. Once they processed the documents at the local office and logistics for a full-scale apprehension were laid on, a large party of marshals, FBI agents under DTED orders, local police, and a representative from the DTED would drive to Rev. Preston's home to serve the warrant. John wished he could be there.

According to procedures developed by John's office in conjunction with the Marshals Service, Pat's house would be placed under twenty-four-hour surveillance. The agents reported to John that no one had gone in or out of the house. By the time the marshals arrived, John knew a surveillance helicopter and a pool television news chopper would be circling overhead. TV news crews would be there to record the arrest. They had done similar arrests across the country, and the media had never failed to show up for the big event.

John made certain the media knew that the person leading the raid on Preston's house had been part of the SWAT team the day Ronnie Lee Jefferson had been gunned down. The deputy marshal would be leading the arrest. He made a point of saying he wasn't about to lose another federal marshal or agent, especially to the preacher that had buried Ronnie Lee Jefferson's killer.

"With all the charges against this man," John told the team, "it's clear he'll never leave prison. He'll never see the light of day again, and he knows it. Take no chances. He's been on hunting trips with members of his church and is known to own a high velocity rifle and some shotguns. Consider him armed and dangerous. He has already fought with law enforcement once—now he'll be desperate."

To reduce the threat of armed resistance, team leaders requested permission from the director in D.C. to use tear gas in the house before going in, and permission was granted. John Knox Smith demanded a maximum-force entry. He told Joel Thevis, "I've invested a lot of my own professional capital in this case, so you'd better not let me down. No injuries, no escapes."

A distant thumping drew Pat from his solemn thoughts. He had done nothing for the last few days except eat, sleep, and pace the floor. He wasn't a psychologist; but he recognized reactive depression when he felt it. He struggled to form thoughts, couldn't work, wanted to sleep all the time, and had cut himself off from friends and family. His body hurt, his stomach had become a churning vat of acid, and he fought tears several times a day. His active prayer life had been reduced to a chant: "I don't understand, Lord. I just don't understand. Please help me."

The distant *thumpa-thumpa-thumpa* grew closer. Then he heard a similar sound. It took several moments for the sound to weave its way through the fog of depression shrouding Pat's mind. "Helicopters."

Glancing out the window, Pat saw a low-flying copter circling his home. Alarms went off in his brain. A motion at the north side of his property snatched his attention. Then he saw them: men dressed in black, each carrying some kind of weapon. They didn't approach the house, they swarmed. White and yellow letters dressed their uniforms: FBI, FEDERAL AGENT, SWAT.

"Blessed Jesus," he prayed. They were the only two words he could force past his lips. He watched as an officer approached the front door in a gas mask, carrying a shotgun with a tear gas launcher attached to the barrel. The next thing he knew, a rocket crashed through the front window. Pat jumped to the side to avoid being hit. Glass crashed to the floor. Something exploded. Smoke and fumes filled the room. Pat dropped to the floor to avoid the gas. His eyes burned and watered so much he couldn't see. The gas choked him, pushing up his nostrils and through his mouth.

What little Pat could see terrified him: four officers in full SWAT gear burst through the door.

"Federal agents. Down! *Down on the ground!* Do it now!" Gas masks muffled their commands.

Pat was already on the floor. For the second time in his life, someone drove a knee into his back, yanked his arms behind him, and pressed metal cuffs on his wrist.

"Stop resisting."

Pat wasn't resisting. He had gone as limp as his convulsing body would allow.

Moments later, the officers yanked him to his feet and marched him to the door, pushed him through, then shoved him to grass-carpeted ground. Agents put restraints on his ankles and linked them to the handcuffs with a chrome chain. Pat was hobbled.

In front of neighbors and news cameras, agents frog-marched Pat to a waiting van.

Pat shook violently from fear and adrenaline. "I'm innocent. I haven't done anything wrong." His eyes continued to burn. His lungs hurt from the gas he had inhaled. He vomited on himself and in the van.

The assault team drove Pat to the airport, placed him on a government transport, and transported him to the Nashville airport en route to the federal lockup at the Ronald Reagan Washington National Airport in D.C.

On the flight, still dressed in his filthy clothes, Pat asked one of the marshals, "Where are you taking me?"

"National Airport in D.C."

"Then what?"

He shrugged. "My job is to deliver you to the jail in the airport, so no more questions. Just enjoy the flight."

"I'm manacled like an animal, and you think I can enjoy the flight?"

The marshal's response was a simple smile.

After landing, they moved Pat to a small jail in some dark corner of the airport.

"How about removing the leg restrains?" Pat said.

"No can do, pal. Not without permission from the judge. You're a high security risk."

"Me?"

"That's what they tell me."

They allowed Pat to call Matt but no one else.

When Matt arrived, the first thing he did was to demand that the authorities show more respect for the human dignity of his client. "Why are you doing this to this man? He is not a criminal. He's not a threat to anyone. His whole life has been dedicated to serving others. This man is a pastor, for crying out loud!"

No one was listening.

Matt was allowed time with his client, and although he had much to discuss, he felt at a loss for words. "How are you holding up?"

"Not good, Matt. I'm scared. I'm confused. I may be in shock. I can't think."

"After the way they treated you, I believe it."

"What now?" Pat asked.

"Tell me about the arrest."

Pat told the story in terrifying detail. Matt could only assume faith was keeping the man from losing his mind.

"I have to ask you something, Pat. The marshals tell me they confiscated a large cache of weapons—*horde* was their word." He pulled a list from his briefcase. "A German-made Colt Sauer 30.06 bolt-action rifle and scope; a well-used Turkish-made Huglu double-barrel shotgun; and a Weatherby Vanguard 7 millimeter REM rifle with a Sightmark tactical laser target-acquisition device. In addition, they discovered three handguns, including a Browning 9 millimeter pistol, a Smith & Wesson .38, and a Glock G32 .357 Sig. They told me the Glock is a favorite of bank robbers and international terrorists. And there were dozens of boxes of ammunition of all types and calibers." He paused and studied Pat. "You own all these guns?"

"Well, yes. Gun collecting is a hobby. I suppose they didn't mention that Glocks are a favorite of law enforcement too? I took an interest in guns after an uncle took me target shooting when I was a boy. Like many men in my community, I hunt. Hunting is a licensed sport."

"The prosecution is going to have a good time with that, Pat. A gun that can kill a deer can kill a federal agent."

"I would never do that."

"Of course you wouldn't. I know that. You know that. But a jury? Well, who knows what they'll believe?"

"Some of the men from the church would go hunting or fishing. It was a way of bonding."

"Please, Pat, whatever you do, don't say that again."

"Why?"

"Because if I were prosecuting this case, I'd make the point that Christians like to bond over dead animals."

"That's not what I said."

"No, but it's what the jury will hear."

"Matt," Pat said, "you need to understand something about American history, the role of firearms, and the Second Amendment. Millions of law-abiding men and women own and lawfully use guns every day. You missed something in your upbringing on this. A Nashville jury will know that."

Matt smiled a little. "I guess I've got a lot to learn besides the facts of your case. However," he added as the smile turned to a frown, "it won't be a Nashville jury. They are going to take you across the Potomac for a trial in D.C."

When Matt made a motion for bond, the magistrate judge noted the weapons inventory, the lifetime imprisonment potential; and said that no amount of bond would be enough to ensure Pat's return. Matt then filed an emergency appeal of the magistrate's order, but that failed as well. He then appealed to the Court of Appeals for the D.C. Circuit and, much to his surprise, got a hearing but only because the arresting federal agents made a technical error in Pat's arrest: Pat had not been given a chance to make an appearance in Nashville before being transported to D.C. Perhaps on that basis, the court set a ten-million-dollar cash bond, which meant that Pat would be sitting right where he was until his case came up for trial.

The next day at his first meeting with Pat, since his client had been moved from the airport jail to a high security facility, Matt made a few things clear. "As you can see, we have an observer." He motioned to a guard a few feet away. "They won't let me meet with you alone. Supposedly, our conversation is secure, but I have doubts about that. Be careful what you say. Think before you speak. Got it?"

"Yes."

Matt quickly brought Pat up to date on the case. "This is like Daniel in the lion's den. Daniel 6:23: 'No wound was found on him, because he had trusted in his God.' It's important that you keep your faith up. I'm praying for you. I'm sure others are too."

"Thank you, but you might be the only one."

Matt heard a measure of strength in Pat's voice. He had a right to despair. He was isolated; denied all calls, mail, and media; and surrounded by dangerous men in the prison, yet he seemed to be gaining strength, and Matt considered that a miracle.

"Are you praying, Pat?"

Pat smiled. It was a forced smile, but a smile nonetheless. "I find I have plenty of time for prayer these days. Lately, I've been a little more coherent in my discussions with God. At times I feel a supernatural presence, a sense of peace, and a promise of God's mercy. But there are times when I'm in the darkest state of doubt and inner turmoil."

"Have you spoken to Becky?" Matt asked.

"Just once. I told her to protect the kids as much as possible. They don't need to be exposed to this."

"She should be by your side, Pat."

"No, I won't let her. She's confused and angry, but most of all she's frightened. I want her left alone."

Matt started to tell him that having Becky present might help the case but decided this wasn't the moment.

"You had hunting photos in the house. A couple of them have appeared on the front page of the *New York Times* and in *People* magazine. You're being called 'that gun-toting preacher from Tennessee.' They're reminding folks of the other Nashville preacher who killed a U.S. marshal."

"I wish I had gotten rid of those things."

"So do I, Pat. So do I."

Eventually Matt, after days of stonewalling by prosecutors, was able to interview some of the witnesses against his client. When he spoke to Bobby Douglas, he discovered that the young man faced criminal charges of his own and had made a deal with the prosecutors for a promise of leniency. Matt wasn't surprised. He had seen prosecutors use the threat of jail time to pressure less-than-honest witnesses to "give up a bigger fish." If the government used Bobby as a witness for the prosecution, all that would come out, along with the terms of the agreement. Matt might be able to impeach Bobby's testimony by showing that there had been a waiver of prosecution. But would it help?

To save his own skin, Bobby had told prosecutors everything he could think of that might help incriminate Pastor Pat. He said he had heard Pat in staff meetings verbally attacking women who had chosen to have an abortion. He said he had also witnessed Pat insulting people of other races and cultures. "One time we stopped at a bookstore," he said. "Pastor Pat went in to buy a book—*The ACLU v. America*, a work attacking the ACLU, as I recall—and there was this Hindu woman there—you know, with a spot on her forehead—standing in line in front of us at the register. Pastor Pat took one look at that woman and said, 'Don't you feel sorry for her, Bobby?' I'm sure she must have heard what he said. I thought that was insensitive."

"You told this to the prosecutors?" Matt asked.

"Of course." Matt suspected someone had been coaching Bobby. "Another time," Bobby told Matt, "Pastor Pat arranged for the men on the church staff to go hunting down near Chattanooga. I was shocked to see all the guns and ammunition he brought with him. He must have had a dozen guns. There were all kinds—great, big hunting rifles; two or maybe three shotguns; at least one pistol that I saw; and a bunch of knives. It looked like he was planning a war. This was just a couple of days after he had been attacking gays and lesbians from the pulpit."

"Bobby, don't you think you're being a little melodramatic? I'm certain you're exaggerating."

"No I'm not. I'm being straight up and honest."

Matt closed his eyes for a moment. "Bobby, I know the kind of crimes the prosecution is holding over your head. A man who fraudulently obtains credit cards using someone else's name and uses chat rooms to solicit young women can't call himself honest."

Bobby went white.

Matt knew the young youth worker felt helpless. The sad part was, so did Matt.

Buoyed by the progress they were making on so many fronts, John Knox Smith stepped up the attacks on other groups that refused to support the new government programs. One of the first targets was David Barclay's group, Nehemiah 217. The ministry took its name from the Old Testament book Nehemiah: "Come, let us rebuild the wall of Jerusalem, and we will no longer be in disgrace" (2:17). Barclay was well-known in Washington circles; he had even lectured on Capitol Hill as part of a forum for conservative congressmen. The preacher's claim that the beliefs of the founding fathers ought to influence how government decisions are made today incensed John.

As soon as they had Pat Preston locked up and safely behind bars, John sent his agents after Barclay, not just for hate crimes but for aiding and abetting intolerance and exclusionary behavior by focusing on the founders and pulling their ancient quotes out of context. "The founders said a thousand things about religion," John told his team, "but that doesn't prove a thing. It's different now. People like Barclay pose a threat to this nation that we can no longer accept. We cannot tolerate the intolerable."

An article by syndicated columnist Herb Roberts, published in the *Los Angeles Times*, expressed John's view well:

> Politicians running for office will say just about anything. They will use the Bible if they think that's what people want to hear. But it's a gimmick, a trick to get them elected.
>
> But even if there were people in those simpler times two centuries ago who attended church services and thought their religion was important, what difference would it make? That may have been the language they used then, but it's meaningless today.
>
> You can be certain that if the founders were here now, they wouldn't be using God talk. The only people who think that stuff makes any difference are hate mongers like David Barclay and his tribe, who want to divide us by compelling people to convert to their beliefs. It's long past time for that kind of intolerance to cease.

| CHAPTER TWENTY-FIVE |

John remained concerned about the reliability of federal judges. He and his staff spent weeks drafting a bill to present to their supporters in Congress, friends who could move new ethics legislation forward. If it became law, then the statute would prohibit any federal judge from belonging to or supporting any organization that advocated, taught, or promulgated any form of prohibited discrimination. With the Judicial Retirement and Expansion Act, this was important guidance in selecting new appointees.

By extension, no judge could belong to any club, community group, civic organization, or church that subscribed to a doctrine of exclusivity. As an added bonus, it also meant that no one would be able to claim that the Bible was literally true.

John knew resistance would rise from some parts of the country. To make sure the principle would be observed by every citizen, regardless of their personal beliefs, John arranged to have dinner with Chief Justice Isaiah Williams. John proposed to his friend that judges at all levels ought to be instructed on the importance of the new policy. "They must impose justice in every case, looking to existing case law wherever possible, but with fidelity to the letter of the law. Judges must enforce the law as rigidly as possible."

Williams nodded.

John took that to be a request for more information.

"To indicate the solidarity of the court system, I suggested that a new image be attached to the judicial robes of every judge in America to indicate solidarity with the policy and to symbolize the nation's commitment to tolerance. It would be a sign of equality and inclusion for all people and lifestyles."

Chief Justice Williams clearly loved the idea. "I've been considering a similar idea, John."

"One of my PR staff came up with a clever design." John pulled a small drawing from his pocket. "I think it is clear and professional, but subtle." He passed the drawing to Williams. "It's a navy blue equal sign on a black field."

"As a professional athlete, I spent most of my career with numbers and symbols on my jersey," Williams said, "so I'm all for it. To me this represents unity, equality, and respect. That's what a judge's robe ought to be about." Williams sipped his coffee. "I remember years ago when Chief Justice William Rehnquist surprised the Court by adding gold stripes to the sleeve of his robe." Williams studied the emblem. "When I first came to Washington, I toured the Holocaust Museum. I was struck by a photo in the exhibit. It was a picture of judges in prewar Germany. They displayed symbols of the Third Reich on their judicial robes."

"This is different," John said. "Their emblem came out of bigotry. Ours is the opposite. Our symbol stems from a desire to see justice for all Americans, including those forced to live on the fringe of our society."

"Yes, of course. I was just making conversation."

Later, when Chief Justice Williams presented the new design in a public forum, he said, "We believe in fairness and tolerance for all. The purpose of the law is the impartial imposition of equality and justice for every citizen. Today we're asking every federal judge and every state court judge, as a sign of their commitment to equality, to voluntarily append to their judicial robe this symbol, which represents the highest aspirations of the American people."

Support for the idea was enthusiastic. However, when it came to actually implementing it, there were judges who resisted the chief's request. Many judges were more than willing to resign their memberships in private clubs, professional associations, and even synagogues or churches, but for reasons that puzzled John, they resisted the new symbol and appealed for more time to consider their options.

An addendum was attached to legislation concerning judicial appropriations already before the House of Representatives. When the bill was passed by both houses of Congress and signed into law by the president, all federal, state, and local judges were required to affix the new symbol of equality to the right-hand sleeve of their robes, halfway between the wrist and the elbow.

There was no formal penalty prescribed for those who failed to make the change, but it was clear there would be eventual consequences for those who refused. Even so, there were a couple of conservative justices on the high court who adamantly resisted the change. They spoke out publicly about their concerns and in the process made themselves a nuisance to the Court, the Justice Department, and the administration.

Chief Justice Williams remarked to John, "Those two just don't get it, do they? They've created obstructions to many of our important initiatives. They ought to resign."

Justices Collins and Grouling were almost always in the minority on the Court's rulings, confined to writing angry dissents about original intent and other ancient ideas. Insisting on hanging on to their own interpretations of the Constitution, they invariably voted to block the progressive rulings of the Court. Now and then they convinced a couple of the moderate justices to cross over to their side, giving them the majority opinion, but such successes were rare.

When that happened, Chief Justice Williams made no secret of his contempt for Collins and Grouling. On one occasion he muttered under his breath, "Wouldn't it be unfortunate if something happened to those two clowns?"

A defense attorney overheard the comment and reported it. Williams quickly apologized for the remark. To show there were no hard feelings, he gave the two conservatives his blessing to make a weekend junket together during the Court's fall term, to take part in a conference in Houston on judicial restraint.

The Houston conference, held at the George Bush Presidential Library, was no ordinary speaking event. Justices Collins and Grouling responded to an invitation by two former presidents of the United States. Conference organizers assured them they could complete the trip and conference in an eight-hour day. With the chief's permission, they prepared their remarks and made arrangements to go.

One made the trip in a privately owned Gulfstream G550 for a quick in-and-out visit. A wealthy patron of the event arranged and paid for the business jet. At the controls were two former air force pilots, one of whom was a flight instructor and the other a former captain of Air Force One during a previous administration. Between them, these two high-ranking officers had more than forty years of flying experience. The other justice took a nonstop commercial flight into George Bush Intercontinental Airport.

The conference took place on a Saturday, but the justices didn't have time to stick around after their talks. It was a breach of custom for justices to fly together, but because of the nature of the event and the time constraints, they decided to do so anyway. On board the Gulfstream were the pilot, copilot, a security officer from the Court, and an aide. The flight to Houston had been quick and uneventful, and their speeches went off exactly as planned. Even though not everyone on the panel shared their views of the Constitution, the justices received a warm welcome and polite applause.

After both had completed their remarks, a driver took them by limousine to Hobby Airport, where they boarded the Gulfstream for the return flight to D.C.

Approximately eight minutes into the flight, the G550 developed engine trouble. The pilots took emergency precautions but weren't especially alarmed. In the history of Gulfstream, there had never been a fatal crash due to equipment failure. Nevertheless, the captain radioed the tower and reported problems with control and response. Then the radio went silent. Two minutes later the aircraft stalled and plunged to earth. All on board were lost.

Predictably, the crash of a private aircraft with two justices of the Supreme Court on board created a sensation in the press. It generated wall-to-wall commentary from television's talking heads. Horrified, conservatives in Congress insisted on a full-scale investigation, to which President Blaine agreed without hesitation. The remaining conservative talk radio hosts raised questions about whose agenda would benefit from foul play.

Clearly something was terribly wrong, but no one knew who to blame. Left-leaning interest groups and activists grew defensive, expressing outrage that anyone would suspect them of something so vile. To John, who had taken the day off at the last minute and gone to the Houston event to attend the conference without any of his aides or support staff, blame didn't matter. There were suddenly two new vacancies on the Court that needed to be filled. It was up to President Blaine to nominate the individuals to take their places.

John made sure information from the FAA and NTSB investigators came to his desk. He read each dispatch with interest, discussing the key events with his staff. When one report mentioned the discovery of a titanium memory stick in a restroom trash bin of the private aviation terminal in Houston, John made a call.

"What else can you tell me?" John asked the NTSB lead inspector on the other end of the phone.

"I prefer to leave the details for a later report, sir."

"As assistant attorney general, I'd like to hear it now." His calm delivery hid none of the heat in his words.

The investigator sighed. John gave him time to weigh his impossible choices.

"An airport janitor was doing a deep cleaning of one of the men's restrooms. While emptying one of the trash bins, he noticed the memory stick. Believe it or not, it was stuck to the back of the bin door above the plastic liner with a piece of gum."

"Someone was hiding it there?"

"Most likely it became stuck to the gum accidentally. The janitor said the bin was packed. You know how it is. Those restrooms are never cleaned enough."

"Go on," John prompted.

"The janitor is a kid working his way through college. He's into computers. He saw the memory stick and took it home."

"He took someone else's memory device home?"

"With all due respect, sir, it *had* been thrown away. The thing had been battered. It looks like someone had stomped on it, but those things are close to indestructible—especially the titanium-cased ones. That made us suspicious."

"If the janitor had it, how did you get it?"

"He plugged it into the USB port of his computer and discovered the thing still worked. It contained technical files on the G550 Gulfstream—the kind of files used by aircraft mechanics. He put two and two together. The two justices died in a Gulfstream G550. Like a good boy, the kid brought it to us. There is no reasonable or innocent explanation for this data being in that location."

John tightened his jaw. "This implies premeditated murder."

"It certainly could be, sir. The coincidence is a little too large to ignore."

"Your earlier reports mention a software malfunction on the aircraft. Does this fit with that scenario?"

"Yes, sir. The black box and cockpit recorder all indicate a software glitch." The investigator paused. "I'm afraid that happens sometimes. Today's aircraft are flown by software. Unfortunately, pilots are becoming too dependent on the computer. There have been a few cases in which accidents occurred while the pilots were trying to reprogram the computer when they should have been looking out the window."

"What's your best guess?"

"We think someone messed with the software, which led to the crash."

John grew impatient with the investigator's vague language. One thing he loved about law was its dependence on precision in oral and written communication. "By 'messed with,' you mean what?"

"Someone programmed the computer to fail."

John's heart beat in double time. "Keep me informed." He hung up and stared at the smooth surface of his desk.

Because the openings on the Court occurred during the busy term, the president's closest advisers, Attorney General Stamper and Chief Justice Williams, suggested that he nominate replacements either from the appellate court system or the Department of Justice. One name on everyone's lips was former federal judge Arthur James Lincoln, who had a distinguished career in the DOJ. Over the previous two and a half years, Judge Lincoln had been tapped on several occasions as a policy adviser to John Knox Smith and the DTED legal team. Before that he had been a judge on the D.C. Circuit and had once clerked for Justice Hadley Brown on the Supreme Court.

The second person receiving near unanimous acclaim was Miriam Lacey McKeegan from the 9th Circuit Court in San Francisco. Prior to her appointment to the bench, McKeegan had served as deputy administrator for compliance at the EPA and had been a professor of reconciliation studies at the University of California at Santa Cruz. She had received a joint J D and Ph D from the University of Pennsylvania and a bachelor's degree in sociology from Rutgers. Her domestic partner, Rosslyn Mirsky, was dean of music at Palisades School of the Arts in San Jose.

McKeegan's credentials were impeccable, and the fact that she was a fairly new appellate judge appealed to President Blaine. Chief Justice Williams and the other members of the Court privately concurred. Miriam Lacey McKeegan was a legendary figure who had already made a name for herself as one of the major advocates of the "kindness doctrine." In due course, both Lincoln and McKeegan received a "qualified" rating by the American Bar Association and were confirmed almost unanimously by the Senate.

With the new justices, the Alliance saw nothing but black clouds on the legal horizon and engagement in confrontation after confrontation with the Justice Department. Alliance head Scott Freeman and his associates challenged the use of foreign law in proceedings of federal courts. It was obvious that all three branches of government—executive, judicial, and legislative—were looking to European courts for both language and philosophy to incorporate into their new policies. The Alliance protested strongly on the grounds that this was unconstitutional and dangerous to the statutory rights of every citizen. To make their case, Alliance lawyers were in the process of building a super-coalition to confront the practice, but they wouldn't go unchallenged.

To counter resistance from certain groups, to educate the newest members of the Supreme Court, and to rally support for all the initiatives the administration was pushing at that time, President Blaine decided to make these issues a centerpiece in his State of the Union Address. To give credibility to his plans, he invited dozens of distinguished academics from America's top universities to be present in the Senate gallery on that occasion.

John hung on every word of the address, which he had helped write. In his speech, the president said,

> There are some people in this country, including some who happen to run taxpayer-subsidized nonprofit organizations, who would say that seventeenth-century concepts of national sovereignty are essential. What does that really mean? The fact is, the United States today is part of an international family of nations, a worldwide brother- and sisterhood of like-minded peoples. This is not 1776, the age of worldwide slavery, violent wars, and religious hatred.
>
> Borders, frontiers, and nationalistic barriers divide us, and this has been a source of conflict for centuries. The ancient concept of "sovereignty" that so many pushed is a seventeenth-century notion that reeks of xenophobia and bias. I would suggest that in this century we can do better. We can put that ancient conceit behind us.

One of the only things boundaries have accomplished, both physically and emotionally, is to promote sectarian strife. Some of our religious organizations have done this by creating walls of separation where they do not belong and tearing down ones that do. Frankly, such actions amount to nothing short of bigotry. I assure you these old tactics are not within the statutory purview of my administration. What I propose is a new climate of cooperation.

Father Jerome Filcher is one clergyman who understands the problem. He said in a recent television address, "We need to get real! We've got to join the family of nations." I say, "Amen." But I would also add, in unison with many of our distinguished guests who are here tonight from some of our great universities, that we need to join the community of persons.

Every day our courts discover new ways of framing age-old issues of community. They're not doing this is in isolation; they're consulting the latest rulings from Europe, Africa, Asia, and the Middle East; and have found a rich storehouse of wisdom. Constitutions from nations as diverse as Kosovo, Germany, Estonia, and South Africa can offer us a wealth of new insights.

Our neighbors in Canada had the foresight in 1982 to establish a Charter of Rights and Freedoms that protects people of all persuasions from insults and slurs. Where have we been? Why haven't we done at least that much?

Today I'm asking Congress to develop new legislation in order to begin a new era of cooperation and understanding. We want to ensure that every woman in America will have access to the full range of mental health services, that no one will be subjected to institutional bigotry or discrimination based on their genetic or racial identity.

As we look at examples from abroad, we are pleased to know that all of the international accords make it clear that some forms of speech must be controlled. Yes, we believe in free speech within reasonable limits. But as a civilized nation we also understand—better now than ever before— that hateful and hurtful speech is never free and cannot be allowed.

Tonight I am announcing the creation of a memorial to the victims of hate, bigotry, and intolerance. In other countries there are memorials of marble, bronze, or stone to the victims of persecution. As we know, Germany has erected a magnificent stone memorial to the thousands of LGBT individuals who suffered at the hands of the Nazis. I want to propose another kind of memorial, not of marble or stone, but of respect, decency, and law.

Accordingly, I have asked Congress to review, systematically and intentionally, our laws and administrative procedures to eliminate any evidence of bias, discrimination, and bigotry toward any group. Part of that review will include a new initiative to provide reparations, not to the descendants of slaves as has been proposed in years past, but to individuals who have actually endured persecution, humiliation, and pain because of the hatred and intolerance of the few.

Many of these individuals have been denied the right to achieve their full personhood because of their sexual identity. Some have suffered physical abuse, incarceration, curses, marriage denials, and personal embarrassment for merely being who their god and genetics made them to be. To express our deepest sorrow and our desire to make recompense, my administration has proposed a compensation package of not less than ten thousand dollars for each person who has suffered in this way.

Representative Frank Burnside of Massachusetts has introduced HR-333 for this purpose. I hope all members of Congress will sign on to this important legislation. There will be some, I'm sure, who will say we can't afford it; but I say we can't afford to wait any longer. Let history record that 'we, the people of the United States' were not too small or too self-centered to admit our mistakes and make things right.

President Blaine shifted the focus of his address to the exercise of state's rights to do more than seize property.

The language of the founders expressed the beliefs of their era and was never meant to be an obstacle for future generations. The Ninth and Tenth Amendments, which some use to restrict the rights of the government, mean very little today. We don't need to live by the standards of an earlier age.

When this administration adopted the International Treaty on the Rights of the Child in 2013, we were thinking ahead about what we wanted this nation to look like in the future. Every child should have the right to grow up in a world that is safe and free of hatred and intolerance.

This treaty makes it clear that every child will have the right to choose certain things about the way he or she is reared, about how he or she is treated at home, how he or she is educated, and what sort of religious instruction he or she receive. It is unacceptable for any parent to force his or her child to go to an institution that teaches bigotry and hatred.

If the biological parents of any child show themselves to be intolerant, bigoted, and a danger to themselves and others, it is only fitting that government should step in, take those children, and make sure they're safely placed so they are raised in a family that will provide the nurture and encouragement every child needs—and to do so in an atmosphere of tolerance and respect.

It is the responsibility of all Americans to make sure our children are raised in ways that allow them to become productive members of society rather than a threat to everyone they meet.

It was clear to John that the threat the White House feared most was the influence of intolerant religious leaders. According to the Endangered Childhood Protection and Training Initiative proposed by the president, the first thing the state would be asked to do was to get the children of Bible-thumpers out of the house before the children could be permanently damaged by the repressive dogma of their parents, pastors, and teachers. These people would lose their children, and church members who stood in the way would lose theirs as well.

John thought Blaine's speech was excellent.

Matt Branson watched the State of the Union address while eating dinner in his home with his wife, Michelle. Holding a plate of pasta in one hand and fork in the other, he consumed his meal while he sat on his sofa, the image of Blaine playing on his big-screen television. Each minute of the speech removed more of Matt's appetite. By the end, he felt ill. He set his dish on the coffee table. He looked at Michelle. There were tears in her eyes.

"Tell me I didn't hear that," Michelle said.

"I wish I could, babe. I really wish I could."

Larry Jordan sat in his home alone, pretending to listen to the news anchors tell him what he had already heard. Marla sat next to him. They didn't speak. Larry slipped from the sofa, went to his office, knelt, and fervently began to pray.

Pat Preston sat alone in his cell.

| CHAPTER TWENTY-SIX |

John monitored reaction to the State of the Union. As expected, there were protests in some places on the children's placement issue. But almost nothing was mentioned on the sovereignty issue. It was either too complicated or too remote for most people to care about. In a couple of towns, some small protest groups took to the streets. The Secret Service ramped up protection for the president. John was receiving reports of increased threats to members of Congress and the president. Trouble also brewed on another front in John's hometown of Colorado Springs, where Bishop Thomas Laroca—fully aware of DTED's earlier seizure of a small number of faith-based hospitals—said in a public forum that he would not allow Catholic hospitals to perform what the government euphemistically called "the full range of health services," meaning abortion, "sex-reassignment" operations, therapy to overcome homophobia, euthanasia where permitted by state law, and the like.

"I will not close our hospitals down. I will not bend to government pressure to force doctors and nurses of faith to do what is offensive to God. If the government wants to arrest me, they know how to find me."

Most Catholic hospitals were independent corporations under the direction of a board of directors composed of both clergy and civic leaders. The bishop could appoint people to the boards of directors, and in some cases he might serve on the board himself. But the Catholic Church had no formal role in the staffing or management of those hospitals. However, the hospitals under Bishop Thomas Laroca still worked under the "old system," in which hospitals were directly accountable to the local diocese.

Laroca had previously assumed direct management of the facility, quoting Pope John Paul II: "Freedom consists not in doing what we like, but in having the freedom to do what we ought." The threats and intimidation from his state governor's office became more intense, but the bishop held his ground.

"Our beliefs, which are based on Scripture, are very clear. The purpose of our hospital is to revere and protect life, not to end it prematurely or provide material assistance to evil. The community needs us, but we will not conform to destructive directives. The only way our hospitals will be closed down is if the government chains the front door."

Bishop Laroca, as his named implied, was a rock. No matter the cost, he refused to compromise on these core principles. He said, "That's not how the scales of God's justice operate. There's no equivalency between God's laws and the laws of a corrupt society." Predictably, the press excoriated him for his remarks.

Another uncompromising clergyman, Bishop Daniel Grace, had stood against the abortion industry for many years. He was an outspoken critic of the compromises that had taken place in the state of Indiana, but what got him into trouble with the DTED was his strong support for a young parish priest in Fort Wayne who had denied communion to the state's governor. When the media and others in the community began complaining about the priest's hate speech and behavior, the bishop wrote a letter defending the priest's position and commending his courage. He laid out the concerns of the church in the diocesan newsletter, which the secular media picked up.

Shortly after the letter appeared in a point-counterpoint in the *Indianapolis Star*, the bishop and the local priest were notified that they were being sued for hate speech and libel with a demand for millions of dollars in damages. The bishop's letter was the centerpiece of a proposed hate speech prosecution to be brought by the DTED with assistance from the ACLU and other equality groups.

At issue was the denial of communion to Governor Rachel Stenson at her home church in Fort Wayne, even though she claimed she was an observant Catholic. The priest said that since she was an outspoken advocate of abortion at any stage of pregnancy and had personally ordered state funds be used to finance abortions for women in prison, the church considered her to be out of fellowship with the Catholic Church and its teachings.

When a reporter from the *Indianapolis Star* approached the bishop, he gave the young man permission to quote from portions of the letter to his pastoral flock without realizing the potential consequences. It was only later that he realized he had made a grave mistake under federal law by allowing a public newspaper to use any part of it. He had the impression they only wanted to mention the letter or to print a short excerpt—that was all the reporter had ever mentioned to him—but they printed every word. The bishop said he had nothing to hide and stood by his beliefs. But when the *Star* published the letter, it became a national scandal, and both he and the governor were embarrassed. The bishop had used Bible verses and passages of the catechism to describe the governor's spiritual failings, and that became the basis of the lawsuit.

When John Knox Smith first read the internal reports describing the case, he was livid. He launched into an expletive-filled tirade that lasted for twenty minutes. He emerged from his office, red-faced with his hair askew, yelling for Andrea.

Andrea met him in the hall and convinced him to let her walk him back to his office. She was clearly worried about his enraged use of profanity and visible displays of temper.

"You're frightening the staff, John." She poured a fresh cup of coffee for him. "Want to talk about it?"

"Talk. I want to do more than talk—"

"Easy, John. It won't do to have a man of your stature in the DOJ making threats."

John took a deep breath. "Okay." He sat down and pulled close the report that had lit his fuse "It's this Stenson thing."

"Governor Stenson?" Andrea prompted softly.

John brought her up to speed and said, "I feel bad for her. Think of the embarrassment." He closed his eyes. "I went to law school with her. President Blaine campaigned for her when she first ran for the Indiana Senate." He looked at his aide. "She was going to run for the U.S. Senate next year, and this condescending bigot is trying to publicly excoriate her. He knows she has the power to shut people like him down. That's what's behind this. We need her vote in the Senate."

"This keeps her from running?" Andrea asked.

"I don't know. I doubt it. It's just . . . it's just that I am sick of these self-righteous, religious nutcases ruining everyone's lives. The idea that this woman is being attacked by a so-called 'man of the cloth' makes me ill."

"Sounds to me like you have a case against the priest and the church." Andrea grinned. "If you can't prevent these things, John, then you can comfort yourself with revenge."

John chuckled. "That, Andrea, is why you're the best assistant a man could ever have."

When announcing his intention to prosecute the offending bishop, John told the *Washington Post*, "If people like the bishop want to practice cannibalistic rites and exclude progressive members of society, they should go right ahead, but they had better do so in the privacy of their own homes."

John watched Reneé X shake with anger. "Is it in the public interest to allow any ministry to exist in America, to use our airwaves or anything else that violates the public trust by claiming they have a corner on truth?" She flashed a picture on the conference room monitor showing the archbishop of Kansas City. "This man is the perfect example of what's wrong with America. He claims to have the truth on his side. He's the head of the antichoice brigades in that place—a sworn enemy of the people."

"The bishop is being defended by a public interest law firm," Joel Thevis said.

Reneé exploded. "They may call themselves that, but it's not in the public interest to grant privileges to an organization that promulgates a doctrine of bias and exclusion. Any group that claims to have the corner on truth ought to have their public entitlements stripped away."

"I agree, Reneé," John said. "The only reason the government granted churches tax-exempt status in the first place was to keep the peace—to keep those rednecks off the streets and out of the way. You're absolutely right. It is not in the public interest for a bishop to scandalize a highly respected public servant like in Indiana. All Rachel Stenson ever did was to stand up for the rights of women and minorities. How dare some monkey in a clerical collar make an example of her! All these right-wing bishops have to go."

Special Agent Bob Maas leaned forward to get the group's attention. "Words can kill, John, and not just statements by hotheaded priests. Columns written by people advocating hate should not be allowed in the newspapers in the first place. We're tracking what's being said on television and radio. Before long we'll be going after what's said on the Internet. We need to get the Commerce Department and the FCC into the act to help shut these people down. We need emergency power over the Internet. If the media won't cooperate with us, we may have to shut them down as well."

Joel looked puzzled. "Hold on a second, Bob. Reneé's legal theories on tax exemption are as unfounded as this media thing. Congress never had the power to regulate churches until we got some modern court rulings changing all that. As to the media, we are not authorized to go after the media. Don't you think that's a little strong?"

"The media uses aspects of commerce for distribution," John explained. "Any communication that promotes bigotry and intolerance, whether by wireless transmission, phone lines, cable systems, fiber optics, or even private e-mails, is a legitimate concern. They operate in the public interest, Joel. I will not allow any organization that impedes our ability to prosecute cases to stand in our way. So far, a lot of folks in the media have been our friends, but Bob's right. If the news media can't be trusted, we will shut those segments down."

"That bishop's newspaper article was clearly a violation of the law," Maas interjected. "Legally, it should never have been distributed. If he wanted to print off a few copies for his personal use, for his parishioners, or for something of that sort, that's one thing. But he can't use the mail or the Internet or any other entity the government regulates for that purpose."

"This was where the Christian Family Forum hit the skids," John said. "There are a lot more ministries of that type we need to be going after."

"They're doing it the right way in Canada," Reneé added. "In Canada they screen the programs of hate groups for offensive material before they're broadcast. If the commission decides the content of a program is unsuitable, they either make them edit the content or shut them down. It's as simple as that. That's what we need to be doing."

After a thoughtful pause, John said, "I believe you're on to something, Reneé. This is exactly what we need with this 'exclusionist' thing. We've been wrestling with the law on prior restraint. Anyone trying to claim they have the only truth needs to be off the air. We can give them the option of changing the message or closing their doors. It's perfectly clear that any such claims must not be mailed or broadcast or published in any form, and the media should not be allowed to quote their contents."

"Your Alliance buddies won a big case in the Ninth Circuit a few years ago called *Canyon Ferry Baptist*," Joel said. "Let me read a section of the decision you need to get overturned to move ahead. 'An unregulated, unregistered press is important to our democracy,'" Joel read. "'So are unregulated, unregistered churches. Churches have played an important—no, an essential—part in the democratic life of the United States. The liberals who applaud their outcomes and live in their light forget the motivation that drove the champions of freedom. They approve religious intervention in the political process selectively: it's great when it's on their side. In a secular age, freedom of speech is more talismanic than freedom of religion. But the latter is the first freedom in our Bill of Rights. It is in terms of this first freedom that this case should be decided.'"

John sat motionless for a moment. "I'm familiar with the *Canyon Ferry Baptist* case, Joel. It's nearly a decade old. Things have changed.

We changed them and we'll change them a lot more." The room chilled to silence. "Sometimes I wonder whose side you are on."

"I started on our side and my loyalties haven't changed, John. I'm just saying that it's all going to come back to the First Amendment."

John stood to indicate the meeting was over, and he looked at Joel. "If we were doing things correctly, Mr. Thevis, the messages from the Indiana and Kansas City bishops would never have been heard in the first place. We've achieved a lot over the last few years, but we still have a long way to go. It's time to turn up the heat."

As John was closing his notebooks and gathering his papers, Andrea came into the room and placed a handwritten document on the table in front of him. "What's this?" John asked.

"Intel," she said.

"Intel from whom?"

"The White House." She closed the door. "I have a good friend in the West Wing. She called a few minutes ago to give me a heads-up. She told me that someone had called this morning, apparently on behalf of a group of big shot Catholic and Orthodox bishops and priests, scheduling a meeting with President Blaine."

"I don't like the sound of this."

"The group wants to express their concern about something you've been saying, John. She told me the chief of staff told the guy who called—who she believes was an assistant to Cardinal Wyeth in New York—that the president's calendar was full, so he wouldn't have time to meet with them. But the caller had some senators and they insisted. He said they wouldn't take no for an answer."

"Get to the point, Andrea; I have a full day. This is about something I said?"

"Yes. The president agreed to a meeting with five big-name members of the clergy for an hour next Thursday. You're the subject of the agenda."

John hesitated. "Okay, so what's the issue?"

"You were quoted in the *Post* as saying Christians are cannibals—'cannibalistic rites.' Remember that? They've taken offense at that. And they brought up something else you said on CNN more than a year ago, that Christians are involved in blood sacrifices. They said . . ." She paused. "Now, John, this is them talking, not me, so don't shoot the messenger. They said the guy running an agency to prosecute hate speech is guilty of the same crimes he's supposed to be preventing." She hesitated then added, "It sounds like they're going after your job on those anti-communion and Jesus-on-the-cross remarks. They say your attack on the Holy Eucharist invades the province of what a religion can believe in violation of the separation of church and state."

"Are you kidding me? I don't believe this!" He stared at Andrea. "Okay, this is good. Here's what I want you to do. Get in touch with our friend out on the West Coast—the Catholic college president I met at the Human Rights Campaign last year—and tell him what's happening. We need some words. I'm going to have to write a letter apologizing to those preachers and also to Cardinal Wyeth to get this thing off the table. We want to head this off before their meeting with Blaine; then we want this thing to go away."

"What do you want me to say, John?"

"Tell him I would be grateful if he would draft something for me, a letter with all the bells and whistles and religious mumbo jumbo—he'll know what I mean—to mollify these guys. I don't want to come right out and say I was wrong, but say that I apologize for any offense my comments may have given, and I will avoid anything of the sort in the future. Got it? We'll doll it up and grovel a bit, but with any luck maybe we can head them off at the pass. How can they refuse to forgive me? It's their job to do so. What do you think?"

She looked up at her boss with emotion. "John, you are brilliant. I thought this was going to get nasty, but as always, you have the answers."

John smiled. "If we can pull this one off, we'll keep the slate clean with Blaine and send those jackals back to their dens. Now let's get back to work."

| CHAPTER TWENTY-SEVEN |

Ever since Mike Alden's report on the Madisonians had circulated through the DOJ, John had been working overtime to bring the full weight of the government down on Scott Freeman, Larry Jordan—especially Larry Jordan—and their associates at the Alliance. As Alden had said at the outset, Alliance lawyers and Madisonians were everywhere, especially in D.C. and New York. John was shocked to see how many cases the Alliance had won over the years, how they had dethroned the once-invincible ACLU, and now how often they had stymied his own litigators.

To turn the tide, John wanted to launch an all-out campaign to evict them, not just the ones inside the DOJ, but in Congress, the Blaine administration, and the media. He wanted to go after their pro bono lawyers scattered hither and yon, and he ultimately wanted their licenses pulled. He met privately with like-minded colleagues in other agencies and departments to flesh out his plans. His internal PR team began transmitting sensitive tips and news leads to their contacts in the media to make sure word got out about their version of what the Alliance had been doing. "By defending religious bigotry," John said, "these people are undermining the most basic guarantees of a free society."

The orchestrated attack and flurry of new challenges from the government and the press had an immediate impact. Suddenly, funding for the Alliance's legal work became a major concern. Some donors were scared off by rumors in the print and broadcast media that the group's corporate charter was being challenged, along with half dozen allied 501(c)(3) policy groups and law firms. Donors feared being targeted for their contributions to an organization that was suddenly in DTED's bull's-eye with the ACLU and other watchdog groups breathing down their necks.

The Alliance board of directors stood strong under the pressure, but some members who served on the boards of other ministries expressed concern.

Larry Jordan spoke to his boss by phone and wondered if John Knox Smith had the phone tapped. Larry wanted to fly to Chicago and meet with Scott Freeman, head of the Alliance. It would be good to share a meal with his mentor and friend, but Larry's caseload kept him rooted in D.C.

"Several groups are facing the same threats we are," Freeman said. "They're having trouble staying afloat. The costs of litigation, not to mention staff salaries, keep going up, up, up."

"Contributions are drying up?" Larry sat at the wide but simple maple desk in his office. The window shades were drawn. He had learned in college that he worked and thought better in a darker environment.

"Contributors are getting nervous. There's a rumor floating around that groups like ours are losing status as a corporation. I've spent the last week sending out e-mails to our largest contributors, pacifying grant providers, praying with some of them, and trying to keep cash flowing."

"Are you hearing anything back?"

"Everyone thinks it's an uphill battle and that we're slipping back down the slope."

"Of course it's an uphill battle," Larry sad. "When hasn't it been uphill?"

"I'm holding telephone conversations with key people around the country. We talk at least once a month. I'm doing a fair amount of teleconferencing."

"I hate to sound paranoid, Scott, but phone and video links are not all that secure."

"In our business paranoia is a needed skill. I'm being careful. Some things have to be handled face-to-face."

"Well, I'm still handling cases here in D.C. Every day seems to bring a dozen new requests. Truth is, Scott, I need a lot more money and a lot more help."

Scott fell silent for a moment, and Larry heard him sigh. "Here's the real reason I called, Larry. You know the IRS paid us a visit recently."

"I heard."

"They took six years of files. Our books are clean, so they will have trouble finding anything to make trouble about. All the money spent on the outside auditors is paying off. Still, it's eating up my time. And—I hate to admit this—I'm going to have to let some of our staff go. We can no longer pay everyone. Some of these people have been with us for twenty years. We are not crushed, but we have been knocked back on our heels. I can't give you any more resources."

Freeman's words were a body punch to Larry. "I pray for you every day, Scott."

"And I pray for you. We have not been beaten, nor will we give up. I'm prepared to fight until God takes me home."

"I'm with you, Scott," Larry said.

"I know you are. In the end it may be two old birds flapping our wings at what's going on, but we will be heard. How goes the Preston case?"

"Slow. Much too slow. The man is being punished, and he hasn't been convicted of anything yet. I'm working with Matt Branson, who represents Preston. He's a good man. Sharp. Dedicated. Money is a problem for him too."

"Money is always a problem. I'm afraid there isn't much more we can do financially for the man, not until things turn around. Do you think Branson will stick with the case?"

"I do," Larry said. "He left his job with the DOJ to take the case. He's committed. He's trying to build a private practice while helping his friend. He let it slip that his father is providing financial assistance to keep him off the street."

"Is he married?"

"He is and has a two-year-old daughter. His wife has taken part-time work to help out."

Freeman groaned. "I wish we could do more."

"So do I, Scott."

To Matt, Pat's situation looked impossible except through the eyes of faith. He had been indicted and jailed pending trial; his lawyer had only been given the barest disclosure of facts. Matt couldn't find out a fraction of what was going on, and he was getting desperate. The Alliance had given him all the help they could, but with the donor base on the verge of drying up, the resources Scott Freeman and Larry Jordan could offer were of little use. They had other cases to worry about, and Matt couldn't hope for much more. Several allied lawyers were doing legal research and writing on a volunteer basis.

At the point of Matt's deepest despair, something amazing happened. A distinguished older gentleman had gone to the federal detention center in Arlington, Virginia, and asked to see Preston. Because of his former stature in the justice system, officials granted him permission to visit Pat in his cell with an officer present. After that short visit, the gentleman placed a call to Matt and asked for a meeting to discuss the structure and strategies of the defense team.

It was an unusual situation. While Matt, Larry, and the small group of Alliance lawyers were doing their best to prepare for trial, they discovered they would have the assistance of a distinguished former jurist, who not only had substantial personal wealth but also the motivation to help field a proper defense. When Matt put all the pieces together, he concluded that it was nothing short of a miracle.

The gentleman, Judge Nestor Holloway, was very forthcoming about himself. The elderly man was the first federal judge to refuse to wear the sign of equality on his robe. He had made no waves with his dissention. He had given no interviews. No one knew why he had stepped down. He had just retired, and many assumed that at his age health issues were involved. But Matt learned that his decision went deeper than that.

Lawyers who had tried cases before Judge Nestor Holloway agreed that he was the kindest, gentlest, most considerate man on any bench—unless you got on his bad side. If an attorney failed to respect the office of a federal judge, he would come to regret it.

Throughout his fifty-year career, Judge Holloway had relied very little on law clerks. He did most of his own research. He had several library tables in his private office, all of them covered with good, old-fashioned printed books. He read voraciously and was a fountain of legal knowledge with an encyclopedic grasp of jurisprudence. He had lectured on the history of Western law at George Washington University and could quote passages from the writings of Livy and Tacitus in English or Latin, the Magna Carta, the Charter of New England, the Constitution, the Federalist Papers, and dozens of Supreme Court rulings. He could do so at great length and with remarkable humor.

Matt thought of Judge Holloway as a Renaissance man who could have been an actor had he been so inclined. He had some interesting habits that amused the young lawyers who visited his chambers. Holloway always had a dozen or more books on his reading table, each marked at the place where he had stopped reading. One attorney Matt interviewed told how he had gone into the judge's chambers to argue a point of law with opposing counsel when he noticed several blue stubs protruding from the pages of the books. When Holloway had to step from the chambers for a few moments, the lawyer had opened one of the books to see what the judge was using as a bookmark. He saw Judge Holloway's government paycheck. He counted ten uncashed paychecks stuffed into the books on the table and was amazed to know that the government still actually issued paper checks.

Another attorney Matt interviewed claimed the judge was so old-fashioned that he loved the look, feel, and smell of books; and had kept a complete set of leather-bound Supreme Court decision casebooks in his study even though no practicing attorney had used anything but digital resources for case law research in years.

Holloway was Ivy League educated. He had relished his position of influence, but, as he confessed to Matt, he didn't need the job. He had inherited a substantial fortune. He had been wealthy man before he finished his law degree but had continued his education and the practice of law. As he aged, he had become more impatient with the nonsense coming from the government. He detested the pride and arrogance of the politically correct young law clerks coming to him from all the "hot" schools. The recent order to modify his judicial robes had been more than he could take, so he had taken retirement at the top of a long and distinguished career.

"What I'm about to tell you, young man, I've never told anyone else."

Matt and the judge sat in an upscale coffee house a few blocks from Matt's D.C. office. The placed buzzed with activity, but soon the hubbub faded behind the words of the elderly man drinking an espresso.

"I understand, sir."

"When I retired, I tried my hand at golf and playing cards with friends. It's all nonsense and a profound waste of time. Three weeks into my retirement I was awash in boredom. Have I told you about my wife?"

The sudden change of subject threw Matt off. "Um, no sir."

"Betty. That's her name. The most organized person I've ever met. When we first met she was working in a law firm, filing and organizing official regulations and legal updates. I guess that's where she became so enamored with organization."

"It's not a bad quality, sir."

"I suppose not. I was in my library a while back, searching for something to feed my mind. I came across a series of binders on the shelf. They held newsletters from the Alliance—the people helping you with the Reverend Preston case. It seems my wife had been sending them money for some time."

"Without your knowledge, sir?"

"Yes, but that's no problem. She has her own money, and she is free to do with it what she wishes. That's not my point. I began reading the newsletters. She had a decade of these newsletters." He chuckled. "She's a collector, that one." He took a sip of the strong coffee. "Anyway, I spent hours reading the material. Of course, it's illegal to send newsletters like those now."

"What do you think of the Alliance's material?"

"It disturbed me greatly. Not because they were writing about such things, but because such things needed to be written out. Do you follow me?"

"Yes, sir. I believe so."

"I came to see that, as part of the system, I had been involved in the suppression of free speech. I didn't see it that way at the time, but my thinking has cleared and I'm old enough to look my mistakes square in the eye."

"Not many men can do that, sir."

"I've never been a religious man, Branson. Never took it seriously, but those articles stirred up something in me. I became curious. I'm still searching, still learning, but one thing I know—it's time I became more involved in fighting the new injustices. I want to help you and Preston."

"That's very kind of you, sir."

"Understand this: I'm not here to take the case from you. I offer my experience, influence, and money. I assume you could use more money for the case."

"Yes, sir, we could. The Alliance has been generous, but they've gone as far as they can."

"My name still carries a lot of weight in this town. Don't be afraid to use it. Maybe when this is all over, we will have a little more understanding about the meaning of truth and human dignity."

"Yes, sir. I'm sure we will."

| CHAPTER TWENTY-EIGHT |

Four months later

I t had taken weeks of planning, studying, rehearsing, and preparing by the entire staff to get John ready for his trip to Italy, but at last he was about to leave for what would surely be the biggest and most important speaking opportunity of his life. He was going to make a presentation to a room full of some of the most distinguished international scholars, diplomats, policy makers, and political leaders in the world.

Andrea pulled the plans together and made the arrangements for travel, accommodations, and entertainment, including a day trip to the Uffizi Palace and galleries, and a boat ride and candlelight dinner on the Arno River. The itinerary pleased John. He was delighted to be getting away from Washington for a while, and it would be a special pleasure to have the three team members who had been most helpful to him—Paul, Reneé, and Andrea—along on the journey. It was a bonus for all of them.

John read over his presentation several times and was satisfied that it would meet all the expectations of the host committee. It was academic without being ponderous, informative without undue boasting, and even had dashes of humor sprinkled here and there. The speech chronicled John's efforts from his arrival in Washington as part of the attorney general's honors program in 2009 and showed how the legal environment in this country had changed so positively for equality over such a short time. He designed it to be an optimistic presentation, focusing on enforcement issues and the implementation process, which were at the heart of transformative justice. With minor changes his paper survived the review processes at the White House, the Department of State, and the DOJ. He was certain it would open new doors for the division and for him.

In order to make sure his wardrobe was complete and that all the travel details were in order, John decided to take an extra day to get ready for the trip. He suggested that Reneé and Paul do the same. Andrea would need to go in on Monday to monitor his calls, but he was sure she wouldn't mind. For his team leaders, however, a three-day weekend would be helpful. They would have the rest of the week in the office and plenty of time to take care of last-minute business before heading to the airport Saturday morning.

However, the news John received when he arrived at the office on Tuesday was not good. Joel Thevis met him at the fifth-floor elevators, and he looked nervous. He avoided John's eyes. "It's not going to work."

"What's not going to work?"

"The Preston case. Chock full of holes. I've been over all the indictments. I've gone back over the procedures several times, from the 302s all the way down the line, and the charges won't hold water. They'll never stick in a court of law. We made major blunders."

John nodded politely at the men and women from other departments who were getting off the elevators, then seized his lead attorney by the arm and led him to his private office. He shoved Joel over the threshold and closed the door behind him. "Are you telling me you've screwed up this case? Are you telling me you've failed on the most important prosecution this division has undertaken? Are you—?"

"Stop!" Joel shouted. "John, please stop." Moving quickly to the other side of the table, he said, "Out of 119 charges against Reverend

Preston, I believe we can get convictions on no more than fifteen, maybe sixteen." He held out his hand with several sheets of paper dangling from his fingers. "Here. See for yourself. It's full of holes."

Someone tapped on the door.

"What? Come in!"

Andrea opened the door and slipped in. Reneé and Paul followed.

"John?" Andrea asked. "Is everything okay?"

"Does it sound like everything's okay?" He raised a hand as if directing himself to slow down. He inhaled, loosened his tie, walked to the corner window, and stared at the traffic in the street. A long moment later, he said, "Sit down. All of you. Joel, you can stand. Our lead attorney has just been telling me that we've screwed up the Preston case. We can't get convictions on . . . what was it, Joel, a hundred counts?"

"One hundred and three of the original hundred and nineteen are flawed."

Paul and Reneé looked at each other and said almost simultaneously, "Are you kidding?"

Joel shook his head. "No. I wish I were."

"Has this been verified?" Paul asked.

"I've checked it," Joel said. "I had a friend who is the leading brief writer for the Court of Appeals on evidentiary issues look at it, and he agrees. We can make the case and probably win on perhaps fifteen counts, but most of these are full of prosecutorial errors. They're dismissals in the making. There was too much energy in this case; people got carried away."

"Carried away? Professionals got carried away? By what, Joel? What could cause a screwup of this magnitude?"

"Chaos. Zeal. Weariness of technicians. Maybe a dozen other factors."

"I'm not following," Paul said. "What happened?"

Joel rubbed the back of his neck. "It's involved and a little complicated."

John's tone turned menacing. "We deal with complicated issues every day, Joel. It's what we do. Perhaps you could see your way clear to give us a bullet list of the problems, if it isn't too much trouble."

Joel's face hardened. "Okay, here it is. First, let me remind you of our original goal—"

"We don't need a reminder, Joel—" Paul interrupted.

"Shut up, Paul," Joel snapped. "I have to take it from John, but I will not tolerate it from the likes of you."

Paul started to rise, but John spoke first. "Just get to it, Joel."

Joel sighed. "We wanted to try Pat Preston in D.C. We stood a much better chance of winning with the venue in our backyard."

"We had grounds to do it since his broadcasts came into D.C. via the Internet." John took a seat at the table.

"Well, yes and no. That assumption was the first mistake. Let me explain how Preston and his church worked their media.

"First, the church has two morning services. The earlier service is broadcast live on local television over a local station. A delayed version of the service is broadcast every Sunday evening on Nashville radio. During every service they take up an offering. I guess that doesn't make very good television, so each week during the offering the cameras do a cutaway to Preston. Remember, this is live. Preston used the time to invite viewers to join them in person at the next service. Sometimes he would promo a special activity the church was doing. All of that went out in real time. Is everyone with me so far?"

The others nodded.

"Okay. Between services Preston did what is called 'live-to-tape.' It's an industry term meant to blur the line between live and recorded material. Basically, it's a recording that's billed as live. Anyway, Preston did these in his office between services. Mostly he promoted material like books or downloadable MP3s and more. Of course, he always asked for money."

"Don't they all?" Andrea said.

Joel ignored her. "The second service would be recorded and stored at an off-site location."

"Off-site?" Reneé asked.

"The video feed was sent to a video studio downtown. There are two organizations. One is the church; the other is a media ministry run by the church. Turns out, this is not uncommon."

John massaged his forehead. He could see where this was going. He let Joel continue uninterrupted.

"On Mondays an employee of the media ministry goes to the studio—off church property, mind you—and edits the two services. The editor pulls the best parts from the first and second service and mixes them. He would also insert Preston's taped appeal and add multimedia elements to the program."

"Multimedia?" Joel said.

"The Internet broadcast often contained links users could click on to get more info about things said in the sermon. The thing to note here is that this is not the old style 'shoot-the-service' approach, where a church sets up a few cameras and records the sermons for playback later. Preston's church and media ministry are pretty sophisticated."

Joel began to pace. "The mixed tape—it's not really tape these days, but you know what I mean—would broadcast on local cable the following Saturday and Sunday for Internet viewing. The Nashville live broadcast was never used nationally. That means a service conducted on June fifth would go live in Nashville. The edited version of the June fifth service would go national the following week—June twelfth—and would be labeled as the June fifth service."

"I know it's because I'm not a prosecuting attorney," Andrea said, "but I'm not following."

Joel glanced at John, who had begun leafing through the documents Joel had given him. After a moment Joel said, "Our people didn't realize that some of the material produced by Preston was local only."

"What difference does it make if only part of the seized material came into D.C.?" Reneé said. "It came in here so we should have no venue issues."

John moaned and buried his face in his hands. "This couldn't be worse." He raised his head and looked at the others. "What Joel is getting at is this: the material we took to the grand jury was taken from the local broadcast only, not the Internet and national broadcasts."

"The techs and researchers," Joel said, "didn't realize there was a difference. The sermons broadcast live locally bore the same date as the one that went out over the Internet and national broadcast the next week. The evidence we took to the grand jury is not the same as what came into D.C. To make matters worse, we took video material only from the church and the on-site office of its media ministry. We seized everything—every computer and the relevant files. What we *didn't* know was that other material was stored in an off-site studio."

"Wait," Paul said. "You said the national stuff is a mix of the two services, so it contains the same material."

Joel nodded. "But that's not what we presented. We didn't gather all the videos, and we didn't compare the local feed with the national feed. We built everything on the local, thinking it was the same material that came into D.C."

"Preston's attorney is going to get hold of this little fact—this first-office-agent-type error—and challenge the indictment."

Reneé leaned over the table. "Can't we go back to the grand jury and show them the right material?"

John let Joel answer. "Yes, we can, but there are three problems. First, that grand jury served well past what most grand juries serve and has been dismissed. It means we'd be starting over with a new panel. We have no guarantee they would hand down an indictment on the same counts, especially after this kind of screwup. Second is time. We spent over four months on the original presentation; there's over thirty hours of video to review alone. Third is—"

"Embarrassment," John interjected. "Preston's attorney is going to kick up a lot of dust and media coverage. We're going to look like imbeciles with such a botch up on such a basic rule. If word of this spreads to the AG, to Congress, or to the press, then our job is going to get a lot more difficult. Everything we do in the future will be scrutinized; everything we've done in the past will be subject to review."

He rose from his seat and cursed loudly. A second later he threw the stack of papers Joel had given him across the room. "Why are we just now finding this out, Joel?" Pointing to the others, he yelled, "You see the four people in this room? Saturday morning at eleven o'clock we're going to be on a plane headed to Rome, and we won't be back here for at least a week. Do I have to cancel my trip?"

"No," Joel shot back. "I'll handle it while you're gone. I'll go over—"

"Don't give me that," John snapped. "If it's as screwed up as you claim, we'll have to start from scratch, and that's impossible. The damage has already been done."

"All the same, John," Joel said, "let me—"

"Stop! Just stop, now. We need to think this through. Give me a list of the charges you say are still okay and then tell Bob Maas and Sandra Evans to get their butts in here. Andrea, get me some coffee. Let's see what I can come up with. Now, the rest of you get out. I need time to think." The office cleared quickly.

There was no way John was going to miss his trip to Florence. It was too big, too important, too large a show to miss, even if this case against Pat Preston fell apart completely. But one way or the other, he was determined not to let that happen. Pat's case was going to be a game changer. He wasn't about to let the opportunity evaporate before his eyes.

Over the next forty-eight hours, John's office looked more like Union Station than an executive suite. Staffers, lawyers, technical experts, DTED, and IRS agents came and went in all directions. They tore apart every case and every count they had spent the last several months building, looking for some way—*any* way—to salvage what they could. They reexamined critical evidence, pored over the interrogation reports, and went back in several cases to the original investigators to see what they could learn from their after-action reports. Even though John feared none of it was working, he refused to give up.

By Thursday afternoon, John had to admit that his case against Pat Preston—as presented to the original grand jury—was on the verge of collapse. He received a detailed report explaining what went wrong. In the effort to regroup and compare notes one more time, John called his team together in his office. The work day had already ended, and the secretarial staff had gone home. The cleaning crew would be coming soon, but none of the key players considered leaving. John had made clear the gravity of the situation. No one wanted to be the first to test John's patience.

"Months of work and prestige down the toilet," he said as everyone took seats. "At this point, I don't know whether to shout or just fire the lot of you. How could this happen? We've lost our most important case, tremendous momentum, our reputation—and we haven't even gone to trial. We look like fools."

Seconds ticked by at glacial speed. No one spoke. John wasn't asking for feedback; he was venting. Paul Atoms, the foot soldier who had gone after the charges on the ground, broke the silence. "John, we can't give up. A hundred and nineteen counts on one guy is a lot. But we don't need that many, do we? If Joel says we can nail him on fifteen counts, then we have fifteen good reasons not to give up."

Over the next hour and a half, others contributed to the conversation, but John's mood didn't change. He didn't blow up. He didn't react. He didn't try to lead the conversation in any particular direction. Instead, he listened and scribbled notes on the legal pad in front of him.

Andrea spoke up. "I'm making notes too, but I need to step out for a minute, if you don't mind. I'm getting a text message that looks important. I'd like to make a quick phone call to follow up."

John nodded. Andrea picked up her notebook and left the room. Ten minutes later, while Bob Maas and Jason Harrier were debating whether to bring in one of the FCC lawyers who was apparently responsible for several serious blunders in the Preston case, Andrea pushed open the office door and said, "John, you need to take this call. It's important."

At that, everyone started gathering his or her pens and papers, preparing to leave, but John stopped them. "No, just stay here. I'll take the call in Paul's office."

When John returned to the office fifteen minutes later, it was obvious to everyone that the news wasn't going to be good. He walked to the end of the table where he had been sitting, bent forward, placed both hands on the back of his chair, and said, "We've got a leak."

Joel almost choked. "A leak? How do you know that?"

"That call was from someone I know very well: Matt Branson, my one-time classmate. He resigned from the DOJ and immediately volunteered to take Preston's case. Our opponent. The defense. He knows."

"Knows what, John?" Reneé asked.

"Everything, Reneé. He knows our case is falling apart and that we have serious procedural and evidentiary errors. He says it's an 'answer to prayer.'"

Joel responded first. "How can that be? There's no way he could know that. You mean someone in this office fed him information?"

John continued dryly. "Mr. Branson said he's heard that we're vulnerable and in danger of losing our case before trial. That would be a huge embarrassment. Because of what he calls our friendship, he wanted to call and let me know before he took the news any further." John clenched his jaw. "Our friendship. What a load of—"

"I don't get it, John," Paul chimed in. "Is he trying to make a deal?"

"He said he doesn't know everything; he hasn't discussed the details with anyone yet, not even his client, but he'll have to share the information with the rest of the defense team. He'll be meeting with them at noon tomorrow. He wants to know if we'd like to quietly dismiss the case against Preston before that happens."

Bob Maas slammed a fist down on the table, startling everyone. "Can you believe the nerve of that guy? Where does he get the audacity, trying to manipulate us like that?"

The room bristled with comments and questions until John lifted his hand and called for quiet. "The fact is, a clean exit may be the only strategy we have left," he said. "But he can just stew in it awhile. I don't intend to give him the benefit of a speedy reply. Everything we've discussed in this room is confidential. Always has been. Always will be. I want you all to hear that. If there is a leak inside this agency, believe me, I'll find it. In the meantime, Reneé, Paul, Andrea, and I have an appointment to keep across the pond, which means we'll have to give it some time and see how it all plays out. I'll call Branson, see if we can meet, and ask for a week. I'll say this is a big surprise, and we need to check out his claims. The four of us will be here most of the day tomorrow. We'll try to sort out a few things before we leave. We head out on Saturday morning, but while we're away, you're not to discuss any of this with anyone. Is that clear? I'll decide what happens next when we get back."

It was shortly before lunch on Friday when John got the news from Andrea. "I just got a very strange call from my friend Gina at OPR."

"You have friends at OPR?"

"Of course. I know lots of people, but I have to tell you something, John. I'm sorry. I know this is going to sound really weird—"

"Andrea, please. Just tell me."

"Matt Branson is dead."

"He's *what*?"

"Metro PD called OPR a half hour ago. This morning some joggers found his body in the water at Founders Park in Old Town."

"You're kidding! Oh my, what happened?"

"Not sure yet. Muggers maybe. His billfold and watch were missing, and pockets were turned inside out. But he had apparently been there all night. And . . ."

"And what?"

"He was shot in the back of the head."

John closed his eyes, groaned, drifted to his desk, and sank into his chair. He said nothing, his hands pressed together, fingers interlaced as if he were in prayer. A moment later, he rocked back in his chair. "They took his billfold? How did they know it was Matt, if there was no ID?"

"His wife called the police during the night. She reported that he hadn't come home. The cops put two and two together, and someone identified the body early this morning."

"Wow! That changes everything."

John had been furious with Matt for deserting the DOJ, for taking the Preston case, and for everything else that had happened, but he never wanted this. Matt Branson had threatened their whole operation and tried to make a very embarrassing deal, but he and John had once been close. Sure, he had gotten angry with Matt. Sure, he'd threatened his career, but murder?

"Can I get you anything?" Andrea inched closer.

"No, thank you." The words came out as a whisper. He looked up. "I'm going to take a long lunch. I know you're ready for the trip tomorrow; I think I am too. But will you please just check through my things one more time? Make sure we've got extra copies of my presentation and whatever else you think we'll need."

"Of course, John. Don't worry and don't hurry back. Anything that comes up here can wait."

"I'll be back to get my things later. If I miss you, I'll see you and the others downstairs in the garage tomorrow morning. Eight thirty. Don't be late."

For the next two hours John was on autopilot. He took his coat from the closet and made his way out of the building, across 9th Street and past the National Archives to 7th Street, where he crossed over to the National Gallery of Art on the other side of Constitution. Ignoring the crowds of tourists, he made his way around to the grand entrance, passed through a security checkpoint, and ascended the seemingly endless, massive granite stairs to the second floor to the fountain with a statue of Mercury the messenger in full stride. He turned left, down the marble hallway, and then onto the resonant wooden floors to the "cabinet rooms," containing the smaller images of the Dutch Masters collection.

There, where it had always been and where Matt had tried to share with him his vision of the delicate-but-strange painting, was Vermeer's *Woman Holding a Balance*. It was Matt's favorite painting. In their earlier days at the DOJ, he and Matt would come here during lunch. After his promotion John had seen Matt less frequently. He never admitted it aloud, but he missed those times with the only person in the world with whom he could have a two-way conversation, someone who wanted nothing from him.

John studied the painting again. A brilliant shaft of light shone diagonally across the image. Matt had tried to convince John that the light was the symbolic boundary of good and evil, God and Mammon, this life and the world beyond. The image of a "painting" hung in the painting—a painting within a painting. On the back wall of the image, behind the woman centered in the picture, the artist had inserted a realistic representation of *The Last Judgment*. The spray of light separated the upper right portion from the lower left. In the lower left, resting on a table, were golden baubles and jewels.

For Matt, this separation of light and dark had been a profound statement about life's choices. There was the image of God and moral judgment on the top half and below that the earthly trinkets and empty jeweler's scale. The woman at the center, holding the balance, was visibly pregnant. Was she, as Matt believed, an image of the Virgin Mary bearing the Christ child? Or was she simply the painter's wife or some other wealthy Flemish woman lost in thought?

It was a riddle—an enigma. John stared at the canvas one more time then backed away slowly and whispered, "Why, Matt? Why did you oppose me?"

Retracing his steps back to the marble hallway, John turned right again and continued down the long corridor to the stairway leading to the subterranean concourse connecting the East and West Buildings. He was surprised that so few people were in this part of the gallery at that hour. He heard the sound of his own footsteps echoing off the tiles—only one set of footsteps this time, not two—and it reminded him again that Matt was gone. He paused briefly at the cascades and reached out one hand toward the mist from the glass-encased waterfall but kept moving.

When he came to the main gallery and atrium of the East Building, his eyes turned upward to the magnificent red-and-black mobile sculpture that hung from the skylights high overhead. The work that had barely fit the large, open space always attracted and mesmerized him. Calder's vision was wild and sweeping and revolutionary. It was his unrestrained passion that John loved. Matt's spiritual journey had always been in reverse, looking backward, focusing on something long dead and gone, to a world that no longer existed; while John's own journey was upward, soaring, bold, inspiring, focused on the future. This was why the Calder was his favorite.

This difference separated the two men. Both yearned for something greater, deeper—something ineffable and sublime. But how very different were their yearnings. *If only I could have broken through the ice and shared the vision with Matt. If only he would have listened to me and believed in something real and vital and dynamic! Maybe he could have been saved. But that's all finished now. Just like those two dinosaurs on the Supreme Court. He's gone. I have to move on.*

John stopped at the restroom on the way out of the gallery to wipe the dried mud he had noticed on his highly polished Michael Kors loafers. The mud sure didn't belong there and was most unusual for this always perfectly groomed man.

| CHAPTER TWENTY-NINE |

J ohn was pensive, Andrea was animated, and Paul and Reneé simply tried to keep out of the way on the non-stop flight to Rome's Leonardo Da Vinci Airport. After a long delay on the tarmac at Washington's Dulles International and nearly nine hours in flight in their government-paid coach seats, everyone but Andrea was ready for a long rest. Arriving at their first-night hotel—the St. Regis Grand on the Via Vittorio Emauele Orlando, around the corner from the Via Veneto and right in the center of the great city—their desire to sleep evaporated, replaced by the thrill of being in Italy.

It was barely 10:00 AM in Rome when the State Department van dropped them off in the porte cochere. Regally dressed bellmen raced to take their bags, and a small crowd of Europe-based State Department and U.S. embassy personnel waited to greet them just inside the main lobby. They had made arrangements for an early check-in, but they had just enough time to go to their rooms and freshen up. The embassy staff had made lunch reservations for the entire group at the hotel's intimate five-star Ristorante Vivendo.

They enjoyed a long, colorful, boisterous Italian lunch, punctuated with multiple wine courses, after which embassy staffers briefed John and the team on protocol and other in-country issues. The embassy staff gave them new travel documents, all in Italian. John was shown how to get in touch with the CIA station chief in Florence, in the event he or any of the team were approached by "curious strangers." The only other request came from Foreign Service staffers, who were eager to hear the latest news from Washington.

None of the travelers had ever been to Rome. Despite their state of near exhaustion, they were so close to so much history that a short walking tour with a couple of quick taxi rides proved too tempting. The Spanish Steps, the Trevi Fountain, and the Via Veneto were minutes away; the Flavian Amphitheater—known to tourists as the Coliseum—and Roman Forum were just a bit farther. Since their stay in the capital was brief, they had to see everything in one tour. Riding on adrenaline and the desire to make a good impression, John and the others enjoyed themselves for a few hours, but by six o'clock that evening they had reached their limit. Returning to the hotel, John slipped from his clothing and crawled on the bed for a long nap. That night he dined alone in his room and assumed the others did the same. He did nothing else until the time came to get ready for an early departure the following morning.

From the Termini train station it was an hour-and-a-half ride to Florence. They were joined in the hotel lobby by two members of the Rome-based staff, one of whom they had met the previous evening. Julian Giordano was an embassy lawyer, a specialist in UN and EU judicial policy. He had finished Harvard Law two years after John but said he knew the assistant attorney general by reputation. He had even heard him speak on one occasion. He told John he was thrilled to be joining them for the conference.

The young man would be John's eyes and ears. He was an able translator, but even more importantly, having lived nearly half his life in Italy, he understood the nuances of European law and custom. He would help John keep track of conference proceedings and the implications of everything that happened there from the DOJ's point of view.

The second person joining the group was Judith Ravenell, an assistant secretary of state and mid-career Foreign Service officer who had been posted at the embassy in Rome for the past five years but was scheduled for reassignment in a few weeks. She was John's counterpart and an avid supporter of his equality initiatives. Judith appeared to be in her early forties with deep brown eyes and exotic Mediterranean features.

Her dark hair flowed gently over the shoulders of an English riding jacket. She carried a small valise in one hand—surprisingly small, John thought, for a four-day junket—and a black calfskin briefcase hanging from a strap over her left shoulder. She spoke with confidence and self-assurance. She completely captivated John. Several times he caught himself staring. He also noticed that Andrea saw him and appeared none too pleased.

He was attracted to Judith Ravenell, not just because of her beauty and charm, but because she had the right connections. She was polished. She was an officer of the State Department at his own level. And she knew the territory. For the first time, he realized the trip to Florence wasn't simply important.

It might even be fun.

The travelers arrived at the Santa Maria Novella Train Station in Florence just after 11:00 AM. To everyone's surprise a police escort, consisting of three motorcycle policemen and an officer in a small, blue-and-white police car, met them. After loading their luggage into two Mercedes limousines reserved by the embassy, they were driven at breakneck speed—with blue lights flashing and horns blaring—to their hotel, a restored twelfth-century mansion in the city center, some twenty blocks away. Once the travelers were safely deposited at the hotel, the escort disappeared as quickly as it had come. John loved it.

Making their way from the bustling entryway to the registration desk at the Westin Excelsior Hotel, however, proved a bigger challenge than the drive from the station. They were surrounded by men and women of all nationalities, speaking every conceivable language and wearing costumes the Americans had seen only in books and films. It was routine for the Rome-based crew, but John was astounded. While John, Paul, and Reneé did their best to take everything in, Andrea glowed. For someone who, until this trip, had never been farther than the Chesapeake Bay—a forty-minute drive from her Washington apartment—this was paradise.

The hotel was the most impressive building John had ever seen. It looked like a palace plucked straight out of the Middle Ages with massive marble columns, high-beamed ceilings, and crystal chandeliers. There were rare and beautiful antiques everywhere. Situated on the sprawling Piazza Ognissanti facing the River Arno, right in the heart of the city's fashion district, it was like something from another era, another world.

Once they had checked into their rooms and put away their belongings, the six members of John's party met in the terrace bar overlooking the river for lunch and drinks before making a quick tour of the premises. The hotel was within walking distance of several of the best-known historical and architectural landmarks in Europe, including the magnificent Ponte Vecchio Bridge, the Uffizi Gallery, and the Pitti Palace, where treasures of the Medici dynasty that had governed Florence in the fifteenth and sixteenth centuries were displayed.

Everything on the official agenda would take place in the hotel. Following the directions she found in the conference literature, Andrea had made reservations for a museum tour and a dinner cruise on the river.

Officially, the four-day event was called "Conférence sur les modèles intergouvernementaux pour la résolution de l'extrémisme international, l'oppression religieuse, l'égalité et la voie à suivre—Conference on Inter-Governmental Models for the Resolution of International Extremism, Religious Oppression, Equality, and the Way Forward."

It was the last part that appealed to John: the Way Forward. It was the reason he had traveled so far. He had come to say that the DTED had found a way forward, that they had and were changing social dynamics in his country. Many obstacles still existed, but the trajectory of his success was promising, and he believed that was a message worth sharing. He knew it was a model the rest of the world could follow: government-mandated equality and hopefully the end of American exceptionalism.

The first day's opening presentations were formal and dry, a showcase of famous politicians and former heads of state, each more venerable that the last; each extolling the virtues of diplomacy and "statecraft," and praising the work of the United Nations to end the impact of religious aggression. Each of the men and women on the dais gave a short synopsis of the sessions and workshops they would be hosting. John's name was not mentioned, although his topic was listed in the program as the main plenary session on the final day.

The most compelling presentations came during the afternoon of the second day. The first speaker after the lunch break was a former Muslim from the United Arab Emirates, who described common themes within Christianity and Islam, and focused on the autocratic nature of these so-called "great religions." Because he had lived and studied in both Europe and America, this man understood how Western culture, beliefs, and society had corrupted human nature.

"The desire to proselytize and control the beliefs of others," he said, "has transformed mankind's innate yearning for transcendence—from hope to human tragedy, from innocence to ignorance, and from tolerance and acceptance to hate." The theme resonated with John. He made a note to mention it in his own presentation. For a moment, he wondered how Matt would have responded.

The second speaker was a tall, stately, former African leader who wore the traditional Babariga robe with embroidered hat, flowing Buba garments, and white cotton trousers. As a child, he had lived in a village frequently visited by Western missionaries. Before he reached the age of six, both his mother and father had died of AIDS, and he had spent the next ten years in a Christian orphanage.

"Instead of teaching us children about AIDS and STDs," he said movingly, "they showed us *The Jesus Film*, over and over. They tried to corrupt our natural values and beliefs and convert us to their religion. They preached abstinence and suppressed our need for sexual growth, which is unhealthy and impossible. All but a handful of the boys and girls I grew up with are dead. Jesus didn't save them; the Holy Bible didn't save them; the American missionaries didn't save them. They all died. So many of them died." His voice broke. He stepped back from the microphone for a moment, composed himself, and then continued. "If the missionaries cared for us, why didn't they teach us about condoms and safe sex and use their money for AIDS research? No. They only talked about Jesus and refraining from our natural sexual expression." When he finished, the speaker received a standing ovation.

The third and final presentation of the day focused on technical issues specifically directed toward participants from the EU countries and the United Kingdom. Since John and his team weren't particularly interested in those topics, they left during the break.

Judith Ravenell approached John. "I wonder if you would join me for a stroll along the river. We can talk privately there."

"Nothing would please me more."

She took his arm, and they slipped away from the conference hall and out of the majestic hotel. For the next two hours they strolled along the fountains and through the lavish gardens on the river walk, making small talk and getting better acquainted. They compared notes on education and where they'd grown up. They found that both of them were passionate about the work they did. Judith's impressive rise in the Foreign Service was similar in some ways to John's ascendancy in the Justice Department. Both had sacrificed family life for professional advancement, and both were compulsive workaholics who put career ahead of everything else.

They also had a highly developed aesthetic sense. They loved contemporary art and modern culture and saw most of classical art, music, and literature as an anachronism—interesting but generally useless. They agreed that history was a record of human failures and missed opportunities, but there was magic in living in the moment. By some miracle of fate they had been put in positions to influence history and perhaps even to change it forever.

John was amazed to meet someone so brilliant who shared so many of his own beliefs. Yet there were differences. While John had grown up in the foothills of the Colorado Rockies and moved east after high school, Judith had grown up mostly in Europe and attended boarding schools in Switzerland. She had lived in Washington for a few years after graduating from Wellesley College and finished at the top of her class at the Foreign Service Academy. But she never considered the United States her legitimate home. In a matter of weeks she would be returning to Zurich, where she was to assume the position of deputy U.S. consul.

"John, the leaders of this continent took the opportunity to officially turn their backs on their dark, religious, Jesus-believing pasts."

"How, Judith?" John asked.

"Back at the beginning of the century, Pope John Paul II asked the EU to include recognition of Europe's so-called 'Christian Heritage' in their first constitution." She laughed and continued, "But with the Berlin Declaration and other actions, that foolishness was soundly rejected. That declaration highlighted European values like democracy and a vision for growth like fighting climate change. That was the official nail in their coffin. Now, let's talk about you."

When Judith asked about the formation of the Diversity and Tolerance Enforcement Division, John told her he would cover it all in his talk on Thursday. He said he had spearheaded the effort with the blessing of the Blaine administration and the Justice Department. When she asked about the caseload waiting for him back in Washington, he hesitated but then mentioned the problems with Pat's Jesus-is-the-only-way case. She had read about the indictment in the *International Herald-Tribune*. John explained the prospect of having to drop the prosecution or at least delay it indefinitely while going back to a new grand jury.

"Why don't you try the case here?" she asked.

"Here? In Italy? What do you mean?"

"No, not Italy. The Hague. The International Criminal Court hears cases like this all the time. Frankly, it would be refreshing to see the American justice system finally recognize the authority of the international tribunal for such hate crimes. The option has been available to us ever since President Blaine convinced the Senate to finally sign on to the Rome Statute of the ICC. We just haven't used it. Your preacher's hate speech has worldwide harm and impact through the Internet, and we still have a lot of Catholics and evangelicals in Europe who believe Jesus is the world's Messiah. A case like yours could be just what we need to advance the quest for religious equality worldwide."

John was speechless. The whole idea of trying a case in Europe was revolutionary. It was something he would never have thought of. "I don't know. I doubt we could do it. We don't have experience with something like that. Our attorneys are not certified to practice before the bar over here, and it would need State and White House sign-off."

"Well, think about it. It's just an idea. But if the ICC wanted to establish a precedent to get the U.S. more involved, I imagine an experienced attorney—someone already admitted to the Supreme Court Bar, for example—could become certified fairly easily. And if someone like a deputy U.S. consul or the United Nations commissioner for human rights, who happens to be the moderator of the conference, were to provide letters of reference for a certain individual, I suppose certification to practice before the European court could be arranged." She looked into John's eyes and smiled. "Just an idea."

John chuckled. "Yeah, just an idea; almost too big an idea. Still . . ."

The following morning John, Paul Atoms, and Reneé X joined a group of conferees and their Italian guide for a private tour of two of the world's most famous art galleries, the Galleria degli Uffizi in the former Medici Palace and the Galleria Dell'Accademia, which housed some of the best-known paintings and sculptures by Michelangelo, including *The Four Prisoners*, the partially finished *Pietá Palestrina*, and the larger-than-life statue of *David*.

The Medici Palace had seen a lot of history over the past five hundred years, but John was surprised to see that this renowned gallery was showing signs of wear. Portions of the building had been flooded years earlier, and one section had been damaged by a car bomb. It was amazing, nevertheless, to see so many famous paintings, sculptures, and mosaics within arm's reach—works John had only seen in books.

During the tour they saw famous pictures by Titian, Caravaggio, Cimabue, Giotto, Michelangelo, and even the Dutch Master, Rembrandt van Rijn. They saw Botticelli's stunning *Birth of Venus* and *The Annunciation,* and *Adoration of the Magi* by Leonardo da Vinci that had appeared in Hollywood movies.

But John thought it was unsettling to have Piero di Cosimo's *Perseus Liberating Andromeda*, an image from classical Greek mythology, in the same collection with Dürer's *Adoration of the Magi*, Raphael's *Madonna of the Goldfinch*, and Raphael's portrait of whom John called a corrupt, indulgence-selling pope in the picture known as *Pope Leo X and Two Cardinals*. There were countless others, but the juxtaposition of secular and religious art were, in his mind, inappropriate and frustrating.

They saw works by Fra Bartolomeo, Andrea del Sarto, and Perugino from the sixteenth century, along with several primitive, two-dimensional works from the third and fourth centuries, most of them with stilted biblical scenes. As historical relics, they were mildly amusing, but the religious allusions reminded John of the tragedy of Western history. By the time they completed their self-guided tour of the Accademia, John and Reneé were ready to head back to the hotel.

As they were leaving the museum, John said, "What a sad, sad shame that the world lost so many centuries to this foolishness. Just think of the countless dollars, the human energy, and the talent wasted on churches and cathedrals and all the paintings and statues devoted to the mythology of Christianity. What if all that energy had been devoted to something real and substantial—housing the poor, feeding the hungry, educating the illiterate and uninformed? Imagine how much more that could have benefited mankind."

When they arrived at the hotel, Paul was obviously way past his capacity for more art appreciation and offered to buy a round of drinks. John planned to attend the afternoon sessions but agreed to stay for a few minutes. There was something on his mind that he wanted to flesh out. On the walk back from the gallery, Reneé had broached an idea that piqued his interest, but there was something troubling about what she had said. He wanted to think it through.

"Whenever I see something like that," Reneé said, holding up her museum brochure, "with all those paintings and sculptures from religious mythology, it makes me nauseous. What we ought to be discussing at a conference like this, instead of paperwork and procedures, is how to regulate and limit this kind of thing. Someone needs to teach these people their history and show them how much damage has been done in the name of religion."

Paul nodded in agreement, but John said it wasn't as simple as that. "I know what you're saying, Reneé, but I'm not sure I entirely agree with you. Not because people don't need to be better educated but because these Christians are so fond of martyrdom. You saw the pictures. Did you count them? Dozens. Christ on the cross, Peter on the cross, Paul beheaded, Jack and Jill on the cross, Savonarola going up in flames, martyrs by the score. The Romans went wrong by helping these people become heroes."

"I see your point, John," Paul said, "but when they start bombing abortion clinics and killing innocent children, they have to be dealt with. Don't you agree? They attack homosexual and transgendered persons. They shoot federal officers. Somehow they must be silenced. If that makes them martyrs, I don't see how it can be avoided."

"Yes, but let's not make them saints, Paul. That's the difference. Putting a stop to their missions and their tricks for converting people is one thing: that's the proper role of government. But we have to stop them short of martyrdom. That's what law enforcement is for. That's what the DTED is for."

"Are you thinking about the Preston case?" Reneé asked.

John hesitated. "It crossed my mind. I think we've done a good job keeping that case in the right perspective so people can see the risk people like Preston pose to free-thinking people. On the other hand, maybe the fact that everything exploded on us isn't such a bad thing after all."

"How so?" Paul asked.

John smiled, "More on that later. I've been thinking about something. It may be our ace in the hole."

John spotted Judith Ravenell crossing the lobby on her way to the conference center. He quickly excused himself from the group.

Andrea and Giordano had been hanging out together, missing most of the sessions. John had never seen his assistant so animated. But since Giordano had done very little to help, he decided to leave them alone. Besides, he thought, the excitement was probably good for both of them.

At eight o'clock that evening, just as the sun was descending over the Arno River, all six members of their party, dressed in their nicest suits and evening wear, met briefly in the hotel lobby. They strolled across the piazza and descended the concrete steps to the boat ramp, where their dinner cruise waited.

The river at night was especially beautiful. Streetlamps, multicolored lights in the restaurants and shops along the river, and the elegant, old bridges all brilliantly illuminated the river as their pleasure boat passed beneath them, making the night come alive. A trio of handsome young waiters entertained them with jokes in broken English and sang to them as they delivered each course to the table. The cruise took them through Florence and past the city lights into the Tuscan countryside, punctuated by small, picturesque villages and large farms. Motorists, bicyclists, and fishermen greeted them along the way, waving a friendly hello as they passed.

During the meal they made small talk. Much to John's surprise, Paul had a lot to say about the gallery tour. He had been paying attention and seemed genuinely impressed by what he had seen. Reneé, on the other, was eager to pick up on their earlier conversation. She said she'd been thinking about his comments all afternoon and couldn't wait to find out what he had meant. "John, you've got to tell us what you're going to do. Don't hold out on us."

John laughed. "You're right. I have an announcement to make. But I think I'll hold off until my talk tomorrow. It involves all of us, and I think you'll like it. But really, that's enough for now." He looked at Judith, sitting just to his right. "Actually, it was Judith's idea. We were talking earlier, and she gave me something to think about. But I promise I'll get into it later. I made some calls, and I'm waiting for a couple of sign-offs."

They teased John, saying that he was afraid to tell them or that they weren't important enough for such a big announcement, but John held his ground.

Reneé turned serious. "I have a question. Why would the UN choose Florence for this conference? Why a city saturated with so much Christian art and architecture?"

"It's the perfect place," John said. "Florence is a world cultural center, a city that has preserved so much art from the past, but in a country that has flushed all the faith restraints that were so oppressive—like marriage and the slavery of women to childbearing. They're past that here. This is a very liberated country."

"That's very perceptive," Judith responded. "That's why international law is so important for your judicial system in America, as President Blaine addressed in his State of the Union speech this year. There is still a lot of resistance in some quarters to getting U.S. judges to cite European, Asian, and African precedents. Just mentioning foreign landmark cases, as the Supreme Court did to decide the *Lawrence* sodomy decision back in 2003, still makes some people in America crazy.

It's important for the American people to find out why Europe has become such a great and free society. We've managed to demystify the mythology and suppress the oppression of religious beliefs that held this continent back for so many centuries."

Giordano and Andrea had spent most of the first three days in each other's company, except for two sessions when John specifically asked Giordano to attend. For much of their time on the cruise, they seemed to be in their own world. While the others were chatting, sipping wine, and admiring the allurements of the Tuscan night, the romantic couple strolled to the bow of the boat and watched like children as they passed beneath each successive bridge.

When they returned to the group, it was apparent that Giordano had been paying less attention to Andrea than to the conversation taking place around the table. As he slipped into his seat, he looked at Judith. "In Italy fewer than 5 percent of the people ever darken the door of a church, except for the artwork or the occasional wedding. I suspect that number will continue to drop."

"In Britain it's already less," Judith said. "Instead of paying homage to the ravings of the religious crowd, most people in Europe under-stand that marriage and family are matters of choice. They don't place unnatural limits on relationships, and they don't make rules that force some antiquated definition of family on everyone. They have children when they want them, not because they believe it's the right thing to do. I'm sure you know the birthrate is low in this country. Muslims are still propagating, but most Europeans are beyond that. We get the picture."

"Wouldn't it be wonderful," Reneé said, "if the United States could be so enlightened?"

John raised his glass of wine. "To enlightenment."

The others lifted their glasses to toast the sentiment.

By the time they returned to the hotel, the moon had gone behind the clouds. The hour was late, and everyone in the group was thoroughly inebriated. When John said goodnight, he noticed that Giordano and Andrea were headed back to the lobby bar. Apparently they were going to make a night of it.

| CHAPTER THIRTY |

The opening session on the last day of the conference focused on the importance of an international justice system and what sort of laws and treaties were needed to end the remaining serious forms of religious oppression. It was a harder hitting session than most of the earlier ones. The young woman from South Africa, who took the platform immediately before John was to speak repeatedly, used the expression "conversion is genocide." It was precisely what Lynn Barrett and the ACLU leaders had been saying for years. To prevent the destruction of indigenous customs and beliefs, she said, her country had recently passed laws banning missionaries who preach exclusionary religious doctrines.

"How can Christian fables be better than our indigenous fables?" the young woman asked to resounding applause and laughter. "Come on now," she said, strolling back and forth across the platform like a street-corner evangelist, "isn't that how the white American Southerners kept their slaves working in the fields, by telling them that if they worked hard enough and long enough, and if they bowed every day to the master, then someday 'in the sweet bye and bye' they might go to heaven? We have a word for that in my country. Poppycock!" As soon as she said the word, the audience roared with laughter.

"I see that our next speaker is from the United States," she continued. "I hope that . . ." She paused to look at the name in the program. "Mr. John Knox Smith knows what I'm saying is true. We have heard that 90 percent of Christian missionaries in the world today are being paid by American evangelicals. Without U.S. dollars, Christian evangelism would pretty much dry up. So they are the ones who are causing so many headaches in South Africa.

"Mr. Smith," she said, wringing the image for all the humor she could get, "please, stop it." Again, there was more laughter and applause, but the young woman turned somber. "You can bring us food, factories, and medical assistance if you like, but no more preaching. If the Americans want to help us, then let them do it with real compassion and without all the Jesus talk. This will separate those who really care for us from those who only want to destroy our native cultures.

"If you examine what Christians believe, you will see they believe that breaking up the family is a good thing." Holding up a black book, she said, "It says in this Gideon Bible, which I found in my room, that if other people hate you, that's a good thing. Do you believe it? Well, I don't believe it. Since the time of the Roman Empire, when Christianity was one of many religions, everything has changed. The Pax Romana under Caesar Augustus—the most peaceful time in all of human history—ended with the rise of Christianity. When the Roman emperors abandoned tolerance and equality for other cultures and faiths, the end had come.

"But they left us a legacy, all the same. The Romans gave us the rostrum—a proper time and place for free speech. They understood that free speech could be dangerous, so they set limits. There were places where free speech would be allowed within certain limits. We also need limits. Before the Christians, the Jews refused to bow to Rome. They arrogantly refused to accept the equality of other beliefs. But Emperor Titus solved that little problem in AD 70, didn't he? And when the citizens of Rome built the Arch of Titus, they gave him a lasting tribute to his victory over bigotry and exclusivity—a monument that still stands in the center of Rome to this day.

"For the past two thousand years, most of the bad things that have plagued our world can be traced back to the exclusivity claims of these two religions. But there is good news, my friends. The world is finally waking up. Change is a'comin'. The question is, how can we liberate what's left, especially in the U.S., with nearly four hundred years of oppression and claims of America being 'exceptional' to overcome?

"I, for one, will be glad to hear what Mr. John Knox Smith has to say. How will America respond? What will your country do, Mr. Smith, to restore sobriety, safety, and sanity to the world?" With that the speaker took a grand bow to thunderous applause, blew kisses to the audience, and left the stage.

By the time John stepped up to the lectern, he had rewritten the conclusion of his speech. He took the first half hour to give a recap of the court precedents, of the enabling legislation, and of DTED's success and the changes taking place in the United States, as he had originally planned. Then he had an announcement. "Ladies and gentlemen, it's an honor to be here. I've learned so much, and I'm very encouraged by each of the sessions. Seeing you all and the wonderful native dress many of you are wearing has been an amazing and eye-opening experience for me and the members of my delegation. Thank you.

"As you know, the United States has been insensitive for too long to international law and the world court. We're a large, wealthy country, but that's no excuse. I believe that's going to change soon. Before coming to Florence, my colleagues and I were pursuing a difficult case on 'exclusivity' claims of a professional religionist that has taken us months of investigation and litigation. This preacher is one of those who still claim there is only one truth, one religion that really works. That means denigrating others. Until coming here, I had planned to try that case in the U.S. courts, knowing it would eventually end up at the United States Supreme Court. But the Blaine administration has changed its mind and decided that we need to try this case of religious bigotry and exclusivity at the International Criminal Court, where true justice can be done. I just received final word of this from my government while I was waiting to speak."

As soon as the words left his mouth, the audience stood, applauding and cheering. "I would say this is a new day, wouldn't you? America is joining the world in this quest for equality!" he said over the noise. Again, the audience responded enthusiastically.

In the time remaining, John described Pat's case and how, over the last few years, his preaching had become more and more forceful and intolerant and how his sermons were disseminated over the airwaves, the Internet, and cable TV. The final series of sermons viciously attacked other world religions as false. John told them how Pat, under claims of "Jesus is the only way," had fought with police and resisted arrest, and then refused to cooperate during peaceful interview attempts.

"We know where this behavior ultimately leads," John said. "I suspect many of you have seen the headlines from my country. Fundamentalist Christians have bombed schools, police stations, and even the FBI headquarters in Washington, D.C., across the street from where I work. They have accosted and fought with policemen outside a public school while handing out Bibles to children. They have shot federal agents and beat peaceful members of the gay community to death on public streets. They continue to resist all efforts at reform. So when we talk about 'transformative justice,' this is the behavior that must be transformed."

By the time he completed his remarks, John Knox Smith had won over the crowd and the young Bantu woman who had spoken before him. She ran onto the stage and threw her arms around John's neck. John smiled broadly and thanked her. She stepped closer to the microphone. "Mr. Smith, you have restored our faith. Maybe now we will see real transformation and change in your country. I asked for sobriety, safety, and sanity; and I thank you for taking a giant step in that direction."

John returned to his seat. The conference moderator returned to the platform for his closing remarks. The moderator lavished praised on the Blaine administration for the decision to bring Pat Preston to Europe to face trial before the ICC. Then, before thanking everyone for their participation and bringing down the closing gavel, the moderator said, "Before we go, I have one more announcement.

"I was asked earlier by a dear friend, Ms. Judith Ravenell, if I would be able to assist her friend, Mr. John Knox Smith, to complete his department's plan. Ms. Ravenell told me that Mr. Smith, who holds certification to argue legal cases before the U.S. Supreme Court and the federal courts in Washington, D.C., would also like certification to argue his case before the ICC in the Netherlands. She has written a letter of reference for Mr. Smith with the imprimatur of the U.S. State Department. I am giving him my own reference as commissioner of human rights of the United Nations. These references will be useful, I'm sure."

The moderator turned to John. "I have just now spoken with the president of the ICC at the Peace Palace in The Hague. She assures me, Mr. Smith, that your certification before that bar will be confirmed within the hour." Once again the room erupted in applause and loud cheers. Several of the conferees reached out to shake John's hand, and the moderator concluded, saying, "And with that good news, I bid you all a fond farewell."

After a death-defying ride through morning traffic, the six members of John's group arrived at the Santa Maria Novella Train Station in downtown Florence, ready for the return trip to Rome and beyond. Judith and Giordano were taking the train north to Milan and would have a short wait before boarding. The DTED team, on the other hand, were right on time. They would be boarding the high-speed train to Rome within minutes.

John and the others felt sad about leaving but none more so than Andrea, who, it appeared to John, had had an exceptional time with her new friend. Before heading in separate directions, she took Giordano's hand and said, "You know you have to write me, don't you? You can e-mail me every day. We can't just say good-bye and never see each other again, can we?"

Giordano glanced at John and the others, looking embarrassed. He said to Andrea, "Well, I don't think that will be possible."

"Why not?" she asked with schoolgirl simplicity. "Surely you can drop me a note or call me at my private number on the government line now and then."

Judith, who had been standing on the opposite side of Giordano, moved closer. She reached over and touched Andrea's arm. "Andrea, Giordano can't do that."

"Why not?"

"His partner wouldn't like it."

Hearing those words, Andrea's jaw dropped. "Partner?"

"His roommate, Carlo. They've been together a long time. Carlo gets jealous easily."

"Julian . . ." Andrea stared at him. "You . . . you came to my room. You . . ."

Giordano laughed. "Oh, that." He shrugged. "I'm Italian, and . . . well, you're very pretty."

"I can't believe you'd deceive me this way."

Giordano blinked and looked confused. "I didn't think you'd mind. After all, you and your friends are fighting to free us from archaic moral restraints. I thought if anyone would understand there are no more 'wages of sin,' it would be you."

Picking up her suitcase and flinging the strap of her handbag over her shoulder, Andrea shook her head and walked toward the depot.

John saw Andrea's humiliation and embarrassment. He didn't like being privy to her indiscretion. He followed at a safe distance.

| CHAPTER THRITY-ONE |

On top of everything Pat had been through, not the least of which was being separated from his family and being held incommunicado for several months, the news of Matt's murder had been a crushing blow. He wept not for himself but for Matt's family.

Not long ago, Pat would have submerged himself in an ocean of self-pity. That was changing. For years he had taught that people who lived for Christ could face persecution even in America. They certainly faced it all over the globe. It had always been that way. From the moment of the church's birth, believers had found themselves in jail. Peter, Silas, John, and many of the early church leaders had spent a lot of time looking at the world from inside a cell. They'd been stoned, beaten, and left for dead. Why should he be any different? Wasn't it an honor to suffer for Christ? The New Testament said so many times.

Still, Pat was human, and his emotions bobbed up and down like a cork on a churning sea. As the days in isolation went on, he decided his feelings no longer mattered; only his behavior and the way he represented Jesus mattered. In fact, he remembered something he had learned long ago: "Faith is not a feeling. Faith is what allows us to overcome our feelings."

A day later, Larry Jordan and Judge Holloway visited Pat in the detention center.

"Are you feeling all right?" Larry asked. "You look like you're losing weight. Are they feeding you?"

"Prison food doesn't agree with me."

"Listen, son," Holloway said. "I know this is your darkest hour, but you have to keep your strength up. Eating is part of that. Your body needs the fuel."

Pat forced a chuckle. "I used to say the same thing to people who'd lost loved ones. I wish I had a nickel for each time I've said that. You wouldn't have to pour your fortune into my defense."

"Don't you worry about my fortune, Pastor. I'm not," Holloway said.

Pat looked at Larry. "Any word on who killed Matt?"

"Not yet. The police are investigating. The bullet was a type not sold commercially. It was the kind manufactured for federal law enforcement."

"How's his family doing?" A few weeks ago, Pat would have kept his gaze down. Now he looked Larry square in the eye.

"I visited them. His daughter doesn't fully understand. His wife is hanging in there." Larry shifted on the fiberglass chair.

"She's putting on a good front," Pat said.

"Do you know her well?" Holloway asked.

Pat shook his head. "I've never met her, but I've seen enough people pass away to know that parents act strong for their kids. Do they have a good church?"

"She said they did," Larry answered. "I know people have been bringing food, and the pastor had been by several times."

"That's good," Pat said. "That's good." He rubbed his eyes. His head and heart hurt for his lost friend. "When's the funeral?"

"They're not sure yet," Larry said. "Since it's a murder, the authorities may hold the body for a while. I think they're planning on going ahead with a memorial service and a graveside service after the body is released."

Pat chewed his lip. "What about that strange bullet? Was he killed because of me?"

"It seems unlikely." Larry said. "It appears to be a robbery, but the bullet type has raised some eyebrows."

"We met a day or two before he was killed. I don't remember exactly. Time in here isn't the same as time out there. He was in a great mood. He said he'd found something, something really big. He said that I'd be pleased to know, but he couldn't tell me yet."

"That's true. He called John Knox Smith to tell him he'd made a big discovery about an evidence issue that he didn't share with us either, one he said might cause Knox to drop everything. He hoped to have you out of here, but he wouldn't tell me a thing; said he'd made a promise to keep his cards close to his vest for a few days. Try as we might, we can't get a clue what this was all about."

"Did they kill him?"

"Who?" Larry asked.

"John or one of his people."

Larry leaned forward. "Listen, Pastor. I've gone toe-to-toe with every one of his prosecutors. We have hammered each other in court. John Knox Smith is arrogant, ambitious, and horribly misguided, but I've never seen anything in him to make me think him capable of murder."

"Why not? He's no longer the young man I knew at Princeton. There's something that seems to have control of him. He's capable of imprisoning me for doing nothing more than repeating the teachings of Jesus. He has a vendetta against Christians, and Matt was a Christian."

"I promise to stay on top of it, Pastor," Larry said.

"We were all friends once," Pat said. "Did you know that, Judge Holloway? We went to college together. John and I used to debate. I used to study the Bible with Matt." Pat ran a hand through his hair. "That was ten lifetimes ago."

"We have to get down to business, son," Holloway said. "I've had a phone call or two with Scott Freeman, head of the Alliance. He agrees that Larry should serve as lead counsel."

"Yes."

Larry said, "Having Judge Holloway sitting beside you would have gone a long way," Larry said.

"Would?"

Larry and Holloway exchanged glances. "Pastor," Larry said, "there has been an unexpected change."

Pat straightened. "I don't like the sound of this."

"Joel Thevis—he's the lead prosecutor on your case—called to ask about who would be replacing Matt. He also told me that there's been a change in trial location . . . and some other things like new charges."

"Changed to where, to what?"

"Out of the country. The International Criminal Court at The Hague in the Netherlands. For engaging in international hate crimes."

Pat felt his spine dissolve. "The Hague? Can they do that? I'm an American citizen."

"I don't know how," Holloway said, "but Smith has made it happen. President Blaine has set the groundwork for such an action; other countries are now trying hate crime cases there. Some of my peers have debated when this would happen. It's happened sooner than any of us expected."

"But why? Why would he do this to me?"

"Must be because his case here is weak," Larry said. "He's afraid of putting it before a D.C. jury. Maybe there are still a lot of jurors who know and believe in Jesus here or at least in real tolerance. Maybe whatever made Matt so excited is troubling them. European countries are more open to prosecuting hate crimes."

"Please stop calling it that. I've never preached hate, just repentance; just the love of Christ."

"It's all the same thing to them," Larry said.

"What do we do now?"

"We fight it," Larry answered. "The Alliance has some good people in Europe who are experienced in international law. We've had an office there since 2008. We have a man in Brussels who has tried cases before the ICC, so we're not walking in blind. I've already contacted two other men, one a Swiss citizen who has participated in Alliance training programs in that country. He's a top-notch trial lawyer and heads his own firm. He's a direct descendant of a cousin of Martin Luther and an active Christian. Another lawyer has represented the Holy See, the Roman Catholic Church in the EU, and won a couple of tough cases, including preserving the right of baptism for children under eighteen. Your prayer partner back home in Nashville, Father John Corollo, who has some big connections in Rome, referred him. You will have six dedicated and enthusiastic lawyers from two continents and two major faith backgrounds, so you'll have both sides of the Reformation, so to speak, working for you."

Pat smiled. "That's an impressive lineup of lawyers and another testament to the mysterious ways of God."

"Pat, slowly—too slowly—the worldwide church has been waking up to what's at stake here for the future of all believers," Larry continued. "You are going to see an outpouring of churches and denominations standing up on this issue more than any of us can now imagine and far more than John Knox Smith could have ever imagined. The outcome of your case will shape what the body of Christ can publicly proclaim about who the Christ is in a way not seen since the days of ancient Rome. A major part of that body will be standing with you at The Hague."

Pat smiled a little more. "Better to wake up now than after the verdict's in. Does The Hague give them a big advantage?"

"I'm afraid so. We lose the impact of having Judge Holloway at our table. His presence could sway most judges in the States, at least to ensure fair rulings on motions and evidence. However, he is unknown overseas, and with his wife's health he can't leave her for the weeks this will take. Smith's case against you had lost all the wind in its sails. What might be thrown out here, might not be there. Do you understand?"

Pat leaned forward. "Will they never learn? C. S. Lewis had them pegged."

"How so?" Holloway asked.

"Lewis said, 'A man can no more diminish God's glory by refusing to worship Him than a lunatic can put out the sun by scribbling the word "darkness" on the walls of his cell.' Don't they understand? No one can put out the light that is Christ. It doesn't matter what they do to me; Christ continues on forever." He straightened. "I'm done feeling sorry for myself. I'm done cowering in the shadows."

Larry grinned. "You know, I think you are."

"I'm not happy being here," Pat said softly. "I have moments when I think I will crumble to dust. I won't lie about that. They've taken everything from me, including my family. I couldn't stop them. But"—he touched his chest—"I will not let them take away my faith. They can strip me of everything but that. We will go across the sea and boldly proclaim the gospel, the good news of Jesus Christ!"

"This is quite a change," Larry said.

Pat gazed at the wall opposite him, seeing something only he could see. "I'm not the first minister in this age to be jailed for his faith. That occurred to me the other night. At first, I was too depressed to leave my bed. I spent hours counting all my problems. That's when the C. S. Lewis quote came to me. I also began to think about men like Dietrich Bonhoeffer, who opposed Hitler and spent two years in prison before they hanged him. Names I learned in church history classes in seminary came forward in my brain."

He returned his gaze to Larry and Holloway. "I also thought of Father Titus Brandsma. Ever heard of him?"

Holloway shook his head.

"I have," Larry said. "He was a priest in Hitler's Germany. He was sent to Dachau, perhaps the worst place on earth."

"Eighty-thousand prisoners died there. Brandsma was one of them. He was overworked, fed too little, and made to endure daily beatings. Do you know what he did? He encouraged the prisoners to pray for the guards. While this was going on, he secretly wrote a book to encourage others. He died in the camp hospital, the result of medical experiments. The more I thought about men like him, the more I realized that things could be worse. If Brandsma could provide spiritual comfort in Dachau, then I can do the same wherever I am. If he could pray for those who abused him, then so can I. I look forward to standing for Christ on the world's stage." After a thoughtful pause, Pat said, "Gentlemen, we need to pray for John Knox Smith."

"We do, but I admit it will be a difficult thing to do," Larry said. He paused and smiled. "I have some other news for you."

"Judging by that grin, it must be good news."

"Judge Holloway may not be able to help us in an overseas trial, but he can still pull a string or two here. I had a long phone conversation the other day with someone you know. I was asked to deliver a message. With Judge Holloway's help, I can deliver much more."

"Why are you being so cryptic?"

Larry rose and Holloway joined him. Larry stepped to the steel door that led from the prisoner conference area to the hall. He opened the door. Becky Preston walked in.

Pat stood on legs that could barely hold him.

Becky broke into tears, sobbing into her hands.

Larry took her by the elbow and led her to the chair he had been sitting in moments before. "I'm afraid you have only a few minutes. It was as much time as we could get."

"I don't understand," Pat said. "How did you arrange this?"

"You don't need to understand, son," Holloway said. "Stop wasting time asking questions and tell your wife how much you love her."

The two men exited.

Becky forced words through ragged sobs. "I'm sorry, Pat. I'm so sorry. I was wrong. I was a fool. I should never have left. I belong by your side."

"I love you, Becky. Now and forever. No matter what they do to me, my love for you will last."

The words drew more tears from her. "I love you too. God hasn't given me a moment's peace since I drove away with the kids. Every time I look in their faces, I see you. Can you forgive me?"

"I already have." Pat put a hand on the thick, plastic sheet that separated them. Tears flooded his eyes.

"I don't deserve it."

Pat smiled. "Nonsense. I handled things badly. I made foolish decisions. Truth is, I've been naïve about so many things. That's changed. I'm ready to stand for Christ wherever I am."

"And I'm going to stand with you." She took a deep breath. "No matter what, I'll never leave your side."

Pat started to speak, but the words would not form. He lowered his head and wept—this time for joy.

The last time John Knox Smith had attended an intimate dinner at the White House was Christmas Eve 2014, the same day Alton Stamper had taken him aside and told him he was going to be nominated to head the Diversity and Tolerance Enforcement Division. Three months later, when the RDTA legislation had passed and the actual appointment had come down, John had been lionized by the media and the inner circles of the permanent bureaucracy.

The engraved announcement lying on John's desk reawakened all the good feelings of that first White House Christmas invitation back before the event's name was changed to the more progressive "Winter Festival." But this time it was addressed to "John Knox Smith & Guest," meaning that he was free to attend the affair with a companion of his choosing, not necessarily his wife. Fortunately, Cathy was far away in Connecticut, pursuing whatever dreams she had left. John thought this was a good thing since Cathy had always embarrassed him with those ridiculous, parochial school dresses she had always worn—at least, that's what he had called them. She had never been cut out for this sort of thing.

He would invite Andrea to join him this time. She would jump at the chance, and he knew she would be appreciative. She had learned to appreciate John even more after the Italian debacle. More importantly, she looked the part. Andrea was a standout in any crowd. John liked having her on his arm, even though their relationship had always been purely professional. Her hair, eyes, jewelry, and evening gown would be splendid, as would be those red-soled shoes she always wore. Andrea knew how to dress. They would arrive in a stretch limousine and sip champagne with the leading lights of D.C. society.

However, there was something else on his mind. As much as John liked his work at the DTED, he didn't plan on staying there forever. For a man of his obvious talents, good looks, and groundbreaking accomplishments, the sky was the limit. He had his eye on the next big appointment. He liked the idea of being "The Honorable John Knox Smith" for life. He liked the perks of high public office. He liked hearing his name on the news and seeing his picture in the newspapers. But he needed another big score in order to continue his upward mobility.

He longed to be named White House counsel, appellate court judge or perhaps a member of the Supreme Court when the time came. Attorney General Stamper was apparently a lock to keep his job in the new administration, but that job would be a perfect stepping-stone for someone like John. From there, he thought, he could go anywhere. An appointment like that could come anytime. Who knew how long Stamper would last? He might be moving up too.

This was another reason why his decision to try Pat Preston at The Hague was suddenly looming so large. To be the first American to win a landmark hate crime decision in that court would be a tremendous accomplishment. John knew that the victory would make him an international celebrity. He always enjoyed the notoriety of winning big cases and making the news. This would be bigger than anything he had ever done. It would be America's first foray on such a grand scale. Trying an American at The Hague for crimes initiated within America's borders was already a front-and-center story in the world's media. It would also mean a new era of jurisprudence since it could end the practice of exclusionary preaching and faith claims in any public forum. The Jesus crowd would finally have a lot less to talk about.

When John spoke privately to the president and mentioned the impact on his administration's legacy for taking the Preston case to The Hague, Blaine's eyes lit up brighter than the White House Winter Festival tree. To John's way of thinking, the president's strong reaction was an extraordinary compliment, particularly when the president asked him to make a private appointment to tell him about it.

"How I would love to be a fly on the wall," Blaine told him. "Can you imagine the fireworks? John, this is a tremendous coup, and you are definitely the right man for the job. I want to know everything, so please tell Roxy to put you on the calendar. When is this trial going to take place?"

"Well, sir," John said, "there are still a lot of details to be worked out on both ends, but with any luck we'll be there by mid-April."

"Magnificent!" Blaine said. "What a fitting tribute. John, you're doing an excellent job. I know you're going to do great things for this country. Thanks in part to you, the poll results show that the religious crowd is lining up with reality. But here's a word of caution—don't attack religious practices so directly. Those Catholic bishops and a lot of evangelicals are still pretty unhappy with your mouth. Who cares what they do inside the four walls of their churches if it has no impact outside? Now," Blaine finished, "I have to get back to my other guests, but I hope you'll keep me informed. I'd like to know what else you'd like to do these next few years."

"Yes, sir. I will."

"Good. I'll take that as a promise."

"Yes, sir," John said. "Please do that."

With the support of President Blaine and Attorney General Stamper, the remaining hurdles that John and the team had to leap in order complete the final details at The Hague and make pretrial arrangements on both sides of the Atlantic proved to be much easier than John had imagined. The DTED team checked and double-checked the forty-count international indictment and charging documents. John knew he couldn't afford another screwup like the last one. The official papers were printed in English, French, and German; and shipped to the attorneys on both sides and to the officers of the world court.

On April 4, 2018, a caravan of five black SUVs pulled up inside the secure courtyard of the federal detention center in Arlington, Virginia. Five officers in black military uniforms, with Kevlar helmets and rifles in their hands, circled the vehicles and stood guard outside a steel-reinforced doorway that was dimly lit by a single yellow bulb. When the door opened, a solitary figure in an orange jumpsuit came forward. He wore handcuffs, and manacles bound his legs. Two federal officers led Pastor Pat Preston out of the enclosed area and placed him in the back of the center vehicle.

With red lights flashing, the SUVs drove off the compound and headed south in a tight column, down the 110 toward Ronald Reagan Washington National Airport, which was being used instead of Andrews Air Force Base to confuse any meddlers. When they had crossed the elevated ramp and made their way past the front of the terminal and around to the military staging area in the rear, a marine guard appeared and opened the gates. The young soldier saluted crisply and stood aside. All five units raced ahead toward the mammoth C-135 Stratolifter parked on the tarmac with its engines running.

When Pat was pulled from the SUV, a team of U.S. marshals took charge of him. A member of the ground crew radioed to the cockpit, and the captain dropped the ramp at the rear of the plane. Reverend Pat Preston was then marched on board. Less than twelve hours later, this preacher, who had dared to say publicly over and over that "Jesus is the only way" and claimed in his ministry's theme verse that "God sent His only Son into the world so that we might have life through Him," shuffled into another cell in another place far from his home and family—frightened, emotionally spent, and light-years from anywhere his soul had ever been before.

Pastor Pat entered the tiny cell that would be his home for the many weeks. He looked at the spartan furnishings, the metal toilet on the back wall, and the worn blankets piled on top of the single bunk and smiled. Turning his face toward the single source of light, a bare bulb in a tiny wire cage directly overhead, he whispered, "Here I stand. I can do no other. God help me."

ALAN SEARS

America on Trial

The Next Installment in the In Justice Series

A murdered defense attorney who held a secret about the Department of Justice.

A downed corporate jet that takes the lives of two Supreme Court justices and a titanium memory device that may lead to their killer.

An American minister facing life imprisonment, on trial at the International Criminal Court for the words of his sermons.

Government-mandated "equality" and "tolerance" enforced with deadly precision.

And more suspense surrounding Pat Preston and the assistant attorney General committed to seeing him silenced.

In Justice took us on a frighteningly real whirlwind adventure through a legal system increasingly unmoored from the Constitution and the rights it was meant to protect. At stake: America's foundational freedoms of religion and speech.

In the next book of the In Justice Series, Alan Sears delivers an alarming yet compelling story of courage in the face of oppression and of the battle to preserve the most basic, historic American rights and national sovereignty; and paints a chilling picture of an all-too-possible future.

In Justice—America on Trial   Coming soon.

| ACKNOWLEDGMENTS |

A special thank you to Coral Ridge Ministries for granting permission to use a portion of Dr. D. James Kennedy's classic sermon "God's Anvil"* within this book. I am so deeply grateful for the impact this godly man had on my life, on the Alliance Defense Fund, and on this country he so dearly loved. In addition, many thanks to those friends and family members who reviewed early drafts of this manuscript for their many helpful suggestions. Finally, I am very grateful to those who helped get my thoughts down on paper. Thank you all very much.

---

* D. James Kennedy, "God's Anvil," Sermon preached at Coral Ridge Presbyterian Church in Fort Lauderdale, Florida. Available from Coral Ridge Ministries, P.O. Box 1920, Fort Lauderdale, FL 33302

ALLIANCE DEFENSE FUND
Defending Our First Liberty

Since our nation's birth, religious liberty has been the bedrock principle upon which our society thrives. The First Amendment to the Constitution is unwavering in its affirmation of religious freedom. Yet the core American values we cherish are under fierce and relentless attack by those who are determined to silence people of faith and redefine the U.S. Constitution. These challenges are more than legal skirmishes . . . they are ongoing, pitched battles for the soul of America. The Alliance Defense Fund and its more than thirteen hundred allied attorneys work tirelessly to see an America whose laws affirm *religious liberty*, protect *life* from conception to natural death, defend the *family*, and preserve *marriage* as being between one man and one woman.

For more information about the Alliance Defense Fund,
please visit www.telladf.org

| GLOSSARY |

ACSFA—American Citizens Safety and Freedom Act
AP—Associated Press
ATF—Bureau of Alcohol, Tobacco, and Firearms
CLAMP—Citizen-Led Action and Mobilization Programs
DOJ—Department of Justice
DTED—Diversity and Tolerance Enforcement Division
EU—European Union
FAA—Federal Aviation Administration
FAC—Faith-Based Action Centers
FACE—Free Access to Clinical Entrances Act
FBI—Federal Bureau of Investigation
HR—Human Resources
ICC—International Criminal Court at The Hague, Netherlands
LGBT – Lesbian, Gay, Bi-sexual and Transgendered
NTSB—National Transportation Safety Board
OPR—Office of Professional Responsibility, DOJ
PPEEO—Public Policy Enforcement Exempt Organizations
RDTA—Respect for Diversity and Tolerance Act
ROS—Return of Service document filed after execution of a warrant
and arrest
UN—United Nations
U.S.—United States

To order additional copies of this title call:
1-877-421-READ (7323)
or please visit our Web site at
www.winepressbooks.com

If you enjoyed this quality custom-published book,
drop by our Web site for more books and information.

www.winepressgroup.com
"Your partner in custom publishing."